# TERRA'S
# FALL

# TERRA'S FALL

## AMANDA D'ERRICO

Silent Mangrove Press

Library of Congress Control Number: 2024916341

ISBN: 979-8-9905802-0-6 (eBook), 979-8-9905802-1-3 (Paperback), 979-8-9905802-2-0 (Hardcover)

Cover design by Miblart

Edited by Lauren Humphries-Brooks

This book contains spiritual and biblical elements. In an effort to portray the characters in the most authentic way possible, it also contains some crude language and dark themes, including addiction, suicide, and abduction.

Life is lived in the contrast between dark and light. To ignore one is to deny the existence of the other.

To Cam & Ev
Never stop seeking the light.


Also, to Ant
Never stop giving me back rubs. Seriously. I need you.

# FALL

## (OCTOBER-ISH)

H e'd be quick to notice her escape, but this was happening one way or another. All she needed was a two-second lead to turn and launch the rock. She would have to come at it with her left hand and hope for the best, considering her right arm had gone on strike since being stabbed a minute ago.

It could work. Take him out with one shot. Then she could be the heroine of her own story. No rescuers need apply.

Terra approached the ledge where the rock lay and had to catch herself from hurtling over like a barrel at Niagara. The narrow waterfall at her feet plunged into the shallow pool far below. The trees encircling it looked like twigs from this height. Light-headed and reeling, she turned away.

He was fifteen yards out and closing in, spittle flying from his curled lips. She dipped down and snatched up the rock —it was as heavy as she'd hoped—and flung it at her pursuer.

But her left arm's aim was a sad imitation of her right's. The rock whizzed over his shoulder in a horrifying betrayal of hope.

Victory gleamed in his eyes. So much for saving the day. With no defense left except her own two (one and a half, really) arms, Terra braced them in front of herself and prepared for impact.

Before he could reach her, a magnificent flash of light erupted between them.

Through half-closed eyes, she caught something familiar within the light: a figure, arms held out protectively. But before she had time to react, the force of the explosion was lifting her off her feet.

She hurtled backward, away from her pursuer, away from the figure in the light.

Back...back...

...and over the edge of the cliff.

# SPRING
(SEVEN MONTHS EARLIER)

*There is no denying that life in this world is a bitter pill. Imagine, had Adam and Eve left the fruit untouched, the billions of descendants spared the consequences of their decision, and their perfect world left untarnished. But then, one could argue, they'd be forever haunted by the question: Is living without those consequences truly better than having the freedom to make bad decisions in the first place?*

*- Elysian Records for the Revivers, Book I: Origins*

# CHAPTER ONE

The doctor had that look on his face—the one they all get once words like *psychosomatic* and *hypochondriac* slip into their heads.

"Don't see anything here that could cause the pain you're describing," he mumbled as he studied the X-ray over the top of his reading glasses. He tapped a finger against the film. "You have some scoliosis here at the T8/T9 level, but nothing to write home about."

Terra Zaragoza gazed in silence at the black-and-white image of her own vertebrae, which looked more like a game of Jenga gone on too long than anything physiologically sound.

He rummaged through the pages of her file. "Could be an extension of the fibromyalgia aches." The doctor looked up and squinted, as if trying to gauge whether she would accept this flimsy hypothesis.

"I've had fibro for seven years, and this pain is not the same," she replied.

"They say it can change from one flare-up to the next. Maybe—"

"This isn't a flare-up. This is searing pain between my shoulder blades."

He sat back and breathed in with a loud whistle of his nose. "And what'd you say you were doing before it started?"

"Carrying boxes down two flights of stairs." She didn't dare elaborate for fear of eliciting a you-know-better look. But she *should* have known better. Solo apartment moves didn't work so well when the only weightlifting you'd attempted involved pulling a gallon of milk from the fridge. She should have known better than to rely on her mom for help. Despite good intentions, the alcohol always got in the way.

The doctor scratched his neck and gazed at the image of her spine again. She sized him up as she waited, the way she did with everyone—imperfections were her sixth sense. He had a slight bend in his glasses, an iron crease in his lab coat, and a questionable mole on his cheek.

"Well, I s'pose it could be the facet joints," he said.

"The what now?"

"Facet joints. Where the bones in the spine meet. Problems with those are harder to see on an X-ray. That's potentially where your issue is."

"What about an MRI?"

"That might help rule out other things. Herniated discs, for example. Though sometimes those have no correlation to how much pain a patient feels. Wouldn't recommend it just yet."

She pursed her lips and stared at him. "I'd like an MRI anyway."

He crossed his arms and held her stare. "I doubt your insurance will authorize that. Not without a round of PT first, at the very least."

Terra's eye twitched.

"Can't put the cart before the horse, young lady."

And so, with the diagnosis of a *potential* facet joint injury of the thoracic spine, Terra trudged to checkout. She tucked the prescription for anti-inflammatory medication into her purse—as if she needed more pills—then frowned at the other paper he'd handed her, an address to a place called Recovery Solutions printed at the top. A three-week stint of physical therapy sounded like the last thing she needed. But the doctor thought it could help.

Potentially.

Shallow puddles from the previous day's rain splashed under Terra's feet as she speed-walked along a paved trail. Indianapolis had several parks, but she came here because it was fairly small and tucked away from the main roads. If she'd wanted to greet a passing stranger every seven seconds (no, thank you) she would have gone to the Canal Walk.

But c'est la vie, Kessler Park was busy for a Friday morning. A group of bedraggled moms gathered near the playground, depositing their toddlers after a long week of rain-induced cabin fever, sipping God-knows-what from their travel mugs. Five yapping huskies pulled at their leads, which were attached to a single, frazzled human, while a line of cyclists angled to get around them. Across the lawn, a bootcamp class dropped in unison for another round of burpee torture. She winced at the instructor's shrill voice and quickened her pace.

To hell with crowds. It was time to blow off steam from this morning's appointment. And yesterday's events. But she didn't want to think about yesterday. She imagined shoving the whole day into a steamer trunk and sinking it to the bottom of Lake Michigan.

She deliberated between the three trailheads at the edge of the woods and chose the one farthest from the park's central pond, exhaling as the noise of the crowds receded behind her. A blonde pony-tailed jogger blew past her on the left. Terra studied her high-end athletic top, which had an unnecessary number of straps holding her torso hostage. The tag was sticking out. But the body to which it clung was perfection, lean and fully functional. Terra knew she'd never be as fit as this woman, who was at least a decade older than her. Probably two.

Even at her spry age of twenty-five, Terra's body didn't get stronger with exercise or reward her with that "good ache" in her muscles. It punished her with pain. It was a crotchety old woman riding her piggy-back everywhere she went. That's why she'd resigned herself to walking. Anything more, and the old hag would find something to complain about.

Walking was good. Walking meant she wasn't disabled—not yet anyway. As long as she walked, she'd never be one of those people who had given up. She would get in her steps, old hag be damned.

A soft ding issued from her sweatshirt pocket. Terra retrieved her phone. Alexis had sent a text.

*Are you mad at me?*

So much for steamer trunks. She jammed the phone back into her pocket and kept walking. She tried to focus on gentler thoughts. Her grocery list. The latest salmonella recall on romaine. The bubonic plague and the socioeconomic collapse of Western Civilization. But yesterday's meeting was already replaying in her head.

Jess, their editor-in-chief, was standing at the head of the table, a hand on Alexis's shoulder, spouting off words like *exemplary editor* and *all-star contributor.* All the while, Terra sat mutely in the corner. Jess never glanced in her direction, as if too disgusted to acknowledge her. The lackluster hiring choice. The glaring typo in need of a strikethrough.

Terra's phone rang. It seemed there was no escaping it now.

She answered. "No, I'm not mad."

"Are you sure? Because it feels like you are."

"I'm just a little..." What was the protocol for when your best friend snagged the senior copyediting position you'd been working toward your whole, brief career? "Caught off guard, is all."

"I'm really sorry about that. I was going to tell you in private, but Jess beat me to it."

"Well…" Terra slowed enough to kick a pinecone off the trail and watch it crash against a tree trunk. "What can you do, right?"

"My point exactly. I just want to make sure you're okay."

"I'm fine. Just not in the mood to talk about it."

"Fine then. Talk Monday?"

"Sure."

Terra returned the phone to her pocket and picked up her pace again. A wooden slat bridge with a creek running underneath lay on the path ahead. She was almost to the end of the trail, where the path opened to a circle of trees with a small pond in the middle. Perfect for a break. Or a nap. Or a long, self-indulgent pity party.

*It's not like you have cancer, for heaven's sake.* Her mother's words from last week knocked through her head like a flaming pinball. *Just take a day off whenever the pain gets bad. ¡No es gran cosa!* (As her mother liked to say, a true Latina always reverts to her native tongue for emphasis.) Terra hadn't bothered telling her the pain was a daily occurrence, and Jess had already granted her well above the company's allotted sick time. She'd been *very understanding*, as she often reminded Terra.

Her legs were growing heavy. The old hag was starting to wail. As she reached the bridge, she saw two cyclists—a man and woman—emerge on the trail ahead of her. She hustled so they wouldn't have to pass her on the narrow bridge.

Alexis had probably deserved the promotion more. It wasn't like Terra had been a stellar copy editor in her three years at Edifice Books. Everyone at the independent publishing house had noticed too. Hiding the aches was one thing, but the fibro fog, which mummified her brain in heavy layers of gauze, wasn't so easy to shake. She knew she was capable, and on her good days, she'd worked twice as hard to prove it. Apparently, it hadn't been enough.

She huffed and took one last step across the bridge, but her toe caught on an uneven board.

And suddenly her body was horizontal.

She threw out her hands to catch herself. As they hit the ground, a sensation like an anvil plowed through her upper spine.

The bikes ahead of her stopped. The man let out something like a laughing gasp and yelled, "Oh shit! You okay?"

Dirt on her hands and in the hair around her face, she lifted her head. "Yeah." The ache between her shoulders was screaming otherwise. She pushed herself upright and picked bits of gravel out of her palms.

"Damn, girl." The woman looked down at her with amusement as they peddled forward. "You do all your own stunts?"

Terra gave a half-hearted laugh and watched them pass. She sat for a couple minutes longer, her ears hot and buzzing as if they were covered in angry hornets.

*It's not like you have cancer.*

Then, completely uninvited, the tears came.

Her sweatshirt dampened as her body convulsed in embarrassing sobs, which erupted from her throat like the guttural barks of a seal. It was ugly crying at its finest. She leaned against the smooth rail of the bridge and watched the creek pass underneath through blurry eyes.

"Help me already," she demanded in a whisper, to no one in particular. There was no one in particular to care. Because she was alone. She was absolutely, utterly—

More footsteps from the trail behind her.

She swiped at her eyes, pulled herself up against the rail, and ventured a glimpse. A man close to her age jogged around the bend, earbuds blasting music. He was disappointingly attractive, which—by way of some residual adolescent instinct—made her want to try even harder to not look a mess.

Lots of people got puffy eyes with allergies, right? It was spring allergies. Yes, that's what she'd go with. She lifted her head and took in one of those cleansing breaths that make everything right again. She was standing here, by the creek, like any perfectly confident and allergy-ridden individual would, enjoying all the amazingness life had to offer. All was splendid. Convinced of this, she let her eyes meet his.

The man half smiled at her, as if drumming up a greeting. *Oh hi, what a beautiful day, totally not hearing anyone cry around here.* But a split second later, the smile fell, and his eyes shifted away. He passed in silence.

Terra clenched her jaw. Had she frowned at him by mistake? Alexis had once accused her of chronic RBF (resting bitch face). Maybe it was her defense mechanism. Sometimes people needed to be told to back off. Or where to shove it. But a defense mechanism was not supposed to go off at random. She frowned at herself, trying to detect the difference in the feel of her face. Whatever. She began walking again, albeit much more carefully.

A minute later, she discovered the true culprit when she lifted her hand to swat a stray hair from her face. Then she lifted her other hand and inspected it. Her legs halted mid-stride. Black smears ran across the backs of her hands.

Long, black, damning smears of mascara.

In disbelief, she snatched her phone from her pocket and activated the selfie camera.

The mascara had collected like dark mud puddles beneath her eyes as she'd cried. Her cheeks blushed with heat as the realization sank in. (Of course, they were covered in black smudges too.) She'd forgotten she'd done her eye makeup this morning.

"Fantastic," she muttered, and threw in a string of profanity for good measure.

She wiped away what she could manage, then charged full speed ahead, ignoring the searing ache in her muscles. Right now, the old hag could be told where to shove it. She was not some sad sack people took pity on. The irrational part of her fantasized about punching that jogger in the face for his unfortunate timing. She quelled the thought when it occurred to her that the end of the trail was ahead; she'd have to pass him a second time when he turned around.

No problem. She smoothed back her hair and lifted her chin. She'd smile like the joke was on him. Like mascara did weird things sometimes, and he needn't get his manties in a wad over it.

When she reached the pond where the path dead ended, an unsettled feeling sank into the pit of her stomach. She glanced around at the tree line that surrounded the water, packed so thick with shrubs and brush, you'd need a machete to get through.

No place to go, and yet...she was the only one here.

*Terra,*

*You don't know me, but I know you. More accurately, I know of you. I had all but forgotten about you until today when we crossed paths in the park. The golden-brown skin, the wild dark spirals...I nearly stopped dead in my tracks. It was all so distantly familiar.*

*Then I remembered. You. You came rushing back to me in a flood of nostalgia. You were so young then, but I could see flashes of the same person in that face. You're older and more attractive now, but with an edge. The way you fixed your eyes on the horizon, the way you set your jaw and walked with determination, I could tell you have been hardened with age and disappointment. Many disappointments. What eats you these days?*

*I followed you for a quarter mile or so, intrigued but not sure what to do with this discovery. I can't help but wonder who you've become. Are you strong? Would you crumble under that hardened exterior if prodded? I thought I caught a sheen of tears in those olive eyes. Have you maintained a semblance of hope all these years? Or has your heart turned cold with apathy? I imagine you lost your faith in humanity a long time ago, considering the events that framed your past. Considering how I framed your past.*

*But these are no more than pointless musings. Eventually, I left you there in the park, alone in your thoughts. I had somewhere to be. I don't have time to chase memories.*

*But if I catch sight of you in the park again sometime, by chance? I don't think I would mind very much at all.*

*- H.*

*Above all else, they must know they are loved, that they have not been forgotten. Trust and follow-through come with time and are of secondary importance to this. For why would they ever allow someone to draw close if they didn't first believe this someone cared for them?*

*- Elysian Records for the Revivers, Book II: The People of Eden*

# CHAPTER TWO

Terra cast a vacant stare over her twelve-ounce mug of coffee in the general direction of her monitor. This was her second cup and the only thing keeping her from face-planting into her keyboard. She didn't sleep well last night, but at least she'd made it into work. On time and everything.

She only needed to plow through this fact check on nineteenth century socioeconomics and fashion. (Would a farmer's wife in 1840s Missouri wear a whalebone corset? And...would anyone care?) Then she could get back to the manuscript. That was the best part, combing the page line by line, highlighting the flaws: a dangling modifier here, an overused crutch word there. She'd been at this since childhood. Back then, whenever her mom got to be too much, she'd lock herself in her room with the newspaper and pore over the Spot the Difference puzzle of the day. Digging up all the incongruities made everything right again.

"Hey."

At the sound of the familiar voice behind her, Terra splattered coffee on her sweater. She whirled around in her chair.

"Too soon to talk?" Alexis leaned against the wall of Terra's cubicle, arms crossed.

Terra took in her red and violet billowy-sleeved blouse and immediately spotted the thread dangling at its hem. Also, the shade of red in her oversized hoop earrings and clanking bracelets was a smidge too orange to match. Incongruities aside, she wore it well. When it came to fashion—and most other things—Alexis stood out like a peacock in a chicken coop. A very professional peacock, though, she would argue.

"Hey, Lex."

"You're still mad, aren't you?" Alexis pursed her lips.

"I was never mad."

"But it's a lot to process. I get it."

"Yeah...oh—" Terra opened her desk drawer, pulled out a paper bag, and plunked it down in front of Alexis.

"What's this?"

"Something for the new office."

Alexis opened the brown paper and pulled out a small flower pot filled with succulents. "Terra!" She flicked Terra's arm with the back of her hand. "You didn't have to get me anything."

"Just sucking up to my superior."

"So freaking cute." Alexis ran her finger over the serrated edges of the aloe plant.

"You're welcome."

"Hey." Alexis set the pot down. "Let's sneak outside." She flashed that wide-eyed grin that Terra had grown accustomed to—a deranged look that was somehow endearing. "I know it's only 10:15, but I'm in desperate need of a break."

Terra took one last begrudging glance at the Missouri Historical Society website. "Screw it. Let's go." She yawned. "But I'm taking my coffee with me."

Terra and Alexis stepped out of the downtown office building into the fresh air of the plaza. Despite its concrete and granite encasement of buildings on either side, the plaza had a secluded garden charm to it. A circle of flower beds, trickling fountains, and gracefully trimmed hedges surrounded a giant tree in the center. The arrangement resembled a carousel, but with ornate benches for the horses and jaded office workers for the riders. Terra and Alexis made their way to a bench near the tree, tugging at the sleeves of their jackets. The full sun did little to thaw the chill in the air.

Terra glanced at her friend as they walked. Though Alexis thought she could stand to lose fifteen pounds—a caveat she frequently worked into their conversations—she had a pretty face with model cheekbones. It made a nice counterbalance to the loud voice and even louder laugh. But why shouldn't she let loose if blessed with the ability? That was something Terra could spend a whole lifetime studying and never get right.

"So, how's it going so far?" Terra asked as they sat down.

Alexis crossed her legs and held a stilettoed heel in the air. "My feet are killing me. Turns out my mantra of *new job, new shoes* was a stupid idea."

Terra shrugged. "They're cute."

"Thanks. Anyway, I don't think it will be all that different. Jess wants me involved with some of the acquisitions going forward, and she's putting me on all the big accounts, but otherwise it's all the same copyediting stuff we've been doing. Oh..." She tilted her head back. "I just found out I'm taking over Lyla Harrison's book."

"I figured." Lyla Harrison was their flagship author; her books regularly grossed over seven figures. Her latest work, an eight-hundred-page tome reimagining Joan of Arc as a Stop & Shop cashier, had occupied the majority of Terra's days the past two months. That is, until Jess put her on a different manuscript last week.

"Sorry about that."

"It's fine. She's kind of a pain to work with anyway." Lyla wasn't the first writer to argue with her editors, but she had made a sport of it.

"Oh, get this." Alexis turned to Terra with a smack of her palm against the bench. "Jess had another one of her massive brain farts this morning."

"Yeah?"

"Like stink-up-the-room, oh-my-God-what-is-that kind of fart."

"Wait. Are we still talking about brain farts or regular?"

"So I was sitting in on a call with her, and she was talking revisions with me for one writer while on hold with another." Alexis placed a hand on Terra's shoulder as if to brace her. "She totally forgot who she was speaking with."

"Oh, Jess."

"She asked the author of *Medical Marijuana 101* whether he was aiming for middle grade or young adult as his target market. The look on her face, though, when she realized her mistake..."

Terra pictured their ever-frazzled boss as she'd glimpsed her this morning, office phone clenched to her shoulder, hair falling in her coffee as she lunged to grab a paper that had slipped to the floor, and—despite her over-enthusiasm for appearing well put-together—the smear of foundation along her jawline contrasting against the white of her neck. "Think it's menopause?"

"Girl, who knows?" Alexis belted out a laugh that echoed off the granite walls of the plaza.

"So a good first day then?"

Alexis nodded. "Yes. But..." She bumped Terra's shoulder. "I miss being next to my Terr-bear."

"Oh but think of the fancy desk you have now. You actually get a view of something other than the printer and Shawn's gnome collection."

Alexis let out a healthy chortle. "You know who I *won't* be getting a view of anymore." Her devious grin gave away the answer. "And lucky you. You still sit right around the corner from—"

"Lex, stop."

"I'm not saying you have to shack up with him or anything. But if you could maybe just get—"

"God, here we go again."

"Just *one* shirtless pic. I mean, have you *seen* Kenneth?"

Terra swatted a pebble off the bench and leaned back on her hands. "It's not like we're going to be chatting it up by the recycling bins, then he's all like, oh by the way, here's a shirtless picture of me for your enjoyment."

"It could happen."

"Sure."

"Or you could ask him out."

"I told you, I'm over dating. Done."

Alexis ignored her and flicked through social media posts on her phone. "Just let it happen, hon. It's going to happen."

"Screw you, it's not *happening*."

"Mm-hmm..."

"And I don't care how ripped he is, I can't have a conversation with that man. Do you know he once said *okey dokey* to me?"

Alexis snorted. "Sexy."

"Besides," Terra continued. "He needs a loud mouth to balance him out, somebody like..." She squinted at Alexis and held her chin as if deep in thought.

"Yeah, no. I have a strict policy against dating in the workplace." Alexis extended her hand and studied her manicure.

"You are ridiculous."

Alexis grinned and did a little dance with her shoulders, swinging her hoop earrings back and forth. "Don't forget fabulous."

"Always."

"So, are we okay?"

"Of course," Terra said. "Sorry I was kind of a jerk before."

"Nah. I get it. You've been here longer than me. Hell, you're the one who got me the interview with Edifice."

"Yeah, but I can't compete with a year in the big leagues. Your experience is better."

"Oh God, don't remind me of New York. I'm glad I got out when I did. Another year in the trenches, and I'd be on Prozac by now."

"Well. I'm glad you came back. And I'm proud of you. Really."

"Thanks." Alexis threw her arms around Terra in that all-or-nothing way that made it easy for Terra to hug back and not notice all the weirdness that comes with entering another's personal space.

They'd been friends long before Edifice, and before Alexis's stint with one of the big publishers. It was freshman year at IUPUI (Indiana University-Purdue University at Indianapolis, though everyone just pronounced it *Ooey-Pooey*), when Alexis had swaggered into First Year Comp wearing slippers and pajama bottoms and sank into the seat next to Terra's. Despite Terra's best efforts to appear busy staring at her blank notebook, Alexis wouldn't stop talking to her. It didn't take long before they were trading grammar jokes and miniskirts. Later, Alexis was the only mutual friend who'd stuck it out after the breakup with Brock, when Terra's life had gone into a tailspin.

Terra stretched and sipped her last drops of coffee. "So, back to work?" She looked over to find her friend engrossed in the study of her own waistline.

"I have *got* to get back into an exercise routine." Alexis sucked in her abdomen and pulled her shirt taut.

"Stop."

"I'm serious. Let's hit the trails this week."

"You know I go at the butt-crack of dawn, right?"

Alexis gagged as if she'd swallowed a bug. "Come on, let's go after work this time. You can handle it."

"I don't know." But she did know. Her body pretty much threw in the towel by five o'clock every day.

"Please?" Alexis shot her another crazed grin. "For your bestie?"

Terra scrunched her face.

"I'll buy you a smoothie afterward. One of those nasty kale ones you like."

Terra huffed. "Fine. Only for you, Lex. And that smoothie."

"Thanks, babe." She gave Terra a squeeze. "It means a lot. Kessler Park, right?"

"Yeah." Terra suddenly remembered last Friday. "Oh my God, I had the most embarrassing moment there last week."

Alexis leaned forward and smiled like a kid unwrapping a full size candy bar. "Tell me everything."

*Always stay alert, for the person you meet next could be the one who has long been aching for a catalyst.*

*- Elysian Records for the Revivers, Book V: Our Charge*

# Chapter Three

Terra stood by the front desk of Recovery Solutions, the physical therapy clinic her doctor had recommended. She scrunched her nose at the coalescent smell of rubber mats, sweat, and hand sanitizer. Through the doorway behind the desk, she glimpsed people—mostly of the silver-haired variety—performing various exercises with the help of their physical therapists. So these were her kindred spirits, it seemed. The elderly and fragile, with joints like old rubber bands that crumbled when you stretched them.

"Terra?" A petite brunette in her twenties popped into the doorway, a small tablet in hand, and Terra made her assessment. Band-Aid on thumb, eyeliner too thick, visible panty line.

"That's me."

"Hey, I'm Piper. You can come this way."

Terra offered a lackluster smile and followed Piper through the door. They passed several treadmills, stationary bikes, and a host of other workout equipment with which she hoped she'd not have to become too acquainted. Three weeks, two times a week, was a big commitment when you had less energy than hours in the day.

The facility was sizable, with therapists ping-ponging back and forth between their patients, calling out reminders for the next set of reps. Others worked at tables, massaging or applying therapeutic ultrasound to patients' injuries. As she scanned the room, she nearly tripped over herself in shock.

At a table near the end, she saw him.

He was wrapping a warm compress around the elbow of a middle-aged woman. He had that same athletic build—muscular but not Hulk-ish—and chestnut hair with dark brows and lashes, deep-set eyes, and an angular jaw. The jogger. The one who had passed her on the bridge last week. Her stomach lurched with the memory of humiliation. Not to mention that weird vanishing act of his that she still couldn't wrap her head around. Worse, he wore a black polo shirt with the Recovery Solutions logo. He *worked* here.

Super.

She studied him from a safe distance but regrettably failed to register any flaws. He had that all-American poster-boy look that told her what she'd learned from experience many times before. It may as well have been a neon sign flashing above his head that read *ARROGANT JERK.* As if that weren't enough, he wore a thin, corded bracelet on his wrist, probably there to accentuate the muscles in his forearm. Men who wore jewelry, in Terra's opinion, were vain.

Fat chance he would even recognize her, but Terra wasn't prepared to find out. She averted her gaze and let her hair fall across her face as Piper led her to a table five rows down.

After Piper assessed Terra's strength and range of motion in her arms and neck, she had her lie down on the table for a therapeutic massage. Then it was on to stretches and strength-building, including a chin tuck that reminded Terra of turtles and double chins. Out and in. Out and in. She performed her tucks like a well-trained circus horse, deciding then and there that whatever Piper prescribed, she would do to the one-thousandth degree. The sooner her back healed, the sooner she could get this over with.

Piper walked her over to a station with an assortment of exercise bands attached at varying heights along a metal rack. "Here. Grab this green band and pull it back until your shoulder blades touch." She placed the band's handles into Terra's hands. "It's called a *row*."

Terra performed a few practice reps until Piper nodded. Easy enough. Terra counted down the seconds until her session was over, each row bringing her four seconds closer to the end. She would grab a chicken Caesar salad on her way back to work. Scratch that. She would order a bacon cheeseburger because she'd earned it, and because she really wanted one. As Terra continued her rows, Piper hurried off to help one of the new therapists with the ultrasound machine.

"Okay, Ms. Hirsch, you have a great day."

A man's voice assailed her ears from across the room. She turned to search for the owner of the voice and found him sitting on a stability ball, watching his patient leave. It was Jogger Guy. He tapped out something on his tablet, then glanced around, his eyes skimming past her. Terra whirled back to her exercises.

Her cheeks burned hot. She glanced sidelong through the corner of her eye as he stood up, set down his tablet, and started in her direction. She continued her rowing exercises, eyes laser-focused on the wall. He was definitely heading toward someone else.

He stepped into her view. "Hi."

Or not.

She forced out a "hi" between puffs and maintained her pace. Two seconds in, two seconds out.

He smiled and regarded her with an inescapable gaze that made her wonder what was on her face. "I've seen you before."

"Oh, really?" She kept her tone cool, disinterested.

"Yeah, I think so. I think it was—"

She prayed he wouldn't say it. With all the positive energy in the universe, she willed him to stop. Willed him to... Shut. It.

"—at the park. You know, the one not too far from here? Kessler. Do you work out there?"

Blazing buckets of turd, he had said it. "No. I don't work out," she answered as she stared down at the exercise band in her hands. "I mean, I don't, um, go to parks." Oh, this was bad.

His smile grew wider. "No..." He pointed a finger at her and shook it. "No, I'm pretty sure that was you that I passed near the bridge last week."

Terra pulled the band back with too much force this time, making her stumble and catch herself. "Yeah, sure. Maybe."

He leaned in a little closer and furrowed his brow at her, his voice lowered. "Were you—"

She needed him to stop. For the love of—-

"—crying?"

Sirens went off in her head. The *indecency* of it. Like he was jabbing at her skin, looking for a way to get under it.

She recoiled from his gaze and tossed the handles onto the floor, then looked around the room as if she had to move on to another exercise. She had no idea what she was supposed to start next, and Piper was still off in the corner fiddling with the ultrasound machine.

In a panic, Terra strode to the opposite end of the room and picked up what looked like a half dome on a circular base. She lifted it over her head for several reps like a body builder on a mission. This was most definitely a good workout for the arms, if she didn't kill herself in the process. This dome thing was heavy.

"What are you doing?" he asked from behind her. And so it seemed *taking a hint* was not on the docket for today.

"My exercises," she huffed.

"You're going to hurt yourself." He came beside her and lifted the dome out of her hands, as if it weighed nothing. "This is meant for balancing...with your *feet*." He placed it back on the floor and gestured for her to step onto it.

"Oh." Terra stared at it for a moment, then decided to humor him. She stepped on with one foot and bounced up and down a couple times. "Yeah, I guess you could use it this way too."

"Hey, I didn't mean to pry or anything." He was giving her that unflinching stare again. And he was definitely prying.

She stared back, resisting the urge to squirm. He had tiny flecks of gold in his brown eyes—no, hazel eyes. There was a thin halo of green around the edges.

"I'm sorry to bring it up. I just wanted to make sure you were okay."

"I'm fine."

"I feel bad now. I should've said something, you know? When I passed you."

"Don't worry about it. It was nothing."

He hesitated, then pushed harder, his voice low. "You don't have to hold it all in, you know."

Terra blinked. "What?"

"Hey!" Piper yelled over the whir of the stationary bikes as she walked up. "Did I say you could harass my patient, Harlan?"

"Me?" He pressed his hand to his chest in a theatrical display of shock. "I tried to tell her I'm on my lunch break, but she won't leave me alone. Can you please make her stop?"

Piper smiled and waved him off. "Go take your lunch break, dork."

He leaned into Piper and hooked a thumb in Terra's direction. "Watch out for this one. She likes to blaze her own trail with the equipment around here." He winked at Terra.

"Sure," Piper droned, checking off the chart on her tablet.

He flashed one last smile in Terra's direction, then disappeared behind a door marked *EMPLOYEES ONLY.*

"You ready for some more work?" Piper drew Terra's attention away from the door. "I've got two more exercises for you, then we'll throw some ice on that back. Sound good?"

Terra nodded, though her thoughts lingered on the man with hazel eyes.

Terra sat at the base of a crooked tree in Kessler Park. The morning sun bounced off the dark water of the central pond, flashes undulating in the wake of resident ducks. She watched it with mild disinterest, too tired to get up and go for a walk. She didn't have somewhere to be anyway, did she? She couldn't remember.

Runners passed on the path in front of her. No one noticed her or glanced in her direction, which was fine. She wasn't much for the *How are you?*s they threw her way, which were basically an obligation to lie. Then again, a *good morning* wouldn't be so terrible. Wait. *Was* it still morning? Confused, she leaned back against the winding trunk. Her mind drifted, aimless as the maple leaves floating in the pond.

Those few crippled leaves. They couldn't just man up and hang on to their branches, could they? No. They'd let the wind rip them away, far ahead of schedule. And now they were dead in the water. They'd never get a chance to show off their glorious golden-orange and fire-red colors in the fall. Too bad for them.

But maybe it wasn't their fault. The wind was a salty bitch after all.

The park had gone quiet. When had she last seen another person on the path? She sat upright and looked both directions. That's when she saw it.

A shadow of a man in the distance. Not stretched out across the ground as it should be in the low-hanging sun, but—incredibly—upright, and walking toward her.

Hilarious. Her brain was foggy enough, and now her eyes were messing with her too.

The vision disappeared as clouds blew in front of the sun and cast darting shadows along the path. Tree branches joined in on the fun, rustling in the wind. She squinted in frustration.

After a time, the wind finally stilled. Her skin prickled as she picked out movement along the path. Deliberate, forward movement toward her. It was a dark shape of a man, and its very existence made no sense. Her pulse hammered out an SOS. She glanced around for help, only to find she was still alone.

She glanced back. The shadow was closer now. Thirty yards away. It stopped as if it had seen her look in its direction. And waved.

Terra threw off the bedsheets and sat up in a flurry of gasps. Her pajamas were damp with sweat. The hard ground lingered beneath her, but as the seconds passed and her breathing slowed, the phantom feeling faded into the soft cushion of her mattress. She settled back into bed.

It was a laughable dream—she'd had scarier dreams about public restrooms—but it had rubbed her the wrong way. Somehow, it had felt real.

*Their relationships are tenuous at best, destructive at worst. Yes, it's difficult to grasp why anyone would choose to hurt another, especially those they love most. You will come to understand with time that they exist in a state of chaos. The unrelenting strain of loss fractures their ability to love.*

*- Elysian Records for the Revivers, Book II: The People of Eden*

# CHAPTER FOUR

"The doctor thinks three weeks should do it... Yep, I started yesterday... No, it won't affect my work. I'm going during my lunch breaks... Mom. *Mom.* Of course I'll eat something. I can eat at my desk."

In the dim light of her apartment, Terra stood at the kitchen counter, cell phone to ear, dropping pills into a days-of-the-week case. Her face was contorted into a grimace, as it usually was whenever her mother called. It was always on a Wednesday night, after her mother's AA meeting. She would call to *check in*, she'd say, but it was really her way of letting Terra know how spectacularly sober she was staying. Like she was looking for a ribbon or something.

"I don't understand how you keep hurting yourself, Terra!" Her mom's mawkish voice, infused with a heavy dose of Latin flair, penetrated her ear. "Weren't you in physical therapy just last year for something—what was it?"

"That was for the fibromyalgia, Mom. I saw a chiropractor for a while. And no, it didn't help." Terra dropped a magnesium pill into the *Thursday* receptacle.

"Just asking." Her mom grew quiet. She never did quite grasp Terra's health issues, but that was expected. Her medical views were informed by a different era and culture, one that looked to home remedies and *positividad* as the solution to all ailments. It was possible she thought you could fart butterflies if you believed hard enough.

But that was Leta Zaragoza. She lived in her own reality, where giving a rip was not required. She'd pilfered the surname of her first and only husband, a fellow stateside Puerto Rican, when they'd eloped at age twenty-two. The marriage self-destructed years before Terra was born, but Leta never took back her maiden name. Zaragoza sounded more "fashionable" than Burgos, she'd said. Nearly gave old Huelo a heart attack.

That's how Terra got her first name too. *Terra, there are a million T-A-R-A's out there. I wanted my daughter to stand out!*

As if a different spelling was all it would take.

"You still have some money left in the trust?" Leta asked.

"Plenty. Don't worry about it." Not that it was her business anyway.

"I know, I know. I just don't think Huelo and Abuelita imagined you'd be blowing all your inheritance on doctor visits."

"It's not like I'm going for fun."

"Still, it *kills* me. You know Abuelita was a descendant of sugar plantation slaves? And Huelo, he worked *so* hard. You wouldn't have known it from the looks of them, but they came from San Juan with only ten dollars to their names. Every penny they earned, it was—"

"You've told me this before. I promise, I'm spending it wisely."

"I don't want you to spend it wisely, Terra. I want you to make it *count*. Live life to the fullest. YOLO, you know?"

There it was: the reason Terra's grandparents had left her a separate trust. Leta had less impulse control than a pyro with a fistful of matches. The drinking had only made it worse.

Terra dropped the final pill, a B12 vitamin, into the pill case. It ricocheted out and skittered across the counter. Terra clapped her hand over it and shoved it back in the case. As she did, ringlets of hair fell in her face, exacerbating her mood further. Her mother had given her this hair. The dark brown curls were like a two-year-old—bouncy and temperamental. She blamed Leta for many things. The hair was a good place to start, as it was a constant reminder, but there were worse things.

After a long silence, Leta spoke with gusto. "Oh! Have I told you about the new diet I've been trying?"

"Um, no, I don't think so."

"My coworker was telling me about it. Hey! Maybe you should try it. You know, for your health. Anyway, I've lost *six pounds...*"

Half listening, Terra pulled the remnants of her kale smoothie from the fridge and retired to the oversized chair in her living room. This was the part where she just needed to offer a grunt of acknowledgment here and there and let her mom purge the chatter.

She thought back to her childhood. It wasn't until late in her grade school years that the drinking got bad. At some point, Terra figured out it wasn't normal for moms to show up at school functions giggling and flirting with all the dads. The teasing from the other kids got so bad that Terra spent most of her middle school years eating lunch with the squirrels in the courtyard. By high school, she'd finally learned to stop telling Leta about school events.

Other times, Leta retreated into herself and became a sad drunk, which was—in a way—worse than an obnoxious one. She was haunted, though by what, Terra could never glean from her mother's ramblings.

Sometimes, though, Leta would stay sober for weeks or months at a time. She'd even show interest in Terra's social life and academics for a hot minute and take her on day trips to the state fair or the Dunes lakeshore. For a long time, Terra believed the *real* Leta, whom she'd glimpsed in these moments, would eventually win out over the alcohol-tainted version. Then Terra grew up and learned life doesn't work that way. Cue the soul-crushing violins.

"Well I was thinking, if you want to have some fun—I mean, if you're *into* that sort of thing," Leta chided, "Marci was telling me about this new home store at the Edinburgh outlets. I need a new rug for the hallway. Maybe me and you could drive down together next weekend?"

"Mom—"

"And definitely lamps for the den. Just for the morning. Not the whole day, of course. I have off next Saturday. We could make it a fun girls' trip. Get our nails done—"

"I don't know."

"Or go see a movie, if you want, honey. What's the big deal?"

"It's just..." Terra rubbed her calves as she worked out an excuse. Her legs were aching from her walk around the park with Alexis. "I have a work dinner that night before, and then I have to, um..." She had nothing to do. She stared across the room at a pair of sweatpants hanging out of the laundry basket. "Go pants shopping...later that day...with Alexis. I should probably sleep in and save my energy, you know? Mom?"

"Since when do you two schedule your *pants shopping*, Terra?"

Terra sighed. "Some other time, okay?" She told the guilt rising inside her to put a lid on it. Despite Leta's best efforts at a reboot, she needed to face the liquor-soaked truth. What was the point in pretending their relationship was something it was not?

"Alright. I get it. You're a busy girl. So, what's new at work? Any exciting projects?"

"I'm actually pretty tired right now. Can we talk about it next week?"

"Of course. I'll let you go."

"Thanks, Mom. Talk later."

"Bye-bye. Love and kisses." Leta emitted a kissing noise through the phone and hung up. The sound grated Terra's ear like a cotton swab full of glass shards.

Terra dropped the phone on the cushion and blew out a hard breath.

*Terra,*

*I didn't think it could happen twice. After all, how many people come and go from that park all day long? A stroke of luck: I saw you again.*

*Okay, so it's true that I spent more time in the park than necessary today. I had no business being there so late. In fact, I was planning on leaving, but then...I turned down a path and there you were. It was unavoidable.*

*You stood next to a park bench, stretching your legs and laughing along with another woman. I nearly didn't recognize you with a smile on your face. The difference in your mood from the last time was like night and day. You seem very comfortable with this friend of yours. I wonder how many people you open up to in the same way? Or was the sullen, tense woman I saw last week the real Terra?*

*I was curious. I trailed you and your friend as you walked past the pond. I was close enough to catch fragments of your conversation. Early 2000s rom-coms, sushi versus sashimi, laser hair removal (what is it with twenty-first century women and their estranged relationship with body hair?), a club downtown closing, and on and on. The drivel of two twenty-somethings. I have to admit, you are much more interesting when you're quiet and brooding.*

*I don't like your friend. That's what it is. She's too—what's the word? Buoyant. It's irritating. Not like you. She upstages you in every aspect. Honestly, it's the subtlety of your personality that draws me in.*

*You are drawing me in.*

*I should stop this. Writing letters to you in my mind, as if you could ever read them, as if you would even want to. It's ludicrous. I have so many more important things to do. Then again, everyone needs a good pastime, right?*

*- H.*

*Accept the likelihood that you will have no life companion in your time here. What they call love is often frivolous and disappointing.*
*- Elysian Records for the Revivers, Book IV: Acclimation*

# CHAPTER FIVE

S he ran her thumb over the smooth surface of the custom pendant and decided it was just what she'd imagined. Better, even.

"Will you be needing a chain to go with that, ma'am?" The sales associate (dodgy eyes, sleeves too short, crooked incisor) leaned over the display case of gold chains with eager anticipation.

She examined the two tiny gold letters in her hand. The pendant was big enough to add some glam, but without screaming excess if she wore it every day. "I already have a chain, thanks."

The chain had lain unused at the bottom of her purse ever since she'd sold the diamond pendant last year at a secondhand jeweler. Good riddance. It was Brock's apology for that one time he'd taken things too far. Like diamonds can make you forget.

She fished out the delicate chain from her purse and brushed off the detritus. It was still intact against all odds, an 18-karat phoenix rising out of the ash. She headed toward a mirror as the sales associate slumped away from the shiny display of chains.

"Let me know when you're ready to check out," he called as an afterthought.

"Mm-hmm," she replied, engrossed in the effort of shoving the astronomically small pendant loop onto the chain. It was funny—she'd had to buy this chain herself after Brock gave her the pendant. What kind of ignorant turd gives someone a pendant without something to string it on anyway? Was she supposed to use pipe cleaners? Make a little craft out of it?

She'd thought they were in love. Oh, the naïveté. They were in *comfort*. They both needed a warm body to sleep next to, a way to save on rent, and an excuse to not eat a whole frozen lasagna dinner by themselves. Problem was, he had a hard time tolerating her and all her issues.

She blew a hair out of her face as she poked at the pendant loop. Her issues. He'd made sure she knew about them. She was lazy. Too sensitive. Not spontaneous enough. Antisocial.

*Fibro-my-ass!*

That was his favorite line whenever she gave him the excuse of being tired or sore. *Fibro-my-ass, Terra! You're just looking for a reason to stay home tonight.* He hated when she didn't want to go out. If she didn't relent, he'd go without her, then return hours later with beer on his breath and some feral female's scent on his neck.

Finally she had the pendant in place. She stood in front of the mirror and drew the chain around her neck, watching the initials flash in the light as they dangled from their new home.

After Brock, she'd sworn off dating indefinitely. Nothing good ever seemed to come of it, so what was the point?

Her mom's warning held firm in her memory. *You gotta make a man earn your trust, Terra. And even then, you only give him five percent. You keep that ninety-five to yourself. You can't trust nobody more than yourself.* Odd, coming from a woman who may as well have installed a revolving door at the front of her house for all the men she had coming and going when Terra was young. Apparently, trusting and screwing were two different things. When Terra had asked about her biological father,

Leta had shrugged and said, *Some gringo in Cancun. I was on vacation.* As if *on vacation* were reason enough.

Once the chain was fastened, she stepped back and took in a deep breath. From now on, her loyalties lay with none other than the bearer of these initials, because that was the only person who knew what was good enough for her. She smiled at the glinting little *T* and *Z*.

Going forward, she would be doing things *her* way.

Terra stood by the printer, listening to the rhythm of papers spitting out into the tray. The warmth from the machine and the integral hum of the printing room made her want to curl up in the corner and doze like a cat on a windowsill.

While the printer spat out its ream of paper one at a time, Terra rolled her shoulders in slow circles. They were looser since her second PT session yesterday. Piper had worked out some knots in the muscles. *You're so tight,* she liked to remind Terra in her chirpy voice, as she jammed a thumb into each painful knot.

Terra had pretended to study the chalkboard of motivational quotes while performing her exercises, but she was really sneaking glimpses of Jogger Guy. What was his name? Hayden or something. Hardy? Haggart? Hobgoblin?

He hadn't seemed to notice her this time. All his attention went to his patient, a woman close to Terra's age, but with prettier hair and an easy smile (and also, to Terra's delight, an obvious muffin top). Toward the end of their session, Jogger did that thing where he stood behind her and guided her arms into proper position for her exercises. All cozy and close, like a scene from one of those nauseating Hallmark Channel movies. He'd probably enjoyed every second of it.

"Hey, Terra."

"Oh, hey."

Kenneth, the team's graphic designer, hovered at the doorway to the printing room as if waiting for permission to enter. His hesitance, that timidity she could always sense in the way he flicked his stylus between his fingers, was all wrong against the backdrop of his physical appearance. He was imposing and easy on the eyes, with ebony skin and a frame just over six feet tall. Even through his dress shirt, his chiseled torso and arms proclaimed their presence. Not that she was staring. Though her eyes did linger long enough to detect a stain on the collar.

Terra offered a smile, hoping to appear non-threatening without being too inviting. "How's your day going?"

He plodded into the room and rubbed the side of his forehead with the flat of his palm. "Man, I've had better. But okay, I guess."

"Why? What happened?"

"Oh, nothing. Just...Jess has been riding me all day to finish the cover revisions for the Lyla Harrison book."

"Oh my God, tell me about it. Must she remind us one more time about the *Big Launch*?"

"Biggest book launch ever." He made exaggerated hand motions, though his voice stayed quiet and restrained.

"Hah. Yep."

He gestured to her stack of freshly printed papers. "You...you keeping busy with her book too?"

"Oh." Terra realized she'd been staring, like a moron, at a completed print job for the last few minutes. "This? No, this is a different manuscript. The author is insisting on a hard copy edit." She rolled her eyes.

"I already finished my part for the Harrison book. Alexis is handling the final revisions."

"Oh, right." He paused and fidgeted with the paper in his hands. "I'm sure you could've handled it all yourself if they'd let you."

"Thanks. I appreciate that." She smiled and gathered up the bundle of printed papers in her arms, then thumbed through them slowly.

He looked around. "Uh, yeah, I've got this page I needed to scan. If...if you're done." He pointed to the machine behind her.

"What? Oh!" Terra stepped away and headed for the door. "All yours!"

"Thank you. Ope! Uh...there you go. Okay."

They engaged in a clumsy two-step, not knowing whether to go right or left, until they finally found their way around each other.

"Thanks for the dance!" she called back to him as she walked away, then immediately cringed at herself.

Terra collapsed in her seat and blew stray hairs out of her face. She set the manuscript on her lap, relishing the residual warmth from the printer. It was always cold on this side of the cubicles, away from the windows. One day, she would have her own office with floor-to-ceiling windows, where she could soak up the sun while she worked on all her high-profile projects, and she could close the door and eat a double pack of Nutty Buddies uninterrupted.

One day.

Kenneth must have felt bad about the promotion. That's why he threw that little compliment at her. Her face contorted. He felt *sorry* for her.

No. She stifled the thought. He was a nice guy saying nice things. That's all.

She chewed on the corner of a fingernail. Maybe that's the kind of guy she'd needed from the get-go. The handful of men she'd dated since high school hadn't fit that profile. But who was she to complain? She'd been looking for attention. They gave it. What use did she have for a *nice* boy when it was always the bad ones who appreciated her ass-hugger jeans and shameless flirting? Looking back on it now, she wanted to gag. It was exactly this kind of dimwitted pursuit that led her straight to Brock.

Terra leaned back in her seat and sighed. She needed to get this fibromyalgia and back injury under control. Then she could focus on being the badass copy editor she knew she was. Knock the socks off Jess. Make a name for herself in this company—no, this industry—and say to hell with all the men. She could do this on her own, with no thanks to Brock, or any other man who tried to butt his way into her life. And no thanks to the universe either. Or karma. Or Buddha, or whoever. They'd all left her high and dry.

The soft staccato of high heels against low-pile carpet shook Terra out of her stupor. She looked up in time to see Jess approach her section of cubicles, marching like she had fire ants in her panties. No doubt she was on edge today. A lot was at stake with this book going to print next week, and they couldn't afford any oversights. Terra steeled herself for a barrage of questions.

"Hey." Jess stopped at Terra's desk and spoke in her usual clipped voice. "Lyla Harrison had a real bone to pick with me about the copyediting today."

Oh, perfect. "What happened?"

Jess's severe expression softened. "She was mad that I took you off the job. Said she liked your work best—something about a *preternatural obsession with detail.*"

"Oh."

"Thought you should know."

"I assumed she didn't like *any* of our work."

Jess cackled. "She's not always a raging bitch. Sure as hell can't handle criticism, but we've all got our hang-ups, right?"

Terra nodded and looked down at her desk, unsure whether Jess was thinking of Terra's in particular.

"She's actually not that bad once you get to know her," Jess said. "Literally, talk to the woman about anything other than editing her manuscript, and it's the loveliest conversation you'll ever have."

Jess's cell rang. She glanced at the screen. "Gotta take this. Seriously though. *Lovely* person. Most people are, under all that junk, you know?" She lifted the phone to her ear. "This is Jess."

"Sure," Terra said as she watched Jess disappear down the corridor, a small clump of loose hair dangling from her butt. "Lovely."

# CHAPTER SIX

Terra lay on a table at Recovery Solutions getting her routine therapeutic massage. She should have been relaxed, but instead, she was mortified.

"Just breathe normally. It helps get oxygen to those muscles."

"I am," she said, her eyes scrunched closed. She thought about her taxes. When that didn't hold her attention, she turned to cat memes, tetherball, the demise of the skinny jean. Anything to keep her mind off Jogger Guy.

Harlan. That was his name.

He had introduced himself at the beginning of her session. As her eyes mounted a frantic search for the nearest exit, he'd explained Piper was out sick, and he would be taking over. Now he stood over her, massaging her upper back and neck, pulling down at the collar of her shirt to reach the skin underneath. Same as Piper's massages. Totally legit. But it was different coming from a man. She tried not to think of the word, but there it was. *Sensual.*

"You stopped breathing again," he said.

"Sorry."

She was here to get her spine in working order—get in and get out—not to feel out the dating scene. Not that he would be interested in her anyway. Little Miss Black-Eyed Susan from the park. He was probably still picturing the scene in his head now.

He dug harder with his fingers. "Wow, your neck muscles are so tight."

"So I hear."

Despite the deep breaths, she'd never felt more like she was suffocating. It was time to get things moving along.

"Ouch!"

Harlan immediately withdrew his hands. "What happened? Are you okay?"

She sat up and rubbed her shoulder. "You hit a tender point," she said in a tone she hoped was convincing. "I have fibromyalgia, remember?"

"Oh." The faintest hint of embarrassment flashed across his self-assured facade before retreating. "I thought I *was* watching the tender points. Sorry. Lie back down and I promise I'll be more careful."

"It's okay. Can we move on?" She swung her legs over the edge of the table before he could reply. Anything to put some space between her skin and his hands. God, why was it so hot in here?

"Okay...I guess we can start your exercises." He led her to the open floor of the facility where a stability ball lay waiting. "*I*'s, *Y*'s, and *T*'s."

Terra knelt on the floor and rested her torso over the ball, acutely aware of her exposed backside. Her face parallel to the floor, she created the letters with her arms held out straight in front of her, then at an angle, then to her sides. He stood over her and watched.

"Don't forget your back."

"Hmm?"

"Keep your back straight. Don't slump over the ball."

"Oh."

"You're overreaching. Here..." He gripped her shoulders and pushed them away from her ears. "Keep these relaxed."

Her skin pulsed with hot flashes under his touch. "Yep, got it." She shifted her shoulders free from his hands and scowled at the floor. This was just what she didn't need. A man telling her what to do, holding her back. Piper never bossed her around like this.

After she performed the prescribed letters for His Highness, they moved on to the exercise bands. Terra chose a red band this time—one with more resistance. As she struggled through her first set of rows, Harlan stepped in front and scrutinized her face.

"Are you sure that's not causing you any pain? Because it looks like it is."

"I'm always in pain. What's the difference?"

Harlan moved toward her. "Pain is okay if it's soreness later on, but pain in the moment is not good. That's your body saying *stop*." He confiscated the band and looked down at her with a furrowed brow. The same way Brock used to feign concern right before he bulldozed over her ego. *You weren't going to eat that last slice anyway, right? I thought you were watching your figure.*

"It's fine," she said through gritted teeth. She reached for the handles of the band, but he held them up higher than she could reach.

"Come on, now. No heroics, okay?" he coaxed. "How about a nice, safe green band instead?"

Now she was on her tiptoes, her face turning the same shade of red as the band he'd stolen away. "Seriously, just—"

"You really don't take instruction well, do you?"

Not from patronizing pretty boys. With a leap, she snatched the handles from his grasp and raised her voice. "*Stop* it already!"

He let out a shocked laugh and stepped back. "Woah, take it easy."

A hairy brute of a man on the nearby stationary bike gave a muffled chortle.

Terra returned to her rowing position in silence, her face hot with embarrassment. It seemed her emotional stability had been put out to pasture for today.

"You do realize I'm here to help you, right?"

She fixed her eyes on the wall. "I'd rather do the exercise part alone, if that's okay."

He leaned against the wall and crossed his arms, observing her for a long moment. It made her skin tingle. Finally, he spoke. "You go ahead and do what you want, but I'm going to stay right here and watch. You know, to make sure you don't kill yourself."

Oh, goody.

"Fine, have at it," she said. Something about his gaze was supremely intimidating. And now her arms were starting to shake. Noticeably.

"Ready for that green band yet?"

"No."

He leaned in closer and spoke so the hairy man on the bike couldn't hear. "I get the sense you're trying to prove something."

She stopped her rows a few reps too soon and let the band fall, her arms like overstretched taffy. "I have nothing to prove to you."

"No, but maybe to yourself."

She scoffed. Unable to drum up a worthwhile retort, she began the next exercise, taking her angst out on the lat pulldown machine.

He continued to watch her in silence. From the corner of her vision, she caught a subtle smirk on his face. Cocky bastard.

An eternity later, when the session had come to its blessed end, she made for the exit without a second glance. As she reached the door, his voice trailed behind her, tagging along like a stray piece of toilet paper on her heel.

"Do you still walk the trails at Kessler?"

She half turned to reply, fearing a full turn would invite more conversation. "Sometimes, if I'm in the mood."

"I'm there at least once a week. Maybe I'll see you again sometime."

"Yeah..." She studied his face. He was wearing that subtle smirk again, impossible to read. "We'll see."

*Terra,*

*In the past few times I've observed you, I've decided something.*

*I like your name.*

*It's very fitting. Your mother somehow knew that when she named you, didn't she? Terra: of the earth. Like the strata of canyon rocks, you have many layers to your personality. You don't like letting people past those first couple layers, though, do you?*

*But I've figured out something else. You crack easily. All it takes is a chisel to that dried up, brittle crust, and all that emotion comes tumbling out like a landslide, rock and mud crushing everything in its path.*

*Am I right?*

*I know your type. One doesn't simply exist since the dawn of man without seeing it a few thousand times. In all my years, I've come to appreciate it most. I enjoy watching you try to hold everything in. The flicker of vexation across those delicate features. It's thrilling. You think you are in control, but I know the truth.*

*- H.*

# CHAPTER SEVEN

The smell of tomato soup and overpriced paninis wafted from the quick-service bistro on the main floor of Edifice's office building. Because it was the only in-house option for lunch, its doors stayed ajar every day from eleven a.m. to two p.m., invariably leaned upon by a human chain of impatience leading up to the service counter. Alexis and Terra stood at the end of this line, waiting to order their lunch.

Alexis shifted her weight back and forth and checked her phone. "Crap. I've got a meeting in twenty minutes and this line is not moving."

"You want me to grab something for you?" Terra asked.

"Nah. I've got a Paleo bowl in the freezer. Hey, you want to carpool to the dinner tonight?"

"Oh." Terra had forgotten about the company dinner. "Yeah, sure. I'll pick you up on the way."

"Sweet, thanks."

"Hey, speaking of driving..." Terra glanced around and leaned in. "So I'm on my way home from work yesterday, and guess who I see in my rearview mirror?"

"A cop."

"Worse."

Alexis deliberated. "Ooh. That weird guy from the fro-yo place."

"No! Never mind. Don't guess."

"Who then?"

"Try...*Jogger Guy.*"

"Oh, you mean Mr. Up-in-your-business Bossy-pants from PT?"

Terra nodded as they inched forward in line. "I'm just driving along and suddenly there he is behind me in this junky old truck." She'd recognize that face anywhere. (It was a fact, apparently, that humiliation could burn superhuman amounts of detail into the brain.) "It's like I can't get away from him."

"Terra, you have a *stalker*," Alexis hissed with glee. "Did he follow you from work?"

"Of course not. How would he even know where I work?"

Alexis thought for a moment. "Doesn't it ask for your occupation on those PT questionnaires?"

"Well, yeah, but all I put was *copy editor*. It's not like I gave an address."

"Hmm..." Alexis tapped her long, tapered nails together as she thought. "What about insurance?"

"What about it?"

"Don't you have to put your company name for the insurance paperwork?"

Terra hesitated. "Maybe."

"See? Stalker," Alexis said, satisfied with herself.

"I don't know. He was only behind me for a few blocks."

"Well, do you think he saw you?"

"Yeah, in fact, he pulled up to my right at an intersection and waved to me before turning down a side street."

Alexis pursed her lips. "Does it still count as stalking if he doesn't follow you to your destination?"

"I don't know. I'm not really familiar with stalker code of conduct."

"I *really* want it to count as stalking."

"Oh, you're enjoying this, are you?"

"I bet he knew his cover was blown, so he was trying to play it cool. Smiling and waving and all that."

"Right."

A woman jumped the line and waved her receipt in the cashier's face. Terra only caught snippets of her whining: "...dressing on the *side*...and double charged me for..." The people behind her slumped like a line of falling dominoes.

Alexis blew a raspberry. "Forget this. I'm going upstairs and heating my frozen dinner."

"Good luck with your meeting."

"Thanks." Alexis exited the line, then called over her shoulder, "Better check the parking garage for sketchy trucks on your way out today."

To celebrate the pre-print completion of Lyla Harrison's book, Jess had chosen a high-end seafood joint in downtown Indy. The editing and design teams from Edifice sat in a quiet cove of the bustling restaurant, with rustic wood floors and portholes along the wall, deep ocean scenes set behind their glass. In case diners didn't get the picture, nets and oars were mounted along the ceiling. The only thing missing was the sloshing sensation of seasickness.

Alexis and Terra sat across from each other at the end of the massive concrete table. Poor Kenneth, the only colleague close to their age, found himself on the opposite end, cordoned off by the resident gossips, Darlene and Suzanne.

"All I know is the beaches on that side of the coast aren't worth going to," the company's design director, Justin, said nonchalantly. He had positioned himself in the center of the table to garner as wide an audience as possible. "The property values aren't even close to what I've got on my beach house. But let me tell you about the Keys. Their economy took a major hit last year after that tropical storm…"

Terra picked at her red snapper and glanced down the table at Kenneth, who was caught in a stilted—and mostly one-sided—conversation with Darlene. She turned back to Alexis, who was looking equally thrilled.

Alexis raised her eyebrows at Terra. "Fun, yeah? At least the company's paying."

Mouth full of fish, Terra nodded. She tugged at the hem of her skirt. It was about an inch too short for a professional setting. She should be beyond mistakes like this. Alexis had dressed smartly in a fitted blazer and black dress pants, and unlike Terra, had not received a disapproving glance from Jess directed toward her thighs on their walk to the table.

As Justin droned on about the Keys, Terra shoveled a bite of lobster-infused risotto into her mouth. She looked up to see Alexis staring past her, eyes wide, toward the entrance of the restaurant.

"Don't look now," Alexis said in a covert tone, "but…*hot damn.*"

Oh, she was going to look, alright. "Where?" Terra whipped her head around.

The risotto almost tumbled out of her mouth. There, sauntering toward the bar, was Jogger Guy himself, looking street-casual and smooth in a fitted jacket and ripped jeans. He stretched out his arm and fist-bumped the bartender, then reached across the bar to give him a hug. Terra turned back and lowered her forehead to her hands. "Oh no."

Alexis was on her like a bloodhound. "What? An ex of yours? No, wait. I would've heard about *this* one."

Terra kept her head down and spoke to her plate. "I keep seeing him *everywhere*."

Alexis sat back, sudden understanding registering in her features. She exhaled an emphatic "*No!*"

"Yes."

Alexis guffawed at a volume that drew the attention of nearby coworkers.

Shawn, whose beard and balding head matched the gnome figurines on his desk, jumped at the sound and dropped his fork in his paella.

Justin paused long enough to glance at the girls before finishing his thought on Florida weather. "And that's why you've gotta fork over extra for the dehumidifier. Duct it right into the HVAC. I'm telling you, it's worth every penny."

Alexis returned her attention to Harlan. She twirled her hair and pretended to wave at him.

Terra smacked Alexis's hand down on the table. "Don't!"

Alexis covered her mouth with her hand and released snorts of laughter that made Terra sink farther into her seat. There were times when having a boisterous friend came in handy. Like when you needed a partner for karaoke, or when you needed a buddy to scream for help over the noise of a madman with a chainsaw. Those kinds of times. This was not one of them.

Terra glanced over her shoulder to discover that—oh yes—Harlan had heard the laughter and was searching for its source. For the briefest of seconds, his eyes traversed the sea of commotion—the diners with clanking silverware, the rushing servers, the steaming chowders, the chaos of fifty conversations carrying on all at once—and found hers. She turned back, but the damage was done.

Alexis tittered a couple more times before settling down, dotting the moisture from her eyes with her pinkies. She leaned forward, arms splayed across the table, and beamed. "Well, isn't this an interesting twist?"

Terra resumed her position hunched over her plate. "Is he still looking over here?"

"Relax. He's not looking anymore. Wait. He's looking at you again. Okay...okay, now he's not. He's talking with the bartender."

"Does he look like he's about to come over?"

"No. He just sat down. He's getting a drink."

Terra sighed and withdrew her white knuckles from the edge of the table.

"Honestly, Terra! De-bunch your panties and go say hello to the guy. He can't be *that* awful, can he?"

"I didn't say he was awful. He's just..." Terra picked up her fork and stabbed her fish with a vengeance. "I don't know...intimidating? And when we talk, I get the sense that he's toying with me somehow."

"In what way, exactly?"

"Like he wants to see me flustered."

"Okay..." Alexis's single raised eyebrow didn't offer the vote of confidence Terra had hoped for.

"I'm serious. He's always asking me questions that feel too personal. And the way he stares at me, it makes me all—"

"Hot and bothered?" Now both of Alexis's eyebrows were raised.

"Uh—"

A smug grin spread across Alexis's face.

"No. Lex, look at me. No. It doesn't matter anyway. I don't want to date anyone. He's not my type. And he's clearly not into me in that way."

"Excuses. Excuses," Alexis said in a singsong voice as she twirled her seafood linguini. "Not into you *that way*."

"Right."

"Terra." Alexis straightened up in her chair and pushed her imaginary nerd glasses up on her nose. "Let's approach this from a logical perspective, shall we? What does Occam's Razor tell us?"

Terra rolled her eyes. Alexis had shifted into useless trivia mode, another fun aspect of her personality best used only in specific situations, like trivia night at the local pub, or belittling know-it-all fourth graders. Terra answered begrudgingly, "The simplest explanation is the best."

"Exactly. Now what do you think"—she pressed her hands to her chest—"in your heart of hearts, is the simplest explanation for this man always *staring* at you, as you say, and talking to you so damn much?"

Terra shrugged.

"The simplest explanation is that maybe—*maybe*—he *likes* you. I mean, you said yourself he's toying with you. Isn't that basically flirting?"

Terra propped her hand under her chin and scrunched up her face. "Nah."

A voice from the other end of the table carried through the crowd.

"Once again, guys, great job." Jess was attempting her polished, toothpaste-ad smile as she addressed the team. "I know Lyla has put quite a few of you through the wringer lately, but it will all be worth it when this book blows up. Thanks for sticking it out."

A few cheers and claps rose from the table, followed by a round of obligatory thanks for the dinner. Everyone stood and pulled on their jackets. When Terra reached for her bag, Alexis was already at her side, elbowing Terra's ribs and speaking through her teeth.

"Talk to him."

"No." Terra pulled away from Alexis and rushed to catch up with their group. She could use them as cover. Harlan was still sitting at the bar with his drink, engrossed in the soccer game on the small TV above. Perfect. She positioned herself behind Darlene's hefty frame and scrambled for the door as if the building were on fire.

Big mistake.

In her rush toward freedom, Terra's shoulder knocked Darlene's oversized purse off her arm and onto the floor. The resulting explosion of cosmetics and coins and stowaway dinner rolls across the restaurant floor turned every head in the room.

"What in Sam Hill, Terra!" Darlene exclaimed as she chased after a runaway tube of lipstick.

"I'm so sorry, Darlene." Terra bent down to rake up the purse vomit, wishing she could shove herself into the bag along with it.

The voice she heard next was unmistakable above the clatter of restaurant diners.

"Terra! I thought that was you."

She froze. Without acknowledging him, she turned her face toward Alexis, eyes pleading. Alexis beamed from ear to ear.

Defeated, Terra rose from the floor and faced her intimidator. "Hi."

He flashed an impish grin. "Wow, what are you doing here? Crazy running into you."

"Yeah. Crazy, right?"

"Well, hey, you want to come have a drink before you go?" He nudged out the bar stool next to him.

Terra drifted back toward the door, her entourage quickly disappearing without her. "Oh really, that's okay."

"I'm buying."

"Thanks, but I mean I can't. I have to drive my friend home." Terra attempted to pull Alexis with her, but Alexis leapt forward and stuck out her hand.

"Hey, I'm her friend." She reached to shake his hand. "I mean, I'm Alexis. And I don't need her to drive me."

"Harlan. Nice to meet you." He took her hand, looking pleased as punch with this friendly little encounter. Terra wanted to kick her friend in the shin.

"I can walk home. I'm just a few blocks down," Alexis said. Terra pinched her in the waist as hard as she could.

"Or you could hang with us, if you want," he offered.

"No really, I've gotta get going. I have my dog to feed...and some murder shows to binge-watch." She let out an awkward laugh and flashed a winning smile at Terra. "But Terra here is *more than able* to stay for a while."

"Alright then." Harlan looked to Terra expectantly.

Terra remained frozen, a polite smile plastered on her face.

"Terra." Alexis was talking through her teeth again. "The man wants to buy you a drink." She pushed her toward the bar.

With lead feet, Terra stepped forward and took the seat next to Harlan's.

Alexis scrunched up her shoulders and talked in a syrup-y voice like a mom dropping off her kids at school. "Okay, nice meeting you. You two have fun!" She opened the door and mouthed to Terra, *Call me later.*

Then she was gone.

Fat chance of that. Alexis would most definitely be getting the silent treatment for the next few days. Or weeks.

# CHAPTER EIGHT

Terra sat with her back rigid against the bar stool.

"Well, you look nice," Harlan volunteered.

"Thanks." She tugged at her skirt hem and looked around, hoping to find a cue card or something for her next line.

Harlan motioned to the bartender and turned to Terra. "I want you to meet my friend." A tattoo-covered man with a pompadour walked over. "Garrett, this is Terra."

Garrett tilted his chin at her. "Hey." He flung a towel over his shoulder and reached across the bar to shake hands. Her fingers ached in his exuberant grip. Terra noted the chapped lips, razor burn, and a scar below one eyebrow.

"How do you two know each other?" she asked.

Garret squeezed Harlan's shoulder with a hand covered to the fingertips in more tattoos. "This guy right here nursed me back from a torn meniscus."

"A wh—"

"Knee," Harlan clarified.

"Went to therapy for a friggin month, and this guy was in my face every time, pushing me to get better."

"It worked."

"It did," Garret said, then added under his breath, "Pissant."

Harlan grinned with pride. "You're welcome."

"But no joke, I was in over my head with some real shit back then, and he got me through it. A true friend." He slapped Harlan on the back. "So how do *you* know him?"

"Small world," Terra said. "We met at PT too."

Garrett snorted. "Man, when you gonna take some time off and make friends *outside* of PT? You work too hard."

"Maybe when klutzes like you stop hurting themselves." Harlan gave a wry smile, then turned to Terra. "Believe it or not, this is the best bartender in Indy. He can make anything. What would you like?"

She deliberated. "Vodka cranberry please."

"Best bartender in Indy, and *that's* what you ask for?" Garrett teased.

"The girl knows what she likes, Gare. Put it on my tab."

Garrett stepped away to mix her drink. Terra summoned her courage. Now that she was stuck here, she was going to pick a fight. And this time, *he* would be the one to squirm.

"You want to explain why you keep following me all over this town?"

Harlan frowned at her. "Huh?"

"Don't give me that look. Just tell me why." She turned toward him, one elbow propped against the bar in an effort to appear relaxed.

"What? Why am I *here*? I was in the neighborhood, so I came to catch up with Garrett."

"And yesterday? When you tailed my car for five miles?"

Harlan laughed. "Five miles? No. You were sitting next to me at an intersection. The end."

"And you were going *where* exactly?"

"A friend's place."

"Bullshit."

"Come on!" He leaned back, his face contorted in disbelief. "You really think I'm chasing you around?"

"Explain to me how I see you at the park, and not even a week later, you show up at my PT appointment."

Harlan took a swig from his glass and set it down. "I *work* there. *You* showed up at *my* place of work."

Her face flushed. This was beginning to look like a very deep hole. Might as well keep digging. "Then you insisted on working with me when Piper was sick."

He gritted his teeth. "I was *assigned* to you. My boss called and had me come in an hour early. *For you.*"

Terra narrowed her eyes at him. "Right."

"Right." He matched her expression and began doing that thing where he unnerved her with a mere stare. "Hey. Who's to say it isn't actually *you* who's following *me?*"

Terra shifted in her seat and faked a laugh. "Original. Did you come up with that theory yourself?" With impeccable timing, Garrett plunked her drink down in front of her. She snatched up the cocktail and sucked it down, washing away the sour taste of self-doubt.

"What then? You think I keep orchestrating all these coincidences to trail a person who obviously dislikes me?" He shook his head. "I'm not a masochist."

Terra faltered. "I—I didn't say *that.*"

"Then why so hostile?"

"I am *not* hostile."

He cocked an eyebrow. "Not at all. You're quite pleasant actually."

"I think so."

"So how do you think this conversation is going so far?"

Terra caught a smirk on his face before staring down at her drink. It was getting harder to maintain eye contact. "It's going great."

"Yeah, fun. We should do this more often."

Terra went quiet, a splinter of shame caught in her throat.

After a moment, he spoke, this time with an earnestness to his voice. "How about we start over?" He lowered his face until he was within her downcast view.

"...Okay."

"Okay."

"I might have been a little..." She forced the confession out of her mouth. "Hostile."

"Don't worry about it. I kind of invite it sometimes." His face lit up with a disarming smile that would have given Nietzsche himself warm fuzzies. There were traces of freckles across his cheekbones. It made him look young, though the faint crinkles at the corners of his eyes indicated he was older. Late twenties? "Tell me more about you—what you do for work. Were those your coworkers?"

"How'd you know?"

He shrugged and adjusted the cuff of his jacket. "It just looked like a work dinner. The business casual attire. The polite conversation and forced smiles. Well, except for you and your friend on the end there."

She rolled her eyes and laughed. "Lex isn't the type for polite conversation. She's a little free spirited."

"I noticed. So what do you do?"

"I'm a copy editor."

"Ooh." He sucked in air through his teeth. "A grammar queen."

"There's more to it than that."

"Like what?"

"I won't bore you with the details. Let's just say there's an infinite number of ways to screw up a manuscript."

"So you point out to people exactly how they've screwed up."

"I like to see it as striving for perfection."

"Can anyone really expect perfection, though?"

Terra's eyes snapped up from her drink. "Hey, I may not be changing people's lives or anything, but it's necessary work. I'm contributing to society."

"I didn't imply you weren't."

"It's hard work too. Especially with the fibro."

"Fibro?"

"—myalgia."

"Oh. I'm sure it's harder to concentrate when you're in pain." His eyes went to her hands, as if he wanted to touch them. Or maybe he was avoiding eye contact because offering sympathy was uncomfortable for him. Or maybe it was because the chips in her nail polish were glaring.

Terra withdrew her hands to her lap. "Yeah, it straight-up sucks. Especially when you get passed over for a promotion because you can barely keep up with the workload."

"I'm sorry," he said in a tone that could pass for sincerity.

"So how about you? I know what you do for work. What do you do when you're *not* at work?"

"Hmm... What *do* I do?" His thumb drew vertical lines through the condensation on his glass as he mulled this over, the corners of his mouth hinting at a smile.

"Sounds like someone needs a hobby."

"Running at the park." He took a drink of his gin and tonic and met her eyes.

"We've already established that." She was tempted to ask whether he'd bushwhacked his way off the trail that time he'd pulled a Houdini, but she didn't want to sound like she'd been keeping tabs on him. "What else?" She glanced down at his hands and noticed the corded bracelet peeking out from under his jacket cuff. An amber stone set in the middle of the twisted cords caught her eye and glowed in the low light of the bar. It looked exotic, like a relic from a distant country. "Do you travel a lot?"

He crinkled his eyes. "You could say that."

"Where?"

"The mountains mostly. I enjoy hiking—when I have the time." His eyes shifted away, and he cleared his throat. "Usually, though, I just hang around Indy, hit up coffee shops, spend way too much money on eating out, mostly to meet up with friends—or patients." He flashed a grin. "I do PT pro bono on Friday afternoons."

"Oh, really?"

"Yeah. I help run a clinic that's open to the public. People who don't have insurance, are underprivileged, underserved, that sort of thing."

"Wow. That sounds awfully noble of you."

"It's standard practice to volunteer at the clinics when you're a student," he said with a casual wave of his hand. "I just decided to stay on after getting my license. Now I supervise and help out where needed. They're required to have a couple licensed therapists, so I figured, why not me?"

"Because you needed a hobby, right?"

"Right." He chuckled.

She stirred her drink and stared at him. He was starting to look very attractive. The thought struck her with equal parts thrill and annoyance.

"So, you from around here?" he asked.

"Born and raised."

"An Indy local. Nice. So then all your family's here too?"

"Just my mom. My grandparents both passed away when I was in high school. I had an aunt I don't remember very well—she died a long time ago—and some second cousins back in Puerto Rico that I met once. "

"No brothers and sisters?"

"No."

"Dad?"

"Never knew him."

"Ran off?"

"One night stand. My mom..." Terra let a disgusted sigh slip out. "Not the most stable person. You? Any family in town?"

"No. I moved away from home a long time ago. Getting back to see them is...a challenge."

"You have a messed-up relationship with your parents too, huh?"

"What? No, I meant the travel part is hard."

"Ah." Terra nodded. The alcohol was starting to take effect. She savored the pain-free buzz.

He broke her trance. "I think I've figured out what your problem is."

Terra put her drink down mid-sip. "My what?"

"You..." He pointed an obstinate finger in her direction and squinted his eyes as if working out a puzzle in his head. "Have some pent-up anger issues."

Her face flushed again. Who would say that? Only someone with pent-up *asshole* issues. "Oh, really?"

"It's perfectly natural," he said. "And fixable. No need to get upset."

Something about that tone in his voice was reminiscent of Brock. *Come on, Terra. You're getting upset over nothing again.* A fiery rage ripped through her.

Terra shoved her bar stool out and slid off the seat, though not as smoothly as she'd hoped. Thanks to her short skirt, the bottoms of her thighs stuck to the vinyl and turned the move into a jerky, undignified scoot.

Unaffected by her reaction, he continued to stare down at his drink. "You know, you're just proving my point by doing that."

Her feet finally made it to the floor. After smoothing down her skirt, she mumbled, "I have to go."

"Don't be like that."

"I'll be whatever I want." She grabbed her handbag and turned to walk away.

He caught her arm. "Hey."

She turned to stare him down, eyes blazing.

"I'm sorry," he said. "Tactfulness isn't my strong suit."

"Wow, was it tough for you to say sorry?" she snapped. "Or do you regularly have to apologize for all the dumb shit you say to people?"

He flinched. "I'm not above admitting my shortcomings."

Terra deliberated. His approach was direct and self-assured, but did that make him arrogant? Had she been unfair? For a brief moment, she considered apologizing, but couldn't face the irony of saying sorry for attacking him on the subject of apologies.

"I'm just..." He hesitated. "Curious. About you. I'm trying to figure you out."

"Well I don't need your psychoanalysis."

"I know. I'm sorry."

"And my *anger issues* are *my* business. They're not yours to 'fix.'" She gave him air quotes, her fingernails held out like claws in the air.

"You're right. Please sit back down."

She glared at him for a moment longer—one last warning— then relented. That vodka cranberry wasn't going to drink itself. Calmer now, she slid back into her seat and looked down at her glass as she spoke. "I know what you're thinking. I'm not especially thick-skinned, but I have my reasons."

He leaned his head against his hand and faced her. "Do you want to talk about it?"

"No."

She felt his eyes boring holes in the side of her face.

"Question."

"Can't promise I'll answer," she said.

"I'll give it a shot. Who's in control?"

"What do you mean?"

"In every situation you face. In the outcome of every best-laid plan. In the trajectory of your life. Who's in control?"

She stared at him for a moment, taken aback. "*I* am."

"Are you sure?"

"I mean, there's always those moments I have to hope for the best, because there's only so much I can do, but...it's that way for everyone, right?"

"Sure." Harlan studied his nearly empty glass and shook it, rattling the ice at the bottom. "So in those moments..." His eyes moved from the glass back to her. "Who's in control?"

"No one."

"So you're saying all you can do is hope for the best."

"Right. I just trust my gut and—"

"But how do you even decide what's best?" he asked.

"Uh...are you saying I don't know what's *best* for myself?"

"It's possible none of us do."

Terra cocked her head. "Where are we going with this?"

"You're avoiding the question. How do you decide what's best?"

"I never promised an answer, remember?"

He cracked a sideways grin at her. "True."

Terra propped a heavy head on her hand, mirroring Harlan.

"You look tired," he said.

"Maybe you're just wearing me out."

Harlan laughed. "Am I keeping you up past bedtime?" He made a spectacle of studying his watch. "Woah, it's almost nine-thirty. You should go."

She grinned and swatted his hand down. "Stop. I'm not tired."

"Well good. In that case, I have an idea."

"Let's hear it."

"There's a place a couple blocks over that I'd like to take you to."

"Where?"

"Down there." He pointed vaguely out the window. "We can walk."

"But what is it?"

"Let's just say it'll be good therapy for someone who has—oh, for example—*anger* issues. Not that I'm trying to *fix* anything." He sank low in his seat and held up his hands in defense.

"I—"

"You have to sober up from that drink before you drive home anyway. Might as well kill some time with me."

He had a good point there.

*Oddest of all is their inclination to conceal their hurts. In Eden, to express pain is to reveal weakness. What they fail to understand is that hurt cannot heal until it's coaxed out of hiding.*

*- Elysian Records for the Revivers, Book II: The People of Eden*

# CHAPTER NINE

They strolled down cracked sidewalks lit by the orange glow of streetlights. The air was biting, a sharp chill that made Terra's bare legs sting. Each new assault of wind was punctuated by the echo of car horns in the distance. She stepped in half-time next to Harlan, hoping the words *one more block* were not an empty promise.

To her relief, Harlan slowed as they passed a strip of storefronts. A Pilates gym, a high-end furniture store, an art gallery for people who liked farm animals. The windows were dark. He pointed to their destination at the end of the block: a large, concrete building with less personality than a parking garage. There were no windows, just an unassuming set of double doors tinted black. The neon writing at the top of the building looked out of place amid the gray, utilitarian walls.

Terra read the sign. "Smash Club?"

"Yep."

The only sign of life was the faint pulse of bass music reverberating through the glass doors.

"You're taking me to a *dance* club?"

"Yes and no." He led her to the entrance. "They have a place in the back for smashing. That's where we're going."

She wheeled around and halted in front of him, one hand stopping him at his chest. "I'm sorry? Am I supposed to know what you're talking about?"

"Smashing. Throwing. You know, like dishes and things?" He mimed throwing something with his arm.

She held her stance. "Is this a joke?"

"No. It's a thing. I promise."

"So...you *throw* things." She pronounced the word carefully, as if it were an entree on a French menu.

"And smash them with sledge hammers. It's great stress relief. And fun."

"People pay money to do this?"

"Yeah. Unless you regularly get invited to Greek weddings or something."

She cast another glance at the dark entrance to the seedy establishment, then back to him.

"The way I see it, you can either stand out here in the cold..." He looked down at her shivering legs. "Or come inside with me and try something new."

Warmth. That's what she wanted. Dammit, he had her.

"Fine," she muttered.

He grinned and reached past her for the door. "Stay close to me. It gets crowded in here."

He opened the door to reveal a dark expanse with painted concrete floors, high ceilings, and flashing lights. The music shot out into the street with explosive volume.

Harlan paid their cover and led her through the dance floor. Throngs of the twenty-one-and-up crowd bobbed and gyrated as if their lives depended on it, dancing to a generic pop song made worse by the addition of a plodding electronic beat. They passed a curved bar lit underneath by bluish lights. Its bartenders worked at a furious pace, avoiding eye contact with the hoard of thirsty people weighing down the bar top.

The pair crossed the length of the room to a door on the back wall. A lanky man with sagging jeans and a soul patch compliments of 2001 leaned near the door. He swigged his beer bottle and leered at Terra with jagged teeth. He opened his mouth to speak, then snapped it shut as Harlan shot him a warning glare.

They stepped into a wide hallway with several doors along the opposite wall. The music quieted as the door closed behind them. Terra squinted in the fluorescent lighting. A homeless-looking man lounged with his feet on a desk at the end of the hall. She took inventory: patchy beard, eyes too far apart, sole separating from right shoe.

He sat up as they approached. "Here to smash?"

"Yes, sir," Harlan said.

"K. Fill out these waivers here. That'll be thirty-nine each."

"Yikes," Terra said as she rifled through her purse. "Next time I'll bring my own dishes."

Harlan waved her off. "I've got it."

After they'd purchased their formal dining set, the employee showed them to a closet. It contained long, gray smocks made of a thick material, rubber gloves, and full face masks that looked tailormade for a post-apocalyptic villain. After they suited up in their smashing gear, he opened one of the doors along the hallway and showed them into the room.

"Here's the rules. One at a time. No swinging the hammer or bat until the other person is standing back behind that blue line on the floor. And no throwing stuff at each other. That wall over there is the only wall you can throw at. Got it?" The man produced a beef jerky stick from his jacket, ripped the plastic top off with his teeth, and spit it on the floor.

They both nodded and stared at the discarded plastic.

"You got twenty minutes. Have fun." He bit into his snack and closed the door behind him. The faint drone from the club died away, replaced by an aggressive industrial soundtrack flowing through the speakers near the ceiling.

Terra turned to Harlan and held out her smock-clothed arms. "We look ridiculous."

"Come on. I know you want to smash something."

She looked around, uncertain. The shelves lining the wall held ceramic dishes, drinking glasses, used electric appliances, and old gadgets that looked like they'd already taken a few hits. A table in front of them held an assortment of blunt objects, presumably their tools of destruction.

"Get out that aggression, Terra. It'll be good for you."

She stepped up to the shelves, picked up a ceramic soup bowl, and turned it over in her hands.

"Throw it!"

"I will throw this at *you* if you don't shut up."

"Stop stalling."

She huffed and stepped toward the smash wall. It was covered in colorful graffiti, and enough dents and scuffs to give it the impression of either a very expensive abstract painting or a very dangerous back alley. Targets of varying heights and sizes were painted across the wall. She focused on one small target at chest height and pitched the bowl at it with a shriek. The ceramic shattered and skittered across the floor in tiny pieces. She stepped back and held her hand to her mouth. "Oh. I feel kind of bad now."

Harlan's hand flew to his forehead. "No! You're supposed to feel a release. Try it again."

"But that was so...wasteful."

"I'm afraid you're missing the point." He walked past her to the shelves and grabbed a dinner plate. "Sometimes..." In one smooth motion, he flung the plate toward the wall at warp speed. Fragments flew in every direction and glittered in the light as they fell. "Things have to break before we can be restored." He turned to look in her eyes, the flecks of gold glinting in his own. "From that perspective, nothing is really a waste, is it?"

She found herself lost in his gaze, absorbing the meaning of his words. They felt significant and disquieting. Too heavy for a Friday night. She shook them off.

"Okay then, Socrates." She walked to the shelves and picked up an ancient toaster. "Behind the blue line."

Harlan obliged. She lovingly placed the toaster on the table and wrapped her small fingers around the enormous handle of the sledge-hammer. With the grunt of a tennis pro, she swung the hammer down on top of the toaster, eliciting a satisfying *crunch*. The casing buckled and the lever flew off. She took another swing. The toaster teetered on its side and relinquished more pieces of metal and plastic to the floor.

"Nice!" Harlan yelled.

Terra smashed the toaster into the table until it lay almost flat and unrecognizable. Satisfied, she chucked the hammer back on the table and snagged a textured glass tumbler from the shelf. She ran her thumb over the dimpled surface. It was the kind her mom used to keep in the kitchen, the kind Terra drank her orange juice from when she was a kid. And there it was: her childhood. She let her mind slide back into the memories. Something inside her released like the safety on a shotgun.

This time when she stepped forward, she didn't hesitate to throw the tumbler with full force against the wall. It erupted in a confetti of silver shards.

She retrieved another glass and threw that one.

Then another.

She continued until she'd lost count. She no longer thought of Harlan behind her or the music that blasted from the speakers or how chemically unbalanced she might appear. Her mind was locked on those kids in middle school who'd ridiculed her. On the chronic disappointment of growing up with an alcoholic mother. On Brock and his snide remarks. On her insecurities. Her pain. Her never-ending health problems. She let out a hoarse yell as she flung a dinner plate across the room like a frisbee.

She finally paused to rest and realized she was shaking. Out of breath, she stepped away from the smash wall and surveyed the damage.

Harlan, who'd been watching in silence, approached her side. "You okay?"

Other than having just lost her shit in front of him? Sure. "Yeah." She pulled off her face mask and sucked in a deep breath. "Yeah, I'm good." She smiled.

"You *look* good."

"Thanks. This is actually kind of fun."

"Cathartic."

"Yeah."

They stared at each other in silence, a tangible energy buzzing between them. Or maybe that was just the fluorescent lighting.

The door to the room clicked open behind them.

"Okay, kids, playtime's over." The scruffy man from the check-in desk ushered them back into the hallway and had them deposit their smash gear in a large bin.

Before re-entering the main dance room, Harlan turned to her. "Need a drink?"

"A water would be great. Actually..." She was feeling fancy. "Club soda please."

"Sure."

They trekked back through the frenetic ambiance of music and lights and undulating bodies. The crowd was now packed tighter than a can of Vienna sausages. Terra kept getting bumped and separated from Harlan as they made their way to the bar. When a fuchsia-haired chick nearly elbowed her in the face, he reached back to grasp her hand and pulled her closer. A warmth shot up her arm, which her brain immediately overrode with thoughts of cold showers.

Since there were no seats open at the bar, they stood nearby while she sipped her carbonated water. It was too loud to have a conversation, so they settled for people watching. Harlan pointed out a girl twerking her hardest while her partner danced with all the enthusiasm of a beached whale, and Terra snorted bubbles up her nose.

As the two of them—pressed by the crowds—shifted closer together, and the music pounded in their ears, Terra decided inhibitions were dumb.

She shouted in his ear, "Dance with me."

Before she could change her mind, he was pulling her onto the dance floor.

# CHAPTER TEN

The TV was too loud. Terra's head throbbed from the shouting of the commentator. She made a half-hearted attempt to reach the remote, but, well, the coffee table was *really* far away. She sank back and covered her ear with a pillow instead.

She lay on her side, curled under a blanket, watching the celebrity chef show in a detached state of mind. For now, this was her lot in life: three chefs scrambling around, trying to cook the most impressive version of palak paneer, while a commentator rushed from station to station proclaiming his observations as if it were an Olympic event.

Throwing dishes and swinging a sledgehammer last night had been great fun, but now the old hag was asking her to pay up. Her neck and back ached all over, and her legs were sore and restless. An unrelenting crawling sensation flowed down her right thigh. With every movement, a sharp pain between her shoulder blades caught her breath and screamed reminders of the injury that had not yet healed. But her head—that was the worst. If she turned it too quickly, it was like her brain was sliding around inside, hitting every pain processing center along the way as it bounced off her skull.

"It appears she's decided to sauté the spinach mixture with sriracha. Now this should be interesting!"

The commentator's voice pierced the pillow. She watched his mouth move but didn't process the words. Her mind was back on that dance floor. She saw Harlan's face. His hand around hers. That look he'd given her after she'd flung her wrenching, repressed pain against the smash wall and laid it out for him to see. That look that said he'd seen into her core and accepted it all. Her stomach kept doing flips, though that was probably the after-effects of the alcohol and she should stay close to the bathroom.

She rubbed her cheek—the one he'd kissed after walking her to her car. He'd left her there, dazed and trying to grasp what she was feeling. On TV, a chef tossed something into the metal pan and a burst of flames sprang up. Fire. That's what it had felt like.

She would probably see him again on Tuesday during her PT session. She sighed as she watched a close-up of the sauté pan.

"And he's adding the cumin seeds now."

Tuesday was an eternity away.

"The key is to wait till they're sputtering a little before adding the next ingredient."

Was it possible she was becoming attached to him? To this man who only twenty-four hours earlier had been as abrasive to her as a cheese grater to the face?

"And it looks like that will be the turmeric. Ah, a generous dose!"

No. Of course not. She had just enjoyed the attention, as usual.

That attractive patient at Recovery Solutions had enjoyed his attention too. Terra couldn't have been the first to dance with him at the club—he was already familiar with the place. How many women had he taken there? How many had he kissed afterward? Or more? She closed her eyes as the stifling weight of disillusion crept over her.

Her cell phone emitted a muffled ring from somewhere under the blanket. She jerked, and a wave of pain broke through her malaise. She flung off the blanket in a frantic search for the phone. When she finally found it under a pillow, she glowered at the caller ID before accepting the call.

"I'm not speaking to you right now."

"Oh, come on. Is that how you treat your best friend after she sets you up on the date of your dreams?" Alexis's voice crooned.

"I didn't need setting up. I needed you to *back* me up."

Alexis sighed. "Terra, I love you, but I had to make an executive decision. Sometimes, you don't know what's best for you."

"Why does everyone keep saying that?"

"Huh? Who?"

"Never mind." Terra rubbed her forehead. "It actually turned out okay. We kind of reconciled, I guess."

"By *reconcile* do you mean *kiss and make up*?"

"No. We just hung out and talked for a while."

"And?"

Terra chewed her lip, deliberating. Finally, she opened her mouth and braced herself. "And we went out afterward."

"Girrrrlll!" The elation in Alexis's voice was about as subtle as a trombone in a string quartet. "I need *details.*"

Terra was dreaming. She was almost sure of it. She sat on a bench in the plaza outside her company's office building with her laptop on her knees. It looked like she'd been typing out an author query, but she didn't recognize the message. Her brain was stuffed with cotton balls. Not even fibro fog made thinking this fuzzy. So it only made sense that she was dreaming...right?

It's possible to know when it's happening. She'd heard the term for it: *lucid dreaming*. She had to be in a lucid dream now because you never think you're dreaming when you're awake...or do you? Terra mulled this over, but the thought flitted away from her like a Kleenex in the wind.

If this was a dream, it was a damn boring one. No people. No cars. Not even a bird chirping. She never had dreams without people around. Her dreams had *hordes* of people. An introvert's recurring nightmare. Even a routine trip to the restroom could turn into a panicked quest for solitude. She would open the stall door to a cocktail party in full-swing, or a panel of ex-boyfriends preparing to heckle her. So what the hell kind of mind game was this dream playing with her now?

The air turned cold. She looked up. A monstrous, dark cloud rolled across the sky. Everything in the plaza turned a shade darker.

Across the gardens, from the edge of the parking deck, she spotted movement. Then she remembered with sudden clarity the last dream she'd had where she'd been alone.

*Oh God.*

She knew what it was before it came into full view.

The shadowy figure was moving toward her again. She recoiled in alarm and tried to call out, "What are you?" but her voice came out as a raspy whisper.

It plodded forward.

She was not okay with this. *Not cool, brain.* She tried moving, but her legs were stuck to the bench, as rigid as a pair of frozen ham hocks. *Really not cool.* This was not going to end well.

She tried another tactic. "Stop!"

But the figure didn't stop.

She'd seen a horror film (what was it?) where the heroine was trapped at the end of a hallway, and the ghost—a gross, one-eyed corpse—drifted toward her. Down the hall. The heroine screaming like a '50s creature feature bimbo. Scratching at the locked door behind her. Splinters driving under her nails. Down the hall, closer. Her eyes wide and fixed on the hollow of his no-eye. Down, down the hall...until it passed directly *through* her.

*Holy shit. Wake up. Wake up. Wake up.*

Her heart pounded, but the adrenaline wasn't waking her this time. She watched the figure advance and cursed the futility of her situation. It climbed the concrete steps toward her bench. Actually, she would have preferred a one-eyed corpse. This thing had no face. Just darkness in the shape of a man.

The shadow now loomed over her. She slapped her hands over her eyes and repeated her mantra. *Wake up. Wake up.*

An ice-cold tingling wrapped itself around her wrists and pulled them away from her face. The thing was *willing* her to open her eyes.

Hell no. She refused to look up. Instead, she looked down at her laptop, which was now glowing eerily. The screen had changed. A single, unfamiliar word etched itself against the greenish-white background.

*HULUM*

She stared at the word as the dream faded to black. She found herself gazing wide-eyed at the ceiling in her bedroom, her wrists still tingling.

# Chapter Eleven

"I think I need to get my sleep meds changed," Terra said over the whir of the single-serve coffee machine. "I'm getting some weird side effects."

Alexis snatched a carton of almond milk from the break room fridge and glanced anxiously at her phone. "What's that?"

"Just having weird dreams. That's all." Terra watched her friend grab her mug the moment the machine beeped, then pour in the milk.

Alexis sipped the coffee and cringed. "Oh God. I'm so sleep deprived these days, I don't even dream anymore. What are you dreaming about?"

"Ugh. This freaky—well—just strange things. Are you in a rush or something?"

"Sorry, yeah." Alexis threw the milk back in the fridge and cursed as she dripped coffee on the floor. "I have an acquisitions meeting in two minutes. Jess will be pissed if I'm late again."

"Again? Better get on that."

As Alexis wiped coffee off the floor, Terra's cell rang. She looked at the screen but didn't recognize the number. Oh good. It had been a while since she'd gotten a call from a scammer. She was starting to worry whether they were okay.

"Hello?"

"Terra?"

A shockwave shot down her spine at the sound of his voice. "Yes?"

"It's Harlan."

"Hi..." She tried to come up with a more pleasant greeting but all that came out was, "*How* did you get my number?"

Alexis froze on the floor and looked up at Terra, eyes wide.

"So I looked it up on your chart when I first came in to work this morning. I know this isn't PT related, but..."

Terra let out a nervous laugh. "You know, you could have just asked me for my number on Friday."

Now Alexis was gawking at Terra's phone and grinning as if Ryan Gosling himself had called.

"Now that I think of it, that would've been a lot less creepy of me, wouldn't it?" He laughed. "I hope you don't mind. Just thought I'd catch up with you on my break."

"No. No, that's—" Terra waved her hand at Alexis, who had apparently forgotten about her meeting, to shoo her out of the room. "That's fine. I can talk for a minute."

Alexis shuffled out the door, flashing Terra a thumbs-up on the way.

"Great. Because I was thinking..."

Uh-oh.

"You really seemed to get a lot out of that *anger therapy* session we had the other night. We should go for another round sometime. It might be beneficial for you."

A girlish giggle rose inside her. She squashed it with a more respectable "Hmph."

"I mean it."

"What exactly are you implying?" she asked.

"I'm concerned for your wellbeing, and I'm offering you my assistance, like any good friend would do."

"Oh, are we *good friends* now?"

"I'd like to think so."

Terra thunked her forehead against the wall and sighed. "Look, I think Friday night was fun, but—"

"So let's do it again. Or I could take you someplace different. Dinner this time? We wouldn't be allowed to throw the plates though."

She closed her eyes. "How about I'll just see you at PT tomorrow?"

"That doesn't sound nearly as much fun," he chided. After a pause, his tone became more serious. "Listen..."

"Yeah?"

"I feel like...there's a reason we keep running into each other. I can't let this go. And I don't want to."

She thunked her head harder this time. "Harlan...I'm kind of taking a break from dating."

"Oh," he said quietly, then chuckled. "We'll see how long that lasts."

"You told him *NO?*" Alexis came to a dead stop in the office building lobby, causing a red-faced man in a business suit to crash into her.

"That's not what I said." Terra pulled her friend toward the exit. It was the end of the workday, and they were rushing to beat the worst of traffic. "I told him we could still be friends."

"Ouch! Might as well have kneed him in the nuts while you were at it."

The man in the suit sidestepped around the girls and cast a glance back at Alexis with obvious distaste.

"Honestly, I don't think his ego was bruised in the slightest," Terra said. "This guy is unshakeable."

"He's banking on wearing you down."

Terra stuck a palm to her forehead. "I'm not ready for any of this. This was supposed to be my year off. Just me, being on my own."

"The Year of Terra," Alexis announced with a sweep of her arms.

Terra slowed her pace to avoid catching Alexis's forearm in her ribs. "You're not helping either, you know."

Alexis pushed open the door to the parking garage with a bang. "I just don't get how you can give up dating when it's so fun."

"Yeah, well my experiences haven't been as much fun as yours."

"You have to pick a good one. Take Exhibit A: Collin Krauss."

"That guy you met in spin class?"

"Right. He's smart. He's empathetic. He only takes me to the classy bars. He's at least a seven out of ten. Oh, and he's got these calf muscles. They're like, so..." Alexis shaped her hands into a giant circle. "Thick."

"Alright."

"And juicy."

"Okay, I get it."

"He's taking me to his cousin's farm this Saturday." She flashed a crazed grin.

"Mmm." Terra raised her eyebrows and nodded dutifully. "How very domestic."

They both slowed as they reached their cars.

Alexis turned to her. "Why can't you just give it another try?"

"I guess I'm not sure what I'm looking for."

"A sign from God?" Alexis asked, her expression dubious.

Terra fingered the gold initials at the base of her neck and stared out past the row of cars, into the city streets below. "I don't know."

*One of the many reasons we've provided you with these accounts is because there, the past has become so convoluted with lies over the centuries, no one knows what to believe anymore.*

*- Elysian Records for the Revivers, Book II: The People of Eden*

# Chapter Twelve

Terra was afraid to go to sleep. She lay in her bed in the dark, midnight approaching, lurching awake each time she started to drift. It was Thursday night, and if it was going to be anything like the last three nights, she was in for another wicked trip.

The shadow had been following her again, popping up in her dreams like freaking Michael Caine in a Christopher Nolan film. She'd been so convinced it was the sleep medication, she'd skipped her pill before bed tonight. But what if she was wrong? Her eyes flicked open and took in the edgeless black of her room. In her mind's eye, formless figures emerged and disappeared before her, blending the real with the unreal. She squeezed her eyes shut again.

What was worse, last night the nightmares had taken a more sinister turn. That shadowy punk had *hurt* her. She would have fought back had she known what was going on, but it had been so confusing. As he'd approached, his dark hand had shifted into a knife-like point. She only had time to stare dumbly at it before it plunged into her abdomen, manifesting a shockwave of intense pain. Only after she woke did the pain fade to nothing more than a prickle. That's when the realization hit her: dreams weren't supposed to be painful. Not like that.

She should probably see a doctor. But who? A neurologist? She pictured herself lying in the coffin-like tube of an MRI, magnetic waves pulsing through her brain. Or worse...a psychiatrist? She cringed. She'd sworn off shrinks after that one she saw in college told her to listen to classical music and buy some house plants. Like that would solve her mommy issues.

Come to think of it, one of the few times during her childhood that her mom felt entirely stable and accessible was after a nightmare. Leta would hold her and tell her long, boring stories about her coworkers until Terra fell back asleep. How that jerk Dave was always swiping her instant oatmeal packets, or how Tricia wore the ugliest blazers. Harmless stories meant to distract. A small part of Terra longed to drive to her mom's home now and crawl into bed with her.

She rolled over and wrapped her arms around herself. And here was the other thing: every minute she fought sleep, that was another minute her mind tried to rehash the events of the day. She didn't want to think of it anymore. But too late.

She'd pretty much embarrassed herself in front of Harlan at PT today. He'd been flirting with her whenever Piper stepped away, hinting at their earlier phone conversation, looking impossibly smoldering in that Recovery Solutions polo, and she'd finally caved. No, that wasn't the embarrassing part.

She hatched a plan to see him without calling it a date. She would go with him to his pro bono clinic tomorrow. Never mind whether she was invited. She was off work and couldn't pass up the chance to see him in a different environment. If nothing else, it could prove he wasn't making up stories to impress her.

*Let me pick you up at least,* he replied.

*It's not a date,* she insisted.

*No, but the streets in that area are pretty rough.* He was being a stubborn ass.

*My car can handle it just fine,* she said, deflecting his stubborn ass-ness.

*I was referring to the people, not the roads.*

*Oh.*

So it was settled: he was driving, and she was an idiot.

And now, she was torn between the anticipation of seeing him tomorrow and the dread of what she might see in her dreams tonight. As she succumbed to a night of fitful sleep, her mind drifted to his question from last week.

*Who's in control?*

At least for tonight, the answer did not point to herself.

She dreamed a memory, every detail as it had happened.

She was in first grade. Abuelita had picked her up from school early. *Your aunt's funeral, remember?* she'd explained.

Terra walked down the long side aisle, led by her grandmother's hand, warm and soft around her own. She peered over the rows of people at the large black coffin in front. All she could see was the shiny surface of the lid, like a grand piano, framed between two flower arrangements. She wanted to pick one of the flowers but had a feeling she wasn't allowed.

Terra's feet hurt. The Buster Browns Abuelita made her wear were one size too small, because Leta hadn't bought her new dress shoes in a while. Terra hated how they looked too. Like baby shoes. She occupied her mind with thoughts of kicking them off as soon as they got home, along with these scratchy stockings.

Abuelita pulled her into a row next to Leta, who sat by herself, stiff and unblinking. *Mommy,* Terra cried in a voice excited children use when they think they're whispering. She hadn't seen Leta all week since she'd gone to stay with her grandparents. She didn't know yet it would be another month before she could go back to living with her mother. Leta stared into a space somewhere beyond her sister's coffin. She was beautiful in her knee-length black dress, long black hair to match.

*Mommy,* Terra said again. She sat next to her and placed her own child-sized hand on top of her mother's, looking up expectantly. Leta's face was severe, almost alien. She said nothing and withdrew her hand to her lap. *Mommy?* Leta's only reaction was a hard swallow, as if something had lodged in her throat. Terra felt Abuelita behind her then, pulling her into her lap.

The moment would burn in her memory with great clarity, replaying over and over again in her dreams. It was the first time her mother's behavior had frightened her.

*Terra,*

*The Boss tells me you are becoming too much of a distraction. He says we all have our rights to a good time, but work should come first. I guess it's true, I've gotten a bit carried away lately, haven't I?*

*You are, after all, a probable lost cause. A shot in the dark. Why waste my time?*

*The thrill of the chase.*

*That's why. You are too irresistible to pass up. I enjoy an uphill battle. The Boss, of all people, should understand this. He's been locked in his own uphill battle of sorts too long to judge me. He calls me obsessive. I like to think of it as focused. When I set my eyes on a goal, I see it through. What quality is more exceptional than that?*

*You aren't the first of your kind. Yanira was a challenge too. I get a little delirious with nostalgia every time I think about her. She had fire in her veins, just like you. She put up an admirable fight, but by the end, her mind was putty in my hands. I only regret that my time with her was so short. I was too strong for her.*

*Maybe I have finally met my match in you.*

*- H.*

# CHAPTER THIRTEEN

Terra slid into the passenger side of Harlan's ancient Toyota pickup, thanking her lucky stars the clinic didn't open until one o'clock. She'd needed the entire morning to recover from a night of fitful sleep. She'd awoken at eight a.m., scarfed down a breakfast of leftover pizza and a banana (to balance out the pizza), then collapsed back in bed for another two and a half hours. A hot shower and two Tylenol later, she was feeling better or—at the very least—functional.

Harlan was dressed down in a T-shirt and athletic shorts, a striking contrast to his usual uniform of black polo and khaki pants. He looked younger, more approachable. Okay, and maybe more attractive too. But she tried not to dwell on that.

They drove to the east side of town, through a section of streets littered with abandoned buildings, liquor stores, and title pawns. A mixed bag of people passed them on the sidewalks, their daily lives a mystery to Terra. What would it be like, living here with her condition, in chronic pain but with limited access to healthcare? She leaned her head against the window and watched the sections of sidewalk fly by.

Harlan pulled the truck into a parking lot peppered with potholes and cracks. Slivers of grass rose from the spaces between like tiny victors in a battle for the city air. He led her to a one-story brick building that had seen better days. The sign above the door read *Grayson Physical*

*Therapy*, and—as an afterthought—in a small, hand-written note below, *Free Clinic Fridays 1–5*.

The gym inside was much larger than seemed possible from outward appearances. Its bare walls were painted a pale yellow. Thick, colored tape marked the utility-grade carpet, sectioning off different exercise stations. Stained ceiling tiles abutted flickering fluorescent lights. A row of windows lining the back wall let in just enough sunlight to make an otherwise dank room feel respectable.

Above the leg press station, a solitary poster hung in a cheap frame. The words *don't let your pain define you* spilled across the poster in a slanted, aggressive font. Terra scoffed silently. How could it *not* define you? Maybe it was only intended for people with temporary pain. The kind of people who, after a little effort and rest, can say *welp, glad* that's *over,* then move on with their lives.

"Harlan, my man!"

A white-haired man rose from a chair in the waiting area and held out his hand to Harlan. His back failed to straighten out as he stood and hobbled toward them, but he spoke with the energy of a classic radio DJ.

"Franklin, how are you?" Harlan gave him a hearty slap-and-grab handshake.

"Almost there, my friend. Almost there. This hip's got a few years left in it yet." He patted his hip and flashed a semi-toothless grin.

"You been doing your exercises every day?"

"Every day, yes sir, I have."

Harlan turned to greet the handful of other patients waiting for their sessions to start. He knew every single one by name. "Another day in paradise, right, Carol?" he called to the receptionist behind the front desk as he and Terra made their way toward a back hallway.

Terra was like the *plus-one* of a celebrity on the red carpet, walking a step behind and smiling sheepishly at curious onlookers. She didn't belong here. Maybe this had been a bad idea.

But she'd made this bed; time to lie in it. She followed him to a break room at the end of the hallway, where physical therapy students were preparing for their day, stuffing their things into lockers and chatting it up. Terra was met with half a dozen quizzical looks.

"Hey guys, this is Terra," Harlan said. "Go ahead and say hi. She won't bite."

Terra offered a modest finger wave, imagining herself shriveling up under their gaze like a slug in the dry heat.

A tall, sandy-haired kid with a name tag that read *Hunter* spoke up. "Which school are you with? I haven't seen you around." He stood at the periphery of the group, leaning against the wall, eyes fixed on his cell phone.

It took Terra a moment to realize he was speaking to her. "Oh, I'm not—"

"She's not a student," Harlan said. "She's just interested in seeing what we do here."

"Prepare to have your mind blown," Hunter said to his phone, his tone hinting at a less exciting reality.

She narrowed her eyes at his downcast face and made her appraisal. Sunburned forehead, neck acne, rude.

The other students offered her brief smiles, their eyes uncertain. She definitely should not have come. Who tags along at a PT clinic for kicks and giggles? She needed to make a recovery. Quick.

Terra turned to Harlan. "I can help out. That's what I came here to do—volunteer, I mean."

"Help?" The corners of his lips turned upward. "I got the sense you just wanted to watch. And make sure I'm not some kind of sociopath."

Bingo. "Uh—"

"I'm kidding. We could probably use some help. Thank you."

One by one, the students filed out of the room to meet their first appointments. Hunter slid his phone into a locker at the last possible minute before slinking out behind the others. Harlan showed Terra to her own locker, where she tossed in her purse.

"Afternoon."

She turned around to see an older man enter the break room. His salt and pepper hair, which matched the scruff on his face, was pulled into a ponytail at the base of his head. She imagined his burly frame on a Harley in full leather, but his clothing didn't fit the bill. The loose cotton shirt and pants gave him more of a tree-hugging, yoga-instructor feel. His eyes—Terra was sure one was slightly higher than the other—crinkled at her with a subdued smile.

"I'm Ezra." He shook her hand.

"Terra. I'm guessing you're not a student."

"Ezra is the lead supervisor here at the clinic." Harlan nodded to him as he spoke. "He's also a long-time friend and mentor of mine. He actually started the program here a few years ago."

Ezra nodded and crossed his arms. "The university hosts some wonderful free clinics, but they're on the other side of town. I felt like the people in this community needed something right here."

"A lot of them don't have the means to travel across town," Harlan added.

"So we opened up a clinic and recruited a handful of students who don't mind the drive," Ezra continued. "The owner, Mrs. Grayson, has been gracious enough to let us use her facility every week."

"Wow," Terra said, feeling substantially less of a person by comparison.

Harlan faced Ezra with a wry grin. "Terra has been so inspired by your clinic that she's volunteering her time today. Also, she has no training whatsoever."

"Zero." Terra elbowed Harlan in the ribs. "But I'm always good for some grunt work, coffee runs, whatever."

Ezra raised his eyebrows and looked back and forth between the two of them. "Okay then." He rubbed his thumb and forefinger across his stubble. "I'll need you to fill out some paperwork over at Carol's desk first, but...I suppose you could work as a standby for the students. Be an extra hand, grab supplies for them, that sort of thing."

She shrugged. "Whatever you need." She hoped she meant it.

The disinfectant used for cleaning the therapists' tables smelled like lavender. By the time Terra had scrubbed down each vinyl surface, she was swimming in the scent. She paused to glance up at the clock.

*4:06.*

One more hour. Then she could go home, stretch out on the couch, and hash out how in the world she had tricked herself into doing manual labor. The work had been grunt work, no doubt: cleaning the tables, fetching ice packs, and running messages between therapists and the front desk. Mostly though, she'd stood awkwardly by the waiting area, trying to make conversation with the hodgepodge of patients that occupied its chairs.

It was one thing to make a stammering fool of herself, but it was quite another to hang in the corner like a dead weight, especially in front of

Harlan. So she damn well made sure to stay engaged. She noticed from afar that Hunter was struggling as well. No. Struggling was the wrong word; he wasn't trying. He was just as skilled with his patients as the rest of the crew, but his work was detached, his stare vacant as a schoolyard in July. She wondered if she looked the same way, then reminded herself to smile more often.

Small talk was not her forte, she was well aware. She had attempted anyway. As it turned out, most of the patients were happy to oblige her efforts. Just ask what brought them to therapy, and the stories came spilling out, occasionally with an exhibition of post-surgical scars thrown in for added effect.

She walked over to the dirty rag bin to toss hers in. On the way, her eyes wandered and caught Harlan staring at her from across the room. He smiled, and her heart rate jumped. She looked away and told her pulse to knock it off.

A moment later, he approached, leaned in close, and—to her utter shock—sniffed her. "Mmm. What is that?"

"What?" Terra kept her damp underarms clamped against her ribcage.

"That smell," he said. "Fabuloso? Lysol? Palmolive? Smells great." With a devious grin, he pulled the sleeve of her shirt to his nose and sniffed again. "Definitely Fabuloso."

She swatted him away. "Would you stop that?"

"But you smell so good."

"The hazards of cleaning tables I guess."

"Hey, I've got another job for you."

"Oh, please let it be rolling around in Pine Sol. That's my favorite scent."

Harlan gestured toward a woman in a wheelchair across the room. "Can I get your help with LouAnne? Just sit with her until her ride comes? You know, in case she needs anything. Her daughter's running late picking her up."

"Oh. Sure."

"Thanks. Oh…" He leaned in. "I should tell you, she's a *talker*." He smiled and led Terra over with a wave of his hand.

LouAnne's broad-boned features were wrapped in a crinkled, papi-er-mâché skin, and her hair—a tinge too auburn to be natural—flowed wildly through a large barrette at the crown of her head. Her fingers strained against a resistance band looped around her hand.

"The bane of my existence, this stupid thing," she said as she finished the last rep and flicked the band onto the table next to her.

"LouAnne's been working to restore full function to her arms and hands the past several months," Harlan explained. "She's the hardest worker I've ever seen."

She let out a chuckle. "Oh, I doubt that, but thank you anyway."

Terra introduced herself and felt the weakness in the woman's hand as she took it, the fingers not quite gripping her own. She noted the lipstick creases, the chin fuzz, and the droop of ear lobes traumatized by a lifetime of heavy earrings.

"I'll grab your ice packs." Harlan said.

"No, please. I'd rather skip the ice today. Makes the nerve pain worse."

"No problem." Harlan gestured to Terra. "Terra will keep you company till your daughter comes. Hey, great job today. Keep doing those exercises at home," he called as he ran off to help another patient.

Terra stood by the wheelchair, biting her lip. "Would you like me to wheel—uh—*help* you back to the sitting area?"

"Well, I'm kinda in the way right here, aren't I?"

Terra gripped the handles—they were worn and sticky—and pushed the wheelchair over to the chairs. "So…good workout today?"

"It was a car accident."

"I'm sorry?"

"I injured my spine in a car accident." LouAnne's voice boomed over the murmur of the clinic. "People are always too afraid to ask, but no big deal. Cut to the chase, you know? I hate small talk."

"Oh..." Terra took the seat next to her. "I'm so sorry."

"They had me over at the Rehab Hospital until the insurance money ran out. Now the kids here are finishing the job."

"Well, you're in good hands. I'm sure Harlan will have you walking again in no time."

The old woman let out a wry laugh. "No. These are useless." She patted her own legs. "The accident severed the lower half of my spinal cord. Sliced through it like a stick of salami. I'm just here to get the rest of me back in order."

Terra caught her breath. The words *oh fuuuuudge* rocketed through her head in slow motion. "I feel so stupid now. I'm sorry."

"Don't be. You can never tell a person's situation by looking at them, right?" She smiled, her skin drawing tight against pronounced cheek-bones.

"True."

"We all have obstacles of some kind or 'nother, and they're not always obvious. Some are physical. But others..." She tapped a finger to her head. "Others are up here. Hidden."

Terra drew back. "You mean, the pain is *all in your head*." She fought the urge to roll her eyes as she said it, the cop-out her doctors liked to say without saying.

"No...no. Pain's very real. What I mean is we make obstacles for ourselves, out of fear or laziness or whatever. Who knows?"

"Oh." Terra fidgeted with her necklace.

"I still remember the day we were out buying back-to-school clothes for my daughter, back when—oh hell—she must've been eight or nine. A song came on in the store. Destiny's Children...or Spice Gals maybe? I get them all confused. Whatever. It was her favorite."

"I think it's Destiny's—"

"Well she *begged* me to dance with her. Of course, I wasn't going to make an asinine fool of myself in the middle of that store. I put my foot down and told her to pick a daggum shirt already. Which one is it? The stars or the polka-dots? And wouldn't you know it, she didn't speak to me the entire drive home." LouAnne palmed the well-loved arm rests of her wheelchair and straightened up. "And now I sit here in this wheelchair, thinking *why?* Why'd I have to be a stubborn ass when I could've just danced with her for two minutes? Sure can't do that anymore now, can I?"

"Don't be so hard on yourself." Terra attempted a reassuring pat on her back, then glanced at the door in search of LouAnne's ride.

"I think that way about everything now. There's a lot of things I'd be doing if I wasn't stuck in this piece of junk." She gestured to the wheelchair. "No more making dumb excuses is what I say."

"Yeah, I suppose—"

"You gotta give people the time of day while you can." LouAnne raised her voice as one of the PT students passed, presumably in case he wanted to hear too. "Know what I mean?"

"Huh...yeah," Terra said. "Makes good sense."

"Hmph." LouAnne laughed at herself. "I'm sharper than I look. Twice as old too." She turned her face to Terra's with a conspiratorial grin. "It's the red hair," she stage-whispered.

Terra returned her grin. This woman was sort of nuts, but in a fun way.

LouAnne launched into another story unprompted. "I made excuses during my recovery too. Hell, did I ever fight with those nurses…"

Terra's gaze drifted to Harlan as LouAnne continued her monologue. He was laughing with his patient as they talked. He seemed to put everyone at ease, like it was his superpower or something.

"And I said to myself, *Lou, you get yourself out of the way already. Stop fartin' around and do what you gotta do.*"

"Ready, Mom?" A flustered woman in her mid 30s popped in the doorway, a couple of adolescent boys in tow.

"Oh good! My chariot is waiting," LouAnne announced.

Her duties fulfilled, Terra stood and pushed the wheelchair toward the door. She bent to LouAnne's side and offered the obligatory, "Nice meeting you."

"Oh stop. I talked your ear off, didn't I?"

"Uh…no, not at all."

"Oh! One last thing, and this is an important one." LouAnne lowered her voice to a near whisper and motioned for Terra to draw close.

Terra leaned in, preparing to be imparted with the wisdom of her elders.

"If you ever end up in the hospital yourself…" LouAnne paused to cast a surreptitious glance around the room, "…just make sure that hospital gown is tied real tight in the back. They don't call it *I-C-U* for nothing."

# CHAPTER FOURTEEN

Terra sat in silence on the ride home, the sky growing dim as the sun gave off its last feeble rays of light. A single question had lodged in her brain after her conversation with LouAnne. Sure, this whole anti-dating crusade of hers was noble enough, but was she just making dumb excuses because she was scared?

In the two years she'd dated Brock, her self-worth had shriveled up like a vestigial organ, a useless remnant she now carried inside her. Even when she suspected him a cheating man-whore, she'd stayed with him. He'd already made it clear no one else would tolerate her problems. She'd been determined to prove her mother wrong about men, that conflicts could be worked out, that relationships weren't a wad of gum you chew up and spit out when the sweetness fades. At least, until that one night. She clenched her teeth and stared out the passenger side window.

That one night. They were out to dinner with a group of friends. *His* friends—it was always his friends. The old hag was playing hopscotch on her back, but she smiled through the pain and stayed engaged, laughing at their moronic frat party stories and downing melon ball shots with the other girls. She was managing pretty well, she thought. Then someone suggested they all go dancing after dinner, and the hag screamed *screw that shit*.

Brock was already leading the charge on which club to hit first when Terra told him she couldn't go.

He curled his lips in disgust. *Forget it then, we'll go without you.*

The sense of abandonment was so overwhelming, she couldn't stop herself. *Why? So you can find some skank to hook up with later?*

That was all it took. Loud enough for everyone at the table to hear, he called her an *uptight mixed-breed bitch* and knocked her water over with the flick of his hand. The full glass hit the table with a *thud*, spilling ice water into her lap. The shock from the wet and cold might as well have been a baseball bat to her stomach. Every muscle in her body tensed, exacerbating her back pain. In that moment, she knew this kind of relationship wasn't sustainable.

It took her two more months to end it. He'd apologized with the diamond pendant, and she'd taken him back. But you can't put a turkey vulture in a white tutu and call it a swan. He was back to his old habits in a matter of weeks. Once she left for good, her heart was as hollow as an old tree stump. He had wrecked her.

Now, here was this man driving her home who knew just the right thing to say to get under her skin. But maybe it wasn't out of malice. Maybe he was breaking down her walls, searching for the real Terra inside. Maybe...she could deal with that.

On their way back from the clinic, they'd stopped for dinner at a counter-service pho restaurant. Then Harlan said the most heartfelt thing ever spoken across a bowl of noodle soup: *You were so caring and kind with those people today. It was breathtaking.*

Boy, he was laying it on thick. *Caring and kind.* The descriptions sounded foreign to her. She was most definitely selfish and lazy—that's what she knew. But it was possible, she hoped, he saw her better than she saw herself.

And *breathtaking*...that was definitely overkill. But not really *her*, right? Just her actions.

Harlan parked near the walkway to her apartment and turned off the headlights. The sky was now nearly dark, and the exterior lighting of the building glowed in diffuse circles along the edge of the parking lot.

"Let me walk you up," he said softly, then strode around to the passenger side and opened her door.

She was a big girl who could find her way out of a car, but her heart thrummed at the sight of him standing there, his hand reaching out. Against her pride and waning resolve, she took it.

As they approached the entrance, two residents burst out the door and headed for the parking lot. Harlan pulled her off to the side among the Japanese maples that framed the front steps, as if she were a secret he didn't want to share. As the sound of the strangers' steps grew distant, Harlan turned to face her.

"We should do this every week," he said.

"I do work every other Friday, you know."

"I'll come to your office and steal you away," he said, then whispered mischievously, "No one will know."

"Right. We'll have to work on our breakout plan, but I think we can throw them off the scent with some cleaning products."

His grin broadened. "Two words: aerosol bombs."

"Ooh, I like your way of thinking."

"I am awfully clever, aren't I?" He stepped closer and tucked a stray hair behind her ear. The back of her ear tingled at his touch.

"Mm hm." She had lost her words. *Words.* The very concept floated around in her head, unfamiliar and disjointed. What were words anyway, if not pointless noises delaying the ultimate goal?

His eyes went to her lips.

She leaned into his space, willing it to happen. She'd given up. Game over. He had her, the sneaky bastard.

Eyes full of intensity, he hesitated, then pushed forward and closed the gap. His lips met hers.

Fireworks. Butterflies. Freaking cows jumping over the moon. All the feels began spilling out of her faster than she could stuff them back down. This was so far beyond what she'd expected for today, but she would take it. She'd take it all and keep it, thank you very much.

He ended the kiss too soon, leaving her breathless and dizzy.

"I should get going," he told her, though his arms continued to cling to her as if they disagreed.

Terra knew if he let go, she'd collapse like a crumpled daffodil onto the mulch below. So she kept her arms locked around him and ran a hand along the back of his neck, feeling the soft prickle of sheared hair against her fingers. *Man hair.* She'd missed this.

He leaned his forehead against hers and cupped his hands around her face. "When can I see you again?"

She smiled and laughed faintly.

"Tomorrow," he said. "Let me see you tomorrow. I'll take you out for dinner."

"Okay," she whispered, "but it's not a date."

"It most definitely is a date."

It had been worth a shot.

"Good." He kissed her one last time before releasing her to wobble away on her limp noodle legs. "I'll call you tomorrow."

"Goodnight, Harlan." She mounted the steps to the entrance and took one last look before opening the door.

He stood where she'd left him. He was watching her, his arms crossed, that same old smirk on his face. She hated that smirk. It was insulting. Obnoxious. Kind of adorable. And it was starting to grow on her.

*Terra,*

*Would you be frightened to learn that I watch you sometimes? It isn't all the time. My work keeps me too busy for that. But why would I choose to spend a minute of my free time anywhere else? You're so much more fascinating than the others. More complex. I know a lot of my kind go for the easy cases, but that's not for me.*

*In fact, my colleagues and I have a little bet going. They seem to think you're impenetrable. I have to admit, I'm very disappointed in their assessment of my ability. They will learn, though, won't they?*

*Today I was too occupied with my assignments to pay you much attention, but tomorrow is another day. Because, see, in my head all day today, I was making plans. The grueling labor of working on all these humans is mindless to me, and so lent me time to mentally prepare. I plan on seeing much more of you soon. I'll be monitoring your every move, finding out what stirs you.*

*Pretty soon, I will be inside your head. There will be no shaking me. To you, I'll be more than just a passing thought between dream and waking. I will speak and you will hear me.*

*Pretty soon, Terra, you will belong to me.*

*- H.*

# CHAPTER FIFTEEN

I t was Saturday, and the weather was perfect. It was the kind of spring day that drew people out of their dusty winter dwellings, along with last summer's sandals and some long-forgotten sunglasses pulled from the depths of a glove compartment. Short sleeves and cropped pants emerged from the backs of closets, while razor blades were dulled in the name of waking legs from their hairy hibernation.

As the late afternoon sun descended through a bold azure sky, Harlan parked the truck at the edge of a clearing all too familiar to Terra's eyes.

She turned to him in surprise. "Kessler Park?"

He cast a sideways grin at her. "The scene of the crime."

"Are you calling our first meeting a crime?"

"No. We didn't meet until PT, remember? But here, seeing you cry. *That* was the crime."

"Right." Yep. Laying it on thick.

"Which reminds me, you never did tell me why you were crying."

Terra crossed her arms and looked out her window. "I thought we were going out to dinner."

"We are. I thought we could have a picnic."

"Oh, well isn't that quaint of you?"

He nudged her in the ribs with his knuckles. "Don't act too impressed."

She let a smile slip out, then glanced around. "Where exactly?"

"There's a perfect spot up on that hill."

She leaned toward him and craned her neck to see out his window. He smelled like clean cotton and sandalwood, but a touch muskier, and—what was that? Thyme? She forgot what she was saying. "That hill with the...the..."

"The...?" He smiled down at her, his face too close for comfort. The truck suddenly felt small, the two of them vacuum-packed together. It was too quiet. And she was pretty sure she'd stopped breathing.

She broke eye contact and pulled herself back upright, her lungs finally remembering what they were created for. "The big tree?"

"Yes," he said. "The hill with the big—"

"Great, let's go." She was out the door before he could finish.

Ten minutes later, they were resting on a blanket underneath the sprawling branches of the massive oak tree, dining on the most elegant menu of all: sub sandwiches and potato chips. Terra had snickered when he pulled the bag of food out of his backpack, but he'd shrugged and said it was either this or sushi, and he wasn't sure if she liked sushi.

They finished their subs, reclined, and stared up at the twisted branches of the oak. It stretched out in every direction, with enough knots and scars to suggest decades of weathering. It must have been there for a century or more.

A shiver shot through her. The wind blowing across the field had felt nice out in the sun, but here in the shade, it was like getting smacked around by an elderly woman with cold hands. She crossed her bare arms and watched Harlan dig through his pack. His hand emerged holding two wine glasses.

"Ooh. What'd you bring?"

He slid a large green bottle out from an insulated cover. "It's a chardonnay." He studied her reaction. "It was either this or a merlot."

"What kind of place do you shop at where you only have two choices for everything?" She bumped his leg with her bare foot.

He kicked her back lightly. "I guess I'll just drink the whole thing by myself since you don't want any." He poured himself a generous glass.

She reached forward. "Not if I drink it first. I love chardonnay. Gimme."

He held out the poured glass to her and proceeded to fill a second one, a smug grin on his face. He leaned back on his arms and sipped his wine. "You like it?"

"Sure beats motor oil."

"That bad?"

She leaned back next to him. "It's perfect, actually."

"Good."

"Hey." She turned on her side to face him, propping herself up on an elbow. "How'd you get the name *Harlan*? It's really...different."

He chuckled. "Not as different as my first name."

"What do you mean?"

"Harlan is my middle name. I go by that because my first name is even worse."

"What is it?"

He turned on his side, bringing his face close to hers. "Rejlukrel." The word rolled off his tongue like crushed velvet. *Rrresh-luh-KRELL.* Like one of those romantic languages she'd always wanted to speak but didn't care enough to learn.

"You're right. That's way worse," she said with a smile.

"It's a family name." His finger traced lines down her own as he spoke.

She shivered. "Where'd you say you were from again?"

"I didn't." His eyes looked up from his glass and pierced hers for an intense moment before glancing away.

"You never talk about your family."

With an expression full of indecision, he rolled onto his back and stared up at the tree. "I don't see them anymore. It's hard to explain."

"I'm a good listener."

After a moment of deliberation, he said, "I'll strike a deal with you. You tell me why you were crying that day when I first saw you, and I'll tell you something about where I'm from."

"Okay." She exhaled and swirled her wine around in its glass. "It was just...stuff. A whole lot of stuff, all at once. You know how they say when it rains, it pours cats and dogs?"

"I don't think that's quite what they say, but yeah, I get it."

She shrugged off the mixed metaphor. Two sips in and she was already becoming *more* awkward. Perfect. "Well, anyway, it was like that." After a reflective pause, she said, "Okay, so where are you from?"

He scowled at her. "Okay." He stared off into the distance as if imagining a scene. "It's a place a lot like this, except very different."

Terra raised an incredulous eyebrow.

"It's very far from here, but closer than you'd think."

"Okay..."

"And, hmm, let's see. It has a lot of *stuff*." He gave a single nod, as if satisfied with his answer. "Just stuff. That's all."

Terra shot him a blank stare, then heaved a sigh. "Alright, fine. I was feeling—I don't know—weak. Like I couldn't get a handle on anything.

My health, my screwed-up relationship with my mom, my career. I just never pictured this was how my life would be at twenty-five."

His expression softened and he drew closer. "I'm twenty-eight, and I'm nowhere near where I thought I'd be."

"You seem like you have it all together."

"No. None of us do. None of us ever could."

"Well, that's a fatalistic viewpoint. Damn depressing too."

He cracked a smile at her and rested his hands behind his head. "I think it's comforting."

"Well, I think if I could get my health back, everything else would fall into place."

"You think?"

"Hell, yeah. With perfect health? I could conquer the world." She downed the rest of her wine. "Okay, it's your turn to answer."

"Where I'm from?"

"You promised."

"One thing. That's all."

"Why so mysterious?"

He ignored her question. "Where I'm from..." He paused. "We never lived in a house."

"So...an apartment?"

"No, there weren't any buildings."

"Shut up."

"We slept outside under the trees like the animals."

Terra scoffed and threw her empty bag of chips at him. "I'm over here baring my soul to you, and you give me that? A friggin' Tarzan story?"

He laughed until she was erupting in fits of tipsy giggles alongside him.

"Man, did I get a bum deal," she said between leftover hiccups of laughter.

"I told you one thing. Now have some more wine with me."

She held out her glass, and he poured.

As the shadows of the trees stretched across the ground, a tai chi class packed up their things and headed home; the last parents on the playground pried their cranky, tantrum-ing toddler from the swing; and a pair of teens emerged from a trail, just before one chucked the other's hat into the pond and made a break for the parking lot with devious cackles. All the while, Terra and Harlan lay on the blanket, taking in the vibrant colors cast from the sinking sun until it was a razor's edge of brightness on the horizon.

Harlan's voice broke through the stillness.

"There's something about you. It makes me want to trust you." He turned his face to hers with a look that was heartbreakingly sincere.

She didn't know how to respond to such a declaration, so returned his gaze in dumbfounded silence.

"There's so much I shouldn't say, but I want to when I'm with you. I—" He faltered.

Her entire body tensed in response to this uninvited weirdness. "About what?"

"Mostly my past. It's a complicated one."

"Oh."

He shook his head. "I'm sorry, I need to stop. I'm making it weird."

Yup. "No, it's okay."

"No, it's not." He sat up and scanned the park with his eyes. From Terra's vantage point, the waning light bathed the lines of his face with an ethereal glow. She admired the dark eyelashes, the gentle slope of his nose, the faintly upturned lips—the ones she'd kissed just last night. Not that she'd been obsessing over it. Much.

"You don't have to talk about your past for us to get to know each other. I don't really like my past either," she said. "Let's just talk about the present. Who are you right now?"

"Alright." He reached out a hand to hers and said, "Come on."

She sat up and felt the dizzy rush that comes with drinking too much wine. "Where are we going?"

"For a walk." He helped her to her feet. "To get to know each other."

"Isn't it getting too dark to walk the trails?"

"We'll be fine. After all, I've got *you* to protect me." He flashed his trademark smirk, then pulled her in close to his side and planted a kiss on her cheek. A million tiny nerve endings in her face rejoiced, while her heart danced the Carlton and her pulse clapped in time.

Hand in hand, they headed down the grassy hill to the deserted trails below. Aside from the bark of a dog somewhere off in the distance, the park was serene, the subtle sounds of evening filling the air. If it wasn't for the intoxicating allure of a moonlit walk, she might have paid more attention to the wrenching sensation in her gut that something was very wrong.

# CHAPTER SIXTEEN

The trees along the trail were only just beginning to bud, allowing light to pass through their branches and illuminate the path below. Everything was painted in the stark contrast of moonlight and shadows. This place Terra had been countless times during the day was now like an alien planet inspired by Rorschach paintings.

She and Harlan walked along the darkened trails at a brisk pace, trying to fend off the cold. They talked at length about inconsequential things like quirks and pet peeves, secret talents and biggest fears. They argued over the best way to eat corn on the cob and whether Bon Jovi counted as hard rock. Terra kept smiling like an idiot—mostly, she told herself, because she was pain-free tonight. It could have been endorphins, but it was probably the wine.

"It's kind of nice being out here at night," she said. "We have this whole place to ourselves."

Harlan's fingers mingled with hers. "Our own Garden of Eden."

"Hm." Terra pictured a naked man and woman frolicking through the jungle and wondered what he was implying.

"Do you know the whole story of Eden?" he asked.

"Something about eating fruit? Temptation and all that. Why?"

"I just think it's an interesting story." His pace slowed as he spoke. "Two people on the verge of making a single choice. One that would ultimately affect everything for better or worse."

She matched his pace until they slowed to a standstill. "Sure, yeah." If this was his way of romancing her, she wasn't getting it. A strange metallic clink registered in her ears, but when she turned to look behind her, she saw nothing but darkness.

Harlan stood before her. The light cast against the darkness on his features created sharp angles and deep hollows. "What if they'd made a different choice?" He stepped closer.

"I don't know." She noticed the faint metallic sound again. "I'm not sure I'm following you."

Suddenly, he gripped her arm with alarming intensity. "Well, I think something is following *us.*" His eyes locked on the path behind her.

She turned toward the sound that was growing louder by the second. A dark figure dodged in and out of the shadows, close to the ground. Two glowing eyes emerged as it approached.

At last, a familiar shape materialized out of the darkness.

"Oh!" Terra called out. "Are you lost?"

She tried to step forward, but Harlan kept a firm grip on her arm.

"Harlan, it's just a dog, see?"

The animal trotted forward without hesitation, the moonlight glinting off the wet of its nose and the shine of its fur coat. It was large with pointed ears, like a German shepherd. Small metal tags swung from its collar and made the jingling sound Terra had heard. Looked like this dog had ditched its owner, maybe jumped a fence. The tags might have a number they could call.

"Let's just check—"

Harlan's fingers dug into her arm until it hurt. "Terra. I don't think that's a dog."

She huffed at him. "I know what a dog looks like. It has a *collar* for crying out loud. Stop—"

With tremendous force, Harlan whipped her to his side and shoved her into a thick tangle of trees and brush.

"Wha—?"

Branches tore at her arms and legs as she stumbled over the uneven ground. He rushed up from behind and locked his arms around her. A single bark from the dog echoed behind them on the path where they'd been standing.

Then, the strangest thing.

Before she could gripe at him for this unexpected rudeness, Harlan carried her forward, over the edge of—*what the hell?* She couldn't see for the lack of moonlight here, but she felt the ground sink away beneath her feet and the sudden, heart-stopping sensation of falling. The dog's bark reached her ears one last time but now sounded far away. Then all went quiet. The wind was still. Only the blinding darkness swirled around them.

Falling. She was definitely falling...very, very far.

Her panicked breaths burned in her windpipe, but her ears didn't register the sound. Harlan's arms still clung to her in a death grip. Had he not seen the cliff before dragging her over it? Was this how she would die? In the arms of a halfwit who had no understanding of the phrase *look before you leap*?

Overwhelming dizziness set in. Then, the pressure of earth met her feet, the moonlight returned, and the sound of Harlan's breath awakened her ears. It was inexplicable, but they were standing still. She wrenched herself free from his arms and looked around. They had landed—*safely*—on solid ground. As if gravity had decided to let this one slide.

This place where they'd landed had enough light for her to take stock of their surroundings. A forest of tall trees—much taller than any she'd seen at Kessler Park—stretched out around them. There was no sign of the path, nor was there a face of a sheer drop nearby. It must have been hidden behind the trees.

She rubbed her face to reorient herself. Her legs stung. She looked down at the welts forming where the brush had scraped her. "Why did you push us off that ledge?"

"What?" Harlan picked leaves off his shirt with a shaky hand.

She gaped at him. "We were *falling*. You didn't notice?"

His brows drew together. "No, I don't think so."

Why did this feel like explaining trigonometry to a two-year-old? "What? You think we just *walked* here? She stumbled over to a tree and leaned against it. "Why am I so dizzy?"

"I—I'm sorry about that," he stammered. "I forgot it can hit you pretty hard the first time."

She turned and gave him a *whoa, buster* look. He stood with his hands shoved in his pockets and eyes on the ground, like a kid who had knowingly broken a rule.

"The first time of *what* exactly?"

He hesitated. "Let's sit down for a moment and take a breath. You need to get your bearings first." He stepped forward and reached out for her.

She recoiled. "How about you tell me what happened back there? That dog wasn't going to attack us. I know what a dog looks like when it feels threatened. And you—" She paused to catch her breath. "You *manhandled* me into a wall of trees." She lifted a weak hand to her forehead. "Oh my God, Harlan. Why?"

He pushed both hands flat against his face and rubbed his eyes. "I'm not sure how to explain it to you."

She wobbled a little and scanned their surroundings again. Why did these trees look so tall? Was she *shrinking*?

She must be hallucinating. Was this weird feeling a product of her racing heart, or was it something she'd had to eat—no, *drink*? She looked back at Harlan. His hands slid off his face, and he met her gaze.

"Terra—"

"What did you put in my wine?" Her vision started to narrow as full-blown panic set in. She began backing away.

"The wine? It's not— You're just in shock. Listen, I was trying to protect you. I didn't mean to—"

"What? You didn't mean to *drug* me?" She began shaking her head as the reality of her situation sank in. "Shit, Harlan. Did you really think your only option was to force yourself on me? Get me all alone out here in the woods?"

"I promise you, I'd never do that."

She continued to back away, feeling her way around the tree. "Dammit. I really liked you too." So much for dating. What a sham. It was only a matter of time now before she resigned herself to a convent.

"You're confused and scared. Let's just talk for a minute." He took a cautious step toward her, as if she were a wild animal ready to bolt.

And that's exactly how she felt. Every ounce of her being quivered with an explosion of energy, and she knew only one word in that moment.

*Run.*

# Chapter Seventeen

Her legs moved at breakneck speed through the trees toward what she hoped was the trail. Better to take her chances with the dog than with him.

She heard Harlan shouting but fought the urge to look back. If he was going to give chase, she would need a monumental head start. Aside from the fact that he was in good shape and much stronger than her, it was possible whatever was in her system would knock her out in a matter of minutes.

Lovely.

She needed to find the trail. But where? She peered through the dense forest while dodging trees. Without her eyes on the ground, she nearly went sailing over a large rock. Her foot landed with a painful twinge in her ankle.

Forget injuries. Her legs would have to detach from her hip sockets before she'd consider stopping. More and more light peeked through the trees ahead, until she came upon what should have been the opening to the trail.

Should have been.

Instead, she stood at the edge of an endless stretch of rolling hills covered in long, thick grass. She must have gotten turned around during the fall—or dizzy spell—whatever it was. But she was committed now.

Kessler was only so big, and she was bound to reach a road soon. Maybe over the next hill.

Without the rocks and roots of the forest to trip her up, she became a human freight train. Her legs pumped and her breath burned in her chest. Only after reaching the base of the first hill did she feel safe enough to glance over her shoulder.

She spotted him at the tree line. He was pursuing her. But not at the frantic pace she was running. Nope. He jogged along like this was a Sunday stroll.

Like there was no rush because he already *had* her.

His confidence incited a fresh wave of hysteria. She let out a madwoman's shriek and forced her legs to work faster.

Any road would do. All it would take was one car, one passerby. But where were the streetlights? All she could see was a planetarium-perfect display of stars above. She'd never seen starlight this immaculate. She might have stopped to appreciate it if she hadn't been busy with other stuff like trying to survive.

When she reached the top of the second hill, her steps began to slow. She couldn't comprehend what she was seeing. There was no road below. There was nothing but more fields of grass, a carpet of emerald that extended to the very edge of the horizon. Miles and miles of it.

In a last-ditch effort, she ripped her phone from her back pocket and brought a shaky finger to the screen. She hit 9-1-1, but the phone informed her there was no network signal. She dialed a second time and received the same response. *No network. (Oops! Looks like we haven't built a tower here yet!)* An embarrassed emoji stared back at her from the screen, the two rosy cheeks taunting her with flippant remorse. She screamed in fury and chucked the uncooperative device into the grass.

Her knees hit the grass as she collapsed under hard, panicked sobs. Looked like this was where the proverbial road ended for her: in a place with no roads. She was going to die in a horrible state of irony. And this man, this *stranger*, had done—was about to do—something so inexcusable, it made her stomach churn. She held her head in her hands and tried to regain control of her breathing.

She'd been gullible. Missed all the signs. Alexis's jokes about him stalking her suddenly took on a darker hue.

Lost in her racing thoughts and heavy gasps, she failed to hear his approach.

A hand seized her shoulder.

She screamed and flailed her arm in the direction of her attacker. Harlan's hand closed around her wrist and hauled her toward him. In her effort to pull away, she lost her footing. Her legs thrashed in the slick blades of grass.

"Terra, stop!"

She sure as hell wasn't going down without a fight. She swung her other arm toward his jaw. With little effort, he dodged and brought up his other hand to catch hers. He jumped out of the way just in time to miss her foot driving into his knee.

She fought with all the energy of a rabid squirrel, but now he had hold of both her wrists. She couldn't get the leverage needed to twist away, and his ability to elude her kicks was maddening. She stretched her head in the opposite direction and searched the horizon. There had to be *something* out here. A Cracker Barrel at least.

"Terra! *Look* at me!"

She turned and looked into his gold-flecked eyes. They were traitorous and achingly beautiful, and she hated him, and she promised herself she'd never waste money on another kickboxing class again.

"I would never hurt you. Can't you believe that?" His voice cracked.

Terra stopped struggling, too racked with fatigue to speak, and allowed her feet to slide out from under her until she was seated on the ground. She hung her head and breathed in the pungent aroma of crushed grass.

"We were in danger. I saw it in its eyes—the dog's—but that doesn't matter now. We're safe." His grip on her softened. "I'm sorry I scared you. I had to get us out of there and had no time to prepare you for it."

She watched, languid and numb, as he dropped to his knees and cradled one of her hands in both of his—so carefully—as if he might break her, the delicate China doll with poor fighting skills.

"I need you to believe me," he said. "Please?"

She wasn't sure what he was asking her to believe. But what were her other options at this point? Now that he had her, he didn't seem to be hurting her. And the scared five-year-old inside her could really use a hug. So she nodded. She would at least play along for now.

Once she got home—got her bearings again and sorted all this out—all bets were off.

But when he embraced her, an involuntary sigh escaped her lips. Her adrenaline began to fade as she melted into his warmth. Damn, he still smelled good.

He kissed the top of her head and held his lips there as he whispered, "I'm so sorry."

She let him hold her for a while, until her heart returned to a steady, non-rabid pace. Then she pulled away and rubbed her forehead. The strange dizziness had faded to a dull headache. The cool air was a shock after being in his arms, but it wasn't at all like the biting breeze she'd felt on the trail.

A glint of reflected light among the grass caught her eye. Oh, right. Her phone. Terra reached forward to retrieve the useless thing, then returned her gaze to the brilliant blanket of stars above.

"Where are we?"

"Let's just say far from home. But we can't stay. I have to bring you back."

"How?" She was starting to believe him now, as ridiculous as that sounded. The realization of this other place was wonderful and horrifying at the same time.

"That's a long story for another evening."

"Of course it is." She scowled. "Just take me home then."

"I'm afraid to tell you you're going to get that dizzy feeling again." He looked at her apologetically.

"Never mind. Home is overrated anyway."

"You'll be okay, I promise." He offered his hand and pulled her up from the ground.

"How do you even know it's safe back there now?"

"Don't worry, we're not going back to the trail." His arms surrounded her. "Oh, and it's going to take a bit longer this time."

"Wait, what?" Terra said, but the sound of her voice was sucked away into a vacuum as they fell into a dark funnel of silence, the grassy fields and stars disintegrating before her eyes.

This time it was pure terror.

Watching everything go black, as if someone had introduced her corneas to a can of spray paint, was a shock almost as sickening as the fall itself. She squeezed her eyes shut and sucked in a ragged breath to counter the agonizing drop in her stomach. Then, the blessed ground met her feet. She opened her eyes. A wooded area with boulders materialized around them, completely unfamiliar. Where were they now?

But no time for speculation. Everything faded to black, and the ground dropped away a second time.

Son of a bitch.

She cursed at the top of her lungs, but it made no difference. The oblivion swallowed all sound. She clawed her fingernails into Harlan's back, pretty sure she'd be drawing blood if not for the thickness of his shirt.

At last, the ground returned to its rightful place under her feet. She opened her eyes to see the oak tree with their blanket lying underneath. A stone's throw away, the truck was parked where they'd left it—what seemed like days ago, though it had only been hours.

"Ow," Harlan said pointedly.

"Sorry. Just *what the holy hell*—"

"Shh!" He hushed her with a finger to his lips, then scanned their surroundings. "Are you okay?"

*Okay* was a relative term. She was dizzier than a bat caught in a windmill, but otherwise fine. She nodded, then teetered slightly.

"Good. Get in the truck while I grab our things. Move quickly and quietly."

The urgency in his tone was enough to light some fire under her rear. Whatever danger he'd sensed before was still nearby, and she'd had enough thrills for one night.

*When you look in the host's eyes, though you may not see anything, you will feel unsettled. It's like an assault on the soul, most often manifesting as a sickness in the stomach. You will be trained in recognizing them, as they are easy to miss and that's how they like to keep it. They fade into the background with ease, making people believe they don't exist.*

*- Elysian Records for the Revivers, Book IV: The Subversives*

# Chapter Eighteen

She found herself on a green hill under the stars. Dreaming. The grass rolled in the breeze like ocean waves, so picturesque she could cry. She turned. The edge of the tall forest lay in the distance, and there, Harlan stood calling out to her.

Oh. This was the part where she was supposed to be running away. But she didn't feel like following the script this time. She wanted to know what was happening. What was this place, and how did they get here? She'd make him explain everything. Beat the answers out of him with a stick if she had to.

She ran toward him. But with each step, her feet sank deeper into the grass. Its long blades snagged and twisted around her legs. It was like running through a vat of fettuccini. In her struggles, she glanced up to see Harlan turn away and walk into the forest.

So much for answers.

She was hopelessly caught in the grass—no, *vines*. (Since when did grass grow into vines?) The metallic jingling of dog tags rang out behind her.

The green tendrils stretched upward. Up, up, until they wrapped around her neck and locked her head in place. She tried in vain to turn and watch the dog's approach. The sound grew louder until it was right on her heels.

A bark or growl would have made sense at this point, but what she heard instead made her hair stand on end.

Something—or someone—was breathing behind her. Bitter-cold air stung her neck. Then, a loud, echoing voice filled her ears.

"STAY AWAY FROM HIM."

Her startled yelp upon waking was loud enough to make the neighbor pound on her wall in drowsy indignation.

The darkness of her bedroom felt oppressive. Terra sat up and squinted at the clock. It read 2:17 in bright red numbers. She switched on the bedside lamp with a groan of disgust, then stretched her legs and winced. Pain greeted her like an old friend pounding on the front door. The fibro was definitely flaring. Chances were good all that maniacal running from Harlan had something to do with it.

Harlan. The drive home in his truck had been a quiet one. She sat in the passenger seat, stiff and unresponsive. Not that he was much for conversation either. Something had broken between them. She'd taken him for a predator, and how do you recover from that? If he hadn't intended to scare her, why couldn't he come clean about what had happened? You know, make himself look like less of a creep?

A darker question ate at her: if he had the ability to change their location in an instant—or, at least, make it seem that way—what kind of person was he really? She thought back to that time he'd disappeared on the trail ahead of her, and suddenly it all made sense. But who could do something like that?

With questions like these, there would be no sleep anytime soon. She padded stiffly into the living room and settled onto the couch. Time to medicate with some LCD-enabled escape. She shuffled through the TV's offerings until she came to Season Six of American Ninja Warrior. Why not. She hit play and slouched against the cushions.

She'd pretended to be a ninja warrior herself last night, hadn't she? What a joke that had been. For all her desperate punches and kicks, he'd overcome her without so much as a hair falling out of place. As she watched the first competitor plow through a gauntlet of physical challenges, she remembered her dream...and the voice. Was her subconscious trying to warn her? Maybe she *should* stay away from Harlan. Then again, her dreams had been so screwy lately, who's to say she could trust her own mind?

But that otherworldly place... She couldn't stop thinking about it. The sheer flawlessness of it.

Terra picked up her phone and began a text to Harlan, then stopped herself. He'd made it clear she'd seen too much. Why would he let her in on his secrets? And he was probably dangerous. This whole situation felt dangerous. She should let it go.

She chewed her lip as one of the *Ninja* competitors lost her grip on a bar and slipped into the water below, immediately disqualified. Terra snatched the remote and turned off the TV. Dammit, he'd roped her into this. He *owed* her an explanation. She would go for broke before letting this slide. She resumed her text.

*We need to talk.*

*Now.*

She hoped the second ding would grab his attention. Sleep could wait.

Five agonizing minutes later, he replied.

*Be right over.*

Well, okay then. Terra rubbed her face and combed her fingers through her hair, trying to make something presentable from the abstract art that covered her head. She hadn't expected him to invite himself over. She peeled herself off the couch and headed toward the bathroom to wash the oily sheen off her face and cover up a zit or two.

Two loud knocks at the door made her heart leap so violently, she had to glance down at her chest to make sure it hadn't fallen out.

Terra froze, calculating the odds someone else had come to visit in the dead of night. (Pretty close to zero.) She gawked at the door as if it had broken some law of physics.

Two more knocks.

This time, the sound propelled her out of her stupor. She went to the door and raised her eye to the peephole.

Harlan.

She flew backward and cursed under her breath.

His voice carried through the door. "Terra, it's me."

She yanked it open. "How long have you been standing there?"

"I just got here."

"You texted like thirty seconds ago. Just how fast do you drive?"

"I didn't drive here, Terra."

"Don't you pull that freaky bullshit on me."

"Sorry to scare you, but I didn't want to waste any time. Can I come in?" He edged forward, wary of her reaction.

She hesitated, then allowed him a wide berth and gestured toward the living room. "Seems you can do whatever you want, so go right ahead."

They chose seats across from each other. As he settled into his chair, she noticed he was wearing the same clothes from earlier, and his eyes were bloodshot.

"I need you to start talking," Terra said. "You can't do whatever the hell it was you did to me, then pretend like nothing happened."

Harlan looked down and sighed. "Yeah."

Terra was already winding up for a retort before she realized what he'd said. "Wait— Just...*yeah*?"

"Yeah. You're not the only one losing sleep over this."

Terra crossed her arms.

His expression turned grave. "What I'm about to say has to stay between you and me. Promise me."

She held up three fingers in a mock-pledge. "Scout's honor."

He blew out a hard breath and rested an elbow on his knee, then tilted his head down to run a hand through his hair. She studied him while he gathered his thoughts.

He was a stranger. The only stranger she was willing to make out with at any given minute, but a stranger all the same. He reminded her of a painting she'd passed countless times in the hallway of Abuelita and Huelo's old house. It was an antique oil of a landscape, with extreme lights and shadows like a Bierstadt replica. She'd always thought it was pretty (in an old-timey way) as a child, until one morning she'd stood in the dusty air of the hallway inspecting it. The brilliance of a sun peeking out from gargantuan clouds spilled over a valley below. It sparkled in a winding river and stopped short of a grove in the foothills at the bottom of the frame. It was there that the painting was dark, almost black. She'd squinted at the faint variations in color and saw what looked like a grotesque beast with sharp fangs and a wicked smile. She knew it could have been her imagination, but she never enjoyed the painting after that. She prayed Harlan's dark unknowns would prove much less sinister, like in a sexy TV vampire kind of way.

He straightened up, as if preparing for a deposition. "I'm not from here."

"No kidding."

"I mean, I'm not from this..." He swallowed hard. "...world."

She narrowed her eyes at him, analyzing. "So, you're an *alien?*" The last word slipped out rather uncomfortably.

"No. Not really like that. I'm human."

"So then, what kind of human are you exactly?" She asked the question as casually as if inquiring about his field of work, but the hairs at the base of her neck prickled.

"I'm what you could call a representative of sorts, for an entirely separate race of people."

"But you're *not* an alien."

"Right. Well, not in the sense that you would think."

Terra blew out a demonstrative sigh.

Harlan's face mirrored her own frustration. "I know. It's complicated. You know how we ended up in that forest after we jumped off the trail?"

"Yeah?"

"That was my world."

"Which is *where* exactly?"

"Um...not here."

"Harlan, I swear to God if you don't—"

"It's an alternate world. It doesn't exist here."

Terra rubbed her face. "And how am I supposed to believe any of this?"

"I don't know." He looked down at his clasped hands. "It's unbelievable. But it's the truth. How else can you explain your surroundings changing in an instant like that?"

That was a good question. Hypnosis? Peyote? But she'd felt so clear-headed sitting next to him on that grassy hill. She'd *felt* that drop in her stomach when they left it. Who was she to say what qualified as real? "So... you can go there—to your world—whenever you want?"

"Yes."

"And return when you want?"

"Yes."

She leaned forward. "Take me back."

"What?"

"Take me back there. If what you say is true, I want to see it again. I want to see more of it."

He was already shaking his head before she'd finished speaking. "Not a good idea."

"What? You expect me to forget everything I saw? Just go on living my life like it never happened?"

"It would be better that way."

"But *why?*"

"You're not supposed to be there. I should've never taken you to begin with. I screwed up, Terra." He stood up and took a step toward the door.

Terra stood, cringing at the ache in her legs. "Damn right, you screwed up. But now you've gotta deal with that. I can't sleep, Harlan. I can't stop thinking about it. Take me back."

"I'm sorry."

"No. *I'm sorry*'s not good enough. Look." She stepped in front of him, blocking his path. "For all I know, everything I saw was a hallucination from the drugs you gave me."

"But I just told you—"

"The drugs you slipped in my wine so you could assault me in the dark woods..." She slowed for emphasis. "Where *no one would see.*"

"You know that's not true."

She picked up her cell phone. "Maybe. But the police don't."

His eyes widened.

"And gosh, I'm pretty sure that's what happened. I mean, unless you can prove otherwise..." She unlocked her phone and pulled up the dial screen.

"I— How— What evidence do you even have?"

She held out her arms, then glanced down at her legs. "I'm thinking all these scrapes might tell a pretty compelling story."

"You're crazy!"

"And you're about five minutes away from the back of a cop car if you don't—"

"Just—" He threw out his hands in a gesture of peace. "Give me till morning."

She lowered the phone.

"I need a little time to...work some things out."

"You mean you need time to ghost me."

"No." He collapsed back into the chair. "No. I promise I won't ghost you. I'll have an answer by morning."

She sat back down. "Fine."

"Fine." He hung his head in a display of defeat, then glanced up at her through his lashes. Defeated or not, his eyes drew hers in a way that felt like being pulled toward a bug zapper. A really good-looking one. "Before I go, you should know I had a good reason for pushing you off the trail like that."

"Not a fan of dogs?"

"That's not it. That dog had something in it."

"What?"

"Something my people call a *subversive*. They're all over the place in your world, but they can't cause direct harm. This one was in a host form though."

Terra's stomach twisted. "What does *that* mean?"

"Subversives don't have bodies. They just kind of...drift around. But there are a few—very few—that are skilled enough to hijack a physical being."

"Like someone's pet?"

"Exactly. Once they have a host, they can inflict as much harm as they want on surrounding people. Or the host itself."

"So you think this thing was *in* the dog and was using it to attack us?" Terra's hands death-gripped the couch cushion.

"Yes, and it was out for blood, because that's what they do. Fear and death and destruction, in one form or another. It's what subversives thrive on. Since we were the last ones at the park, it probably saw us as easy targets."

"To *kill* us?"

Harlan backpedaled at the sight of her blanched face. "Or to give us a good scare. It's possible that's all it was."

Terra shook her head. Nope. She refused to be dragged onto this crazy train. "It was just a dog. And you're telling me these things are *all over the place.* How's that even possible if no one's ever heard of them before?"

"You have heard of them, Terra. Your people call them by a different name."

"Don't tell me you mean—"

"Demons."

*Terra,*

*I followed you all day yesterday. Forget my other assignments, I finally had my full focus on you. At least, until he showed up. Unbelievable timing. I am still reeling.*

*I have a sneaking suspicion of who he is and where he comes from. What else could explain the repulsive aura surrounding him? Your impossible escape? Or the fact that I can barely draw within earshot of you when he's nearby? You know how to throw a wrench in my plans, don't you? And the funny thing is, you don't even know you're doing it.*

*But I'm not that easily intimidated. He's hardly begun to comprehend who he's dealing with. He probably didn't even realize it was him I was after on the trail last night. Yes, I had to sink so low as to slip into the form of a slobbering canine and jump a fence. That's how badly I needed to get you away from him. But if he's going to cross over every time I come close, then physical force won't get me very far. I need something more powerful.*

*I can still get in your head. I know that much because I managed to do it again last night in your dreams. This time, I'm almost sure you heard me. You heard my voice. That's why you woke up so suddenly, isn't it?*

*This isn't over yet.*

*- H.*

# CHAPTER NINETEEN

This time, Terra was sure her nails were drawing blood.

Once the intense sensation of falling subsided, she stepped back and glared at Harlan. "I thought you said it would get better after the first couple times."

He tweaked her chin. "Don't look at me like that. I said *maybe* the first couple. And you need to trim your claws, Cat Woman." He rubbed his wounded back.

She huffed and kicked the dirt, relishing the feeling of solid earth beneath her.

"I'm sorry the journey wasn't pleasant, but..." He nudged her shoulder to turn her around. "Was it worth it?"

Terra took in the vista before them. They stood on a rocky slope scattered with tufts of grass and wildflowers, bursting in violet, blue, and fiery orange. Clusters of subalpine fir trees lined the top of the slope and stretched upward like viridescent stalagmites, touching an impossibly blue sky. Far beyond the line of trees was a range of jagged mountains topped with flecks of snow, as grand as something she'd expect to see in the Pacific Northwest.

But this was not the Pacific Northwest, nor did it bear the slightest resemblance to the hill she'd collapsed on last night. It was most definitely not her sorry little apartment in central Indiana, where they'd been standing a minute earlier.

Terra caught her breath and laughed.

Harlan turned to her. "You think it's pretty funny, huh?"

"No, it's...*beautiful*, but it doesn't make any sense."

"I know."

Terra bent down to touch a spray of vibrant blue flowers, their petals as tiny and delicate as a newborn's fingernails. She brushed her fingers through the thin strands of grass surrounding the flowers. "Where is this? I thought we were going back to where we went last night."

"Same world. Different region."

"Oh."

Harlan took her hand and pulled her up. "Let me show it to you."

They hiked up the slope, his hand steadying her along the rugged terrain as if she were his great-grandmother. She may as well have been with these body aches. With Harlan's unnerving revelations still whirling around in her head, the events of last night seemed like a lifetime ago. Still, her back and legs begged to differ.

She'd woken from a restless sleep around eleven that morning, groggy and stiff. After a shower and breakfast—which probably counted as lunch—he reappeared at her door with his answer, leaning against the frame all cool like James Dean, but without the cigarette breath. *Ready for an adventure?* was all he had to say, and she was done for.

He'd said last night she wasn't supposed to be here. Now something had changed his mind, but what?

Harlan caught Terra's arm as she stumbled over a rock, jarring her out of her thoughts. They were nearing the top of the slope.

"Sorry, your apartment happens to coincide with an area of uneven ground," he said. "I could've jumped us to someplace with an easier walk, but I figured you wouldn't appreciate the extra-long jump."

"Um. What?"

Harlan cringed. "Sorry. I've never had to explain all this to anyone before."

Terra steadied herself against a boulder, lest her granny-body should fall and break a hip. "Wait, you mean I'm the *first*?"

"Shhh! Hold still." He stared past her at the boulder.

She turned her head, following his line of vision, until she spotted a grayish-brown ball of fur three feet from her hand. She sprang back with a yelp. The thing was a rodent of some kind. It looked like a rabbit, but fun-size, with short, rounded ears. Its whiskers twitched as its dark eyes took her in.

"It won't hurt you." Harlan stepped closer. He held out an upturned palm to the rock, and—to Terra's bafflement—let the giant hamster scurry onto his hand. He pulled it in close to his body and stroked the soft fur.

"What is that?" She squirmed at the sight of it but couldn't help leaning in to get a closer look.

"I think it's a pika. I've seen a few around here before. They live in the mountains."

"Why isn't it running away?"

"None of the animals run away here. They aren't afraid because there's nothing to be afraid of."

The creature's soft nose nuzzled into Harlan's shirt. She reached out a tense hand.

"Really, it's okay," he said. "Just be gentle."

She ran her fingers along the pika's back and felt the silk-like fur and delicate spine beneath. The animal turned its head and sniffed at her hand, then let out a greeting that landed somewhere between a chirp and a squeak.

Terra made her own chirp-squeak when Harlan placed the pika in her hands. Once she recovered from the feel of little rodent toes on her palm, she decided he was, in fact, pretty damn cute.

"Hey."

She kept her eyes on the pika as she stroked its fur. "Yeah?"

"Can you please not threaten me with the police next time you're upset? That wasn't cool."

She looked up. "Will there *be* a next time?"

"Not if I have any say in it."

She studied the sincerity in his expression for a long moment. "Deal."

They reached the crest of the ridge several minutes later and found a gentle slope on the other side. Beyond that was a field of densely packed wildflowers. A herd of elk grazed in the distance. They lifted their heads to observe the pair's approach with impassive interest.

"Need a break?" Harlan gestured to a boulder that sort of looked like a recliner, one intended for people with well-cushioned butts.

"Actually..." The nagging ache in her legs conceded for her. "Yes."

They sat together on the boulder and watched the herd's lackadaisical stroll through the field below. As Terra searched for a more forgiving spot on the rock for her minimally cushioned butt, Harlan spoke.

"So, every point in your world is parallel to a point in this one. That's how we ended up in a different place today than last night."

"Parallel. Sure. Cool."

"But this world is bigger. So much, in fact, that to get from one place to another around here, we don't usually walk. We jump."

"And by *jump*, we're talking...?"

"Travel," he said. "Instant travel over vast distances. I can't do that in your world. But here I can. That's how I got to your apartment so quickly last night, and again this morning."

"I don't get it. Give me some Power Point slides or something."

"Look." He turned to his side against the face of the boulder and placed a finger at the base of the vertical wall. "If I'm here, in your world, and want to get to"—he moved his finger along the base of the wall to a point about a foot away—"here, that means I have to cross over first."

"You mean to your world?"

"Yes. To this one." He moved his finger back to the starting position and, from there, jumped in a straight line to the top of the wall. "Say this top section is *my* world. Once I'm here, I can jump to whatever location in this world I want in an instant." He ran his finger along the top of the wall. "And then..." He dropped his finger back down in a vertical line to the base. "I cross back over to your world, to the corresponding location."

She followed his finger with her eyes, transfixed. "How long does it take?"

"Seconds."

"But...how?"

He pulled back the cuff of his jacket. The corded bracelet with the amber stone in the middle—the one she'd mistaken for a pretty boy's vanity statement—glowed in the sunlight. "It's more than just a piece of jewelry."

"That makes you jump? Or teleport or whatever?"

"Yes. All I have to do is press the stone and envision where I'm going, and I'm there. It was a gift."

"From who? Elon Musk?"

"Who? No. From Iam. The Creator."

"Of the bracelet?"

"Of the world. Of everything."

Terra frowned. "Come again? There's a guy named Ian who made everything?"

"No. *Iam* with an *M*."

"Huh." She leaned back against the rock. "Didn't know the Creator had a name."

Harlan pulled his sleeve back over his wrist. "*Here* he does. It's been long since forgotten in your world."

Terra massaged her temples. A headache was beginning to sink its teeth into her skull. *The creator of everything*? She'd been hoping there was an easy scientific explanation for all this. Something about bending the space-time continuum and maybe a government coverup thrown in for good measure. But what he was talking about was...*God?*

She registered a movement behind Harlan. Something brown and massive lumbered through the trees in their direction.

"There's a lot you still don't know, Terra, and I'm trying not to overwhelm you. But now that I've cleared it with Iam, I want to share it with you. All of it."

Terra nodded blankly, but she wasn't listening anymore. Her jaw went slack. Her hand gripped Harlan's knee. It was all she could do to point toward the monster that now loomed over them.

*When Iam gave our ancestors a choice, it was because he understood*
*the duality of existence. As difficult as it is to comprehend, he knew it was*
*unavoidable. Evil is like darkness. Just as darkness is the absence of light,*
*evil is merely the absence of good. It exists by default because good exists.*
*- Elysian Records for the Revivers, Book I: Origins*

# CHAPTER TWENTY

It struck Terra as comical how many thoughts can race through one's mind in the heat of a panicked moment. But laughter was hard to come by. She was too busy racking her brain for proper protocol on surviving an encounter with a grizzly bear.

Were they supposed to stay still and not make a sound? Or was it the opposite of that? Jump up and down and make lots of noise? Don't run or climb a tree—she knew that much. What was that joke about being chased by a bear? *You don't have to be fast. You just have to be faster than the guy next to you.* Funny. Oh God, if she died here, would anyone ever find out what happened to her? Would she be filed under a missing person report? Even worse, the police would go through all her possessions looking for answers. Oh, perfect. She still had that yeast infection cream from three months ago sitting in her medicine cabinet.

As her mind whirled, the bear—it had to be a full-grown male—let out a guttural grunt. Harlan finally turned to face the beast, now only a few feet away.

"Oh, hey, bud. What are you up to?"

Harlan offered a good-natured pat on the shaggy fur of the grizzly's shoulder as if it were just a dog with a bad case of gigantism. The bear grunted again and sniffed the air.

"A...friend of yours?" Terra choked out.

"I told you, there's nothing to be afraid of here." His smile faded when he saw her face. "Are you okay?"

She eyed the beast with suspicion as it stretched its giant head in her direction and sniffed. "Not really. What's he doing?"

"I think he's just checking you out. He hasn't seen you here before."

"Can you tell him to check me out from farther away please?" She leaned back as far as the boulder allowed.

"Terra." Harlan turned her face toward his with a gentle hand. The gold flecks in his eyes caught the sunlight. "It's okay. Give me your hand."

With blind obedience, she let him pull her hand (her less favorite of the two, just in case) toward the bear. She cringed as the bear stepped forward, brought its nose to her palm, and made soft snuffling noises. To her shock, it pressed its forehead into her hand like an affectionate house cat. Puffs of warm air from its snout spread over her arm. For a long moment, she looked into the bear's almond-shaped eyes and sensed something she'd never encountered before. Something innocent and pure, an acceptance that transcended language and species. She held her breath and felt the beginnings of tears sting her eyes.

Then, as suddenly as it had happened, it was over. With a final snort, the bear turned and wandered off toward the trees.

She stared after it in a daze.

When her eyes returned to Harlan, he was watching her, his lips parted as if he had something urgent to say but couldn't capture the words.

"What?" She ran a hand through her hair to check for remnants of bedhead.

Without a sound, he pulled her into him and planted a full-blown kiss on her lips.

When he finally pulled back, she gazed at him wide-eyed. "What was that for?"

"I—I guess you could say I'm as captivated by you as the animals here." He looked down and breathed out a hesitant laugh.

Was she sure what she was seeing? Oh, yes. She only wished she'd gotten it on video. For the first time, Mr. Swagger himself was overcome with self-consciousness. Her heart gushed with a quiet thrill.

He was human after all.

They continued on through the field of wildflowers, past the elk, and into a grove of fruit trees. The fruit, hanging like fat ornaments from their branches, resembled pink and gold pears. A tangy fragrance filled the air and made Terra's stomach growl.

Harlan plucked a piece of fruit from one of the sagging branches. "Hungry?"

"Yes."

He tossed it to her, then chose one for himself. They sat underneath the tree and leaned against its trunk while they ate. The pear-fruit tasted like plums. Interesting. They watched as a pair of sparrows pecked at a piece of fruit that had fallen on the ground nearby.

"Harlan, where are all the people?"

"What do you mean?"

"I see animals everywhere here, but no people. I mean, you weren't raised by animals, were you?"

He placed the well-eaten core of his fruit on the ground. "They're around. Just not here."

"I just love your cryptic answers. I feel so satisfied by each and every one."

"I'm getting there. This place we're in is quarantined from the rest of the world. The people who live in it can't come here. It's only safe for us."

"How?"

He leaned forward, resting his arms on his knees. "That's a loaded question. I'd better start at the beginning."

She reached out her hand to offer the remnants of her fruit to the birds. "Alright."

"Okay. Do you remember last night when I brought up the Garden of Eden?"

Her arm froze in midair. "Oh. You mean *that* beginning."

"Right. *The* beginning. You've probably heard the basics. God created Adam and Eve and gave them a very significant choice."

Terra dropped the fruit. The birds hopped over to it with delighted little twitters. "Right. The fruit. Wait. *Why* are you telling me this under a fruit tree? Harlan, did we make a bad choice?" she asked with a sly smile.

"This fruit tree carries no moral consequences, I promise."

She nudged his shoulder. "So they had a choice: to eat or not to eat. So what?"

"Well, as the story goes..." He returned her nudge. "God created Adam and Eve, each with their own unique identity and desires, having the ability to make decisions for themselves."

"Free will. So I hear."

"Exactly. He put a tree in the Garden. It was called—"

"The Tree of Good and Evil." She was no Sister Maria, but she'd shown up for her World Religions class in college. Most of the time.

"Almost. The Tree of the *Knowledge* of Good and Evil. God had created this new world and everything in it, and he called it *good*. If they wanted, they could keep living in this world and *only* know the good."

"Sounds like a pretty sweet deal to me."

"It was. But the other option was for them to be *like God* in the sense that they could know the natures of both good and evil. Up until that point, they'd never experienced evil. They'd never seen death or felt sadness, or had so much as a bad hair day, as far as they perceived it. Everything was literally perfect for them. So God warned them that eating the fruit and gaining this knowledge would mean losing all that perfection. Their immortality too."

She leaned her head back against the tree. "That's a steep price to pay for a little curiosity."

"Oh, it was more than curiosity that drove their decision."

"Well...yeah, there was a snake too, right?"

"The Deceiver. That's what we call him."

"Well, whatever you call him, I know he told them the fruit was tasty and eating it was no big deal. And they decided, *hey, maybe this random talking animal has a good point*, and chowed down."

"Sort of." Harlan plucked another fruit from the tree and examined it.

"Personally, I think there was no fruit. It's all just a euphemism for sex."

"This had nothing to do with their physical or sexual appetites. It was their appetite for *more*. The snake made them question whether they were missing out, and whether they could trust God at all. Because if God really loved them, he wouldn't withhold anything from them, right?"

"Huh." Terra picked a small flower and rolled its stem between her fingers.

"They bought into this lie and took the fruit, and—consequently—took the Fall."

"So the Fall of Mankind all stemmed from a major case of FOMO," Terra said as she crushed the flower in her hand. "That's some riveting shit."

"It got them banished from the Garden forever."

"One mistake, and they're kicked out forever, then they die." She dropped the wilted flower with a scowl. "There's a reason I never liked this story."

"It was much more complicated than that. When they made the choice to take the fruit, it's like...a complete shift happened. In themselves *and* their world. And they knew it right away. They got their first taste of evil, coexisting side by side with the good. But it was too late to undo what they'd set in motion."

Terra stared at him in profound confusion. Who was he to talk like this? As if he'd written the story himself? She shifted on the ground and shook her head. "That's just dumb. And it doesn't make any sense. If they broke themselves and their world, then why didn't God fix it for them? No one's that heartless."

"Again, it wasn't that simple. When Adam and Eve made their choice, it wasn't only for themselves, it was for *all* people, all generations to come. Now they would have to let that choice play out. And God wasn't heartless about it at all. He had a plan to rescue them, but it was going to take some time..." He trailed off as Terra abruptly stood up.

"I'm still not getting where you're going with this." She ducked her head as she stepped out from under the tree. "Philosophical debates aren't my thing. Plus, you're talking about all this stuff like it really happened. That makes you a nut job in my book, just so you know."

"It did happen, Terra," he called after her. "A long time ago. That's where I'm going with this. It's been written off as myth and legend, but it's actual history. And the craziest part is, that's only half the story. No one—at least, very few people—in your world has ever heard what I'm about to tell you."

"Oh?" She stopped walking and let him catch up.

"There was another garden."

"Say again?"

"A *second* garden, with a second Adam and Eve."

*Because evil cannot exist on its own accord, it relies on things that are inherently good, but twists them until they are no longer as intended. Even the Deceiver was good once but chose to believe his own distorted version of the universe where he existed as an equal with the Creator, not under his authority. So he and several others of his kind separated themselves from Iam, and they came to hate everything that was good, because Iam had made it.*

*- Elysian Records for the Revivers, Book I: Origins*

# CHAPTER TWENTY-ONE

*Second garden?* The internet would have a field day with this one. Flat Earthers, move over.

"When you say another Adam and Eve," she asked, "you mean God called a mulligan and scrapped the first ones?"

"No," Harlan said. They began walking through the maze of trees. "He made two separate creations at the beginning of all humanity. Same premise, but separate. Adam and Eve, then Korej and Gimmal. This second pair...they're my ancestors."

Terra inhaled sharply and pressed her palms against her eyes. "Man alive, Harlan. This is a lot to take in."

"I know. I'm sorry. Let me simplify it for you." He pointed to her. "You: Eden." He placed a hand on his chest. "Me: Elysia."

"Yeah, and you Tarzan, me Jane. We can do this all day."

"No, listen." He squeezed her arm to get her attention and gestured to the land around them. "This is Elysia, my home."

"Okay."

"Your home is Eden. You don't call it that anymore. Somehow it came to be associated with just the Garden in the beginning, but it's all part of the same world."

Terra paused to watch a family of vibrant blue and black jays fly over their heads. "Alright. I'll take your word for it, but you still haven't explained why there are no people here."

He sighed and took his time answering. "This part of Elysia is only for the ambassadors to visit. The rest of Elysians can't come here, because if they did, they might be exposed to our illness."

She cocked a questioning eyebrow.

"People like me are called *revivers*, because we come to Eden to help revive the sick, so to speak. But in the process, we become infected like everyone else in Eden. It's like a virus of the heart." He stared out past the grove and into the foothills beyond. "Somewhere out there is a barrier between us and the other Elysians that can't be crossed, not even with the bracelet. I'll never be able to see my family again—not in this life anyway. That's the sacrifice we make as revivers."

Her chest tightened in pain for him. "I'm so sorry."

He nodded and looked away.

"So, the people on the other side of Elysia, they're not *infected*?"

He turned back to her. "Exactly. They made a very different choice in the beginning."

"To drop-kick the snake and run like hell?"

"They completely avoided the fruit."

"But that would mean nothing changed for them, right?"

"Bingo." A smile pulled at the corners of his lips. "The first two people, along with all their descendants, the animals, their environment, the world...they all remained as Iam had intended. They were—"

"Perfect." Her eyes widened as the realization sank in. Perfect, as in no natural disasters, no murder, no disease, no traffic, no slow wi-fi...

"Yes."

"But...the implications of that are..." She shook her head. "*Staggering.*"

"You have no idea." Harlan's mouth stretched into a broad grin. "Come with me. I need to show you something."

Terra's head throbbed and her back pain screamed at her like a hot-tempered banshee. She guessed it was late afternoon by now. Her body was spent, but she felt wired and giddy. Reality had been cast to the wayside in favor of the most incredible crackpot story she'd ever heard, and...she was pretty sure she believed it.

They had hiked through rolling hills and valleys, past bison and, strangely, a pack of wolves. The wolves had been lounging side by side with the bison, all good with each other, as if they did weekly potlucks together or something.

According to Harlan, all the animals in Elysia lived this way. (In harmony. Not potluck-ing.) There were no carnivores because the plants provided every nutrient needed to thrive. Death did not exist. Even the grasses and trees continuously regenerated themselves.

"What about the bugs?" Terra asked.

"Bugs? They're around, but they were created for very specific purposes, to tend the gardens, pollinate, till, prune, groom, lots of things. They don't swarm like they do in Eden. The ecology here's always in perfect balance."

"So they don't crawl all over you and bite you?" She eyed him sideways and rubbed her arms at the thought of mosquitos.

"No. Of course not."

"Good. In that case, I think I could stay here a whi—" Her last word was throttled by a sudden lurch forward as she tripped over a tuft of grass. Her ankle throbbed with reminders of the previous night's stumble.

Harlan caught her arm. "Woah, you okay?"

"Yeah, thanks." She shrugged him off and kept walking. She'd been betrayed by her own candy-ass legs. The aches were getting harder to ignore, but no one likes a buzzkill.

"We can stop if you need to." He was watching her with a furrowed brow.

She sighed. "Just tell me how much farther it is."

He stared out into the distance and scratched the back of his neck. "Maybe another mile?"

*Another mile?* She'd have rather dropped a frozen ham on her toe.

"I figured you wouldn't enjoy jumping there, but..." He trailed off, his worried eyes holding hers. "Sit down. I have a better idea."

No point arguing. She sat her rear on the ground with all the grace of a drunk giraffe. "What are you going to do?"

"Give me a few minutes. I'll be right back." He lifted his sleeve and unveiled the bracelet. Before she could question him further, he pressed the amber stone and vanished soundlessly in front of her eyes, like the air swallowed him up.

Terra blinked and continued to stare at the empty space where he'd been standing. There really should have been more warning for this sort of thing. She pulled her legs into her chest and hugged them. This other world had a dream-like quality. And she was here all alone now.

Uh-oh.

She thought of the shadow man. His creeping figure. The tingling pain. Anxiety rose from the pit of her chest. Who's to say she wasn't dreaming right now? What if everything since last night had been one long dream? She took a deep breath to calm herself, but her eyes darted around in search of shadows.

*Stop freaking out,* she told herself.

Her heart raced anyway. Terra pinched her eyes shut and brought her head down to her knees. Now she was hyperventilating. Awesome. *Stop. What is wrong with you?*

Then, there was a second voice inside her head. It wasn't quite audible—more like a thought—but it spoke with such force and urgency that it overwhelmed every other thought in her head.

*You're safe.*

She opened her eyes and glanced around, half expecting to see someone standing there, but she was still alone. It spoke again.

*You're safe.*

Her heart rate and breathing slowed, and her frenetic thoughts came to a standstill.

She listened for the voice again, but nothing more came to her. Mystified, she sank into the grass and leaned back on her elbows. A hawk cried out. She tilted her face to the sky and watched it glide on the air currents in wide circles.

"Hey!"

She turned at the sound of his voice. On the crest of the hill behind her, Harlan approached.

Riding a bison.

"Need a ride?" he yelled from atop the lumbering steed. He held on by the dark, shaggy fur that covered its colossal shoulders. The bison ambled down the hill and stopped a few yards away from Terra. With a pat on the shoulder from Harlan, it lowered itself to its knees.

Well, this was new.

"Come on. There's room for both of us up here."

She gave a weak laugh and shook her head.

"What's wrong? I promise it's a smoother ride than it looks."

"It's not that. Harlan, something happened while you were gone. I'm still trying to wrap my head around it. "

He climbed down from the beast and sat beside her in the grass. "What happened?"

She looked down and shook her head. "Maybe I imagined it." Then again, pretty much everything she'd experienced today could fall into that category. "I heard a voice. In my head."

Harlan's face lit up. "He spoke to you."

"What?"

"And you heard him. Terra, that's wonderful!" He gripped her arms, his eyes dancing with more exuberance than the cast of a Broadway musical.

"What are you talking about? Who?"

"Iam."

*Unlike their counterparts in Eden, Korej and Gimmal chose trust over control and goodness over all-encompassing knowledge. Because of this, they continue to live in the Garden with Iam, possessing a connection with him that the people of Eden lost long ago.*

*- Elysian Records for the Revivers, Book I: Origins*

# CHAPTER TWENTY-TWO

"It's called *second hearing*," he said, "though it's not anything we can detect with our ears."

Terra shifted her weight, trying to find a comfortable position atop the bison's spine. It wasn't ideal, but it was more enjoyable than walking at this point. The ribs beneath its thick hide strained against her legs as they rose and fell with each labored breath. She sat behind Harlan, clinging to his waist, extra vigilant of not falling a full man's-height to the ground.

Harlan continued. "It's how he communicates with the revivers and Edenites, since we can't stand face to face with him. Otherwise, the perfect good in him would demolish the evil in us instantly and kill us in the process."

"He sounds like a super nice guy."

"I mean, he is, other than that."

The bison let out a low bellow as they climbed a steep grade.

"Is he okay?" She bent over to try and glimpse the animal's face. All she could see was its ear jutting out from a wall of wooly fur.

"He's just working hard." Harlan patted the bison's neck. "Take it easy, bud. No rush."

"So...what's the point? I mean, of Iam speaking to anyone?"

"If you could connect with the creator of the universe...the one who created *you*...wouldn't you want to?" He paused, letting the question sink in. "The fact is, he already knows everything that's going to happen before it happens, so he can help us navigate our circumstances."

"Like *don't order the chicken tacos or you'll regret it later*? Because that would be extremely helpful."

"Sort of. Take for example all those times we ran into each other, when you thought I was following you."

She scoffed. "*Stalking* was the word."

"Whatever you want to call it, I can see now that most of that was at Iam's prompting. That run in the park...I'd planned on going for a run in Elysia that morning, but Iam pushed me to go to Kessler instead. That night we had drinks together...he told me to go catch up with Garrett, which led me to you. That time I was behind you on the road..."

"Okay, I get it. Iam was *making* you stalk me."

"He wanted us to meet."

"That's weird."

He turned and flashed a grin at her. "Call it what you want, but I'm glad he did."

She offered an unsure smile in return. What would Iam care whether they met? Was Harlan supposed to be her guardian angel or something? Oh...wait. Wait just one holy, harking minute. "Harlan?"

"Yeah?"

"If the subversives are demons, does that mean revivers...Does that mean you're an—"

Harlan was laughing before she could finish the sentence.

"What?" she asked.

"That's a very generous assessment. I'm flattered."

The bison slowed as they reached a cluster of trees, stepping forward and backtracking several times. It seemed to be searching for a clear path through the branches that would avoid knocking its passengers in the head. Apparently animals here were more conscientious than most people back home.

"So I guess angels aren't real then?" she said. Probably just a marketing ploy by the makers of porcelain figurines and toilet paper.

"Oh no, they're real. They just don't interact with humans much, because every time they do, they scare the bejeezus out of them."

"I thought angels were supposed to be beautiful and kind."

"They are. But they're so magnificent, they're *terrifying*. Haven't you ever heard the stories where they appear to people? They always start by saying *fear not*. Otherwise, the people are too busy groveling on the ground to hear a single word they say. That's why Iam recruited us revivers to do most of his face-to-face work. We're a little more relatable, I guess you could say."

"Then what do the angels do?"

"Extreme interventions." He reached down to pet the bison's thick coat.

Terra tightened her grip around his waist and leaned her head on his shoulder. "I don't know, this feels like a pretty extreme intervention to me."

"Hey, don't get too comfortable. Not that I mind, but we're almost there."

"And where would *there* be?"

"Just beyond these trees is one of the reasons revivers return to Elysia."

"Just tell me already."

"I don't have to. See for yourself."

As if on cue, the trees ahead of them began to thin out, their branches separating enough for her to glimpse what lay beyond. She drew an involuntary breath as if she'd been sucker punched.

It was the epitome of perfection.

The two of them sat on a rocky bank next to the clearest body of water Terra had ever seen. It was only the size of a pond, but the water was transparent instead of a murky brown. And instead of a layer of slime and dead pond animals at the bottom, she could easily make out a carpet of tiny pebbles that extended from one end to the other. Their shaggy steed stood nearby, grazing among the halo of fronds and flowers that surrounded the pool. The plant life was more vibrant here, like a Rousseau painting come to life (except without the lions everywhere.)

As inspiring as the view was, so was the prospect of a nap right about now. Since that seemed like an inappropriate reaction, Terra forced herself to sit up straight and take in the moment.

Harlan sat next to her with his arms folded over his knees. He squinted into the flashes of sunlight that ricocheted off the pool and danced along the bank, then he turned to her with a troubled smile. "Iam told me that leaving my home to become a reviver would be a great shock. Like a rebirth." He hung his head, a few strands of his chestnut hair falling into his eyes. "He was right."

Terra tried to think of a comforting response but came up empty. She watched the water with him in silence.

He continued. "It's like an infant leaving the womb. You're warm and protected at all times. Then suddenly, it's cold and too bright. Nothing is familiar. Everything is uncomfortable. That's the best way I can think to describe the transition."

Terra shifted on the rock and stretched her aching back. *Uncomfortable.* She was used to that word by now, but she felt bad for the sorry sucker who had to experience unbridled pain for the first time. What a slap in the face.

"But Iam gave the revivers this one allowance. He knew without the power to retreat to Elysia, we'd all be lost in despair. The burden is too much."

"I can't think of a better place to visit," she said. "Sure as hell beats squeezing a stress ball."

"True. But it's not just a pretty place to sit. The real beauty lies in what happens *beneath* these waters."

"Oh yeah?"

"Come and see." He bent down to pull the shoes from his feet, then stood and motioned for her to do the same.

She sighed. This game of show and tell was getting old. "Harlan, I'm exhausted. You can't just tell me?"

"It will be worth it, I promise."

At a funeral pace, she shed her sandals, and together they walked to the water's edge.

She stood there, water lapping the tips of her toes, and searched the pool for whatever secret lay hidden beneath. All she could see were the tiny pebbles, the occasional sprout of green plant life, and—when the light hit at just the right angle—flashes of her own reflection, looking like a smudge on a painter's masterpiece.

No escaping the truth. She was a stranger here. No matter how flawless the environment, she'd never be able to shake the flawed person that stared back at her.

Harlan strode forward into the pool and held out his hand to her.

"Um, Harlan. Your pants." She nodded at the soggy denim.

"It's okay. Come on."

"No, thanks." She didn't want wet clothes. And while she was no pearl-clutcher, skinny dipping seemed out of the question in such clear water, where every imperfection would only be magnified. "You didn't tell me to bring a swimsuit."

"You're overthinking this," he told her, his hand extended and waiting.

She eyed him.

"I want you to trust me."

That was a tall order. But one long look at that outstretched hand, his willing patience, the promise of adventure in his eyes, and Terra was transported to her childhood. She stood on the beach of the Indiana Dunes, her mother in the water before her with arms held out. The waves were nearly as tall as her five-year-old frame, jostling against her legs. But her mother coaxed her farther in.

She could still see her mother's face, that smile that seemed to stretch from one horizon to another. Strands of wet hair were plastered against her neck in ringlets. Like Terra's. She wore a bikini in sunset colors of gold and vermilion. Droplets splashed on the brown skin of her shoulders and sparkled in the sun like that craft glitter you keep finding for three months after you thought you've cleaned it up. Terra remembered clearly how her mother looked in this moment. She was lovely.

*Terra!* She laughed effusively and reached for her daughter. *No tengas miedo. ¡Ven conmigo!* Leta was never one to coddle a sissy when there was fun to be had. At this prompting, young Terra finally set aside her fear of the waves and shuffled forward into the safety of her mother's arms.

Now, here she stood at the water's edge again, entertaining the possibilities of the unknown. Who needed dry clothes or respectable hair? She reached forward and took Harlan's hand.

The water was warm. As he pulled her in, it soaked through the legs of her jeans. She tensed as if she'd been whacked on the backside, but she was committed now. She inched forward. The smooth pebbles shifted beneath her toes like sand. Seven more steps, and the water was swirling around her waist and soaking upward through her shirt. She congratulated herself on the choice of a dark-colored T-shirt today.

When the water neared her chest, Harlan stopped and turned to face her.

"Terra."

"Yeah?"

He wrapped one arm around her shoulders. "This is Iam's gift to you. You will be healed."

"Pardon?"

"Here, in this water."

"I'm sorry, but that doesn't clear it up at all. What are you talking about?"

"Once completely submerged, your body will be healed. All you have to do is accept it."

She studied his eyes and pursed her lips, deciding whether this was a real thing or if his sense of humor was really that awful. "A gift from Iam?"

"Yes. Are you ready?"

She had no idea. She looked down at her hands through the glass-like surface. Miracles were a sham, weren't they? Not real and close up like this.

Then, the urgent voice was there again, pushing past every thought in her head to the forefront.

*Trust me.*

It was hard to argue with someone who could talk to her in her head. She nodded to Harlan.

He positioned himself beside her. "Hold your arms to your chest, like this." He crossed one fist over another and pulled his elbows in close, bringing his hands up to his heart. When she did the same, he clasped one hand around her wrists and placed the other on her back. His breath was on her cheek.

"Take a deep breath and hold it. It takes a few seconds to start working once you're under."

She nodded again and sucked in all the ever-loving air her lungs could hold.

And she was plunging backward.

*Describing to them the character of Iam is as fruitless as building a house with no doors. They will never understand until they have experienced his mercy for themselves.*

*- Elysian Records for the Revivers, Book II: The People of Eden*

# CHAPTER TWENTY-THREE

S low motion.

Water breaking around the back of her head. Spilling over the top of her forehead, her neck, her hands. Her skin registered every ripple.

She closed her eyes and yielded to the gentle push of Harlan's hand against her wrists. The warm water wrapped around her and took control. She floated in its transparency, suspended between earth and sky.

The tingling began in her back, between the shoulder blades.

It was filled with heat, but not burning. The warmth and tingling spread outward from there, washed down her back, and wrapped around her abdomen. It spilled down her legs and up through her neck, until her entire body vibrated with warmth. She could get used to this, other than the not-breathing part.

From her chest, a burst of energy shot outward in every direction. It reached her fingers, her toes, and finally, her head. Beneath the surface of the water, her eyes flicked open in response.

Above, Harlan watched her through the warped-glass surface of the pool. She could just make out the subtle change in his face, the corners of his mouth turning upward.

Then a pressure was on her back, pushing her up and forward: his hand guiding her home. Water broke around her face and poured off her hair in streams. Her feet found the bottom, and finally, she breathed.

The pain was gone. All of it. Even the fatigue. She laughed out loud, and for the first time in a long time, it didn't hurt.

"How do you feel?" Harlan asked.

"Like I just crawled out of the grave and punched Death in the face."

"So...better, I take it?"

"Yes." She laughed again and wrapped her arms around him, nearly knocking him over. "That was awesome. You should try it."

"I have."

"No, really." She shot a teasing glance at him. "Have some." With that, she slammed her hand into the water, sending a spray of healing power in his direction.

With a shocked face, he shook his dripping hair. "I think we're going to need to dunk you a second time, young lady."

She shrieked and paddle-jogged away from him. But he paddle-jogged faster and snagged her with both arms.

When she turned to face him, his expression turned serious. "Hey, hold still a minute."

She stopped squirming long enough for him to place a hand on the side of her face and brush his thumb underneath one eye, rubbing gently, then repeat the process on the other side.

"What is it?"

"Your eye makeup is everywhere."

Oh, the irony.

But she didn't care. She allowed him to wipe it away. Her self-consciousness was gone, just like the pain, washed away in the water.

As he continued to rub off the last of her raccoon face, an honest-to-goodness tear emerged from the corner of her eye. "Is this real?"

"Yes," he said. "It's all real."

*Terra,*

*I know where you've been. You have some nerve coming back here after what you did.*

*There was a shift in you when you returned. I sensed it. Not a mood, but something deeper. Something that reeks of the Adversary. It's disgusting. That, along with the lingering stench of your Elysian boyfriend, has put my plans to infect your dreams on hold, at least for tonight.*

*Yanira would never have done this. She was too smart to fall into the Adversary's trap. She knew his religion is a guise—he doesn't truly care what happens to people here in Eden. That's why he's in Elysia, after all. He gave up on the fools of this world a long time ago. She understood all this. She was determined to exert her independence, to prove her strength. I expected the same of you, Terra, only more so. That's why this new twist in your story is especially revolting.*

*But let me get back to my point. There are consequences for what you've done. Edenites don't laze around in the waters of an Elysian healing pool and get off scot-free. That was not part of the deal after the Fall. This is our world, and the people of Eden belong in it, under our sway. Do you know what the payment is for Edenites who cheat the Fall and partake in Elysia's luxuries? A swift death, you'd think?*

*Wrong. A slow, mind-meltingly painful death. Suffering in its purest form. The very thing you, of all people, seem to fear the most. And it's not as hard for us to exact this penalty as you might think. We influence your own kind for most of our dirty work. Ironic, isn't it?*

*The Boss will be quick to intervene once I report you. He doesn't take kindly to the Adversary's infringement on his domain. And when word gets out, I'll be the envy of my colleagues. The one who brought you down, you cheating whore. But...*

*Not yet. Maybe...I'll have a little more fun with you first.*

*- H.*

# CHAPTER TWENTY-FOUR

The fibromyalgia had been debilitating, but this infatuation was worse.

Terra stared in the direction of her monitor, not so much at it as *through* it, until the words on the screen turned fuzzy and separated into two distinct images floating in and out of each other. It was like that book Huelo used to keep on the lamp table by his chair, with the colorful, wavy pictures that looked like an artist's acid trip until you adjusted your focus to the perfect point in space beyond the page. What were those called? Stereotypes? No. Stereograms.

For the longest time, she'd glare at those pictures, angry at herself for not getting it. Then her eyes learned to relinquish their hold on the page—a sort of surrender to the unknown. That's when it clicked. The image was there, popping off the paper in front of her. A pirate ship, a city scape, a wonky-legged emu. An entire world hidden in plain view.

She forced herself to sit up and refocus her eyes to see the time on the screen: *9:33.* She'd only been at work for an hour. This day was going to be excruciating.

She couldn't *not* think about him. About his world. About the miracle pond that completely shattered her view of reality. Her pain was gone. But in its place were an erratic heartbeat and a queasy stomach. Forget butterflies—this felt like baby pterodactyls.

She kept wondering about Iam too. Not that she was complaining, but why had he singled her out for healing? An even dicier set of questions lurked in the back of her mind: What did she owe him now? A polite thank you? A lifetime of loyal service and rule-following? If he was truly a god, or *the* God, was he watching to make sure she didn't screw up? Could he withdraw his gift at any time? But thoughts of impending doom were kind of a drag, so she let her mind drift back to Harlan. And Elysia.

"Ask me how it went."

She swiveled in her chair. Alexis was standing by her desk with an expectant grin.

"How what—oh yeah, how was your...uh...*farm* date with Collin?"

"*So* good. Terra, this guy is perfect."

Terra's mouth drew into the tiniest smirk at that word. "Oh yeah?"

"His aunt and uncle have this little creek at the back of their place where we took a walk. Their property is huge..."

Her mind flashed back to the rocky ridge lined with trees, where she had touched the bear. Its almond eyes. Harlan's kiss on her lips.

"...well water. He said they eventually want to go completely off-grid..."

How soon could she see him again? Would tomorrow be too obsessive? But she should give herself some time to digest everything. Keep her feet planted in the real world. Then again, the real world sounded so boring.

"...place is legit, Terra. Like, straight out of Doomsday Preppers. Living off the land and— Hey, are you hearing me?"

Terra realized she'd been staring down a speck of lint stuck to the cubicle wall. She snapped her eyes back to Alexis. "Sorry. Yeah, I'm listening. Sounds like it was all very, uh...enlightening."

Alexis shifted her weight and propped a hand on her hip. "You're acting weird."

"Am I? I don't think I slept well last night." Actually, she'd slept like a sloth in a coma, and it had been glorious.

"No." Alexis contorted her lips. "No, it's gotta be more than that."

"You know I have a hard time sleeping."

"No, you're hiding something. I can tell."

"Phhft." Terra took a sip of her coffee.

Alexis's eyes widened. "You *did* end up going out with him, didn't you?"

*And here we go.* "It's possible."

Alexis sprang up from her perch on the desk and punched Terra in the arm. "I *knew* he was going to reel you in." The shrill glee in her voice caught Kenneth's attention as he emerged from the copy room. His eyes met Terra's for an uncomfortable second then darted away.

"Shhh!" Terra gestured for Alexis to sit down. "Yeah, it was great. Now dial it down, Sparky."

"When did you two go out? I can't believe you didn't tell me. Was it Friday? No, Saturday." Alexis read Terra's face with mixed results. "Yesterday?"

Terra looked down and grimaced. "Kind of all of those."

"I seem to recall just last week asking you to give the guy a chance, but..." Alexis raised her voice, loud enough for half the office to hear. "I didn't expect you to *move in with him.*"

She was running through the rocky field, her toes kicking up sprays of tiny flower petals as she went. They flew past her face like miniature firework displays. She marveled at her legs as they moved. Her body was a freaking powerhouse.

The wolves and bison rose from their grass beds and watched her approach. The wolves howled in excitement, and the bison made a grumpy *mmmm* sound that she could only assume was their way of encouraging her. A pair of overachieving wolves ran alongside her, jowls pulled back in grins, tongues lolling to the side. She kept running, her eyes fixed on the snow-capped mountains in the distance.

The wolves fell behind as her steps quickened and her stride spanned impossibly long, enough to make Stretch Armstrong jealous. She discovered with a thrill that the mountains were racing up to meet her. She was almost there. One step, two steps, and now she was climbing and bouncing along the steep slope as if she weighed nothing, like a ping pong ball on the moon.

Near the summit, she glided across the snow and bared her teeth in victory. *World, meet your conqueror.* Before her lay the edge of the peak and all of Elysia in its splendor below. Without a second thought, she bounded into the emptiness and took flight.

This. This was the life. Coasting on the wind like a bird, dodging white puffs of clouds. She lifted her face toward the warm sun and closed her eyes, then wondered when Harlan would join her out here.

Where was he? She'd forgotten. Wait. How the hell was she flying?

A sudden strike of pressure above her jolted her eyes open. Something was riding on her back, weighing her down. She craned her neck around, but all she could see was the sky. It wasn't until she felt the cold, tingling hands wrap around her arms that she knew what it was. That's when a healthy dose of panic set in.

And when she began to free fall.

"Stop it!" Her voice cracked as the wind pummeled her face.

The shadow's grip tightened around her. She tried wrestling herself free, but in a sickening twist, the sky was upended, and her back was now turned toward the fast-approaching ground. She could see nothing but the sun and clouds above. The shadow man continued to drag her downward from underneath like a three-hundred-pound, frozen corpse strapped to her back.

From the corner of her eye, she glimpsed the mountain peaks drawing closer, then rising past her. She screamed in outrage and thrust her elbow at the shadow's face. When it grazed nothing but air, she knew this was a game she couldn't win.

Now the tops of trees rose around her. Branches flew by. Her heart thudded painfully as she fell.

Down...

Down...

Down...

Then, the savage end.

The impact was like a thousand hammers to her backside. Pain. Exquisite pain vibrated through her body.

Terra shot out of her bed and scrambled onto the cool, hard floor of her bedroom. A faint buzz of pain lingered in her back before slowly fading, blurring the lines between dream and waking. Not sure what else to do, she crumpled into a miserable pile against the wall and punched it with her fist. She spent the rest of the early morning hours there, sobbing inconsolably.

*Even though he had separated from the Creator and taken his subversives with him, the Deceiver was unable to start his own creation. He wasn't that powerful. He quickly discovered the only power he had apart from the Creator was the power to destroy. That's why he began to target the humans. Humans were the prize of Iam's creation: the ones he loved above all others, and the ones the Deceiver hated the most.*

*- Elysian Records for the Revivers, Book III: The Subversives*

# CHAPTER TWENTY-FIVE

Terra chewed a hangnail compulsively as they sat at the edge of the pool, their bare feet submerged in the water under the light of the moon. This place had a decidedly different feel at night. Then again, this was a different healing pool than the first.

Harlan said they were all over Elysia. Used to be everywhere in Eden too before the Fall. She wondered if the pools could be used for curing anything, even anxiety. She was too anxious to ask.

Harlan's muscular arm pressed against hers, while his large man feet played a game of footsie with hers in the water. She noted with great appreciation that his were nice-looking as far as feet go. Not hobbit feet like with that one guy she dated.

He smiled at her and leaned back, his hands resting on the rock behind them. "Uh-oh." He jerked his head back and pulled away a hand. An iridescent blue and green beetle lay twitching on the rock, sending flashes of reflected moonlight in every direction.

"Oh, gross!" Terra leaned away in repulsion.

"No, not gross," Harlan said. "I mean I accidentally crushed him with my hand."

"Oh." She tilted her head and stared at the convulsing insect, trying to reframe it in her mind as something adorable like the pika. It wasn't working out too well.

"Sorry little guy," he said as he scooped up the beetle. "Good thing we're right here." He put both hands together, enveloping the beetle, then dipped them into the water.

Terra watched in fascination as Harlan waited a couple seconds, pulled his hands out of the water, then released the bug back onto the ground behind them. The beetle righted itself with a couple wriggles, then scampered off into the grass like it had somewhere to be.

"Wow. The water works on everything, huh?"

Harlan resettled himself, this time checking behind him before leaning back. "Anything that's alive. Can't raise the dead, of course, but nothing dies in Elysia anyway."

"Interesting. Why do Elysians even need the pools? I thought they were already perfect."

"Free of bad intent, yes. Free of error, no. They still hurt themselves by accident all the time. But they can't die. They just go into a deep sleep."

She scrunched her face. "Really?"

"My younger brother was playing in the treetops with the tamarins one time. He slipped and fell the height of six men. Knocked him right out. Until I carried him to a healing pool, then he ran off like nothing happened."

"Bizarre."

Harlan ran a hand through the water, then flicked shimmering droplets across its surface. "Not all that crazy if you think about it. When Edenites and revivers die, we may be buried in the ground, but it's really just an extra-long sleep. We'll all eventually wake up again with restored bodies. Once evil is expelled from the world, not even death can remain."

Terra stared out across the clear waters and rolled the words over in her mind. *Not even death can remain.* Like it was no more than a temporary inconvenience.

"Hey." He turned his face to hers. "It's getting late."

Her heart began banging in her chest as they stood.

"We should go."

She kept her eyes on the water. "Yeah." But she couldn't go back to that empty apartment.

He leaned in for a slow kiss. Once she was sufficiently wobbly-kneed, he pulled away and smoothed her hair back with his hand. "Well..." He gave her a reluctant smile.

Panic thrummed through her veins. He began to reach around her, and she knew he was aiming for the stone on his wrist.

"Wait. We could stay here for tonight."

He rubbed his nose against hers. "You have work in the morning. So do I."

"I don't care. Or stay at my place awhile?" Flashes of her dreams ran through her mind. She leaned into him, summoning what little power of seduction she had. "Or stay all night?"

He looked down at her with eyes full of yearning. "Terra."

"Please?" Now she was sounding too needy. Dammit, she was going to scare him off.

He let out a strained sigh. "You know I can't do that."

He'd already made it clear he didn't want to rush things. She'd thought it endearing at first, but now that he was sticking to his guns, it was more like a sanctimonious thorn in her side.

He brought his arms around her again. "Come on. We'll talk tomorrow, okay?"

She stiffened and pulled away. "Okay, here's the deal."

"What?"

"The truth is..." She began pacing. What was the truth? She was a scared little girl who couldn't handle her own imagination? "The truth is

I've been hearing weird noises lately. Like someone's been trying to break into my apartment."

Genius.

The crease in Harlan's brow deepened. "Are you serious?"

She nodded.

"Did you call the cops?"

Oh. Right. "Well...no, but I called the landlord, and she said they'd check the security tapes from the parking lot."

"They didn't see anything?"

"Still waiting to hear back."

Harlan's jaw clenched. Oh yes. He was torn now.

"Just for tonight. I'd feel better if someone stayed with me."

He sucked in a lengthy breath and ran a hand along the back of his neck.

"You can have the bed. I'll sleep on the couch," she reassured him. "I'll only come and get you if I hear the noises."

After a long deliberation, he finally spoke. "Don't be ridiculous."

"Wha—"

"I'll take the couch. You can have the bed."

Score one point for her mastery of persuasion, and negative five hundred for her dignity.

It was a little after noon on Friday, and Terra's section of the office looked like a tile-carpeted ghost town. She had purposely delayed her lunch break, knowing most everyone else would be out for lunch by now. The weather was too nice to stay inside.

Terra leaned back in her chair and tuned her ears to the sounds of the office. Muted footsteps receded down the main hallway. One coworker called to the other. "Mexican today?" Somewhere on the far side of their floor, an exit door clicked shut. The hum of the HVAC system combined with the symphony of buzzing office lights seemed to grow louder as all other noises ceased.

Terra tapped a fingernail on her desk, hammering out some nervous energy. It was just a phone call. It wasn't like she was having herself committed. And the sooner she could get this appointment in, the better.

Harlan would get suspicious if she asked him to stay a third night. He was already threatening to knock down the door of management's office for not taking her concerns seriously. She would tell him today they found the source on the security tapes. A raccoon or stray dog maybe. Or a rat with really loud teeth. She'd figure that part out later.

So definitely no sleepovers tonight. It was a shame too. She'd slept well, without nightmares, the past two nights. It was odd how that seemed to happen any time he came by.

She looked down at her phone. *Just dial already.* The doctor would probably prescribe her a different set of meds, tell her to schedule a follow-up in a few weeks. Or there was the worst-case scenario. She would finish describing the violent nature of her dreams, and his reaction would be stiff silence, perhaps a raised eyebrow or an incoherent murmuring to the P.A., something about psychiatric disorders. She'd be on her way to a shrink faster than she could say *but really, I'm fine!*

All this after finally ditching the fibromyalgia: her physical maladies had been replaced with a mental one.

She sighed and dialed the doctor's office. Maybe just stick to the high-level stuff. No getting into the details of the dreams. Then again, that was another hallmark of all of them: so much detail. And there was that one dream in particular...

The office plaza. The letters on the laptop were still seared into her memory: *HULUM*.

Terra abruptly ended the call and pulled up a browser on her screen. It couldn't mean anything, could it? She typed the word into the search bar all the same.

*Did you mean:* **Hulu***?* appeared at the top of the screen. Google was just trying to be helpful. She scrolled through the first few search results, mostly all articles in another language or profile links to foreign-sounding people. Then, at the bottom of the first page was a link that caught her interest: a baby names website. She clicked it.

A highlighted section at the top of the screen read:

*Name:* Hulum

*Gender:* Male

She stared at the words, dumbfounded. It was a name. Not a random word her mind had pulled from the recesses of her imagination. But she'd never heard it before. If it wasn't from her own memory, then where had it come from?

She continued scanning the bullet points.

*Origin:* Urdu

What was Urdu anyway? Indian? Something too exotic to be familiar to her. She kept scanning.

That's when she saw it. Her body tensed. An ice-cold sensation crept down her spine.

*Meaning:* Dreams

No way was that a coincidence.

*Terra,*

*Did you know that my kind used to live among your people? Not as spirits, but physical beings. We coexisted with them.*

*We dominated. We fought battles and conquered territories. We wielded great power and influence over men's ideals. We took women as our lovers and fathered children with them. Our offspring were called* Nephilim. *They were giants among men, true specimens of brute strength, and together we ruled. We enjoyed every pleasure this earth had to offer.*

*But the Adversary saw fit to rob us of these things. And for what? To reclaim a world that he had abandoned long before? The greedy bastard. He murdered our descendants in his Great Flood. Mercilessly, he did not stop there, but banished us from our own bodies. Now we are resigned to live as spirits adrift in your world, observing from a distance all the things that once belonged to us.*

*Oh, there are still ways of getting some of the things we want (wait and see, Terra), but we now seethe with fury at what he has done to us. So we find every way possible to wreck his creation where we see fit. We reveal its hideous underbelly. His perfection is an illusion. A construct. To live in his perfect world is to die inside, to become a hollow shell of yourself. He wants all the control.*

*We never bowed to his arrogant will to begin with, and we certainly don't intend to do so now. When he comes after the things we value most, we fight tooth and nail.*

*My mind is made up. Yes, your days are limited. I will report your trespasses. But until then, I'll be coming at you with the force of a tidal wave, Terra. I'm going to descend on you, pummel you, flip you around until you don't know which way is up anymore. See if your Elysian or his god can steal you away from me then.*

*- H.*

*They work under the authority of the Deceiver, often taking direct orders on whom among the Edenites they should manipulate next. However, they are a rebellious bunch by definition, and many of them deviate from their assignments as often as they are able.*

*- Elysian Records for the Revivers, Book III: The Subversives*

# CHAPTER TWENTY-SIX

"Mom, you're going to be late."

Leta lay face down, tangled in the sheets of her bed. If Terra hadn't seen it a million times before, she would have thought Leta were dead. She placed her hand on her mother's shoulder and shook her as hard as she could. A groan of protest arose from somewhere under the mess of hair.

Terra glanced at the digital clock on the shelf above the bed. An empty bottle of Bacardi sat next to it.

"Mom. Now!"

"Mmmmrrph."

"How you going to pay rent next week if you don't go to work, huh?" Terra hauled her mom by the leg until she was hanging halfway off the bed like a broken teeter totter.

"Mmm-nooooo."

Terra headed to Leta's closet, nearly tripping over a full laundry basket on the way. She yanked open the folding doors, hoping to find something respectable to dress her in. Instead, the closet housed a fully stocked bar, complete with a bartender standing behind the counter. He sneered and winked at her.

Terra rolled her eyes and forced the doors shut.

It was another stress dream. She'd had this particular one more times than she could count.

"Terra, mmmaybe I can call in sick today." Leta struggled to push the hair out of her face. "S'no big deal. Really."

Through the cloudy lens of her mind's eye, Terra studied the pitiful manifestation of her mother. She was younger than in real life. Early forties probably. Her hair was long, past her shoulders—the way it had looked when Terra was a teenager. Just a memory. This bedroom was a memory of the old house. But she couldn't turn and walk out. Not with the familiar burden of responsibility pulling her in. Terra sighed and stepped forward.

"Come on." She pulled Leta up from the floor and toward the bathroom. "You're going to need a shower."

Leta rubbed her face and started moving on her own accord. "Fine, Terra, fine. I'll go."

"Good. And please, hurry. They'll fire you if you're late one more time."

Leta turned at the door and placed a hand on the side of Terra's face. She patted it lightly. "My daughter. Always taking such good care of me."

Terra stared at her mother. They both smiled genuinely at each other, and for a fleeting moment—Terra contemplated hugging the old boozehound. Then, Leta's face dropped into a grimace. She swore like a sailor.

"This headache kills. Terra, can you get me the Advil?"

"Sure."

Terra headed to the kitchen, where Leta used to keep an ample supply of pain killers. On her way, her mother yelled, "Thanks, sweetie!" and shut the bathroom door.

When she reached the kitchen entrance, she stopped. A wave of nostalgia hit her. Details of their past life were strewn around like confetti after a New Year's party. The little dish on the counter Leta used for holding her rings when she baked cookies with Terra—almost always Abuelita's recipe for *coconetes*. Terra's green backpack, hanging on a hook by the back door, the black mockingjay pin proudly displayed on the zippered pocket—she'd forgotten all about her *Hunger Games* phase, but her subconscious hadn't. A valentine Terra had made for her when she was four, stuck haphazardly to the side of the fridge, that read *I luv you Moomy.*

Just memories.

Enough with waxing nostalgic. Terra grabbed the bottle of Advil and headed back to the bedroom.

"Mom, I got it."

There was no response.

She stood outside the bathroom door, listening. The shower wasn't running. The house had gone deadly quiet. Terra sucked in a breath and bolstered herself. Slowly, she opened the door to reveal an empty bathroom. She was alone in her dream now. He would be here soon.

She walked back into the kitchen and sat down at the table. Right away, she stood up again. Waiting around for his punk-ass would only prolong the inevitable, and she had better things to do.

"I know you're here," she called, her voice shaking. She wasn't scared. Just peeing in her pants a little.

The rhythmic ticking of the clock on the kitchen wall was her only answer.

"Hulum!" she yelled.

The clock stopped.

With her heart thrashing like a wild animal, Terra scanned the room. She caught a darkness in the far corner. As her skin crawled in hot flushes, the shadow emerged. It made its way across the room at an unhurried pace, disappearing and reappearing as it passed through the shadows of the kitchen. The lack of features on its face was wholly unnerving.

"Where did you come from?" She stared it down—as much as you can stare down something without eyes.

It continued toward her in silence.

"Answer me!"

Its murky hand shot forward and clamped around her neck, forcing her to walk backward until she was up against the wall. It leaned in close and made a noise more like a hiss than a breath. Then, it spoke.

"YOU ALREADY KNOW."

The deep vocalization reverberated in her ear like a chorus of dissonant voices. The statement was followed by a dog's bark and the clanging of metal dog tags outside the back door. As Terra strained to see out the door's window, the pressure around her neck tightened.

The dog barked again. And that's when it registered. That night at the park. The thing that was *in* the dog. What was it called? The sub— Subservient? Substandard? Sub sandwich? She tried to speak again, choking out the words.

"Why...are you...doing this?"

The figure spoke deliberately, punctuating each word with the jab of its thumb into the soft hollow at the base of her neck.

"FEAR. ME. TERRA."

The pain in her lungs and throat was agonizing. As the chokehold intensified, the dog's barks devolved into wild yipping. Through bleary eyes, she saw the dog stand on its hind legs and glare at her through the window. It scraped its claws on the door—feverishly—as if it wanted to join in on the kill.

Terra stopped resisting Hulum's grip. In her last rasping breath before waking, she uttered the only reply she would allow herself.

"No."

The morning sun hit the blinds of her living room window with a tenacious brightness, painting glowing stripes along her walls and chasing away the predawn gloom. *Don't worry, life is peachy,* it seemed to say. At least this much was true: she'd survived another night.

She stood at the kitchen bar, no more than an extension of the small living room, and typed out her text message.

*I'm ready.*

It wouldn't take long for him to show. It was a little earlier than they'd planned, but she'd have to claw her own eyes out if she stayed in this place any longer. Standing up to a demon did not make her brave any more than doing a cartwheel made her a gymnast. It was an act, one she couldn't keep up for long. It was time to tell Harlan.

The microwave beeped. She opened the door and removed her breakfast burrito from its packaging, burning her fingers in the process. *Idiot.* A curse word or five flew from her mouth. She turned to run her hand under the cold water of the faucet.

"Those are some ugly words for such a pretty mouth."

Terra glanced up from the sink to see Harlan sitting at the bar, watching her. She cursed again.

"Geez, Harlan. You scare me every time you do that."

"Would you prefer I show up in a closet somewhere and knock on the door?"

"No. I wish you'd knock on the front door, though, like a normal human being."

"But this is more fun." He shot her an ear-to-ear grin, then hopped down from the stool. He was in a good mood this morning. Bubbly. She hated that she'd have to ruin it. He walked around the counter and encircled her in a zealous hug. "Hey."

"What's up?"

"Let me take you out tonight," he said, combing his fingers through the ends of her hair.

"But I thought we were going to Elysia."

"We are. I mean later. I'll come back here with my truck and take you on a normal date. You know..." He winked. "Like the Edenites do."

She smiled. "Sure." She'd go anywhere with him. A restaurant, a garbage heap, the DMV. Anywhere sounded better than being here alone.

"Great. You ready?"

"Just a sec." She lunged for the burrito, wrapped it in a napkin, and brought it close to her chest.

He looked down at her to-go meal with amusement. "You bringing that with you?"

"What?" she said.

She leaned into his embrace as they fell and welcomed the soundless dropping sensation as an old friend. Soon enough, they were strolling through the grassy meadows, gathering Elysian dew on their shoes as they went.

"It's so warm here, even in the mornings," she said after swallowing the last bite of her breakfast. She shoved the wrapper in her pocket, seeing as Elysian trash cans were in short supply.

"That's because of the veil."

"Hmm?"

He looked up toward the sky. "It insulates the atmosphere. Keeps the climate steady all day long, all year long."

She squinted her eyes at the infinite blue dome above them. "No seasons...strange."

"It's a layer of water vapor, so it's not easy to see." He stopped and turned in a circle, surveying the horizon. "There." He pointed to a patch of clear sky that looked the same as the rest of it.

"Where?"

"You've got to catch it at just the right angle. It has a kind of reflective sheen."

She stared, tilting her head left and right, until she caught the slightest hint of luster curving across the horizon. "Woah."

"It's a beautiful design, isn't it? The things he thought of."

"Yeah..." Terra's voice trailed off. "Harlan?"

"What?"

"I need to talk to you about something."

"You're kidding me!"

"No, I'm—"

"Of all the times I come here and our paths finally cross!"

Terra frowned at Harlan, but his eyes were on something in the distance. She turned to see a figure seated on a ledge a hundred yards away. A man with a gray ponytail peeking out underneath a worn ball cap. He turned and stood in response to Harlan's voice.

Harlan picked up his pace and yelled again. "Ezra! What are you doing here?"

Terra ran behind Harlan, trying to keep up, literally and figuratively. Ezra, the guy from the PT clinic? Were all physical therapists Elysian or something?

Upon meeting, the two men embraced and slapped each other on the back. Terra stood back, thoroughly confused.

"You found my favorite sunrise overlook," Ezra said with a good-natured grin. "I come here all the time."

"You been here all morning?" Harlan asked.

"Just the past hour." Ezra's steel-blue eyes shifted to Terra. "A woman of Eden on Elysian soil. Now that's something you don't see every day."

Harlan turned to Terra. "You remember my mentor from the clinic, right?"

"Sure, though it's a little unexpected seeing him here."

"I'll bet it is," Ezra said with a hint of a smile.

"When I told you before that he was my mentor, I didn't just mean with PT," Harlan said. "He was my mentor way back when I became a reviver. He's a reviver too."

Ezra held up his arm.

Sure as tornados like trailer parks, he had a bracelet identical to Harlan's, complete with an amber stone in the center.

"I think my mind just exploded."

Ezra seemed to be enjoying her state of shock. "We usually try to avoid exploding any minds, but I guess you're an exception to the rule. Harlan told me all about your close encounter with the dog."

Harlan was already scrambling over the boulders to reach the overlook where Ezra had been sitting. "I can't believe we found you out here," he called back to Ezra.

"Dumb luck, I guess," Ezra said. "Elysia's so big, revivers rarely run into each other," he said to Terra.

"How many of you are there?" she asked.

Ezra glanced at Harlan. They both shrugged. "Lots. All over Eden."

"*Incognito*," Harlan added with a sly smile.

"Wow, okay." She looked at Ezra. "So do *you* go around rescuing people from possessed dogs too?"

Ezra frowned. "Harlan, you've been bringing her to Elysia on a regular basis, and you haven't even told her what we do?"

Harlan threw his hands up in defense. "What? Explaining the existence of another world was complicated enough."

"What *do* you do?" she asked, glancing between the men.

Ezra gestured to the mantel of rock where he'd been sitting. "Have a seat and I'll tell you."

# CHAPTER TWENTY-SEVEN

T he two men settled on the ledge and let their legs swing beneath them, while Terra decided to sit back a couple yards and keep her feet on solid ground. The view of the valley below was spectacular, and tumbling over the side of this rock would make for a spectacular death.

"Did Harlan tell you about second hearing?" Ezra asked.

"Yes," Harlan and Terra answered in unison.

"Okay. "Imagine second hearing is like a radio station. You have to be tuned into it."

"Sure," Terra said, watching the eagles circle the sky in front of them.

"But in Eden, there's a lot of static, so it's very hard to hear. We...help people tune out that static."

"How?"

"Well..." Ezra leaned forward and cast a pebble into the open air below. "Static is distraction. Fear, pride, resentment, greed, jealousy. You can't hear Iam when all these negative thoughts are raging through your head. We work with people individually to overcome these things. Everyone in Eden has the ability for second hearing. They just forgot how to tune into it a long time ago."

"And why do you care if people tune into it?"

Harlan answered. "Think about it. If everyone tuned into Iam, seeing things through his perspective, the good would finally win out over the evil. After centuries of struggle, your world would finally be restored to the way it was intended. That's what we're working toward."

"Wow, is that all?"

"It's a tall order, but not impossible," Ezra said.

"Well I guess I'm ahead of the curve. I already heard Iam's voice the first time we came to Elysia."

Ezra shook his head. "Elysia's a different ballgame. The static is the product of the subversives' influence, and Eden is their playground. They make sure Iam's voice is drowned out there."

"But not Elysia?"

"Subversives can't come here. Once our ancestors chose Iam's way, he put a barrier around Elysia and trapped the subversives in Eden. If they ever tried to cross over..."

"Let me guess..."

"Poof." Ezra mimed an explosion with his hands.

"Dead?"

"For all eternity. So that's why it's easier to hear his voice here. It's also why revivers are allowed to travel back to this place, so we can hear him clearly when we need to. Even revivers struggle with the static sometimes."

Terra watched as an eagle dove into the trees, then launched back into the sky, seemingly for the thrill of it. "So, in short, you help the deaf hear."

"Yes."

"But how exactly do you do that?" She was betting it involved a couch and lots of questions about childhood trauma.

"It's a delicate process." Ezra stared at her for a long moment, brow furrowed, like he was about to launch into a dissertation. Instead he rose from his place on the rock. "Listen, you two are welcome to stay here, but I was going to head out for a hike. Get some blood flowing through these rusty legs."

"Hike away," Harlan said.

Terra squinted up at him in the sunlight. "You didn't really answer my question."

Ezra removed the hat from his head and rubbed at the crease left behind on his forehead. "The simple answer is you have to care about people. Knowing how to help them comes with time." With that, he replaced his cap on his head, tipped it in an old-fashioned gentleman's farewell, and took off down the path.

Terra turned to Harlan. "Any other surprise Elysians I should know about?"

"No one you know anyway," he said with a crooked grin.

"Guess I'll have to take your word on that." She watched the trees below bowing to the wind, and a familiar anxiety began banging at her chest. "Hey. I need to tell you something."

His smile wavered. "What is it?"

"The dog at the park. That demon thing."

"The subversive?"

"Yeah, that. Harlan, I think it's been following me for a while. In my dreams."

"You keep dreaming about it?"

She shook her head. "I mean it's been getting in my head at night. I don't know how." She wrapped her arms around her legs, which felt like they might bounce away from her with the jitters. "It's been showing up in my dreams since even before the night at the park."

He sat up, his body rigid. "Every night?"

"Mostly." Terra had been hoping he was used to this sort of thing, hoping he'd say *oh they do that all the time, the little rascals.* Then he'd tell her the Elysian secret for keeping them at bay. Instead, he seemed unsettled.

"For how long now?"

"A few weeks."

He was quiet, thinking. "What does it say to you in your dreams?"

"It's not really the conversational type. I mean, mostly it just tries to kill me." She forced a laugh. It was a hollow, sad excuse for one, though, so she quickly gave it up. "But it did tell me one thing. Its name—*his* name—I mean, I think it's a he. It's Hulum."

Harlan stared at her with a look of such shock, she may as well have just smacked him in the face with a mackerel.

"What?" she said.

He stood up from the rock ledge and began pacing, rubbing his face with both hands.

"You're scaring me, Harlan."

"I'm thinking."

"I looked up his name and saw the meaning—"

"*Dreams...*or *nightmares* or something, right?"

She jerked her head back. "How did you know?"

"This is not good, Terra."

"Harlan, *how did you know?*"

"Most subversives..." He exhaled a ragged breath. "They have no names. The Deceiver made them shed their given names when they broke away from Iam in the beginning. But there's a special class of subversives that operate at a higher level."

"And *they* have names?"

"Yes. The Deceiver gave them names based on their abilities. Their methods of attack. Most subversives struggle to get more than a single thought into a person's head, let alone inject themselves into someone's dreams. But this one seems to have a knack for it."

"You could say that." She stared numbly at the ground.

"And if it's the same one that slipped into a dog's form, then we're dealing with a very powerful subversive."

"Awesome."

"What I don't understand, though, is why he would call so much attention to himself. Why even tell you his name?"

She bunched up her shoulders. "I don't know. How *would* I know?"

He stopped pacing and pulled her into his arms. "I was just thinking out loud. I didn't mean to upset you." He ran his hand along her back until her shoulders relaxed. "This is a problem neither one of us can solve."

"So I guess I'm screwed then."

"No. Let's take it to Iam."

*Terra,*

*Sometimes I fantasize about enforcing your penalty myself. Inhabiting that dog again. Running it straight toward you. Knocking you over and tearing your throat out. Feeling you writhing in pain beneath the weight of its paws, hot canine drool dripping onto your petrified face. And slowly, so slowly...your feeble struggles give way to the pull of death.*

*But then I stop myself from thinking such things. This would be completely unfair to you. You've hardly had the chance to get to know me first.*

*If you were to slip away in the grand finale of my pursuit, I'd want you to know who it was that brought you to your knees. I'd want you to know you were one of the lucky ones, one of the few who caught the eye of creation's most masterful and cunning being. In your dying breaths, Terra, I'd want you to feel* honored.

*Perhaps I will bring the dog to you again, but only to torment you. Rake its claws across your belly. Watch you come gradually undone with each attack. There's a visceral quality to real-world touch that I can't attain in dreams.*

*But no. The Boss hates it when we engage with the physical realm. He says it's bad for business these days. Not subtle enough, attracts the wrong kind of attention. He never let me touch Yanira, even though I begged for it.*

*I find myself detesting him more and more by the day.*

*- H.*

*Little is known of how subversives go about choosing their victims. What is known is their ability to study their targets with an assiduous rigor. In fact, a few have been observed to turn quite fanatical after they've latched on, only releasing their victims once they've followed the path of self-destruction to its bitter conclusion.*

*- Elysian Records for the Revivers, Book III: The Subversives*

# CHAPTER TWENTY-EIGHT

Terra scanned the horizon and wondered if Harlan had accidentally jumped them to a different planet. There were no traces of Elysia's green lavishness; just cracked, dried-out earth covered in a shallow layer of sand.

"I come here when I want to talk with him," Harlan said. He squatted down and pinched some sand, then rubbed it between his fingers. "I don't know why, but I hear him clearest here."

"Well...it's definitely quiet," Terra said in polite approval.

"This is where I came that first night after I brought you to Elysia. To talk with him. Find out if I could bring you back."

"That's why you couldn't give me an answer til morning?"

"Yes."

"How'd you convince him?"

Harlan smiled and looked away. "I didn't have to. He wanted you here."

"He did? Why?"

He kept his eyes focused on the horizon. "He didn't say."

"Huh." Iam was clearly the strong, silent type. "So what do we do now?"

Harlan knelt and gestured for her to follow suit. "Tell him what's bothering you."

She lowered to her knees and looked around them, bewildered.

"Say it out loud."

"Hulum," she blurted, then scowled. "I don't know. This feels weird talking out loud to no one."

"It's not *no one* you're talking to."

"You know what I mean."

"Go on."

She took in a deep breath. "Hulum is in my dreams, and I don't know what to do." She resisted the urge to recoil as she said it, like she was reporting on the news. *This just in...* "I can't fight him off. I can't...I'm not strong enough. I need help." She looked to Harlan.

He whispered, "That's good."

They sat in silence, eyes on the ground, because what else would they look at. Terra traced her finger along the cracks in the ground beside her knees. The wind was warm against her face. Harlan had told her it might take a while. She presumed that meant her message was still uploading into the great beyond. As it turned out, Iam had already received it. She just needed a minute to take notice.

As she studied the individual granules of sand falling away from her finger, a tremor rushed through them, as if an earthquake had struck in the distance.

She withdrew her finger and watched as the sand began vibrating like a nervous chihuahua. She opened her mouth to tell Harlan but was interrupted by an insistent voice catapulting out of the recesses of her mind.

*You're safe.*

Her shoulders slumped. She'd heard that one before, thanks. "I know," she said aloud, "but I can't go on like this."

Harlan cast a glance at her.

The sand in front of Terra was now trembling at a fever pitch, spilling outward from a single point. She bent forward and watched, completely rapt with this new magic trick.

There, in the middle of the quaking sand, a tiny green shoot sprang upward.

At impossible speed, the shoot grew several inches tall and unfolded an array of leaves, and at last, a single round bud at the top. It bloomed before her eyes into a magnificent flower, a desert rose in the palest shade of coral, darkest at the ruffled edges of its petals and fading to white at the center.

Terra wrapped her fingers around the delicate stem and tried to pluck the flower from the ground. It resisted her pull. In disbelief, she tugged with more force, but it held fast. The voice spoke again.

*Strength comes from the unseen, from where you are rooted.*

Her brows drew together. What did any of this have to do with her dreams?

*Take root in me.*

"Take root?" she said.

*Take root in my name.*

The flower burst into a thousand tiny grains of sand and fell back to the earth, the only evidence of its existence a lingering floral scent in her nose. For a moment, she stared at the sand, waiting. When nothing else happened, she sat up and frowned.

"What?" Harlan asked her. "Did he speak to you?"

"Yes, but..." She raked her fingers through the sand. "It didn't make any sense. I don't get what I'm supposed to do."

"Hmm." Harlan paused. "Maybe it has less to do with what you're supposed to do, and more to do with what *he* will do *for* you."

"But he said *take root in me.* What does that even mean?"

"I think it means to put your trust in him."

She squinted at him in the desert sunlight. "But what else?"

"That's it."

"I need to know more. Dates, names, points of interest..."

"He gives you what you need to know, when you need to know it. Nothing more."

"And when will that be?"

"I don't know. That's where the trust comes in."

Right. Because guessing games were so much more fun than just knowing. "Well anyway, I think that was the most beautiful flower I've ever seen."

"What flower?"

That's when she realized it had been for her eyes alone. The maker of the universe had created something just for her, had spoken just to her. The thought was stupefying.

# Chapter Twenty-Nine

"**O**h my God, Terra!"

"Mom, stop."

"How long has it been, anyway?"

"It's not a big deal. We're just hanging out."

"But you're dating again!" Leta stabbed another triangle of pancake and made a show of swirling it around in the syrup. "I can't remember the last time you mentioned any man in your life."

Terra clobbered her omelet with her fork while she waited for her mother's excitement to blow over. They sat at the two-chair dinette set in Terra's kitchen, catching up over Leta's surprise brunch.

After a full night's sleep, it would have been nice to relax with her coffee while she pondered how she'd managed to dodge the nightmares. Maybe Iam had come through for her, just as Harlan had promised. Was it really that easy? But Leta had tap-danced all over this blissful discovery by showing up at Terra's door at ten a.m., uninvited.

*If you're going to keep yourself too busy to come see me, then I'm coming to see you*, Leta had said, putting on a smile laced with rebuke. She'd stood at the door, one hand on hip, the other holding out a bag of groceries and cooking supplies for Terra to see.

They both knew Leta's brunches were pure witchcraft. She may not have been much for cooking when Terra was young, but she'd recently acquired the hobby as a diversion from more inebriating activities. These days, Leta could whip up an omelet like nobody's business, and Terra was defenseless against its magic.

The conversation hadn't been all that bad—not until Leta had spied Harlan's jacket hanging from the kitchen barstool. Terra glared at it now over her forkful of eggs, the Judas of all outerwear. Harlan had taken it off after their date and forgotten to bring it home. Now it was the sole focus of Leta's attention.

"So who is he?" Leta asked. "And when do I get to meet him?" She swept her thick, black hair off her face with a ring-studded hand. Terra's eyes homed in on a broken fingernail with a jagged edge. She hadn't even bothered to file it.

Terra shrugged and shoved a lone sausage around on her plate.

"Well at least tell me where he took you last night. And did he pay for you? I don't care if it's old fashioned. I think the man should pay." For her petite build, Leta had a big voice. A big, fat, meddling voice.

"I can pay for myself." It was none of her mom's business that he had, in fact, paid. "Fountain Square. We got some burritos and went bowling."

"Burritos and bowling with a boy—all good Bs." Leta's dark eyes gleamed. "Did you have a good time?"

Terra took a long sip of orange juice. A *good time*? The words didn't do it justice, not that she would say that. Nor was she going to mention the charm of the little cantina, or the way Harlan had held her hand as they walked through the square. How he'd stopped and pointed to the top of a brick building with the words YOU ARE BEAUTIFUL spread across the bricks in large, white letters. *I had them put that up there just for you,* he whispered in her ear. She'd seen the artwork a hundred times before, but she decided to play along. *I had them put that up there just for you,* she would say to him later as they passed a billboard for air duct cleaning on the highway.

They went to the vintage bowling alley after dinner for a couple rounds of duckpin bowling. She didn't care about her low score. Watching Harlan throw a dainty little ball at dainty little pins was amusing enough in its own right. Later, he kissed her by the fountain, the lights of the nearby theater flashing on their faces and the distant music of a street-side guitar solo filling their ears. The moment was so disgustingly perfect, she nearly dry-heaved with delight.

"Yeah, it was good."

"Alright." Leta paused, waiting for more. "Well, keep me posted on this one."

"Yep."

"Can't wait to meet him," she sang under her breath. She stood and carried her empty plate to the sink.

Terra ignored the comment. "So are you still seeing that one guy you met at AA...what's his name?"

"Who, Tim? No, he stopped going a couple months ago. We don't really talk anymore."

"Oh, sorry, I thought—"

"But I met someone else—oh, I have to tell you this—of all places, Terra..." With dramatic flair, Leta dropped a mixing bowl in the sink. "We met at the *grocery store.*"

"Hm."

"I know! Right? His name is Jeremy. He said he recognized me from somewhere. We got to talking and realized—get this—he and I went to *high school* together."

"Really?"

Leta was practically googly-eyed now. "He said he used to have the biggest crush on me."

"Cool." Terra rolled her eyes as her mother ducked under the sink to grab more dish soap out of the cabinet.

"Yeah, he was best friends with Scott Wakefield back in the day. You remember him?"

"Sure. He used to come to Huelo and Abuelita's cookouts when I was a kid."

"That's right. He taught you the ukulele, remember?" Leta puckered her lips to form the word *ooh-koo-lay-lay*, like she got bonus points for the proper Hawaiian pronunciation.

"Yeah, I do. That guy was alright." Terra smiled at the memory. "Wait. Didn't he also date Aunt—"

"Oh, how would I know?" Leta said, the smile falling from her face. "He was popular with all the girls." She shrugged as if bored with the topic and began scrubbing the mixing bowl with added aggression.

Despite the burning desire on Leta's part to quash the memory of her older sister, Terra still had fleeting impressions of her aunt from when she was young. Painting Terra's nails with purple glitter polish. Helping Abuelita in the kitchen during Sunday family dinners, tossing Terra a few tostones, still hot from the skillet. Teaching her to dance the Macarena over and over until everyone begged them to stop playing that godawful song.

Abuelita had talked about her a handful of times over the years after she'd passed away, but never about the day it happened, only the happier times. She'd mentioned once that her older daughter was sick toward the end, but that was it. Nobody ever wanted to elaborate.

"Anyway," Leta continued. "It's a small world, right? Jeremy and I have been dating for three weeks now."

"Congrats." Terra mashed the side of her fork against her last pancake like it deserved to be punished.

"In fact, the four of us should go on a double date sometime."

"Um, I don't know. I think that might be weird."

"Don't be such a wet blanket. God, you act like I'm just here to ruin your good time."

Terra dropped her fork with a clatter. "Mom, why don't you ever talk about her?"

Leta jerked her head back as if she'd been slapped in the face. Grimacing, she placed her hands on the edge of the sink for support, then turned her head away in stark silence.

Oh shit.

"Terra." Her voice was stern and distant. She paused a long time, allowing Terra's stomach to work itself into a pretzel of regret. "I have told you before, and I will tell you again, as Abuelita once told *me*: the older generation does not talk about their problems with the younger generation, because it's not the younger one's burden to carry. There is too much pain, too much horror there to even speak her name." Leta's voice wavered with restrained intensity. "My heart is already broken. Do not bring it up again, unless you want to kill me."

Stand down. Retreat. Be a good girl now and shut your trap.

"I'm sorry," Terra mumbled. She supposed it was only fair. There were details of her life she withheld from her mom. How could she expect anything different in return?

The thought struck her with immense sadness.

Terra woke in the middle of the night. Her bedroom light was on.

In a daze, she wondered how she'd forgotten to switch it off. She spent an indeterminate amount of time staring at the ceiling, too lazy to get up and remedy the situation. That's when the shadow appeared at the foot of her bed and crept toward her.

Before she could pull herself upright, he was on her, pinning her down at the arms and legs. An unbearable pressure sank onto her chest. The faceless sleaze bag was going to crush her in her own bed. She struggled to scream under the shadow's weight (surprisingly heavy as far as shadows went) but found she couldn't breathe.

Lungs burning, she focused her gaze on a spot on the ceiling and waited. It would come soon. The slow creep of death. She stared unblinking into the dim white of the drywall until everything appeared to be moving. The ceiling looked like shaking sand.

But now something churned in her vision. It was more than the dancing of visual static across her retinas. Something bloomed.

A pale desert rose.

Then, the words bloomed in her mind.

*Take root in my name.*

This time, it made sense. Despite the nauseating pain in her chest, she forced her lips to form the word. A squeak of voice came out her throat.

"Iam."

The shadow's pressure on her body eased just enough for her to take a breath.

Now when she expelled the name from her lungs, she found the strength to shout it. "Iam!"

Hulum's weight above her diminished to featherlight. She threw the dark figure off her and watched as he sailed across the room like a discarded sock. The shadow hit the wall soundlessly and slipped into the cracks of the baseboards, leaving the wall painted in the soft glow of the ceiling light. She was alone.

She sat up in bed panting. Now the room was dark, and she was awake.

"Thank you," she whispered, knowing exactly to whom she was speaking. Now she was certain he could hear her.

# Chapter Thirty

Terra sat cross-legged in the tall grass, basking in a state of perfect tranquility. She burrowed her fingers in the soft fur of the serval stretched on the ground next to her. It purred like an overgrown cat and butted its head up against her knee. Before Harlan had told her it was a serval, she'd assumed it was a juvenile leopard with jackal ears—an incredibly cute freak of nature either way.

Harlan sat next to her, plucking blades of grass from the earth and tying them together. The breeze of the Elysian savanna blew across the striking contours of his face and feathered his hair away from his forehead. He frowned with concentration and squinted his eyes in a way that reminded her of a boy band music video—the part where they clutch a fist to their chests and sing with utmost sincerity about their broken hearts. God bless him, he was adorable.

It was hard to ignore the gaping difference between the two of them. Here was a first-rate Elysian slumming it with a lowly Edenite. Was he simply settling for what he could get?

From what he'd told her about his past relationships, they never lasted long. Big surprise, all his secrets eventually got in the way. (It's hard to keep the conversation going when there's a gaping hole where your childhood should be.) The only reason Terra knew about his double life as a reviver was thanks to a frantic escape. Was that all that set her apart from the other women? A German shepherd and an impulse jump?

She was no longer feeling so tranquil.

"What?" He roused and returned her gaze.

"Nothing." She turned her eyes to the serval and scratched its chin. "I just wish we could stay here all the time."

She'd waited all week for today, when Harlan would bring her back here. Her world was celery; his, a seven-course meal, amuse-bouche and all. But the fact that Harlan was her only ticket to Elysia gave her pause. If—no, *when*—she lost him, her connection to Elysia would be severed. It would be like that helium balloon she'd gotten at the school festival in second grade, when the string snagged in the bouncy house motor and suddenly the fickle ball of gas was rising into the great unknown as she cried after it. Gone forever. The thought made it hard to breathe.

"But you have nothing to be afraid of back home anymore," he said.

True. She'd managed to kick Hulum to the curb. All it took was two more calls to Iam during her dreams, and the attacks had stopped. Iam was turning out to be a pretty competent exterminator.

"I know, but it's so much nicer here," she said, as if the argument were over ambience.

He kept his eyes down as he worked the blades of grass into a complex cord of braids. "We aren't meant to live our lives here. You know that. We're meant to live with other people."

"I know."

He turned to her and held out the cord of braided grass he'd created. "It's about time I gave you your own bracelet. What do you think?" He wrapped it around her wrist and tied it at the base.

She regarded it with amusement, turning her arm to study his hand-iwork. It was well made. "Almost as cool as yours. It just needs a certain stone right here." She pointed to the center.

He tweaked her chin, as he was in the habit of doing whenever she uttered something preposterous. "Only Iam makes those."

She ran her finger over the intricate braids. "What would happen if I had one like yours? Could I jump too?"

"Hmm...with some practice, I guess."

"Yeah, but..." She shot a devious glance at his wrist. "What if I borrowed *yours*?"

His smile strained at the edges. "You're serious, then?"

"Yes."

"That's a risky proposition."

"It would work for anyone, right? For whoever is wearing it at the time?"

"I would think so." He scratched his jaw pensively. "My concern is if something goes wrong and you need help, I'd be stuck in the other world with no way to get to you."

"Can't I bring you with me? Hold you, like you do me?"

"Okay, yeah, but..." He shifted on the ground, kicking out his legs in front of him. "There's also the challenge of knowing when and where it's safe to jump."

"What do you mean?"

"Oh, you don't think I do it blindly, do you? Oncoming cars and revivers don't mix. Neither do steep drop-offs, uneven terrain, lakes, concrete walls. But there are other important factors."

"Like?"

"People are everywhere in Eden. If I jump in or out while someone is there to witness it, we've got a big mess on our hands. Things have to be explained. People get suspicious or start to think they're losing their minds. I always check my surroundings before jumping out of Eden, and when jumping back, I use the extra second to check again."

"Extra second?"

"When jumping into a world, you always get a second to view the surroundings before merging with it. If I see trouble, I can pull back by letting go of the stone. It's a failsafe that Iam put in the design."

"Why's he so guarded about people finding this place anyway?"

"Isn't it obvious? If everyone knew about Elysia, they'd all want to come here too. That's not what it was meant for."

"So then it still doesn't make sense to me." She eyed him with one eyebrow arched. "Why am *I* here?"

He looked down at the bracelet. "Iam has his reasons. That's all I know."

They both watched as the serval stood and stretched, arching its spine and flattening its spotted ears against its head. She ran her hand along its back, and the cat leaned into it with a contented mew.

"It's getting late," Harlan said. "I promised Hunter I'd hang out with him tonight."

She rubbed her cheek against the serval's velvet head. "Hunter from the PT clinic? Why?"

"His girlfriend dumped him. I figured he could use a little encouragement right now."

"That kid's got an attitude problem."

"Oh, you noticed?" He shot her a wry smile.

"Hard to miss." Hunter had less personality than a cardboard box. At least around the patients. In the privacy of the break room, he was kind of a douche.

"Those are the ones that need help the most. You know, the whole *tuning out the static* thing."

"Ah," she said with a slow nod, as if this nebulous component of Harlan's life made any sense. Terra unfolded her legs and stood with reluctance. "I guess I'd better get back too." She was sure Alexis was having palpitations by now, waiting to give her the dirt on her date with Collin. They'd planned to go to a bonfire at his cousin's last night.

She held up her grass imitation bracelet. "Are you driving, or should I?"

"This is your stop," said Harlan.

They stood in her apartment taking their time with their good-byes. He lifted her chin to meet his gaze. "Can I ask you something before I go?"

"As long as it's not a math question."

"Are you— Do you plan on seeing anyone else?" He fidgeted with the pendant on her necklace and added, "Or can you maybe *not* see anyone else?"

"Hmm?" She tilted her head, looking as clueless as possible. She wanted to hear him say it.

"Because I'd kind of like to keep you for myself."

She smiled. "Feeling a little possessive, are we?"

"Uh, well—"

"Yes, I'm okay with that."

He sighed with relief. "Good. I was afraid I might have to coerce you with my indomitable wit and charm."

"Oh please. Not the wit and charm." She smirked as she lifted onto her toes and pressed her lips to his. She would delay his departure in this way as long as he would allow.

But she knew it was coming anyway.

He kissed her then pulled away, as was his habit.

She wasn't having it this time. Boundaries were made to be pushed, dammit. She went in for a second kiss.

A tug-of-war ensued. His hand went to her shoulder and nudged her back. She slapped it away and wrapped her arms around his neck. He stepped back. She pushed forward. When Terra had him in her embrace again, he shot her a crooked grin and disappeared, leaving an armful of air behind. He reappeared on the other side of the room a couple seconds later, a self-congratulatory look on his face.

"That's hardly fighting fair," she said.

"No one said anything about fair."

Terra flopped down on the couch. "I wish you wouldn't go to such great lengths to protect my virtue. There's not much left of it anyway."

"Hey, what makes you think it's *your* virtue I'm trying to protect?" he teased.

Before she could respond, he lunged forward, pinned her wrists to the couch, and kissed her on the forehead. As she struggled to free her hands, he whispered in her ear, "Good night, sweet cheeks."

Then he was gone.

She frowned. "*Sweet cheeks?*"

She sat on the couch, taking in the empty room, and wished she could steal that obnoxious piece of jewelry from him. Teleporting, she decided, was grossly overrated.

Still melting like a hot candy corn in the afterglow of his presence, she peeled herself off the couch and walked to the kitchen. Her phone was on the counter where she'd left it this morning. The screen showed three missed calls and a text message, all from Alexis. Terra allowed herself a smug grin. Called it. Alexis was dying to dish.

But as she read over the text message, her stomach twisted into knots.

*Terra, this is Alexis's friend, Collin. Please call as soon as you get this. There's been an accident.*

*Terra,*

*I find it pathetic, the degree to which people can be impressionable. Behold, the all-knowing, ever-independent human race of Eden, blown over by a single breath. A whisper, really, in their ears. All I have to do is come up with an idea and then feed it to them, like scraps from a table to the dogs. They don't even realize where it comes from. They think,* I have a great idea. *Then all hell breaks loose.*

*That's what I'm here for, Terra. To bring hell to your world.*

*What? The fire is dying down? The firewood is too damp? I can help. How about some gasoline? Yes, gasoline gets fires going again. Brilliant idea. Oh, Terra. I just wish you could have witnessed it. The explosion was flawless, as if I had dumped the can on the bonfire myself. And your repulsively carefree friend, well...it turns out she* does *care about some things. You should have heard her screams.*

*You might think you've overcome me, that this new thing you have going with Know-It-All himself will solve all your problems. Keep telling yourself that, Terra. Whatever lulls you into the idiotic complacence you humans always return to. It makes you much more malleable that way.*

*But know this: if I can't haunt you in your dreams, I will haunt you in your waking.*

*- H.*

*After the Fall, everything in Eden rebelled in its own way. Some plants grew thorns, others became poisonous. Some animals began killing others for food. Almost all abandoned humans. Even the wind and the rain turned savage, and the ground itself quaked with rage.*

*- Elysian Records for the Revivers, Book I: Origins*

# CHAPTER THIRTY-ONE

T erra plodded down the sterile corridor of the hospital. The utilitarian lighting added to the otherworldly feel and gave her the sensation of drifting into a blue abyss. This was the opposite of Elysia, and worse than the Eden she knew.

At the entrance to the burn center, a young man waited by the reception desk. He was tall with dirty blond hair, an unshaven face, and—Alexis hadn't been kidding—fantastically thick calves. When Collin greeted her, Terra caught a whiff of bonfire and cologne, a sordid combination of high romantic hopes and bitter tragedy. She took inventory: ruddy complexion, peeling skin around the fingernails, scratches on the forearms.

Collin waited as she signed in, then led her to Alexis's room. Halfway down the hall, he halted and pulled her aside. His eyes were fixed on a family lingering outside a doorway several rooms down. "Let's give them a minute," he said, a grave expression on his face.

Terra kept her head down as she glanced at the three people in front of them. A teenage boy was wiping his eyes with a bandaged hand and shaking his head, while an older man, presumably his father, hovered over him and spoke under his breath. A woman—Terra guessed the mother—stood nearby with a consoling hand on the boy's back, the other hand clutching a vase of flowers.

"Who's that?" Terra whispered.

"My cousin's neighbor, Reed. The young and dumb seven-teen-year-old I was telling you about on the phone."

"Oh. It was him?" She sized him up through covert glances: untied shoe, wrinkled shorts, pale lips.

Collin had already filled her in on the high-level details, how the kid thought he was helping but didn't think to consult anyone else before grabbing the gas can from the shed. When Collin had told her about it, Terra had pictured a teenage punk with a sneer, the type who might laugh after the fact and say *well ain't that some shit luck?* as if he couldn't be held responsible for which way the fire blew. But this kid was petrified, like a mouse staring up the nostrils of a boa constrictor. She imagined he would disappear through a crack in the wall if he could.

His father was still speaking in his ear, pushing him toward the room. Alexis's room. Then, the mother spoke up. Terra barely caught what she said over the clamor of the burn unit's echoing halls. "Jason, he's not ready. Please don't force him."

Jason scowled at his wife, then gave that little head-tilt-eye-roll combo husbands give when they know they can't win the fight.

Terra and Collin straightened up and started down the hall again as Reed and his father turned in their direction. Reed's mother disappeared into Alexis's room with the flowers.

"Hey, Reed," Collin mumbled as the two passed.

"Hey," Reed mouthed, though his voice seemed to be stuck in his throat. His father put an arm around him and led him out of the burn center.

As Collin and Terra reached the room, Reed's mother stepped out, a meek version of Alexis's voice floating after her. "Please tell him it's okay..."

At the sound of her voice, Terra's throat wrenched. Screw this. Screw all of this.

"I'll do that, honey. You know he feels too terrible for words right now. We'll be back another time." In turning away, the mother met Terra's eyes for a fraught moment, a sheen of wetness glistening in her own, then took off down the hall.

Terra didn't want to see what the woman had seen. She didn't want to be here. She'd rather be driving toothpicks under her nails. Or worse, shopping for swimsuits. She nearly stopped at the edge of the door frame, but Collin was behind her, pressing forward, and suddenly she was inside the room.

Alexis's parents sat in the corner, lines of weariness on both their faces. They looked up and nodded to her in acknowledgment. In bed lay the patient, wrapped in bandages from head to fingertips on her left side. But the fire had left most of her face untouched.

Most of it.

"Terra, *where* have you been?" Through the gauze and drugs, Alexis still managed to reproach her friend like a Catholic school nun with ruler in hand.

Terra stepped forward, ignoring the sting of tears, and reached out to hold Alexis's one good hand. "I'm so sorry. I was with Harlan all day and didn't hear my phone."

Alexis made a sound that Terra surmised to be a snort, though her expression didn't change—the bandages along the side of her face were too restrictive. "We need to put you on a leash so you can't keep disappearing with that boyfriend of yours." Her words were slow, a bit slurred.

"I know, I'm sorry." Terra kept steady eye contact, as if there were nothing wrong with Alexis. But there was. Everything was wrong. The singed and sheared hair on the side of her head. The day-old eye makeup crusted around her eyelids. The raw, red skin peeking out from underneath the bandages. This was not a meaningless list of incongruities Terra's mind had singled out for the fun of it. Nor was it a grammatical error that could be deleted and rewritten. Terra couldn't fix this.

Alexis cracked a hint of a smile from her right side. "It's okay. Thanks for coming."

Terra sat down by the bed. "How are you feeling?"

"Great. Drugs are the *best*."

Terra forced a smile and swiped a swell of moisture from the corner of her eye. "You sound like a junky already."

"Do you blame me? I was on fire, Terra. Flames. Fuh-luh-*ames*."

"I know."

"Actually, I got lucky."

"How's that?"

"When the gas hit the fire, I was turning to grab another marshmallow."

"A marshmallow?"

"The fire only got me on the side. Would've been way worse if I'd been facing it. But I wanted another s'more." She let out a lethargic snicker. "Never thought the drive to stuff my face would be the thing that saved me."

Terra exhaled a laugh, though it was more of a release of anxious energy than anything genuine.

The fatigue sank back into Alexis's features. "Everyone else was luckier than me. Reed got a few burns on his hand, but the explosion went in my direction. My burns are mostly second-degree, they're telling me. My arm got the worst of it. Will probably need some skin grafts." She paused for a moment, her eyes shifting to the window. "The doctor said I'll have scarring. But that's it. My lungs are okay. Should have full use of my arm eventually. My ear is still in one piece. Just scars."

"That's a good thing, then, right?"

"Yeah. It is," Alexis said, though the glum tone in her voice betrayed her.

Collin piped in from the doorway. "I'm grabbing some chips from the vending machine. Anyone want anything?"

They shook their heads. Alexis watched him turn and leave.

"He seems like a good guy," Terra said.

"Barely left my side since the accident. And he got to meet the parents, lucky him." Alexis nodded to her parents in the corner, who had resorted to reading magazines pulled from the reception area. "Isn't he great, Dad?"

Her dad glanced up from his issue of *Arthritis Today*. "Hmm?"

She let out a labored sigh. "Oh, stop acting like you don't know who I mean."

"I think he's very nice, sweetheart," Alexis's mom offered, her eyes still glued to her *People* magazine.

"So as you can see," Alexis said to Terra, "they are both thrilled."

"When's the wedding?"

"Probably right after yours."

Terra scoffed. "Right." The thought made her miss Harlan immediately. And Elysia, where freak accidents didn't happen, and people didn't go up in flames. Where the only kind of shit storm you'd ever see was if the bison ate too much grass.

She stayed another twenty minutes, until the very sight of Alexis's bandages made her skin crawl and her eyes water. "I have to get home." She rose from her chair by the bed, hands fidgeting with the strap of her purse.

"Oh. Are visiting hours over already?"

"Um…" Terra looked around for a clock. Seeing none, she shrugged. "No. I just can't stay."

"Oh." Alexis stretched the unburned side of her body with a languid yawn. "I guess I'm pretty tired anyway."

"Call you tomorrow, okay?"

"Yeah."

Terra waited until she'd reached the safety of her car before letting the curse words fly. She fumbled with her keys and missed the keyhole several times before jamming them in the ignition with an enraged cry. The engine came to life, but her hand hesitated over the gear shift. She stared out her windshield at the pock-marked concrete wall of the parking garage, frozen in thought.

Where was Iam in all this? Seemed like he was content to galivant around Elysia, ignoring the other half of the human race. But if he really knew everything that went on in Eden, as Harlan had said, then why had he been silent? Why no warning, or call for help? *Something.*

Terra put the car in reverse and began the long drive home. All the while, a bitterness seeped through the cracks in her heart.

*Terra,*

*I'll be withdrawing for a while. I've raised enough red flags with the Boss now that he's started monitoring my activities. He knows about the bonfire incident, though he doesn't realize the connection to you. He even commended my ingenuity with that one. But he isn't happy that I've gone rogue on my assignments. And he's not the sort you want to piss off.*

*I'll need to fly under the radar for a time until he eases up. It won't be long though. When it comes to complacence, he's no better than you idiot humans. I'm sure somewhere deep down, he recognizes he would be incompetent without me. Not even the others in my rank command as much power as I do. Soon enough, I'll be able to prove it to them. And to you.*

*That brings me to my plan. It won't be easy by any means, and it will take the utmost perseverance, restraint, and patience. But when it comes time to execute, the results will be nothing short of spectacular.*

*I've made my decision. I'm not reporting you to the Boss. If I do, he'll have someone else deliver your punishment. And I can't have that. Not after all I've invested in you. I'll be doing it myself. I'm the best fit for the job, after all.*

*I can't wait for the day, Terra. Yes, it is coming. The day when I am standing before you, face to face. Just try ignoring me then.*

*- H.*

# FALL
## (SEPTEMBER-ISH)

*Their susceptibility can vary. Some lean whichever way the wind blows them. Others are nearly impervious to the subversives' manipulations, either having been born with or developing over time a firmness of will and questioning mindset. Unfortunately, this also makes them hard of hearing to Iam's voice and multiplies the complexity of our work.*

*- Elysian Records for the Revivers, Book II: The People of Eden*

# Chapter Thirty-Two

Terra willed her eyes to stay shut and took in another cleansing breath, as if it would help. The wind grazed her neck and taunted her like a delinquent schoolboy.

Focus. Sound was her only companion now. She clung to every auditory parcel. Rustling leaves. Lapping water. The far-off laughter of children. The not-as-far bickering of a couple. The subtle patter of sneakers hitting concrete.

Nothing. She grimaced in frustration.

"I'm not getting anything." She opened her eyes and raked her hand through a tangle of hair.

"It's not always about getting, you know." Harlan sat nearby, studying the palms of his hands where the grass had made indents. It was beginning to dry out and turn brown with the cooling weather. All the lawns overlooking the downtown canal were starting to look dismal, but at least this patch was in a wide-open space away from the roads.

Terra leaned back with her hands in the grass and watched as city dwellers made their way along the path below. Nearby, the dark water rippled in the wind and sloshed along the canal walls like a sinuous eel trying to escape its enclosure. She inhaled slowly and said, "I figured."

"Sometimes it's about *giving* too. Stilling your mind and surrendering whatever you're holding on to."

"Like the static."

"Exactly."

"But I don't have any of that."

"That's a little presumptuous, don't you think?"

"What?"

"You're telling me there isn't anything you're hanging onto?"

She narrowed her eyes at him. "I'm free as a flipping bird."

"Are you ever afraid of what others think of you?"

"Isn't everyone? What does that have to do with anything?"

Harlan stared at her at length without answering, as if the answer were obvious. "Or afraid of what might happen if things don't go the way you planned?"

She shrugged.

"And what about bitterness?"

"What about it?"

"Do you ever feel bitter toward anyone?" He leaned his head into her field of vision and caught her eyes. "Like your mom?"

She looked away. "That's not fair, Harlan. Parent-child relationships are always complicated." It was a fact of life, wasn't it? Not that Mr. My-Parents-Are-Literally-Perfect would understand.

He drew his fingertips along her arm. "I'm only pointing out the things that might be bogging you down. It doesn't make you a bad person."

"I know."

"And once you can stop holding on to all that stuff, your hands will be open and ready to receive." In demonstration, Harlan took her hand and rolled her fingers outward. Then he pulled something from his pocket and placed it in her open palm.

She gawked. "Where did you get this?"

"Found it under a tree on our walk over here."

"Really? They grow like that?"

She turned the half shell of what looked like a walnut around in her hand and studied it closely. The inside housed a deep indent in the center where the nut had once been nestled—probably foraged by a small animal some time ago—in the perfect shape of a heart. It looked like it had been expertly crafted by a woodworker—or at least a chipmunk with some serious artistic flair.

"I guess sometimes they do," Harlan said. "Just a reminder that not all is lost in this life, or that maybe somebody loves you."

She eyed him with a sideways grin. "You're such a flirt."

He turned his face away without speaking, a cocky smile playing at the edge of his mouth.

She slipped the walnut shell into her purse like it was no big deal, but she knew she'd keep it forever. They'd been dating since the spring, and he still gave her that baby-pterodactyls-in-the-stomach feeling.

"So remind me again why we're doing this?"

"Practice," he said.

"I'm supposed to sit here and listen, whether or not he has anything to say to me?"

He watched the water below. "Yes."

"What if I have questions and need some answers?"

"He's not Google."

She scoffed and shifted her legs beneath her. "But why can't we do this in Elysia, where it's so much easier to, you know, *hear?*"

"Because this is where we live our lives. This is where we make our choices. He speaks to us in the moment. We have to be ready for that." He returned his gaze to the grass marks on his palms and spoke quietly. "Besides, there's another reason."

"What?"

"The sooner you get used to connecting with him here, the sooner you can *remember*."

Terra squinted up at the clouds as they raced over the canal. "Remember what?"

"Who you really are. Kind of...seeing it all at once. But not like a regular memory—it's a memory of the soul."

"Can you explain that a little better? Use your big boy words."

Harlan leaned back. "I wish I could, but it's not something Elysians get to experience. We can't uncover memories that were never lost to begin with. It's an Edenite thing."

As Terra's left eyebrow reached new heights in the name of skepticism, her phone vibrated on the ground next to her. She picked it up and groaned. Alexis had sent multiple texts.

*Come on spill it*

*What REALLY helped with your fibro*

*These nerve pain meds are making me loopyyyy*

Well, crap. Alexis had noticed months ago that Terra wasn't exactly shuffling around like an invalid anymore. Terra had offered a vague answer about yoga stretches and getting to bed earlier, but that wouldn't cut it this time. She racked her brain for new excuses. No inspiration came.

"What's wrong?" Harlan asked.

She exhaled a labored breath. No easy way to broach this prickly subject. "You said the healing pools can heal *anyone*, right? As long as they're still alive?"

"Yes. Why?"

"Lex needs help."

His face turned grim. "Terra."

"Harlan. She's in pain. And the medicine isn't cutting it. If we could just heal the pain—"

"You know that's not the answer."

"But why the hell not?"

He glanced around and lowered his voice. "There are rules. You know that. We can't bring anyone else into Elysia. We can't—"

"You brought me." Her eyes pierced his and held them.

"I hadn't planned on it, but we were in danger, and I panicked. It was a moment of desperation."

"And isn't *this* a desperate situation too?"

"It's not the same, Terra. After I brought you home from the park that night, I couldn't sleep. I'd messed up. Thought I was done being a reviver for good. And when I finally talked to Iam about it, he told me it had been in his plan. That it was okay somehow. But *this*...we have a chance to really think about this first."

She eyed him skeptically. "How exactly is getting chased by a demonic dog part of his plan?"

"It's not as complicated as it sounds. He knows how things are going to work out before they happen. He knew we'd be safe, that I'd bring you to Elysia, and that's what he wanted. I never told you, but it was Iam who gave me the idea to take you to the park that night."

"Huh. Well...maybe bringing Alexis to Elysia is part of his plan too."

"We don't know that. You can't force your own plans on him. Trust me, that never turns out well."

"Then we'll ask for permission."

He shook his head.

"Yes, we will," she said. "*I* will."

He sighed. "Fine. You can try." His tone suggested the same level of optimism as if she were attempting to summit K2 in flip flops.

"You just wait," Terra said with an air of confidence. "And when I ask him, I want to go to Elysia to do it. No more of this sitting around in silence like a monk, waiting for answers to float in on the breeze."

*If they could see reflected in our eyes even a fraction of what we have seen, this great undertaking would be finished before it ever began.*

*- Elysian Records for the Revivers, Book V: Our Charge*

# Chapter Thirty-Three

T erra knelt in the supply closet of the Grayson Physical Therapy clinic, organizing resistance bands and barbells by color and weight. It was a tangled mess, the work of therapists in a hurry. She was willing to bet no one here suffered from OCD. Absorbed in her task, she overheard the banter of two PT students speaking under their breath.

"And what are you doing this weekend? Getting wasted on Jello shots?"

"Hey, shut it, bruh. That was *one* time."

*Wasted,* she thought. They didn't know the meaning of the word.

*Wasted* was when you could no longer pour your own drinks, so you asked your eight-year-old to do it for you. *Wasted* was spending the night on the couch because you couldn't get up to go to bed. *Wasted* was the mother who spent her daughter's childhood with one foot in reality, the other in a bottle.

She remembered the first time Huelo and Abuelita caught her mother drinking. It was about a year after the funeral. Before that, Terra never knew that Leta was a drunk. But that's the word Huelo used: *Look at you. You're drunk.* As if this was not supposed to be a nightly occurrence.

She'd crouched by her bedroom door, listening to their accusations, biting down the nails of her fingers until they stung.

*We're all moving on in our own ways, but you have a daughter.*

*My daughter is fine. She's not neglected.*

*We didn't say that, but if we ever have to pursue custody...*

*Don't you hang that over my head! I am in my right mind. I am not my sister.*

*God as my witness, Leta, if you don't get your act together—*

*God! What God? If there was one, she would still be here.*

Terra bristled at the memory of the exchange, the grownup words that children should never have to hear. It was a miracle they didn't rip themselves apart fighting over her—and rehashing the death of her aunt, when it seemed everything had changed. But things had gotten better after that first incident. Leta had always managed to pull herself together just enough to maintain the appearance of motherly duty.

Terra wondered if it would've been better going to live with her grandparents, though she knew they couldn't have been up to the task, what with Abuelita's heart condition and Huelo's emphysema. The old custody argument was only a threat, a motivator, for her mother's sake. And if she had...then what? Probably after Huelo's passing—most definitely after Abuelita's—she would have been packed up and sent straight back to Leta's as a teen, massive attitude in tow. That would have been worse. At least living with Leta all along had helped Terra build up a tolerance to all her bullshit. And learn independence. At least she had that.

"Dinner at my place tonight?"

She looked up from her task to see Harlan poke his head in the supply closet. "You're cooking?" she asked.

He snorted. "Of course not. Takeout."

"One of these days, I will teach you to cook." That was one thing she'd learned out of necessity growing up.

"Believe it or not, Hunter told me he likes to cook too." He tilted his head toward the sandy-haired student. "Good thing, 'cause with me it will have to be a team effort."

Terra watched Hunter behind them, chatting it up with his patient as he worked out a trigger point in her shoulder. "Hunter seems like he's enjoying himself more these days."

"Yeah, he had a lot of angst to work through, but he's getting better."

"Let me guess. You took him to the Smash Club?"

Harlan flashed a mischievous grin. "No. I only took *you* there because I wanted to dance with you." He winked and turned back to his patients.

She stared after him. What had he been doing all these months to make Hunter pull a one-eighty? She knew he'd been spending time with Hunter regularly, but it's not like he was chanting spells over him. Just spending time. Was that all it was?

She kept at her volunteer chores as the afternoon drew to a close and the last patients finished their allotted times. As she wiped down the leg press with disinfectant, she heard Hunter saying goodbye to a patient who looked the age of her grandfather when he'd passed.

In a sincere gesture, the man placed both hands on Hunter's shoulders and squeezed. "Thank you," he said. "I feel like I've been made new again."

As the patient plucked his jacket off the table and headed out, Terra almost turned back to her chore. But Hunter's reaction caught her eye.

From across the room, she could see a glint of something different in his eyes. He stared after his patient in a daze. Then she realized. He wasn't staring at anything in the clinic. He was somewhere else altogether.

Then, as if he'd been struck behind the knees with a billy club, his legs buckled and he fell. From the reception desk, Carol gasped. Another PT student called out, "You okay, bud?" A few others turned to see what the commotion was all about.

His trance broken, Hunter slowly pulled himself back up and nodded. "Yeah." He brushed off his pants. "Yeah, I'm good."

Another student called, "Looks like Hunter needs to lay off the sauce," eliciting a round of chuckles.

Hunter smiled sheepishly and wandered toward the break room.

The incident was over as quickly as it had begun.

Terra turned to Harlan and saw him exchange a glance with Ezra. Chills raced down her back. Something had happened. What did they know?

The students didn't linger after their patients left. Taking a glance in the supply closet just long enough to notice the neatly organized rows Terra had established, they raised their eyebrows in approval, then tossed their equipment in a pile on the floor anyway. They were clearly anxious to get started with whatever it is students do on a Friday night. Making Jello shots, maybe.

Terra crept down the hall to the break room and stopped at the door. Ezra sat with Hunter at the round table, talking in hushed tones. Harlan leaned against the doorway, listening.

"What's going on?" she asked.

The two men at the table looked up at her, suddenly mute. Harlan walked her back into the hallway and leaned close.

"Hunter *remembered*."

"Remembered what?"

Harlan offered a strained smile and answered patiently. "The thing that happens when you connect with Iam. The memory of the soul that I was telling you about."

She vaguely recalled something about that, right before their argument over Alexis. "But how?"

"We don't know how it happens. It just does. Without warning." He looked back at Hunter. "He's still in a bit of shock, but it's okay if you want to talk with him."

He led her into the break room, where they took a seat across from Ezra and Hunter. Harlan nodded toward them. "It's okay. She knows."

"Quite a trip, right?" Ezra said.

"Kinda feels like I just woke up for the first time." Hunter replied. He ran his hands through his hair, his eyes burning bright like he'd just downed five energy drinks.

"What was it like?" Terra asked.

"Like everything coming together all at once. Like being born and dying at the same time."

"All that in a couple seconds?"

"Yes."

As far as trips went, this one sounded like the motherload. Terra couldn't manage to wrap her mind around it. She tried a different approach. "When you were staring off into space—when you *remembered*—what did you see?"

Hunter opened his mouth and closed it again, as if too overcome for words. He hung his head for a moment, then brought his eyes up to hers.

"I saw God."

# CHAPTER THIRTY-FOUR

The sky was tumultuous, the clouds rolling like a stampede of fluffy rhinos.

"I thought Elysia was perfect!" Terra yelled as they ran for cover, abandoning their impromptu picnic by a creek. Giant raindrops splattered against her face. The creek, no more than a trickle before, was beginning to rush and swell.

"I never said it didn't rain here." Harlan flashed a smile at her as he reached back to grasp her hand. "I know somewhere we can go."

They were both sopping wet by the time they reached a hollow at the base of a solid rock prominence. The low entrance forced them to bow their heads as they passed through, their footsteps echoing in the dank atmosphere. The ceiling rose high enough for them to stand. The floor was made of smooth earth. A coffee maker and some curtains, and this place could double as a vacation home.

They sat against the wall of the cave, watching the rain break across the landscape in gentle sheets. Terra tilted her head against the rock and panted from the exertion of their run. They should have used the bracelet to get here. A little late now. The rainwater from her clothes dripped down her arms and back in tiny streams, parting and converging again as they made their way to the dirt below. Harlan wasn't any better off. He wrung out the bottom of his shorts, and a puddle formed beneath.

He turned his face toward hers and smiled a helpless *what now?* She drank in the features of his face, the wet shirt clinging to his chest, and her mind started going places it probably shouldn't.

She projected her voice over the cacophony of rainfall. "What are people like in your world?"

He studied her face, then gazed out into the rain, as if tapping into the psyche of the ones who lived beyond the boundaries, the mysterious *others.* "They're selfless. And honorable."

"But do they...date...like people do in our world?"

He raised his eyebrows, then leaned close to her ear, as if the rain were an unwelcome eavesdropper. "No. It's better than that."

"Oh? Is it like a lottery system?"

His lips grazed her ear. "No. Dating is all trial-and-error. And marriage is a contract, a substandard one at best. But there's no need for that in Elysia."

He stopped to wipe a raindrop from her brow, and she leaned into his touch.

"In Elysia, people are given to each other while they're still children." He paused as she shot him a look of disgust. "Don't look at me like that. They still act like normal kids. The romantic love happens later, as they get older. And when they're both ready for love, they're already there for each other. There's no waiting for *the one.*"

"So the parents arrange it?"

"No. Iam pairs them from birth."

He had to be joking. She pulled back to meet his gaze. "But what if two people fall in love that he didn't pair?"

"That wouldn't happen."

"But why not? Why can't someone choose who they want to be with?"

"I think you're missing the point," he said gently. "They have no desire to be with anyone else, because Iam's choice for them is the most perfect choice."

"The *most perfect* choice. Is that even a thing? Isn't love perfect enough in itself?" Terra's raised voice bounced off the rock walls like angry hailstones.

"It was Iam who made it that way."

"But then..." Her voice faltered. "Where does that leave *us*?"

He was stunned into silence. Outside, the rain slowed. Harlan looked down at their joined hands and fixed his jaw in a frown. "You're afraid Iam doesn't want us to be together."

"No—or yes...maybe." She ran her hand along a patch of moss on the cave floor, little flecks of green shedding from it like a cheap carpet. "I'm not exactly the perfect Elysian woman."

"Terra." He met her eyes pointedly. "You forget there's no one perfect this side of Elysia. We're all broken here."

"So he *does* want us to be together then?"

Harlan sighed and leaned his head back. "He hasn't been entirely clear on that, but I think so."

"What do *you* want?"

He gave her an unsure smile before looking away, then rubbed the back of his neck for a long moment. "I want *you*. Sometimes so much I can't stand it."

She laughed. "Am I that unbearable?"

"Every minute is torture."

"Then why push me away? Why all the boundaries?"

"I don't want to make any mistakes. I've made enough in the past."

"I'm on board with you there."

"I've always expected things—especially love—to be certain, to be spelled out. But this...this feels like jumping out of a plane, not knowing whether the parachute will open."

She looked at him with a crooked smile. "You really are new to this, aren't you?"

"The whole true love thing? Or soul mates—whatever you want to call it—it's uncharted territory," he admitted.

"Didn't Ezra ever explain any of this to you?"

"Ezra always thought it best to go it alone."

"Well, allow me to educate you." She sat up on her knees and faced him. "Love..." She paused for dramatic effect. "Is all about *faith*. Faith that the other person will love you no matter what. And that you can manage to keep loving them no matter what." It also required the patience to pick out furniture without screaming at each other, but she kept that part to herself.

"Yeah?"

She leaned in to whisper in his ear. "And guess what?"

"What?" His hand grazed the side of her waist, stirring a frenzy of hot sparks inside her.

"I love *you*, Harlan. No matter what. Always and forevermore." She let out a self-deprecating laugh. Spewing sentiments made her squeamish.

They'd used the *L-word* with each other a dozen times over the summer, but she was still warming to the idea of sharing feelings. That they weren't something you stuffed down until you had nowhere else to hide them. And this time, something in his reaction gave her pause. His eyes were troubled.

"What's wrong?" she asked.

"Forever is a long time."

"Does that bother you?"

"No." He ran a hand along the wet ringlets of hair framing her face. "I just didn't know you were ready for forever."

"Maybe I am." She leaned in and brushed her lips against his, then pulled back to look in his eyes. "Are *you*?"

"I can't imagine being with anyone else but you."

"Oh yeah?" Teasingly, she ran her fingers down his chest, skimmed the muscles of his abdomen, and twisted the bottom hem of his shirt into her hand. "Prove it."

When she tried lifting the damp cotton away from his skin, his breath hitched, and he seized her hand in a steel grip. His voice came out strained. "But how do we know for sure?"

She sat back, her levity blown over. "We don't. It's...it's a decision we make."

After a long moment of consideration, he lifted a hand to her neck. "Then let's make one." The backs of his fingers incited goose bumps along her skin as they moved downward and lingered at her collarbone. "I'm going to love you for the rest of my life." In a heartfelt tone that could coax tears from a cardboard cutout, he asked, "Can you promise the same?"

Her eyes locked with his. His expression was desperate. His willpower was teetering like a one-legged bird on a fence. Good God, he was caving. In a cave, no less. As a resident of her own world for twenty-five years, she knew—better than him—that a pronouncement of commitment coming from any flawed person was just words, flimsy and subject to the whims of fallen hearts. But she also knew she wanted him. She wanted to make this work. Hell, she'd give up Elysia for him. Or wine. Or eating after eight p.m.

"I promise," she said. "I'll love you forever." She didn't laugh this time. She wanted it to mean something. No takebacks allowed.

He didn't waste any time. She found herself locked in his arms in a way that set fire to her core, his lips pressing against the delicate skin under her jaw. God bless America, she thought she might cry.

But why waste time on sentiments when they had so many better things to do?

They spent the rest of their afternoon there, boundaries more or less an afterthought. And much like that first night Terra set foot in Elysia and took in that immaculate canopy of stars above, the realization of this moment—and all its implications—was terrifying and beautiful all at once.

# CHAPTER THIRTY-FIVE

Terra sat in the bistro on her lunch break amid the bustling crowds of office workers, an empty chair across the table from her. She tapped her fork against the side of her salad bowl at a rabid pace.

Alexis was going to go berserk when she found out. If, that is, she ever showed up so Terra could tell her. She didn't need to say much. Just a hint. Tell her things were going *exceedingly* well with Harlan. Then Alexis would connect the dots. Flip out. Buy her a greeting card or something that said, *Congrats. It's about frickin' time.*

To Terra, Alexis's reactions were top-shelf, liquid energy. They woke her up to life whenever the numbness was beginning to creep in. But these interactions had become few and far between lately. Since the accident, Alexis had had a hard time smiling. At first, she'd blamed all the bandages and scarring that pulled at the skin on her face. But the bandages were gone now, and the burn wounds healed over. Terra was starting to suspect the worst of Alexis's scarring lay far deeper than skin.

She took another bite of seared salmon and arugula and thought of Harlan. She'd been a bit heady and disoriented ever since that day in the cave, her thoughts as organized as a kitchen junk drawer. It had jarred her how little convincing he'd needed. How long had he been ready to make a commitment like that, but had kept quiet for her sake? What else had he been hoping for in their future together? When she tried to imagine what forever might look like with him, her mind went blank. It was too overwhelming to process.

A figure in the sea of business casual attire caught her eye: a face with discolored patches of skin along the jawline, an angry, ridged scar peeking out the top of her shirt collar like a topographic map of pain, and long sleeves to hide a compression garment, which protected the much more obvious, gnarled scarring that stretched from shoulder to knuckles. Alexis had expressed many times since the accident her insecurities about her appearance, but Terra would always reassure her. Alexis could be dressed in a trash bag and clogs and still look gorgeous.

Alexis waved and came toward the table with a look of self-reproach. "I forgot I had a deadline at noon today." She pursed her lips. "Sorry. I did it again."

"It's okay." Terra pushed out the chair for Alexis with her foot. "Have a seat. You can watch me finish my lunch, I guess."

Alexis collapsed in the chair. "Ugh. I know I've been awful lately."

"Of all the awful friends, you're still my favorite."

"Aw, you really mean that?"

Terra rested her head on her hand. "You want to tell me what's going on?"

"Nothing. I swear. It's just the same old stuff since..."

"Yeah, I hear you."

"I just can't get back to where I was, you know? I can't concentrate. The nerve pain, and the itching—it never stops."

"What'd they say at your last appointment?"

"She thinks the damage in my arm is permanent. Fried the nerves like an egg on a hot sidewalk. Of course, not enough to numb them."

"But I thought the methadone was helping."

"It did." Alexis stopped to rub the delicate pink tissue on the side of her neck. "But they started tapering my doses a couple months ago. You know. Can't have the narcs coming after me." She huffed. "Already tried all the nerve pain drugs. Hated them. The doctor said to just take an ibuprofen when the pain's too much."

"I'm so sorry, Lex."

"Problem is, I've got pain all the time. I can deal with it during the day. It sucks, but I can push through. It's at night though that I can't deal. It keeps me awake. I've been taking sleeping pills to help. You know how that is."

Terra shook her head. "I don't really take them anymore, but even when I did, I tried to keep it to a half dose. They say those things are addictive."

"Oh, honey, I'm way beyond half doses. I had my doc bump it up to the max amount."

"For how long now?"

"A month." Alexis finger-combed the hair that draped over the scarred side of her face. It was a habit she'd started ever since she'd parted it that way to cover the burns. "I think it's one of the reasons Collin left."

"You think?"

"Well it sure as hell better not be because of how I look. It's not, is it?"

"Absolutely not. But why would he leave you over sleeping pills?"

"He said he didn't like the way I act when I'm on them. All groggy and out of it during the day, and just weird at night. Sleep walking, sleep talking, completely blacking out on whole conversations we had. But he doesn't get it. It's not like I have a choice."

"This is sounding kind of serious, Lex."

Alexis picked at the week-old polish on her nails. "I once woke up standing in the parking lot with car keys in hand, like I was about to go for a joy ride or something. What the hell?"

Terra put her fork down. "You need to stop taking those pills."

"Wish I could. I'm on such a high dose now, I can't sleep without them. The doctor wants to send me to a cognitive behavioral therapy program at the pain clinic. Sounds like a racket to me."

"You're not going to try it?"

Alexis looked at her with the hardened face of a war veteran. "Terra. Do you really believe the power of *mindfulness* is going to fix me? I'm broken. For good. Game over."

Terra opened her mouth but failed to conjure any semblance of encouragement. Behind Alexis, a middle-aged man with a limp hobbled past the bistro and into the elevator lobby, his left dress shoe dragging at an angle with each step. She'd seen him in passing a thousand times before. He'd had that limp for as long as Terra had worked here. This time, it occurred to her with bitter clarity that he would probably always have that limp.

She thought of a patient at Harlan's clinic with a similar limp. And LouAnne in her wheelchair. Broken. There were so many broken people here that deserved better than the lot they'd been given. If this state of the world were a manuscript, she'd have scrapped the whole thing. The flaws were glaring. And no one was fixing them.

Were these people meant to stay this way for the rest of their lives? Was this all Alexis had to hope for too?

Terra stood up and threw what was left of her salad in the trash. She had suddenly lost her appetite.

*The right to free will is a precarious thing. It gives the bearer of this right the chance to gain everything—or lose it all—in the wake of a single decision.*

*- Elysian Records for the Revivers, Book I: Origins*

# CHAPTER THIRTY-SIX

The word *no*. It was borderline offensive.

Terra sat in her car's driver's seat, rolling the cords of the bracelet between her fingers. A *not right now* or a *no, but...*would have been acceptable. But the single-word answer comprised of those two obstinate and final letters, *N* and *O*, got under her skin with a pernicious tenacity.

After taking a long pause in the darkness, mostly because her heart was still hopping like a jackrabbit in her chest, she cranked the engine and flipped on the headlights. He hadn't woken up. She was sure of it. She'd been careful. Tediously so. She'd watched the numbers on the digital clock change three times as she'd eased the slipknot open and stretched the bracelet over his hand. As the cords finally brushed past his fingertips and into hers, the glowing clock had read *1:59*. She still had plenty of time.

The clicks of the turn signal on her dash sounded ominous as she made her way through the empty side streets to Alexis's apartment building. Like driving a ticking bomb. But this would be the easy part. Getting the bracelet had been the biggest hurdle. That required convincing Harlan to stay the night after he'd dropped her off from their date, then staying awake long enough to catch him in a deep sleep. By comparison, getting Alexis to Elysia would be a cakewalk, especially if she'd used the sleep meds tonight. Terra patted the apartment key in her pocket to make sure it was still there. Alexis had given her a spare a long time ago for dog sitting whenever she was out of town.

She should've worn all black. Thrown in a ski mask and crowbar for full effect. She choked out a high-pitched laugh at the thought. She was like a criminal. An eyepatch-wearing, cat-stroking villain. But every time she second guessed herself, there was that word again scratching its way under her skin: *no*.

Harlan had warned her, but she'd still had to ask. When she'd finally heard the soundless, iron-fisted answer as she sat on the bank of an Elysian river, she'd felt nothing short of rage. It was an injustice to Alexis. An irrational injustice. That's when she'd begun quietly plotting her rescue.

After parking the car, she glanced at herself in the rearview mirror and caught a glint of gold from the pendant on her neck. The *TZ* gleamed like a statement of defiance. Damn straight. Terra Zaragoza was calling the shots tonight.

All was quiet at the entrance to Alexis's apartment. Without knocking, Terra slipped the key in the lock and opened the door. Hoots, Alexis's terrier mix, picked his head up from his sherpa-lined doggie bed and watched her in silence.

"Hey Hootsie," she whispered to the small dog. "Stay."

His tail thumped the cushion in response. He slowly turned his head, tracking her with bright eyes as she made her way toward the sounds of deep breathing in the bedroom.

Alexis lay sprawled in the middle of her bed, sheets twisted beneath her, a prescription bottle and empty glass on the nightstand at her side. Good. So long as Alexis was on her medication, chances she'd remember any of this were slim to none.

"Lex," Terra whispered. "Wake up."

Her friend continued breathing deeply.

"Lex."

No response.

Terra flipped on the light and shook the bed. "Alexis!"

Alexis popped up in bed like a turkey timer. "Huh?"

"Where are we going again?" Alexis mumbled from the passenger seat, one arm draped over her face to shield her eyes from the streetlights.

"I'll tell you later." Terra was still catching her breath from hauling her friend to the car. She'd known Alexis would be groggy but hadn't anticipated having a deadweight on her hands. She may as well have been rescuing a sack of bowling balls. Shame she hadn't taken the time to learn how to jump across distances. If that were the case, they'd already be there by now.

Harlan had actually offered to let her try the bracelet the first time. After that, it had been easy to ask. He let her wear it whenever they crossed over, convinced she was simply amused by it. Like it was a toy to her. With his unwitting help, she'd gotten enough practice under her belt to trust she could use the bracelet on her own.

A more problematic venture was the mapping out of Elysia in correspondence with Eden's locations. She'd tried to remember the few healing pools they'd come across in Elysia, most of which they'd found by jumping across distances instead of direct from Eden. But there was the very first one they'd visited by walking, so she could mentally retrace their steps. Because distances were so much greater in Elysia than Eden, it was hard to estimate how far they'd gone from the original jumping point in

Eden. Her best guess was next to a grocery store loading dock not too far from her apartment. It was also a safe place to cross over without being seen.

Terra pulled up behind the empty loading dock and glanced at the passenger seat. Alexis was slumped over and snoring like an elephant seal. Great. It'd better not be too far from here.

Alexis grunted an unintelligible "Hmmph?" as Terra hefted her onto her feet outside the car. This was the moment she'd prepared for. Rife with nervous energy, Terra brought her hands together behind Alexis's back and reached for the amber stone.

Alexis's body stiffened at the sudden drop. After what felt like a few seconds too long, the magic of the stone dumped them out into a thicket of small trees and brush. Alexis shrieked with alarm. They stumbled over broken branches under the Elysian moonlight.

"Did we crash? Did the plane crash? I don't want to die!" Alexis wrestled with a bush like she was breaking out of imaginary wreckage.

Terra untangled her from the shrubbery. "It's okay, Lex. You're fine. We just have to get you to..." She scanned the wild landscape. "To..." She caught what looked like a flash of the moon reflected in water. Half a mile away. "Shit."

Alexis sat on the ground in exhaustion, her light blue pajamas and bare feet getting soiled in the process. "To where?" Her eyelids began to droop again.

"Dammit, Lex. I'm gonna need you to walk."

"No, leave me here...I'll meet up...with you later," Alexis said between yawns.

Terra heaved a frustrated sigh and pulled her friend up to her feet. She wrapped Alexis's arm around her shoulders and began the arduous hike down to the healing pool.

"No really, I don't have to—"

"Trust me, you *need* to. This is the most important thing that will ever happen to you." Terra panted as she pushed forward over the uneven ground. "I promise this will all be over soon, and when it is..." She paused to breathe. "You'll be good as new. Better than new."

Alexis leaned her bobble head against Terra's. "Aw. That's cool."

They continued on in silence for several minutes. Terra stopped to catch her breath and adjust her grip on Alexis. The waters from the healing pool glinted in the light another twenty yards away.

"Home stretch," Terra whispered. A smile of victory spreading across her face, she took another step forward.

A blinding flash exploded in front of them, knocking them backward off their feet.

Terra squinted into the white light. The figure of a man stood before them with a powerful frame and outstretched hands. He looked like he was on fire. And like he was totally cool with it. A thunderous voice emanated from the light.

"*NO!*"

There was that damn word again.

And they were falling through the darkness. Down, down, and onto the cold pavement.

Terra lifted herself off the ground with trembling hands, her mouth sputtering inane sounds of surprise, and looked around. Alexis lay in gentle slumber next to her, as if a flock of doves had carried her in gathered sheets and deposited her on the ground while cooing lullabies. Terra, meanwhile, rubbed her sore tailbone.

They had landed back in Eden, about twenty paces from the loading docks where they'd first crossed over.

She brought her hands to her head. "Holy shit."

# CHAPTER THIRTY-SEVEN

Terra trudged down the dim hallway to her apartment door. Her hands were still shaking. Someone had known what she'd planned. *I am* had known. Sneaking through the darkness like a cat burglar in the night had gotten her nowhere. Worse, she still had to return the bracelet to Harlan's wrist without waking him. She dreaded the thought.

She opened the door to a soft glow from the living room. She bit her lip and swung the door open wider, hoping it was just a streetlight in the window. Or a possessed lamp that had turned itself on. But no. There, sitting in silence next to the glowing lamp, was Harlan, and he was very much awake. He was leaning forward, elbows propped on his knees, hands clasped together in a fist below his chin, a faraway look on his face.

"Late night," he said, his eyes fixed on the wall.

She threw her keys on the counter. "Hey...you're up." She tugged down her sleeve to keep the bracelet hidden. No sense in reminding him of his naked wrist that he almost certainly hadn't noticed yet. *Probably* hadn't noticed. There was a small chance. She wasn't going to think about it.

"Where'd you go?" His voice was reserved, almost weak.

"Lex needed me. I didn't want to wake you."

"In the middle of the night."

"I know it sounds crazy, but she was...having a panic attack and called—"

"Terra, I've been sitting here for the past twenty minutes trying to come up with a reasonable explanation for what happened, and I've been very generous in my willingness to believe the best." He rested his forehead on his knuckles and closed his eyes. "But see, there's one problem I still can't wrap my head around." With great reluctance, he pulled back the sleeve of his sweatshirt and showed her the damning evidence that was his bare wrist.

Terra feigned surprise. "Oh, you lost it."

"Terra."

She breathed a sigh of defeat. "I'm sorry." She slipped the bracelet off her wrist and dropped it on the counter, the last of her hopes sliding away like a melted ice cream cone.

"You tried to take her there, didn't you? To the pool?"

"Yes."

"He told you no."

"But I had to at least *try.*"

Harlan straightened up and raised his voice. "You *had* to? You *had* to break the rules? You *had* to lie to me to do it? Do you always have to do things your way, without even considering how it might affect someone else?"

"I didn't mean to go behind your back, Harlan. I just knew you wouldn't—"

"Wouldn't agree to this plan of yours? You're right about that."

Terra matched the volume of his voice. "Don't you ever think for yourself?"

"Of course I do."

"I mean for the things that actually matter."

"You mean without going to Iam."

"I mean without Iam telling you what to think," she retorted.

His face turned reflective and his voice quiet. "You know, I did once. I'm starting to regret it now." He looked sidelong at her in a way that made her chest hurt. "That time in the cave, when you told me to prove to you..."

She recoiled and shook her head. Oh hell no.

"I should have known better. It was too rushed."

"Are you kidding me? We're both adults. We talked it through first."

"We're also both human."

"What are you saying?"

He looked down at the floor. "I'm saying maybe we made a mistake."

Terra shut her eyes as the tears began to well. The world was suddenly unstable, a mountain of sinking sand under her feet. "Then why'd you go through with it?"

He clenched his jaw, mulling over the question like a piece of gum in his mouth. Finally he spoke. "A moment of weakness maybe. You just kept pushing—"

"Bullshit, Harlan!" she screamed. "Don't pin this on me. You're the one who was asking for promises. *Forever*, remember?"

"It doesn't feel like I can count on that anymore."

By *that* she knew he meant *you*. Her cheeks flushed. He was giving up on her. The quitter. The gutless bastard. "You know that's unfair. I didn't mean to—"

"You completely broke my trust, Terra." He stood, and as he did, her heart fell to the floor. "I just don't know how to reconcile that with the person I thought you were."

She folded her arms and watched him slip on his shoes. "And I guess I can't reconcile how you sided with Iam on this one." She turned her face away to wipe a tear from her cheek.

As he reached the door, he called back to her. "Well, did it work?"

"What?" she asked glumly.

"Your plan. Did you *heal* her?" The words came out caked in bitterness.

She took her time answering. "No. Something stopped us before we got to the edge of the pool. There was this...flash of light."

"An angel." He nodded, then swiped the bracelet and his keys from the counter. "You can go behind my back, but you can't go behind Iam's." Without another word, he stepped through the door, leaving her alone in her apartment.

Terra watched in numb shock as the door latched shut behind him. It clicked with a finality that resonated in her bones and made her temples ache. She stood in place, half expecting the door to reopen.

As the minutes passed, the silence of her apartment became crushing. She covered her ears, as if it could stop the angry mob of thoughts storming through her head. How could he have been so unfair? How could he have expected her to act any differently when he'd left her with no choice? What did he know about the hopelessness of chronic pain?

She realized now that she was glaring at the front door, calling it names in a colorful array of curse words it didn't deserve. "Who are you to judge?" she hissed to the inanimate panel of hollowed wood. When she failed to gain any reaction, she turned and kicked the lamp table instead. The flimsy lamp perched atop rattled under its now lopsided shade. A stack of unopened junk mail slid off the edge of the table and onto the rug below. Something small that had been buried beneath the stack dislodged and rolled across the tile with a soft clatter. Her toe throbbed in pain.

She turned her attention back to the door and screamed at it in one last projection of anger. With nothing to show for her efforts, she fell into the living room chair and huffed. She should go back to bed—it was the middle of the night. But she was still too worked up.

Screw it. She would sit here forever until something changed. Until he came back on his knees apologizing, using words like *overreacted* and *moron*.

From her position in the chair, she spotted the small object that had hit the floor in her rage. She crossed the room and stooped to pick it up. It was the walnut shell that Harlan had given her. She stood staring at the heart shape in the center for a long, impassioned moment, like an archaeologist discovering a relic from a distant past, hoping that if she held it tightly enough, if she studied every line and curve, maybe then she could bring the past back to life.

But who was she kidding? You can't resurrect the dead. She let the walnut slip through her fingers back onto the cold floor.

# CHAPTER THIRTY-EIGHT

This was not how most women would choose to spend their time the evening following a catastrophic breakup. Terra would have been much happier in bed blasting something heavy and hypnotic from her playlist, feet propped up against the headboard, staring into oblivion. She could've cared less for company, though if forced to choose, she would've had Alexis be the one to show up at her door with a box of tissues, a sleeve of cookie dough, and a big-ass bottle of wine.

But Leta had been insistent. And as it turned out, Jeremy (white pock mark on chin, belt buckle off-center, vague smell of Listerine) made for enjoyable company. Terra liked the little steak-and-seafood joint he'd chosen for their double date. Ah, but there it was again. Not really a double date. More like a three-legged animal—a sad, crippled reminder of what it should have been.

"I'm so sorry Harlan couldn't make it tonight," Leta crooned.

"Yeah," Terra said. "The laryngitis..."

"It sounds just awful."

Yes...an awful lie.

"That just gives us an excuse to do this again sometime," Jeremy said. His dazzling grin doused some of the burning in Terra's heart. He was, by all accounts, an idealist. He *had* to be if he was dating her mom. Any

other self-respecting man would know better than to get entangled
with a recovering—and periodically relapsing—alcoholic.

Despite this flaw, Terra liked him. He was kind, personable, and
unusually adept at following her mother's meandering train of
thought. He had a faintly crooked nose that only added to his rugged
appeal. She imagined he'd broken it when he was younger, probably
defending a friend in a fistfight. He seemed like that kind of friend.

"Tell me more about this mystery man of yours, Terra," Jeremy
said. His gray eyes had a mischievous glint to them.

Terra fidgeted with her napkin under the table. Leta had met
Harlan twice—the first time when she finessed her way into joining
them at the Strawberry Festival in June, and the second on Terra's
birthday—but Jeremy had not and very likely would never meet
him. Talking about him now was as pointless as watering a dead
houseplant. "There's not much to say. We met in physical therapy,
and he kind of hounded me for a date."

To Terra's relief, the server interjected with a bottle of Malbec held
out for the table to view. "Again, our sincere apologies for the delay
with your entrees tonight," she said in a voice smooth as elevator
jazz. "Can I offer any of you a glass of wine to enjoy with that steak?
Compliments of the manager."

Terra shook her head. Jeremy eyed the wine with interest but
demurred.

"None for me, thank you," Leta said to the server, then turned to
Jeremy. "Go ahead, enjoy yourself." She rubbed his arm reassuringly.

"Alright then." He patted her hand and accepted the wine.

Terra watched in cold silence as the wine poured into his glass.
Perfect. It seemed she was the only adult at the table.

With the breeze of the server's departure still stirring in the air, Terra turned to her mother. "Why do you do that to yourself?"

Leta stared back. "What?"

"It's like you're choosing to be oblivious to your...your..." Terra held up a flailing hand. "Problems."

"Jeremy's aware of my *problems*," Leta responded calmly. "And everything is fine. You let me worry about that. But I don't appreciate you saying I'm obliv—"

"You just love to push it, don't you?" Terra's pulse quickened. She knew she should stop, but there was too much angst buried under this junk pile she'd just unearthed. "Every time. You push it *all* the way to the edge and then pretend there's not a cliff there."

"That's ridicu—"

"It's reckless, Mom. You and I both know you have zero self-control. The question is..." Her eyes shifted to Jeremy. "Does *he* know that?"

"You are treading on thin ice, *chica*. I have more self-control than you know, and I don't have to sit here and explain to you all the conversations he and I have already had. And this?" Leta gestured to the wine glass. "*This* is called self-sacrifice, Terra. It's something you do for the people you love. I'm not about to make this relationship all about me."

"How about self-sacrifice on *his* part, huh? I don't think anyone should be drinking within twenty yards of you."

Until this point, Jeremy had been listening, his hand frozen around the glass. Now, he made a display of pushing it away. "Hey, I don't have to drink this if it's an issue for any—"

"And don't think I don't know about all the times you promised you were sober, but you were hiding that bottle of Tito's under the bathroom sink."

Leta's eyes widened and her mouth fixed itself into a narrow line of reproach. Jeremy's eyes were trained on his lap, his mouth twitching. The untouched Malbec sat at the edge of the table, each step of passing servers creating shallow, expanding rings on its liquid surface. The low buzz of the restaurant patrons' conversations continued as if the world hadn't stopped turning for a full second.

But it had. Terra had felt it. She'd gotten under her mother's skin and right into her core. It was a victorious, queasy feeling. She lifted her fork and dampened the sensation with the taste of baked potato and sour cream.

"Terra." Jeremy spoke with caution. "Leta's right. She isn't the person she used to be."

Through her potato, Terra mumbled, "Give her five minutes."

Jeremy leaned in. "What was that?"

"Phew, I need to visit the ladies' room," Leta announced breezily. "Terra, how about you come with me?"

Terra kept her eyes on her food. "I'm good."

Leta stood up from her chair, ramrod straight, and slammed her napkin down on the table, causing the silverware to clatter against their plates. "Come with me, please."

The ladies' room was a single-stall bathroom with a pedestal sink, peeling silver wallpaper, and an oversized silk plant in the corner. Leta locked the door behind them, then leaned back against it. Terra stood against the opposite wall with her arms crossed like an adolescent bracing for the lecture of her life.

"In what alternate universe do you think it's okay for you to talk down to me like a child and embarrass me in front of my date?" Leta's eyes were wild, her voice spilling out in a wavering tremolo.

Terra kept her mouth firmly shut. She knew this was a rhetorical question. Leta was just getting started.

"I am your *mother*." Leta began pacing in front of the door like a caged tiger. "I did not raise you like this—to see this level of disrespect. *¡Dios mío!*" She brought her hands to her forehead. "I am so embarrassed. I can't— Listen, I know I was far from the perfect mom when you were growing up, but I know I taught you wrong and right in the way you treat people. And Jeremy! What did he do to deserve that, huh? Shaming him for taking the wine. Shame on *you*, Terra!"

"Mom."

"He is paying for our meal. He is paying for *your* meal. And you treat him—"

"*Mom.*"

"*¡Callaté!*" Leta yelled sharply. She held up her hand and waved it in dismissal. "I don't want to hear from you right now, I'm so disgusted."

"Just answer one question."

Leta folded her arms and stared into the mirror.

"How long have you been sober?"

She pulled at a wayward strand of hair, taking a long time to answer. "Six months this Tuesday. That's the honest-to-God truth."

"Six months. So he hasn't seen you drunk yet."

"He *won't* see me drunk. I'm doing everything I can to make sure of that."

"You're going to slip up again, Mom. You always do."

Leta turned to her daughter with a stunned face. "Where is all this coming from? Do you *want* me to fail? Because that's what it sounds like."

"No, but—"

"When's the last time you've seen me drunk, hmm?"

"I—" Terra huffed. "I can't remem—"

"Do you want to come to my house right now and check the cabinets? Do you want to see if you can find any Tito's under the sink?" Leta narrowed her eyes and held up her fingers, ticking them off one at a time. "I've been going to my weekly meetings religiously for three years now. I've had a steady job for the past two. I've paid off my debts. I have a support network of friends that hold me accountable. I have new interests and hobbies to fill my free time. I feel better mentally and physically than I have in years. Have I fully recovered? Probably not. I don't know if it's even possible. But I'm damn well close, Terra. I'm closer than I've ever been."

Terra stared at her mother, speechless.

Leta was right. The change had been gradual, but Terra had seen it. She just hadn't allowed herself to believe it. Believing the best when it came to her mom had only ever left her disappointed. *Best* wasn't really Leta's thing. So how in the hell had she pulled it off this time?

Terra should have been proud of her mother. But pride was not the emotion she felt as she dug her fingernails into the skin of her palms. Her eyes began to sting.

"Why now?" she yelled. "Why now after all these years?"

"Terra, it's a process."

"Why couldn't you fix your life while I was still at home?"

The bathroom door rattled in its frame as another patron tried to enter.

"Go away!" Leta yelled. She turned back to her daughter, eyes glistening. "Oh, honey. You know I would take it all back if I could." She turned her eyes to the floor and said, "You didn't deserve the mother you got."

"You didn't even try," Terra said, her voice weak.

Leta shook her head, lips quivering. "When my sister...when she passed away...I had a hard time coping. I couldn't get any closure—or peace—over it. Those years...I'm sorry you had to witness it, Terra, but those years were some of the darkest years of my life."

"She was my aunt. I lost her too."

"Yes. I know." Leta dotted tears from the corners of her eyes. "Oh, sweetie, I know. But you can't even begin to imagine what I went through after what happened. The dark thoughts that made me question myself—"

"Because you won't talk to me about it!" Terra shouted. "You never want to talk about it."

"I can't, Terra."

"But why?" she pleaded. "Don't you think I need closure too?"

Leta blew out a sigh and hung her head, pinching the bridge of her nose. Her voice was barely audible. "We're not going through this again." She held up a hand. "I can't."

The two women stood in silence. The flush of a commode on the other side of the wall let out a muted roar. Cooking utensils in the nearby kitchen clattered. The leaky faucet dripped, ticking off the seconds like a countdown. ...3...2...1...

Terra snapped.

"Fine then. We're done here." She blew past her mother and jerked open the door.

"Terra, don't you walk out on—"

"Tell Jeremy I said thanks for the meal."

*Pain is many things. It can be a physical affliction, yes, but it is more often a psychological one, brought on by the circumstances and people around us. Nothing can prepare you for it, other than to simply know that it will be a necessary (albeit temporary) companion.*

*- Elysian Records for the Revivers, Book IV: Acclimation*

# Chapter Thirty-Nine

F ive days.

It had been five long, miserable days since Harlan had walked out her door. With each passing sundown, the breakup became all the more solidified, like concrete poured into the cavity of her chest. What she'd first struggled to believe was now blindingly evident. He'd meant what he'd said. Every word.

Terra trudged through the lobby of Edifice's building in a numb state of mind. It was his silence that killed her. She would have taken anything at this point; a passive aggressive email or a Post-it note with chicken scratch would have been more welcome than the silence. To receive no response at all—and she'd tried everything short of making threats to provoke one—was as good as a dismissal.

She stepped out into the plaza and found Ezra sitting on a bench by himself. He looked up and lifted two fingers to wave her over, like a diner summoning the check. She sucked in a breath and made her way toward him.

Calling him hadn't been the hardest thing she'd done. That honor went to making the confession about her little bracelet heist. Turned out, he'd already known. Harlan must have told him over a stiff drink, or maybe Elysian style, with a perfect sun rising over perfect mountains in the background, Ezra consoling him while he looked on with that pensive stare. In any case, her pride was long gone. She just wanted closure now.

As she sat down, he pulled a container from a brown bag and opened it.

"I hope you don't mind," he said. "I've got a short lunch, and this sandwich won't eat itself."

"Knock yourself out."

He took a bite and spoke through a mouthful of turkey and rye. "No word yet, huh?"

"Nothing."

"He does this, you know." Ezra swiped a crumb from the side of his mouth. "Retreats to Elysia anytime he's had enough of this world."

"I guess I don't blame him." At least he *had* a way to escape. Lucky bastard.

Ezra took a moment to work through another large bite before speaking. "I don't think he's doing it to spite you. It's just an old habit. Goes all the way back to acclimation."

"Acclimation?"

"That's what we call the first few years of being a reviver. It's a rough transition. Did he tell you what age he was when he came here?"

"He told me he was young."

"Eleven," Ezra said squarely, then took a swig of water. "Eleven years old. So while most kids get to deal with social anxiety and puberty, Harlan had the extra hurdle of adapting to a world drowned in its own depravity."

Terra jerked her head in reaction. *Depravity* was an awfully harsh word. Then again, compared to the perfection of Elysia, Eden's *okayness* did seem pretty depraved.

"I was his legal guardian during those years. Tried to walk him through it, but I think he had a harder time with it than most revivers. He would disappear all the time. I'd find him asleep in Elysia curled up next to an ox or bear or something—I guess the big furry animals were the most comforting. Anyway, he said he couldn't get the evil thoughts out of his head."

"What evil thoughts?"

"We all get them. The bad things you think about other people that you'd never say out loud. The selfish thoughts. It's scary the first time you cross over, and these things enter your mind. You have to remember, that's not something we ever experienced before coming here."

She watched an ant crawl over a leaf on the ground nearby and wondered whether it had selfish thoughts too, like ditching the queen and running off to live its best life. "What's it like?"

"Brutal." Ezra shifted on the hard bench and stretched his back. "You get to a point after a while where all you want to do is protect yourself from other people's horrible behavior, and that just compounds your own selfishness. Then you start to realize the full meaning of this commitment you've made, and by the time you really understand it, well, there's no going back."

"Damn," she said quietly.

"Yeah, Harlan didn't take it that well. He got angry. Raged to Iam. And Iam wouldn't speak to him."

"I'm guessing that didn't help things."

"Two whole years Iam stayed silent." Ezra popped the rest of the sandwich in his mouth and slid the container back in the bag. "I tried to tell him Iam was using that time to prepare him, but he wanted no part of it. He eventually found a way to get by on his own here in Eden, but it was a reckless way of living. He was no better than your average teenager." He smiled wryly. "Those were some tough years for the *both* of us. But finally, after he'd been wandering around Elysia in a real mood for a couple days, he stumbled into this desert...and there Iam was. His voice clear as day."

"The desert." Terra remembered the rose. "I've been there."

"Yeah, he's been going back there ever since. That first day was the day Iam showed him who he'd become."

"What do you mean?"

Ezra gazed across the plaza. "If you can imagine a fortress in disrepair—it's kind of like that—with the walls all crumbling and defenseless. All of us revivers experience..." He gestured with his hands in search of the words. "This erosion of the soul. The evil always finds its way in. But Iam can put the broken pieces of wall back together. Those ugly cracks that are left, they stay with us the rest of our lives, and they're what help us connect with everyone else here. The shared brokenness, so to speak.

"So after that, Harlan's whole perspective changed. His heart ached for the Edenites. And he realized it was in this world's mess and chaos that he could fulfill his purpose. To show them that they didn't have to be perfect to be loved, but that, because they were already loved, they could be made whole again."

Terra fought back a surge of sadness. "He never told me how much he struggled."

"It wasn't a phase of life he was too proud of." Ezra leaned forward and rested his hands on his knees. "My point in telling you all this, Terra, is that he still struggles. I wish I could tell you he'll move past this bump in your relationship and everything will be fine, but it's not my place to say. Most revivers never marry. Putting your total trust in a fallible human being is a difficult thing to learn."

Yes. Yes it was.

"What I can say for sure is that he's come to love people the way Iam does. He'll always care about you, regardless of how things work out."

"Hmm," Terra replied. That didn't sound too reassuring.

Terra slid into her chair and tried to remember what she was supposed to be doing with the manuscript on her screen. Something about a continuity error. She picked up a pen and flicked it against the desktop rhythmically as she waited for her mind to re-focus.

Ezra hadn't been too hopeful about Harlan. He couldn't ghost her forever though, right? She threw down the pen. The lilacs. That was it. The main character's mother had planted lilacs in the garden, but in a later chapter, she called them hydrangeas.

Ezra had said Harlan was in Elysia *seeking answers*. What did that even mean? Like it was a damn scavenger hunt or something. And how much longer did he need? She pushed her fingers into the inner crease of her eyelids and crammed her eyes shut as if the endless reel of thoughts were a river she could dam, if done with enough determination and wads of bubblegum.

"Headache?"

She removed her hands and blinked her eyes several times until her vision cleared. Kenneth stood over her with his elbow resting along the top of her cubicle wall, something only Kenneth could do, given his stature.

"Looks like you need a break," he said, his deep brown eyes catching hers.

Terra's stomach gurgled. The lunch she'd downed in a hurry after meeting Ezra was not settling well. Of course, nothing had settled well since Harlan had left. She clutched her midsection, embarrassed. "Just resting my eyes for a minute."

Kenneth smiled at her for a long moment, like he knew more than she'd let on, the way his eyes lingered. She wondered if he'd heard about the breakup.

"What?"

He shook his head. "Nothing. Hey, I want to ask you something."

"Shoot."

"What are you doing tomorrow?"

She shrugged.

He hung on the wall and leaned toward her, voice low. "I'm going hiking at Hemlock Cliffs with a couple others from the office. Want to join us?"

This was new. "Really? Who's going?"

"Blake and Allison, you know, from upstairs?"

Blake and Allison worked in the real estate firm one floor up. They were both young and outdoorsy and energetic. The kind of nut jobs who signed up for half marathons for the fun of it. She'd never hung out with them outside of the occasional happy hour. Then again, she'd never hung out with Kenneth either.

"We can go for the morning and get back in time to beat rush hour," he said. "I can drive." He tapped the side of the wall with his fingers.

Tomorrow was Friday, their off day. Normally, she'd be spending it at the clinic with Harlan, but she knew that wouldn't be happening. Might as well find a good distraction. And she was dying to visit Elysia again. Or at least some knockoff version of it. Give her some nature and wildlife, and maybe a hint of falling sensation too, and she'd be hunky-dory.

A faint smile cracked the plaster of gloom on her face. "What time?"

Kenneth picked her up at eight o'clock Friday morning. As she rushed out the door, she paused at the mirror in her hallway to smooth down the pieces of hair that had chosen to misbehave for that day. She stopped herself. Why was she primping before a hike?

Because she'd been holed up in a state of semi-hibernation for too long, that's why. Time to wake the hell up and live life again. She peeled herself away from the mirror and grabbed her jacket.

As she stepped out of the building, Kenneth called from the window of his black sedan, "Ready for an adventure?"

The words hit her like a battering ram to the chest. It was the same phrase and tone Harlan had used that first morning he'd taken her back to Elysia. Or was it? Her moronic heart was probably projecting false memories onto the present. The breakup had done a hell of a job messing with her head. She shook it off.

"Yeah, but can you handle all this hiking prowess?" she quipped and gestured to herself.

"Only if you can handle my mad driving skills," he shot back as she climbed in.

Terra eased into the passenger seat and looked askance at Kenneth. "Uh...I'll do my best." She was suddenly fresh out of quips. He was kind of—dare she say?—confident today. He had his arm resting along the open window and his head tilted back like he picked up chicks and took them hiking every day. Like his in-office persona was just a Clark Kent cover, and now he was finally whipping out the red cape and tights.

She glanced at the empty backseat. "Are Blake and Allison meeting us there?"

"Naw, they had a big closing come up at the office."

"Oh. Just us, then?"

"Yep."

"Cool." Cool? Had she been hankering for a one-on-one wilderness date with him? "I mean, that's fine."

He gave her a cursory smile as he pulled the car out of the lot.

A small part of her hoped he'd try to make a date out of it, or at least, keep it up with the non-awkward conversation. It was going to be a long car ride after all. But as the miles ticked away on the odometer, a heavy blanket of silence descended. She shrugged off her false hopes, stupid as they were, because she knew they'd been born from a state of loneliness, and she refused to play that game with herself anymore.

A low-stress, quiet ride was fine with her.

# Chapter Forty

They pulled into the Hemlock Cliffs trailhead parking lot, which was wide open, save two other cars.

"Finally," Terra said. The country roads had been charming at first, but she could happily go the rest of her life without seeing another cornfield. "I was starting to think we'd landed in the middle of nowhere."

"Technically, we have." Kenneth steered his car into the far corner of the parking lot. Without warning, he drove off the edge of the gravel onto the dirt and pulled into a wooded section behind some low-lying branches.

"What are you doing?" Terra braced her hand against the passenger side door as the car bounced to a stop over the uneven ground.

"I don't want people parking next to me and putting dents in my car. I like my space."

"Park any farther away and you'll be in your own galaxy."

Kenneth said nothing, his eyes trained on the rearview mirror.

"The forecast probably scared most people off anyway," she said.

"You think?"

"Scattered showers. You didn't see my text?"

"No."

"This morning. I said make sure to wear a poncho or something, because of the rain."

"Oh, yeah, I didn't see that. I sort of forgot my phone at work yesterday."

"Well that sucks."

"Yeah, but it's fine. I can pick it up later." He climbed out of the car. "You ready?"

Terra opened the car door and paused. "But wait. How did you get my address then?"

"What?"

"My address. I texted it to you last night."

Kenneth rifled through his trunk and pulled out a large backpack. "I was at work late."

"Oh. Burning the midnight olive oil, or whatever it is they say?" She immediately felt the urge to bang her head against the car. Had she said *olive* oil?

He slammed the trunk closed and began walking toward the trailhead, stepping over rocks and fallen twigs while dodging branches from above. He turned to look back at her. "You coming?"

"Oh. Yeah." She snagged her small pack that contained a water bottle and power bar from under the seat and closed the door behind her. No point in lollygagging when her pretend Elysia awaited.

The air was cool and damp against her face as she plodded along the trail behind him. She knew Kenneth was not the talkative kind, but she hadn't expected to be eating his dust. He was clearly a class or three above her in terms of his athleticism.

The fallen October leaves crunched under her boots as she tried to match his pace. "Can you slow down a little?" she called to him.

He grinned back at her. "Sorry, I keep forgetting your legs aren't as long as mine." He slowed down, though not by much.

They hiked through a forest of sprawling trees and saplings, some mostly bare now, having lost their leaves in the previous weeks. It was still nice to look at. Serene. This was one thing Eden had on Elysia. Elysian trees never lost their leaves. The people there must have been so tired of the color green.

They soon came to a set of steps cut into the rock. The steps curved down into a narrow ravine, where the faint trickle of water echoed below. As they made their way down, the canyon wall of sandstone towered above them, an impressive feat of natural creation. She paused to rest on a rock and admire it. A thin dribble of water cascaded down from the top of the 150-foot wall. She tilted her head, studying the giant pattern of gaps and crevices where water had eroded the sandstone.

"It almost looks like a face, doesn't it?"

Kenneth didn't reply.

She turned to discover he was already barreling down the trail like a Mack truck with a deadline.

"What the—" She ran to catch up with him. "In a hurry?" she shouted.

"There's an even better canyon farther down. Come on." His body was a machine of iron and sinew, moving with maddening speed through the ravine. So much for a leisurely hike. Terra huffed to herself at the surprising lack of—what was it? chivalry? camaraderie? a single shred of common sense?—that would cause any other person to slow down and wait for their hiking partner. It occurred to her why Kenneth was still single.

She leapt over fallen trees and scurried around giant rocks in her effort to keep up. The walls of the ravine rose around them on either side as they hiked alongside a shallow creek. She gradually became aware of the cool spray of rain droplets against her face. The leaves under their feet turned slippery with moisture.

Kenneth stayed ahead, occasionally remembering she existed long enough to glance back at her. She glared at the back of his head, trying to work out the puzzle forming in her mind. What was it about him that seemed different? Lots of little things. Behaviors that didn't quite fit.

She'd bet Allison and Blake would have noticed too. She frowned. And what had happened this morning? They were *both* needed, for an *emergency* closing meeting? Had they even planned on coming? She remembered saying hi to them on the elevator yesterday afternoon, and they'd never mentioned the hike to her. As if they'd never been...invited...to begin with.

Her footsteps slowed. She pulled her phone from her pack and scrolled thorough her texts. She checked the time on the text she'd sent Kenneth last night with her address.

"Keep moving," Kenneth called back to her. "This drizzle could turn into a downpour at any minute."

She stopped and stared at her screen. The time of her text was 8:08 p.m.

"Hey," she called out. "What time did you say you left work last night?

Kenneth stopped and looked behind him. He scrunched up his face in agitation. "I don't know. About 6:30, I guess." He turned back and started down the trail again.

Midnight oil, her ass.

The patter of raindrops became increasingly louder on the surrounding brush. A large, wet raindrop splatted against her cheek. She returned her phone to her pack and pulled her jacket hood over her head. The air was turning colder against her skin, but a heat was beginning to simmer deep in her chest.

"How do you know where I live?" She had to yell over the quickening cadence of the rain to be heard.

Kenneth stopped once more. "What?" he shouted.

"You never got my address last night. I texted it to you after you left. So how do you know where I live?"

He froze in place and stared back at her in silence.

The question hung in the air between them like a guillotine blade suspended by the thinnest of strings.

At that moment, the steady fall of raindrops transformed into an all-out deluge. It filled their ears with the roar of water pelting the ground at full force. Kenneth remained still, water pouring in streams down his face, dripping down his neck and off the knuckles of his clenched fists. Through the sheets of downpour, Terra saw his eyes go dark. A cold, unflinching stare that pierced her at her core. Her stomach twisted sharply. Something unnatural was hiding inside those eyes.

She hadn't anticipated this.

The heat in her chest burst into flames and raced through her limbs. It was fear. All-encompassing, carnal fear, catching in her throat and sending her into a panic. She pivoted on her heels and launched into a sprint in the opposite direction, pumping her arms to gain momentum.

She slid on soggy roots and splashed through the mud. The rain was deafening, but she didn't need to hear his footsteps to know he was already on her heels. One, two, three more steps, and one muscular arm whipped in front of her collar bone and clothes-lined her like a running back.

The impact took her breath away.

She lay flat on her back among the mud and leaves, struggling to fill her lungs with air. His shoes tweaked her hair as he stepped close and pinned her head to the ground. He leered down at her from above with an expression she'd never seen on Kenneth's face before. This was not Kenneth.

"You're a smart one, Terra," he spoke into the rain, "but it's a little irritating at times."

Terra fought to turn her head far enough to see her pack, which had flown off during her fall. Her fingers splayed out across the ground, feeling for the strap. Nothing. Raindrops hit the bridge of her nose and coalesced with the tears of shock sprouting from her eyes.

"You could've at least waited till we got off the trail," he said. His head tilted to the left and right, a wolf sizing up its prey.

A high, feral whine escaped her lips. It was a distant noise, as she felt detached from her own body, each pound of her heart pushing her further into a daze. But this was no time for an out-of-body experience. She needed to focus.

What would she do if she could get to her bag? Chuck her water bottle at him? The absurdity of the thought made her dizzy with fear. She still had her phone in there, but if she could use it when he wasn't looking, who would she dial? Harlan was without question still sulking in Elysia. The police were the obvious answer, but they wouldn't get here fast enough. She needed someone with a bracelet...

Ezra. She had his number. He could get here in an instant.

She stretched her fingers farther. The heel of Kenneth's boot struck the back of her hand with sudden force. She yelped in pain.

He bent down to pull her phone from the bag and pushed the button to power it off. Then, for good measure, he tossed the phone into the creek.

Welp.

She watched, helpless, as he kicked her pack far into the brush. Then he leaned over and hefted her up by the arms, nearly pulling her shoulders out of their sockets in the process. He whirled her around to face farther down the trail and pushed his lips to her ear. Her back was pulled against him, her arms still in his iron grip.

"You belong to me now," he whispered with a vicious intensity. "I've waited a long time for this moment, so don't screw it up."

She hadn't wanted to believe it. Lips shaking, she said his name aloud. "Hulum."

His fingers sank deeper into her arms, eliciting bruises and making her writhe. "In the flesh." His lips curled into a smile against her ear, his breath unnaturally cold on her face.

Didn't this douchebag from hell know when to give up?

"Iam!" She hurled the word at him like an insult.

"This isn't a dream, Terra." He let out a husky laugh into her ear. "I'm grounded in a physical body. Invoking your god's name is a waste of your breath."

Terra slumped in his grip. This was turning out to be the worst hike ever.

"Now," he said, bringing out a terrifying depth to Kenneth's voice she'd never heard before. "Walk."

He thrust her forward. She stumbled and caught herself. Then, with shaky legs, she began walking.

They continued down the trail, their only witness the forest of hemlocks.

*Nuanced interference is their work, but extreme affliction is their passion, and they gravitate toward the latter when tempted.*
*- Elysian Records for the Revivers, Book III: The Subversives*

# CHAPTER FORTY-ONE

T erra began to shiver. The rain was slowing, but now her clothing was soaked through to her underwear. As it turned out, her discount *all-weather* jacket had been on discount for a reason.

She could hear Kenneth's heavy footsteps behind her, driving her forward. Toward where, she was still unsure. The trail was a loop that led back to the parking lot, so they couldn't be staying on it much longer, unless his plan was to march her in circles to death. She forced her legs to keep moving, despite the numb and cold, and tried to figure out how she'd gotten to this point.

Kenneth. When had Hulum overtaken him? When had she noticed the change? If it was Hulum's plan to bring her out here, then it must have been yesterday, before he invited her. How long had Hulum been plotting this? And poor Kenneth. Was he aware of what was happening right now? Was he trapped somewhere inside, silently screaming for help? She shuddered. But here was the most nagging question of all: where on earth was Iam?

Abruptly, Hulum grabbed the back of her jacket and drew close to her ear.

"Not...a...word," he whispered.

"Wha—" she said. Then she saw what he'd spotted in the distance.

A lone hiker, a forty-something-year-old man wearing a backpack with rappelling gear dangling from its clasps, was walking toward them along the trail. She'd assumed the other two hikers that had parked in the lot this morning were traveling along the loop in the same direction, which would mean they'd likely never cross paths. But this man must have started at the other end.

"Do you want him to live?" Hulum's grip tightened.

She took in the weight of his words as she stared at the man, and a single tear pushed past the edge of her eyelid. This was someone's husband. Or father. Or drinking buddy at the very least. She remembered the force Hulum had used to knock her down and yank her back up again as if she were an inflatable tube man in the wind. How easily could he do the same to this man, or worse?

"Yes," she whispered.

"Then don't give me a reason to kill him."

Terra sucked in a ragged breath and wiped her eyes. He was right. Unless this man was packing heat, or had some wicked-awesome ninja skills, there was nothing he could do to help her. Finding out was not worth the risk of his life.

The feeling began to sink in that she was very alone.

"Crazy day for a hike, huh?" the man shouted as he approached.

Terra stayed focused on the ground in front of her.

"Yep, how 'bout that little sprinkle we just had?" Hulum shouted in reply.

The man let out a good-natured bellow, blissfully unaware he was making small talk with a demon. "Well, good news is the waterfalls should be flowing now. Will make for some nice pictures."

"Absolutely."

As the hiker neared, he frowned at Terra. "Hey, you look pretty cold. You have an extra layer you can put on?"

She looked down and realized she'd been hugging herself and shivering. "Oh. No, I'm fine."

"Are you sure? Your clothes are soaked. You could get hypothermia." The man stepped closer, and Hulum drew to her side.

"Don't worry about it. We'll get her to the car right away." Hulum kept his tone light as he stepped between her and the hiker.

"Well you guys have a ways to go." He squinted down the path. "You know..." He unzipped his pack and dug around inside. "I have this extra sweatshirt I brought. I'm not using it." He held it out to her. It was blue with an obscure company logo in white lettering in the upper righthand corner. Probably swag from some corporate event. The kind of stuff you're excited to get for free in the moment but then have no idea what to do with.

"That's really generous, but I can't take your shirt." She shrank away from it as if it were a live wire, unsure of what Hulum might try if she got any closer to the man. What if authorities discovered the shirt on her lifeless body days (months?) from now, and it implicated the man in her murder? But now she was being ridiculous. She wasn't going to die. She wasn't going to—

"No really, you look freezing. Please, take it." He pushed it closer to her.

Dammit, this aggressive kindness was going to be his downfall. Terra could see Kenneth's fists beginning to clench. "No, thank you."

"Please."

For a brief moment, no one said a word. Terra's pulse quickened. Kenneth's nostrils were flaring. The man's eyes shifted back and forth between the two of them, his face registering the rising tension.

Hulum broke the silence. "You know what? That's a great idea." He snatched the shirt out of the man's hand and tossed it to Terra. "Put it on, babe." He lunged forward to shake the hiker's hand and said, "We appreciate it."

"You're welcome. Just trying to help." The man nodded with a look of unease in his eyes, then resumed his hike down the trail.

Terra pulled the men's size XL sweatshirt over her head. It hung like a tent around her body, the hood drooping halfway down her back. Aesthetics aside, it was warm, and she was thankful for that. She felt terrible that he would never get it back. But Hulum had let him go. He would return home to his family (or drinking buddies) none the wiser.

She glanced back down the trail and watched the hiker fade into the distance. Hulum was also watching with a wary eye.

He turned back to face her. "Next time, just take the damn sweatshirt."

They plodded on until they came to a junction with a *YOU ARE HERE* sign. The map showed the squiggly main loop, with a much smaller loop jutting out from the place they were standing. Next to the smaller loop, a warning read *HIGH CLIFFS. RAPPELLING PROHIBITED.*

Hulum directed her toward a narrow spur trail, presumably leading to this other loop. She took one last glance down the main trail in either direction in hopes she might see a group of hikers headed their way, or preferably, a Navy SEAL team that happened to specialize in exorcisms. She saw nothing more than damp trees and rocks and a gray sky stretching in every direction. All was dishearteningly silent.

"Where are we going?" she asked, though she wasn't sure she wanted to know.

At first, Hulum didn't acknowledge her. His heavy footfalls and the snapping of twigs were the only sound. Then: "Do you know what lies beyond the top of this ravine?"

"Enlighten me," she muttered.

With a hiss, he seized her arm and whipped her around to face him. He stepped close, Kenneth's shoulders meeting the top of her head. His eyes burned with ferocity as he looked down at her. "Miles of dense forest. Wilderness that we could get lost in for weeks and never be found."

She arched backward to create space between them, her back muscles straining. "You know they'll eventually send out a search party." Her stomach churned at the word *eventually*. No one would notice her absence until Monday morning at work.

Three days away.

He grinned. "I told half the office yesterday that you and I were going hiking in Eagle Creek Park. That's over a hundred miles north of here. How wide of a radius do you think that search party will cover?"

She flinched. Had she mentioned to anyone where they were going? She'd told Alexis they'd be going hiking, but the conversation had then turned to Alexis requesting multiple revenge selfies of the two of them together so Harlan could find out on social media. (Alexis was going to be very disappointed.) Terra tried again. "They'll track us here. With cell phone signals."

"Kenneth's phone is back in Indy. Yours is dead."

She racked her brain. What other evidence had they left behind? "But Kenneth's car—"

"Is parked in the woods." He brought a giant hand to her face and caressed her cheek. "Give it up, Terra. By the time anyone figures out where you are, I'll be long gone, and you and Kenneth..." He slid his hand beneath her chin and wrapped it around her throat, squeezing gently. "You'll both be dead."

Panicked, she clawed at his hand. He kept it locked firmly in place.

"I can't wait for your Elysian boyfriend to hear about it and wonder what the hell happened." He chuckled and released her. "He'll never forgive himself for leaving you, you know."

Terra rubbed her neck and swallowed a rising sob. *Dead.* She was still caught up on that one word. She didn't have the stomach to ask what his plans were prior to death. But this was not her dreams, where he could kill her repeatedly. He would want to make this one count. *We could get lost for weeks*, he'd said. Oh God. He was planning to take his time with it.

The fact he'd known Harlan had left meant he'd been following her. For weeks. Months? Watching her every move like one of those creeps featured on *Dateline*. Bile shot up her throat. She dropped to the ground, bracing her hand against a tree.

"Oh, did I say too much?" He sneered at her as she retched. "It's amazing the power words can hold over a person, isn't it? I tried for months to get through to you in your dreams and had almost nothing to show for it. You blocked me at every turn. But now that I have a voice...look at you."

Terra heaved deep breaths, eyes closed, and tried to shut out his voice. But it was like stuffing cotton in a bull horn.

"You're not as strong as you think you are, Terra. A little pressure and you snap like a twig."

Her breathing slowed. Lies. She knew she was plenty strong. Sarah Connor strong. Though if Kyle Reese showed up right about now, she wouldn't mind the help.

"All I needed was a human form and a way to separate you from the Elysian. You took care of that second one yourself, didn't you? And Kenneth...his mind was so pliable. It took a few months, but he let me right in." He pointed to Kenneth's temple with two rigid fingers.

Rage ripped through her. "Kenneth doesn't deserve this," she spat as she lifted herself to her feet, holding the tree for support. "He had nothing to do with this. If it's me you want..." She tried to offer herself up in his place, but the urge to vomit was starting up again. No. She was stronger. She could fight through it. "Take—"

Nope. She dry-heaved against her hand and gave up on verbal sparring.

Hulum gave her a look of mock pity as her gag reflex went to town. "Terra, you haven't learned by now? Do you really think you have any control over this situation? As if you could change a demon's mind. Especially after what you did."

"What did"—she fought back another gag—"I do?"

"You broke the rules, Edenite. Bathing in an Elysian healing pool?" He clucked his tongue. "That's not allowed. There's only one punishment suitable for that."

She didn't ask.

He answered anyway. "Death with extreme pain. The slow, agonizing kind. That's what I'm here to deliver."

She glared at him.

"Don't worry." He snatched a strand of hair peeking out from her hood and flicked it in her face. "You're in capable hands."

Terra bristled with contempt.

"The *anger*!" he responded in rapture. "I can feel it radiating from you." He drew close. "I like the fiery ones best."

# Chapter Forty-Two

S he could hear it before they saw it: the echoes of water splashing off rock walls.

Before them, the forest opened into another box canyon with a massive stone wall stretching up from its floor like a scaled-down Hoover Dam. Midway up the wall, the path curved along the canyon in a semi-circle. It passed through a natural rock shelter that cut several meters deep into the wall and was tall enough for a person to walk beneath its ceiling with ease. A delicate waterfall, over seven stories high, spilled over the precipice above, passed in front of the rock shelter, and tumbled into a shallow pool below. Current situation aside, this place was breathtaking.

They followed the path as it banked left through the cavernous rock shelter. She stared into the dark, narrow crevices of the rock shelter, and imagined they would be an excellent place to hide a dead body. No one would find it until the spring thaw when hikers might begin to smell it...

She snapped her head to the other side and looked out at the waterfall instead, its shimmering droplets passing by as if from a pint-sized raincloud. Did everyone have morbid thoughts like these leading up to their death? What else was she supposed to think? The crushing reality was Iam was not coming to rescue her. No one was. She would have to fight for herself.

She looked out beyond the waterfall into the ravine and noted the irony of meeting death in such a scenic place. In her peripheral vision, Hulum was unaffected by the charms of nature. His cold eyes were fixed straight ahead. Kenneth's body was the human equivalent of a jaguar, every muscle bulging. Damn, he'd chosen the perfect host. And he was smarter than she'd credited him. How could she outfight him, outrun him, or outwit him?

As they neared the end of the canyon wall, the path split in two. On their left, a steep jaunt headed back down the loop. On their right, an even steeper path led up and around the back of the wall.

"Up." Kenneth's voice pushed her onward.

Terra turned to the precarious path, inlaid with giant tree roots, rocks, slippery leaves and moss, and hesitated. The ledge above, to which she presumed this path led, was a smidge too high for her taste.

"Now."

She began to climb. Boulders on either side made the trail narrow and jagged. Rocks hampered her footing and tumbled down the hillside as she stepped and skid her way along the path. The grade was unforgiving, and she soon found herself hunched over and panting as she forced her legs forward. She glanced back to see Hulum working his way up at a slow, methodic pace, not out of breath, but not enjoying the climb either.

Suddenly a slick mass of leaves gave way under her foot and slid down the slope, taking her foot with it. She fell to the ground, which wasn't all that far, thanks to the steep angle. But her knee had the misfortune of banging against a bulbous root in the process.

"Get up," he barked.

As she tried to regain her purchase in the earth, Terra felt a rock the size of a racquetball wobble beneath her palm. She closed her hand around it and stood up, clutching it close to her chest, out of Hulum's sight.

After an arduous slog that made her wonder why anyone would *want* to come up here apart from murderous intentions, they reached the top of the trail. Here, it opened up to a wide plateau overlooking the canyon. Trickles of water converged into a single stream near the edge and fell into the abyss below. It was much quieter here. Probably because they were seventy-odd feet above the splash of water in the basin.

She froze when she saw the dense forest beyond the plateau. If she let him take her any farther, she might not be able to find her way out later.

She collapsed on the ground, breathless. "I have to rest."

He stood over her and glowered but said nothing.

As she sat there panting, she thought through her plan again. It would never work. No. It had to work. She was out of options. Her legs began to shake. She just had to be quick enough. And accurate.

Hulum crossed his arms and began to pace. Adrenaline found its way through her veins. This was her chance.

Hands in her lap, she let the rock slide from one palm to the other. As he strode about ten feet out, she stood quietly, checked her angle, and drew her arm back, channeling her inner major league pitcher. When that brought up nothing, she settled for her inner grade school softball player.

As he swiveled on his foot and turned back toward her, she launched the rock with full force.

It was dead on.

Hulum flinched as it struck the upper corner of his forehead and bounced to the ground. A single trail of blood emerged from the soon-to-be welt and dribbled down the side of his face. Hulum reached up and touched the wound, then contorted Kenneth's features into a look of confusion and disbelief.

Before Terra could high five herself on the perfect aim, she noted with despair that he was still standing. The rock hadn't been heavy enough. She may as well have just bitch-slapped him with a Barbie hand.

Now Kenneth's face was showing a different emotion altogether: rage. He stormed toward her. She had no time to turn away before he was on her, walloping the side of her head with a punch that made her teeth rattle and her eyes roll strangely in their sockets. She flew sideways from the force of his strike and landed on a pile of leaves with a groan.

Terra was lost in a world of black. She felt the leaves beneath her hands but couldn't see them. Searing pain ate at her head. She brought her hand up to it to make sure nothing was there, because it felt as if his fist were still drilling into her.

"The hell you trying to pull, Terra?" His voice came through one ear. Her other ear was consumed with a high-pitched ringing.

She clambered around, trying to right herself despite the dizziness. Her vision started to return. She blinked several times until she could see him: a blurry shape standing over her. He bent down and snatched the collar of the man's sweatshirt. Her head rolled as he yanked her to her feet.

"Don't test me," he hissed in her good ear. He walked her backward and pushed her up against a tree trunk.

She tried to focus her eyes on him as he pulled something from his bag, but the images from her two eyes kept separating and drifting before her like disembodied spirits. She slumped against the tree.

To her alarm, he clapped a cold hand over her mouth and whispered, "Wake up, Terra." Then a blinding pain struck her right arm.

Terra let out a muffled cry of agony. The pain ripped her back into full consciousness. Her eyes came into focus. Something was piercing her right biceps.

Hulum held her there a moment longer, his hand still locked over her mouth, pleasure dancing in his eyes. "You want to get started early?" He smirked. "I'm game."

He jerked his hand away from her arm, evoking a fresh jolt of pain, and stepped back. Wetness and warmth soaked her sleeve, and she gripped her arm to stop the bleeding. In his hand she glimpsed a compact jackknife, the blade glistening red with her blood. He flicked it closed and stuffed it into his pocket.

Hulum pulled her away from the tree and ordered her to start walking. She stumbled forward, still disoriented. The thick cover of trees loomed over them. A point of no return. She glanced out over the plateau and the valley below.

Before Elysia, she'd thought this was a good world. Not perfect, but good...*ish*. It had potential anyway. Now, she'd had enough of it. This place. God, this awful place. It fostered the deepest of misery, the most horrific of tortures. How could it still be good? It was a skeleton of what it should be. Dried and dead bones with no heart.

Terra restrained a whimper that had clawed its way to her throat. Impatient with her trudging pace, Hulum was now a step ahead, glancing over his shoulder to ensure she followed. At the edge of the tree line, she cast one last glance back at the precipice, where the waters all converged and fell. In the thin stream she spotted another rock, larger than the first—grapefruit-sized—and her heart began to thrum.

It was near the ledge, but not too far if she turned back now. Her legs were weak, her head woozy, and her right arm useless, but maybe...

Hulum tripped over a root, which forced him to look down and right himself.

In that moment, one that seemed to float in time and space, where the trajectory of everything can change like train tracks at the flip of a switch, and where ludicrous ideas become reality, Terra decided she had nothing left to lose.

She made a break for the ledge.

# Chapter Forty-Three

He'd be quick to notice her escape, but this was happening one way or another. All she needed was a two-second lead to turn and launch the rock. She would have to come at it with her left hand and hope for the best, then she could be the heroine of her own story when all was said and done. Forget Iam, and forget Kyle Reese too.

Terra approached the ledge where the rock lay and had to catch herself from hurtling over like a barrel at Niagara. The narrow waterfall at her feet plunged into the shallow pool far below. The trees encircling it looked like twigs from this height. Light-headed and reeling, she turned away.

Hulum was fifteen yards out and closing in, spittle flying from his curled lips. She dipped down and snatched up the rock—it was as heavy as she'd hoped—and flung it at her pursuer.

But her left arm's aim was a sad imitation of her right's. The rock whizzed over his shoulder in a horrifying betrayal of hope.

Victory gleamed in his eyes. So much for saving the day. With no defense left except her own two (one and a half, really) arms, Terra braced them in front of herself and prepared for the impact.

Before he could reach her, a magnificent flash of light erupted between them.

Through half-closed eyes, she caught something familiar within the light: a figure, arms held out protectively. One of Iam's angels. But before she had time to react, the force of the explosion was lifting her off her feet.

She hurtled backward, away from Hulum, away from the angel.

Back...back...

...and over the edge of the cliff.

*The purpose in helping them remember goes beyond divining the wisdom of what to do and not do. Unlike us, they never knew a world without evil, and they've scarcely witnessed the full power that Iam wields over it. From their perspective, there appears to be no end to its dark hold on them. What they need, even more than direction, is hope.*

*- Elysian Records for the Revivers, Book V: Our Charge*

# CHAPTER FORTY-FOUR

S he was walking through a desert.

Her bare feet stirred a faint cloud of dust as she trod across the dry earth. She looked down and smiled at the sunlight glinting off the tiny flecks of sand on her toes. It seemed to glow when she squinted. The dress she wore had ruffles at the bottom that tickled her knees, and this made her smile too.

To be honest, she didn't have a clue where she was going. She took a look around. Desert and blue sky stretched in every direction. She couldn't remember how she'd gotten here. Not that she cared. The sun felt warm on her shoulders, but not scorching. The wind was strong, but not in its usual pushy way.

On the horizon, a figure appeared, walking toward her at a steady pace. He wore the clothes of a desert traveler, with a light-colored tunic and pants, and a shemagh wrapped around his face. She should be afraid—*stranger danger*—but for some reason, this guy seemed alright. She shrugged and went with it.

Time moved fluidly. While one minute, he seemed to be a mile away, the next he was within ten yards of her. Their steps slowed until they stood facing each other. The man nodded to her and unwrapped the shemagh, revealing a sun-worn face and an olive skin tone near the color of her own. She tried to scan him for flaws, but her mind refused to focus, like she was staring into the shifting colors of a kaleidoscope.

"How did you come to be all the way out here?" he asked. There was a gentleness in his eyes.

"I'm not sure." A hazy memory danced through her mind. Something about the woods. "I thought I was..." She trailed off. Going camping? She didn't even like camping.

He smiled at her, a kind smile that turned the corners of her own mouth upward in a sort of reflexive action. "It's easy to lose track of where you're heading sometimes, isn't it? Until you're already there."

"Yes." She looked down at the white cotton dress she was wearing, sure she'd never seen it before.

"That's why it is better to not walk alone." He held the crook of his arm out to her. "May I walk with you, Terra?"

He knew her name. She sensed that maybe she should be weirded out by this, but instead, she reached out her arm and threaded it through his. "Sure."

Together they continued on for an indefinite period of silence. Then he spoke again.

"Your mother loves you very much, doesn't she?"

He knew her mom too? "I guess so, in her own way."

"Do you love her?"

Terra winced. The question pressed on an old wound in her heart. "What does it matter? It doesn't make up for all her mistakes."

"She made a lot of mistakes, didn't she?"

"Um. Yeah."

"She's been wandering here alone for a long time."

"She has?"

"She needs your help, Terra."

"Screw that." The rebuttal came out as a knee-jerk reaction. "I mean...not that I don't want the best for her, but she was a *horrible* mom."

"Perhaps." He looked into her eyes as they walked. "But you have to let that go."

"But she doesn't deserve it."

"Deserve what, exactly?"

"My forgiveness."

"You're right. She doesn't. But forgiveness is never about deserving."

Terra remained silent and fixed her eyes on the miles of desert before them.

"How do you walk with so much weight on your shoulders?" he asked.

"Hm?"

"That bag looks awfully heavy."

She glanced over her shoulder and saw she was carrying a large backpack. She hadn't noticed it before, but—yessir—there it was, the straps digging into her shoulders.

"You should take it off."

"But I need it."

"Do you?"

"Don't I?"

"What is in there that's so important?" He stopped walking and let go of her arm.

That was a good question. She shrugged the bag off her arms and immediately felt the release. She heaved it onto the parched earth and stooped down to unzip the top.

Inside were rocks.

Dozens of large, jagged rocks. She rummaged through them, finding only more of the same beneath. Like she'd just shoplifted souvenirs from a geology convention.

"Why do you carry all that extra weight?" She heard his voice above her. "Leave it here."

Terra's mother appeared in her mind's eye, as if he'd spoken her image into existence in that moment. *Leave it here.*

She considered the contents of the bag for a minute longer, and the implications of his words, then stood. She took his arm, and they resumed walking, the backpack lying in the dirt where she'd left it. Her entire body felt lighter, so much that, if she skipped, she might accidentally crash into a bird or the sun itself.

After a time, he spoke again. "Your mother is not the only one who has made mistakes."

"True. Everybody makes mistakes, as they say."

"And everyone must answer for their own mistakes, right?"

"Yes."

He stopped and turned to her. "Why did you break my law, Terra?"

Terra's feet stopped moving. Even the air around her, as if overcome by the gravity of the question, seemed to freeze in place.

Suddenly her heart registered what her mind could not.

She fell to her knees and lowered her head. She was a total sham. A sad representation of the person she was supposed to be. She dug her fingers in the sand, hoping to burrow away from the scrutiny of his stare. But she couldn't, so she shut her eyes on the swelling tears and uttered the only thing she could think to say. "I'm sorry."

He shifted to her side, crouched down, and put his hand on her shoulder. "Tell me why you did it."

"I just thought..." She paused to wipe her nose with the back of her hand as a rogue tear made a break for it. "That if I could get Alexis to the healing pool, she would be saved. She wouldn't need the drugs anymore because the pain would be gone." She sniffed. "I didn't want her to end up an addict like—"

"Your mother."

"Yes."

"But you knew it was wrong."

"I did. I'm sorry, but...*why* is it wrong? To want healing for someone, I mean?"

"It's not." He patted her hand. His own hand felt rough and warm on hers. "But it was not Alexis's time for healing yet. Enduring pain and struggle is a transformative process. While her outward body is damaged, her inward soul is growing in strength and depth. She is finding me in the desert, just as you have now. Believe me, she has not been forgotten."

"But...*I* was healed. Harlan brought me to the healing pool."

"Harlan did so because I commanded it. It was in my plan for you. Terra, there are many different types of healing. While your physical pain was healed, you still have many other hurts that are in the process of healing, and many struggles ahead. Everyone has their own path they must follow, and it involves trusting the one who has laid out the path before them."

"You mean...trusting *you*."

He acknowledged her with a single nod.

"Yeah. I sort of have a hard time with that."

"That's why you broke Harlan's trust. You took control of a situation that was never meant to be in your hands."

She twisted the hem of her dress between her fingers, avoiding his gaze. "I guess I don't deserve forgiveness any more than my mom, do I?"

"Terra." He lowered himself to a seated position and took off his sandals, shaking the desert dust from them. He waited until she looked up. "What do you think I love more: the rules I created, or the people for whom I created them?" His eyes gleamed as he spoke. "There is always room for forgiveness."

This should have made her feel better. She should have been grateful. Instead, she wanted to lay down on the desert sand and wait for the buzzards to find her. If she couldn't help Alexis, then what was the point? What was she good for? "I wanted so bad to fix things for her," she sputtered.

He unwrapped his shemagh from his neck and used the end to wipe the dampness from her cheek. "Do you know that I created you with a heart full of compassion and courage? And those are the traits you expressed to the fullest when you empathized with Alexis and brought her to the healing pool. What you did was reckless and defiant. But it was also brave and selfless." He leaned in and whispered, "You are going to do *great* things, Terra. *Worthwhile* things." It wasn't a demand, but a promise.

Somewhere deep within her, something pulled free, like the click of a latch as a door is opened. Peace slipped in and wrapped itself around her. She was speechless as he clasped her hands in his and kissed them.

"Now the question is," he continued, "once you are healed, what will you do with the time you have left?"

He smiled warmly at her. Then, the wind picked up, whipping around her face and deafening her ears. It was cold and somehow fluid. It took on a vaporous quality as it passed in front of her eyes and blurred her view of him. Her eyes widened in alarm.

His expression remained calm. "*No tengas miedo.*" *Don't be afraid.*

He faded out of her sight, and his words echoed and drifted away on the wind, until she realized she was no longer sitting in the desert. She was on her back, floating, water swirling around her in every direction, her eyes closed tight. Someone was holding her, pulling her upward through the water.

Then, the water parted. Air met her face and filled her lungs. She opened her eyes to see the hazy shape of a man staring down at her, supporting her in his arms. She blinked a few times as the waters of the healing pool settled around her, then finally recognized the hazel eyes returning her gaze.

In a state of unadulterated shock, she inhaled water, coughed it up, and reclaimed her voice. "You found me."

# Chapter Forty-Five

They sat on the bank of the healing pool, waiting for the sun to dry the clothes on their backs.

Terra had her arms wrapped around her knees. She had no memory of the injuries she'd sustained. Fortunately, neither did her body. It felt fantastic, if not a little chilly from the wet clothes. Harlan sat an arm's length away, his expression dismal.

"I can't believe he came for you again," he said, "and in that way."

"He said I'd broken a rule," she replied in a daze. "Because I used the healing pool. He was going to kill me as punishment."

Harlan shook his head. "That's not how it works. That's just what they've convinced themselves is fair. Iam never agreed to that."

"Do they usually choose a person as a host?"

"No."

"Well I can't say I saw that coming. He's good."

"Too good."

They fell silent. Harlan looked down and brushed some sandy dirt off the rock where he sat, while Terra occupied herself with watching the sunlight skate across the water's surface. The situation felt utterly ironic. After a hellish week apart, she finally had the chance to talk with him, to maybe get some closure, and she couldn't think of a damn thing to say.

Harlan finally spoke. "That giant hoodie of yours must have snagged a branch on the way down and slowed your fall. I think that's what kept you alive." He lifted the sweatshirt off the rock where it lay drying and studied it. "Where'd you get this thing anyway? Boyfriend of yours?" He smiled half-heartedly.

"You know the saying...a hiker with a heart of gold."

"That's not the saying."

"Whatever. How far did I fall?"

Harlan gaped at her. "All the way."

"What do you mean?"

"You don't remember?"

"I don't remember anything after seeing the angel at the top of the cliff."

"I found you unconscious at the bottom of the ravine. You must have hit your head pretty hard. I could barely find a pulse."

"How'd you find me?"

"The bracelet brought me there."

She lowered her brow at him. "You *tell* the bracelet where to take you."

"Not this time." Harlan flung a pebble across the water and watched it skip three times before slipping beneath its surface. "I was walking through Elysia when my wrist started burning. When I looked down at the bracelet, all I could hear was the word *Go* over and over again. So I pressed the stone, and it brought me straight to you."

Terra stared off into the distance.

"I thought for sure you were already dead when I saw you lying there." Harlan sniffed quietly and looked away. "You looked like a rag doll."

"Do you think that's how he planned it?"

"Who?"

"Iam. Do you think I was supposed to go sailing off the edge like that? Not that I'm in any position to complain, but it was kind of a weird rescue." She plucked one of her sopping-wet socks off the rock and shook it a couple times, hoping the airflow would dry it faster.

"He doesn't make mistakes. But yeah, I guess getting pushed off a cliff is the last thing you'd expect."

"Why would he do it that way?"

Harlan furrowed his brow. "Maybe he wanted Hulum to think you were dead, so he'd leave you alone."

"I guess that makes sense. Sort of."

"At least, I didn't see any sign of him by the time I got there."

Terra jolted upright. "Ohhhh no."

"What's wrong?"

"Kenneth."

Ezra nudged Kenneth's lifeless arm with the toe of his boot while the other two watched. "Yeah, he'll be out for a while, considering how long he was a host. Possessions really do a number on people."

"But he's okay?" Terra asked. She stood far back from the cliff, not in any particular mood to revisit the plummet she'd made earlier. Harlan stood beside her.

"Oh sure. He'll be right as rain when he wakes. Won't remember a darn thing from the past couple days, but it's better that way." Ezra crossed his arms and stuck his neck out to see over the ledge. "Your subversive must've given up and ditched him here when he looked down and saw you'd fallen in the ravine."

"So he thinks I'm dead?"

"Probably. And I'll bet he moved on a while ago. Subversives have no use for a dead person."

Terra hugged herself and stared at Kenneth. "What do we do when he wakes?"

Her question was met with dumbstruck silence.

Harlan piped up. "I don't know, but I doubt we could just blame all this on a bad trip."

Terra eyed the bloody welt on Kenneth's forehead and narrowed her eyes. "Good idea."

"What?"

"How about he *did* have a bad trip...over a stump?" She pointed to the welt. "Explains the bump on his head *and* the short-term memory loss." Voila. This recovering-from-a-demon-abduction thing was a cinch.

Ezra cracked a smile. "I like the ingenuity."

"But how do I explain you guys being here too?"

"You don't," Harlan said. "We'll make sure you're the only one here when he wakes. You tell him about how you guys were hiking together—no sense in leaving that part out when all your coworkers already know—explain how he had a little altercation with a stump, then drive him home in his car."

Terra baulked. "Do I have to?" Just looking at Kenneth's face was giving her flashbacks of Hulum's leer.

"Nah," said Harlan. "So long as you're cool with being accused of manslaughter—or at best, of being a really lousy friend—for abandoning a bleeding and unconscious man."

She sighed. "Point taken."

They'd asked Ezra to keep an eye on Kenneth while they hunted down her things along the trail. Harlan could bring her back to the cliff the second Kenneth started to regain consciousness. In the meantime, she reunited with her pack and a very wet cell phone in need of CPR.

"I should have never left you like that," Harlan said as they walked together. They had nowhere to go at this point, and nothing left to hunt for. But neither one wanted to admit it.

"Ezra told me you were searching for answers," she said. "Did you find any?"

"Mostly self-reflection. I realized I'm still learning what it means to forgive."

"I know the feeling."

"And what it means to live in a place where nothing is permanent."

Terra kept her head down. Didn't sound like he'd be taking bets on their relationship anytime soon.

The trail narrowed through an encroachment of gnarled trees. The two grew quiet and walked single file through the bottleneck.

Terra finally worked up the nerve to say the thing that had been gnawing at her stomach like hunger. "I'm sorry I hurt you."

Harlan swatted a wiry branch out of their way, then guided Terra through with his hand on the small of her back. "I know."

"What I did was stupid."

"What you did was understandable, given the situation."

She stammered, "But...I thought you said—"

"I was upset about a lot of things. I blew up, and it wasn't entirely fair to you."

"What do you mean?"

"There was something else I never told you that made me question everything. You remember how I said Iam wanted me to bring you to Elysia?"

She nodded.

"He eventually told me why, and it led me to believe we were supposed to be together, that it was part of the plan. Believe me, Terra, I wanted that to be true more than anything else. But then you did something I never thought you'd do."

Terra's throat swelled painfully at the mention of it. The theft. The betrayal. The chasm between them.

"So I thought I'd been an idiot, jumping to conclusions that Iam had never said, committing myself to a relationship that wasn't supposed to be. Then I started to question the truth of what he *did* say."

"Wait. What did he tell you exactly?"

"I haven't told you yet because I didn't want to scare you. I didn't think you were ready."

"*What?* Just say it." If he dragged this out any longer, it would require its own drumroll.

He slowed his pace and looked her in the eyes. "You were intended to become a reviver. I was supposed to be your mentor."

Terra stopped dead in the middle of the trail. "What? I'm not even from Elysia."

"Doesn't matter. He chose you."

"But *why?*"

"I don't know. Ezra told me he's heard of it happening before—Edenites becoming revivers."

She shook her head. "I think Iam's really reaching on this one."

"Terra."

"I'm the last person he needs on his team. Come on, you said yourself you started to question it."

"I did," he admitted, "but as you've seen firsthand, his plans aren't always straightforward. Forget that you're not Elysian by birth. You have a lot more to offer than you think."

"It's not that," she said, though it was true she'd probably royally bomb at the task. "I'm still not sure what to believe, even after everything he's done. Even after seeing him face to face in the desert. Some things...I just can't reconcile with real life."

"Real life?"

"You know. The dumpster fires and shit-covered fans. Where is he in all that? And don't tell me about *second hearing* again. That's a weak excuse. If I was in a major car accident, I wouldn't call up a doctor and ask, well, what do you think I should do? I'm going to go *see* a doctor and have him do everything in his power to fix me. Better yet, I'd like him to make me a time machine so I can go back in time and stop the accident from happening to begin with. Is that too much to ask?"

Harlan watched in stunned silence as she blew out her frustration and collapsed on a nearby stump. When she was settled, he said, "Here's a question for *you* now. Let's say there was a way to go back in time and stop the car that caused the accident—before it even left the parking lot—and let's say someone else did that for you. Would you have ever known?"

"What do you mean?"

"Would you know that you narrowly missed being in an accident that day, if the car that was supposed to hit yours never left the parking lot?"

She ruminated on this. "I guess not."

"So how many times do you think Iam may have caused you or someone else to do something that completely changed the course of your day, preventing the worst possible outcome, and you had no idea?"

"I hear you, Harlan. But, come on. Bad stuff still happens. *All* the time."

"True. We can't always avoid it. That's why we have each other."

She glanced at him, dubious. "I don't think hugs and rainbows are going to make it all better."

He crouched next to her, resting his arms on his knees. "But if someone offered your favorite dinner or a shoulder to cry on...that wouldn't be so bad, would it?"

Terra's mind revisited the hospital room with Alexis all those months ago. Had she been a shoulder to cry on for Alexis? If so, she hadn't done a bang-up job of it. And who *could*, really? Circumstances like that sucked too much to be conquered with a fruit basket. She glowered. "So he wants us to do all the work for him, is that it? When I met him in my dream, it's like he genuinely cared, but everything I see in this world says otherwise. And he sends the revivers in his place, because why? Because he has better things to do?"

"You don't understand." Harlan said. "He was the first."

"First *what*?"

"He gave up everything to pave the way for the revivers. We're just following the example he set."

Before Terra could respond, Harlan's phone dinged. He pulled it from his pocket and read the text.

"That's Ezra. I need to get you there now. Kenneth's waking."

*It was because of his actions that we could cross the barrier. Iam was the Original Reviver. It was not without great cost to him, however. Knowing it would be a danger to the Edenites, he chose to leave his power in Elysia and live and die as a human. His return to Elysia marked the beginning of a new age, when Elysians became revivers, and Edenites' ears were opened once more.*

*- Elysian Records for the Revivers, Book V: Our Charge*

# Chapter Forty-Six

Terra held her toothbrush in midair and paused to study the reflection in the bathroom mirror. Iam's words ran through her head like a news ticker on repeat. *Breaking News: You are going to do great things. Worthwhile things.* Her reflection looked washed out, unremarkable, about as enchanting as a piece of plywood.

*Great things.*

*Worthwhile things.*

And on and on it scrolled.

If she'd had to guess where she would be half a year after her first healing pool encounter, it would not be here in her current state. Her chronic illness had been the lynchpin of all her problems. So why did her life now feel like it was on a downward spiral? Her relationship with her mother was strained, teetering on the verge of nonexistent. She'd failed miserably to help her best friend. She had betrayed the one man she'd wanted to spend the rest of her life with. Absorbed in her own pity party, she'd walked headlong into a subversive's trap, placing not only herself, but also Kenneth in danger. And all the while, her performance at work had been a distracted mess, putting her on precarious terms with the boss. If she'd been trying to sabotage every part of her life, well, mission accomplished.

Her thoughts were interrupted by the insistent brush of something furry against her ankle.

"Hey, Hoots." She bent down to pat the dog on his head. As she did so, Alexis popped her head in the doorway and gave Terra a once over.

"Pajamas already? I guess you're not coming out."

Terra jammed the toothbrush in her mouth.

"You know the girls are going to ask about you."

"Sorry, Lex," she said through a mouth full of toothpaste. "I'm sure you'll still have fun without me."

"It's not the fun I'm worried about. It's you." Alexis watched, arms crossed, as Terra spit into the sink. "You can't wait around for him forever."

"I'm not waiting around. I'm just tired."

"Alright." Alexis shrugged and pulled at the sleeve of her top, which wasn't quite long enough to cover the compression garment she wore underneath. "Hey, I'll stay home tomorrow night and we can watch a chick flick or something. I mean, if you're still here. Did they fix the gas leak at your apartment yet?"

"I'll check tomorrow. You know I hate chick flicks."

Alexis snorted. "Fine. We'll watch one of those depressing indies you like. I'm heading out." Her curled hair bounced as she turned and slipped down the hall in her thigh-high velvet boots and black sweater dress.

"Miss you already," Terra called out in a mock-cutesy voice.

"Miss you more, roomie," came the sing-song response before the front door banged shut.

It was nice to see Alexis getting out tonight. Almost like she was back to her old self. *Almost* was the operative word here, as the nights Terra had stayed at her apartment had proven otherwise. Twice she'd woken

Terra up in the middle of the night by ransacking the kitchen, mashing random foods like crackers and gummy candy in a bowl, and eating them with a spoon. *Sleep snacking*, she called it. Last night, Terra dreamt of bad karaoke bars and woke to the sound of Alexis belting out "Party in the U.S.A." in her bedroom. Alexis remembered none of it, of course.

Terra took one last glance at the sullen figure in the bathroom mirror and switched off the light. She trudged into Alexis's living room and flopped on the fold-out, which had served as her bed for the past week. Her phone glowed with one missed text from Harlan.

*All good?*

She typed her reply.

*Still alive.*

It had been exactly one week since the possession, the kidnapping, and Harlan's return into her life, if she could call it that. His daily checks for a pulse didn't exactly count as conversation. As long as she replied with anything other than *help me I'm dying*, he seemed satisfied to end the exchange there, able to live with himself for another day.

There was no gas leak at her apartment. (Only, perhaps, a demon with a mind for vengeance.) Harlan had insisted she stay away for the week, in case Hulum came back to look for her. She was basically playing possum. It had also been Harlan's idea to take some sick days from work. Lying to her friend and coworkers was never on her list of life aspirations, but *hiding from a demon* didn't seem like a credible excuse for taking off.

She turned on the TV as Hoots jumped up and curled his wiry-haired body next to hers. The typical *Law-and-Order*-style drama was playing, with the best second-rate acting TV had to offer. This was exactly the kind of show her mom would let all calls go to voicemail for. Terra could imagine her now, watching from her armchair, making an inane gasping sound when the bratty rich kid turned out to be the culprit.

They hadn't spoken since the steakhouse. She picked up her phone and scrolled through the contacts list until it landed on Leta's number. Her finger hovered over it for an uncertain moment before hitting the Off button instead. She tossed the phone back on the fold-out and returned her attention to the TV, then sifted through channels until she found an old comedy with Will Ferrell. Good enough.

On the television, Iam's desert appeared. She sat up and stared before realizing it was just an ad for a luxury SUV with 0% APR the first twelve months. She sunk back against the pillow and thought about her conversation with Iam again. Why hadn't she asked him what to do about Hulum? Or how to help Alexis? Somehow, she hadn't felt the need at the time. Even now, she was weirdly calm about it. Still, one of his comments kept eating at her. He'd said *once you are healed, what will you do?* Not *now that you're healed...*

She touched the gold initials at the base of her neck, warm from her skin, and wrapped her fingers around them. Only the sick needed healing.

*Who's in control?*

The necklace suddenly felt too tight, like she was being strangled. She unfastened the clasp and held it out in front of her. Hoots sat up to watch the dangling *TZ* with interest, his head bobbing with the sway of the chain. She scratched behind his ear and said, "Maybe it's time to give this thing a rest. What do you think, Hoots?"

His tail waggled like a fuzz-covered slinky.

She dropped the necklace on the end table next to her, then returned her attention to the screen. Breathing was somehow easier now.

In the gray light of dawn, Terra woke to a panicked shriek.

The thin mattress of the pull-out squeaked and pitched against its piddly springs as she turned to her side. She lay still for a moment and allowed Alexis's dim apartment to come into focus. All was eerily quiet.

Terra rose to her elbow to see Hoots standing at attention in his bed, ears perked up and tail held frozen in the air. He'd heard it too.

A second shriek carried down the hallway from Alexis's room. Then Terra heard Alexis call her name.

She pushed out of the bed, stumbled over a chew toy, and bounded toward the bedroom, terrier on her heels. She halted at the door when she saw Alexis sitting up in bed, inspecting her right forearm.

Terra leaned against the door frame and pushed her hair away from her face. "Holy crap on a stick, Lex. I thought someone was attacking you in here. What's wrong?"

Alexis held up her arm, the one without the burns, and her face went Wonder-Bread-white. "I thought it was a dream, but it wasn't."

Terra stepped closer. Newly crusted scabs extended from Alexis's elbow to palm, a bloodied mess that Terra noted with terror had left a foot-long smear of reddish-brown stains in the white bedsheets. "Oh my God."

Now even more frantic, Alexis threw off the covers and checked the rest of herself. She patted her hands down her pajama pants, pausing over the knees where the cloth had been torn. The ragged edges were smudged with blood. She drew up her feet, which looked filthy on the bottoms, like she'd been shuffling across tar. Then Terra saw the top of her right foot. More blood. Red speckles and splotches reaching from toe to ankle. Like road rash.

Alexis brought her hands to her forehead and swore. "Did you see me last night?"

Terra felt pinpricks of heat under her skin. "What?"

"In the middle of the night, Terra. Did you see me leave the apartment? Did you hear anything?"

Terra shook her head. "I slept pretty hard."

"Shit." Alexis emitted an unsteady laugh that dissolved into hysterical gasps. "I think I got hit by a car."

Terra lowered herself onto the bed next to her, gripping the bedpost with white knuckles. "Lex, what are you talking about?"

"I had a dream I was running down a road. I don't even know where. I was just...running. Then I saw—ugh, no, Hoots!"

Hoots had jumped on the bed and was licking her wounds with the utmost sincerity, as was the job of any good dog who loved its owner. Alexis nudged him away.

"Freaking vampire dog. Anyway, I saw lights, and something screamed at me. At least, that's what I thought, but it was more of a screech—it had to be a car. It knocked me off my feet." She rubbed her arm and winced. "That must be where I got these scrapes. And..." She yanked down the side of her pajama pants and exposed her left hip. "Oh God. This bruise."

"Alexis," Terra whispered. Her stomach lurched at the sight of the deep purple mass of skin above her waistband. "They should have taken you to the hospital."

"Maybe the driver tried. But when he came toward me, I flipped out, like he was chasing me or something. I ran away. I don't remember anything after that." She crossed her ankles and hugged her knees. "Terra, I was asleep the whole time. I only remember parts of it, but holy shit, it happened." Her voice cracked and a tear raced down her cheek. "I don't even know how I got back here."

Terra looked over at the bottle of sleeping pills on the nightstand, then back to Alexis. "This has to stop."

Alexis buried her head between her arms. "I can't."

The words *yes, you can, dammit,* nearly tumbled out of Terra's mouth. But she stopped herself. If hopelessness were a sewer, Alexis was already swimming in it. What good would it do to tell her to think positive or try harder? Isn't that what Terra used to hear all the time about her fibromyalgia? *No es gran cosa.* Like it was so easy to rise above it. So easy to pretend it was fine. So easy to stop taking a pill.

They would need to take Alexis to urgent care to get checked out. And she would need to see her doctor immediately about changing her medication. Find a better way to manage the pain and sleeplessness. Possibly enter an addiction program if the doctor called for it. But for now, none of those things were what Alexis needed most.

Without a word, Terra edged closer and wrapped her arms around her friend, feeling the pulse of her sobs beneath.

They wept together.

# Chapter Forty-Seven

Terra inspected the empty shelves of her fridge, then slammed the door (a difficult feat, considering the door was built to make a pleasant *thunk* upon closing). The Sunday dinner hour approached, and she was finally back at her own place. But she'd forgotten to get groceries.

There was a light knock on the front door.

She answered it and found Harlan standing there, his eyes trained on the floor.

"Harlan." Two scenes played in split-screen across her mind. In one, she fell forward and kissed him. In the other, she kicked the door shut in his face.

"Hey." He sounded about as delighted as a kid who'd gotten a Werther's Original tossed into his trick-or-treat bag.

"No text first?"

"It was faster to jump. Can I come in?"

She stepped to the side and held the door open for him. "I'm fine. No subversive attacks today."

"That's not why I'm here." He stalked into her living room, glancing around as if he were, in fact, looking for a subversive.

She crossed her arms. "Well then?"

"Iam wants you in Elysia."

"Oh." She took a moment to process. "What for?"

"He wants to meet with you."

"Really? Why?"

"That's not my department to say. I'm just the transportation, so to speak."

She cast a furtive glare at his back as he gazed out her window. "So the only reason you're here is to give me a ride to Elysia?"

"More or less."

"Huh. I'm actually starving. Can I grab some dinner first?"

He swiped a hand across his jaw. "Of course," he answered, his brow creased. "Sure, I can take you somewhere first."

She tilted her head. "You sure?"

"Yeah...yeah. Let's go."

Terra took another bite from her sesame rice bowl and chewed at an expeditious pace. Harlan sat across from her in the booth, stiff as a department store mannequin, his eyes averted toward the parking lot.

"I'm sorry I'm such a slow eater," she said, breaking the unbearable silence.

"No, it's okay. Take your time." He clasped his hands and sighed heavily, the table empty in front of him. She guessed he'd had dinner earlier.

Terra continued to eat, though she was quickly losing her appetite. A high school kid behind the service counter was using the selfie-cam on his phone to inspect his braces, intermittently digging bits of food out with his finger. So much for ambience. She stopped chewing when she noticed Harlan's leg bouncing like a jackhammer under the table.

"Judas Priest! I'll get a to-go box." She began cleaning up the table in a frenzy, then he placed a hand on top of hers.

"Don't," he said. When she ignored him, he grasped her other hand and held her in place. "Terra. I'm sorry."

"No." She threw his hands off hers. "Stop trying to be nice. You're doing a piss-poor job of it anyway." She turned to a nearby counter and reached for the stack of empty to-go boxes.

"I'm not trying to be nice. Well, I mean, I hope I am, but—"

"I'm just one big walking guilt trip for you, aren't I?"

He paused, half standing at the table. "What?"

"Give it up, Harlan. You're only here because you *have* to be. The only reason you've been checking on me is because you feel guilty about leaving me alone with Hulum." She dumped her dinner into the to-go box, spilling rice on the table. "Oh, and let's not forget the crap-load of guilt I apparently used to *force* you to sleep with me." Time to make a grand exit before she came fully unhinged. She gathered her things and headed for the door.

She could hear him hustling behind her. "Terra, wait."

This was childish, running away from him. She could feel Braces Boy watching from behind the counter as she jerked the door open and hurried outside. Why did Harlan have this effect on her? God, it pissed her off.

By the time she turned the corner of the building, he was already on top of her. "Terra." He latched onto her arm until she stopped and whipped around. "I'm sorry. I did this all wrong."

"Damn right, you did. Wait. What are you talking about?"

He glanced around the parking lot. "This is not how I planned it at all. I was going to bring it up after you met with Iam, and now I'm all thrown off."

"Well, so sorry to throw off your plans." She crossed her arms to guard against the biting cold. "Bring *what* up?"

Harlan shook his head. "I'm sorry, I suck at this. Let me start over. Terra...I really screwed up before."

She slumped against the brick wall and watched him fumble his words. Might be entertaining if nothing else.

"I—I shouldn't have shamed you the way I did. That day in the cave was every bit my decision as it was yours. What I said about you pushing me into it...that wasn't fair to you. I'm sorry."

She wasn't an idiot. Apologies almost always came paired with a *but*.

"You're not a guilt trip to me. You're not a burden. And I want to tell you I forgive you for what you did. I'm not mad anymore."

Terra's heart pulsed in her throat. Harlan had stopped talking and was now staring, waiting for her reaction. She stared back, debating whether to turn it into a contest.

Maybe this was it. He wanted to be with her too. She could see it in his eyes. He was about to push her up against this brick wall and kiss her with enough force to make her drop her dinner on the pavement. Well, she would make him grovel a bit longer first.

"Anything else?"

"No," he said. "I just didn't want that rift between us any longer." Then, like a guidance counselor giving a pep talk, he put a hand on her shoulder and said, "It's important you know I accept you as you are."

Dumbfounded, she glanced sidelong at the offending hand on her shoulder and quelled the impulse to smack it off. "Great. Thanks."

"Come on. Elysia's waiting."

She tensed as he wrapped his arms around her, then clasped his arms with weak hands, no longer sure of how to hold onto him. As the amber stone plunged them into free fall, she let out a single, dejected sigh. The black silence obscured the sound from his ears.

*Many times it has been asked: if the angels can fight the subversives, why haven't they cast them out of Eden yet? Unfortunately, until Edenites learn to trust their creator, the subversives will maintain the lion's share of power in Eden. The fact is, what humans choose to believe wields more force than an army of angels.*

*- Elysian Records for the Revivers, Book V: Our Charge*

# Chapter Forty-Eight

S unset was making its grand entrance across the Elysian sky when
they landed on a rocky shore at the edge of a mangrove forest.
The lavish purples and pinks and golds that spread outward from the
horizon cast a radiant glow on their faces and the water below. Any
prettier, and she'd have thought they'd overshot Elysia and jumped
straight to Heaven.

She stopped shivering when the warmth of the salty air hit her.
The to-go box was still in her hand. Not quite sure what to do with it
here (*Don't suppose Iam has a fridge?*), she set it down on the ground
at her feet, then turned to take in their surroundings.

A brackish body of water surrounded their little vestige of gravel,
a maze of mangrove trees running through it. Their interlacing roots
jutted out above the waterline and took on the appearance of dripping candle wax that streamed outward from their trunks in every
direction. They plunged into the sea, supporting their bodies on a
jumble of aquatic stilts. The trees themselves were no more than six
feet tall above the water, but their collective branches formed a green
wall that all but obscured the horizon.

"What part of Elysia is this?"

Harlan peeled off his jacket and tossed it among the rocks and sand. "It's a sort of meeting place. Ezra brought me here when I first became a reviver."

"I've never seen anything like it."

"You'll want to take your shoes off," he said, and bent down to remove his own.

"Will I?" Iam sure had a thing for impromptu pool parties. Mentally bracing herself for water-logged clothes, she slid her shoes off. Together they stepped barefoot to the edge of the water and let it lap at their toes.

"It's hidden in there, through the trees." He pointed into the mangrove maze, where the water was several feet deep.

"What?"

"The meeting place. I'll walk you partway, then you'll go the rest alone. This meeting is just for you and Iam."

"Do I have to swim?"

"No, it's all shallow." He strode into the water ahead of her. It was a hazy turquoise, but clear enough to see the color of sand and gritty soil at the bottom.

Legs tottering, she waded in after him, watching her step among the larger rocks on the sea floor and wondering how many people had face-planted in the water right before meeting Iam. She followed Harlan into a section of mangroves that lined either side like the walls of a hallway.

They plodded forward, kicked-up sand swirling around them like an underwater mist. The water rose until it reached their waists, and the shoreline receded behind them until it disappeared among the bramble of mangrove leaves. Harlan turned left, then right, down different corridors of trees and stopped when they came to a much narrower segment. Here, they could no longer stand side by side without brushing up against branches. The trees arched inward as if trying to embrace them, giving a whole new meaning to the term *tree hugging*.

He turned to her. "It's not much farther from here. Just follow the path to the end. I'll wait for you on the shoreline."

She nodded and watched him wade back through the hall of trees. Then she was alone.

This section of the mangroves was darker. Only a thin strip of sky shone through the gap at the top of the arch formed by their leaves. The water was calm, aside from the gentle sloshing noises it made against the gnarled roots at her sides, but her heart was experiencing turbulence like a propjet in a thunderstorm. She pushed on and watched her feet through the cloudy water, wondering how much longer.

It was only when the turquoise of the water brightened that she looked up and saw the trees formed a circle ahead of her. The canopy parted to reveal a dazzling display of sunset clouds above, their edges catching fire in the sun.

As Terra stepped into the halo of trees, she was knocked upside the head with a powerful sense of something mystical. This place was sacred: Iam was here.

Once she'd waded into the center, her foot hit something hard. She would have fallen forward into the water, except her hands landed against the large object blocking her way, and she caught herself. She searched the water and, as the churning sand cleared, caught a glimpse of an embankment of rock that rose to just beneath the surface. There was something lying on top of the rock.

Two pieces of jewelry, arranged side by side, confronted her.

On the left, the gold necklace with her initials. She'd left it hanging on a hook near her dresser back home. But, oddly, here it was, moonlighting as an Elysian artifact. On the right, a bracelet, identical to Harlan's in

every way except smaller, meant for a slimmer wrist. Its amber stone
glowed under the water.

*Choose.*

The word came to her, and she didn't need to ask why. This wasn't
the combos menu at a local Mexican joint. She could ask for a chalupa
and burrito on one plate, but these two pieces of jewelry were mutually
exclusive, no special orders allowed.

She reached her hand into the water and hovered over the bracelet.
Then she turned her attention to the necklace, its gold links glinting in
the wavering light. If she left behind this part of her...would she still be
herself? Her eyes flitted back to the bracelet. Or was she only now starting
to become the person she was meant to be?

Fate. Destiny. Free will. It was all a funny thing. Did she want this
because she knew it was what Iam wanted for her, or would she have
chosen it anyway?

Did it make a difference?

Terra pictured her own will like a wave in Iam's ocean. It would rear
up, stretch its fingers to the shore, struggle against the current with
impressive but waning strength, then fall back into the great undulating
sea. There it would reconvene and find rest for a while, then inevitably
engage in tug-of-war again. But it would never escape the sea because a
wave is nothing without it. The sea breathes life and force into the very
particles of its being.

She was certain now.

She wrapped her fingers around the token of her choice and pulled it
dripping from the salty water. As she placed it on her wrist and pulled
the cords taut, a warm breeze swept across her face. She looked upward
and watched the clouds racing high above. And the voice was speaking
to her again.

*Now, my reviver, go.*

She stepped out from the mangroves, flaunting the bracelet on her wrist like a golden ticket winner. Harlan stood at the water's edge waiting.

"So. Crazy story..." she started.

His eyes flashed to her wrist, and his reaction was immediate. He charged toward her, sending saltwater splashing in every direction. By the time he met her in the ankle-deep shallows, she had to brace herself for the collision.

"I'm a reviver now," she said, her legs straining under the weight of his embrace.

"I know." His hold on her tightened, and he was planting kisses on her hair, then her cheek. As far as congratulatory hugs went, this was the strangest she'd ever had. It got even stranger when he began shaking under her arms.

Good God, was he crying?

"Harlan, what's wrong?"

"I had to be sure first." He sniffed and kissed her head again. When he finally released her, his eyes were tinged red. "I needed to know it was your choice, and not something you felt you had to do for my sake."

She frowned. "Of course it was my choice."

He fell to his knees in the sand and water. Head down, he reached out and grasped her hand in both of his and rested his forehead against it. He held it there, clinging to it like a shipwrecked mariner clings to driftwood. "I'm sorry for earlier at dinner. I'm sorry for the past week. I had to keep my distance until you'd made the decision for yourself."

She stared down at him and her hand, which it seemed she would not be getting back any time soon. "Well, I guess that explains a lot."

For a moment, he looked up at her, a desperate yearning in his eyes, and she thought he might be preparing to beg for forgiveness. Then, he brought one foot forward, balancing on his other knee in the water, and reached a hand back into his pocket. He looked absolutely ridiculous. She opened her mouth to tell him to stand up, that he'd hit his groveling quota for the day and could relax already. But then he fished something out of his pocket and brought it out into the light.

And said the unthinkable.

"I love you, Terra. Marry me?"

She gazed down at the ring between his fingers as if he'd just whipped out a severed toe.

"*What?*"

# Chapter Forty-Nine

"Will you marry me?" Harlan rephrased his question, as if clarity were the only issue.

Terra gaped at the ring. She wanted to say something. *Tried* to say something. He was kneeling there, waiting for her to speak, for God's sake. But her voice was caught somewhere between her throat and disbelief in this big fat joke of his.

Harlan's smile wavered and he let out an awkward laugh. "Did I say it wrong?"

She shook her head and brought a hand to her face. A swelling ache pierced her eyes.

"Oh no." He retracted the ring and stood. "I screwed this up too, didn't I?"

She withdrew her hand from him. "We were broken up, Harlan. It's not like flipping a switch."

"It's okay if you need more time. I know this is sud—"

"Oh, you think?" She sloshed her way out of the water and onto the gravel. "You don't go from broken up to married. That's not how it works." She kicked a pile of gravel with her bare foot, then cursed at the pain.

Harlan stood still and rubbed his face. "Definitely screwed up," he muttered under his hands.

"I don't know how they do it in Elysia, but in *my* world, you don't jerk a woman's heart around like a cat toy, then give her a ring."

"Tell me what to do. I'll do anything."

She stared at him for a long moment, this man who had crawled under her skin and made a home there. He stared back, his clothes dripping with salt water. He had no more words, and neither did she.

Her face twisted into a grimace as the tears broke through.

He trudged onto the shore and took her in his arms. "What can I do? Please."

She shook her head and mouthed the word *nothing*.

"What was that?"

"Nothing," she whispered. She drew close and laid her head against his shoulder, hating herself for loving the feel of it. "I've missed you so much, you jackass."

He coughed out a quiet laugh, his warm breath on the back of her neck. "I've missed you too. I haven't stopped thinking about you since I last saw you."

She sniffed and wiped her cheek. "You know, I would have chosen to be a reviver whether or not we'd gotten back together."

"Yeah?"

"Yeah. Congratulations. You just wasted a whole week."

"You mean all that time, we could've been doing this?"

He dipped his head and kissed her. Slowly at first, then with passion. Like a soldier coming home. She gave up the fight—at least, until she could figure out a way to make him pay—and kissed him back. If there were a brick wall nearby, she would most definitely be up against it now.

When they came up for air, he held up the ring and asked, "Well?"

She hesitated. "I thought you said marriage was just a substandard contract."

"I did." He smirked. "But what do I know?"

"So you're saying you were wrong?"

"Maybe I thought I knew better than the Edenites. Thought I didn't need marriage to substantiate my love for you." He grazed her cheek with his fingers. "But you were the one who took it seriously when we made a commitment to each other. You tried to work it out, even when I'd given up."

"Yeah, pretty much."

"And now I'm ready to start trusting another person, even though I know that person will make mistakes. Because I know I'll make mistakes too, and you'll—I hope—still give me another chance every time."

She grinned. "So the Elysian has finally learned the ways of the Edenites." She stepped back and held out her hand, fingers poised and waiting. "Okay."

"Okay?"

"I'm saying I'll *marry* you."

"Usually a *yes* to a proposal is a bit more spirited than that."

"And usually a proposal doesn't have such weird-ass timing. So this *yes* comes with a huge *but*."

"Then you'd better get it some huge pants."

Terra smacked his chest with the back of her hand. "I'll marry you, *but*...only if you know for sure Iam's good with it. I don't want you to have any reason to second-guess this."

"We're good."

"What? How do you know?"

"I already talked to him."

"And?"

"He said it's our choice."

"That's it?"

"Yeah, though I'm pretty sure he already knows what we'll choose." He flashed a crooked smile and took her hand. "Hard to surprise the all-knowing." He slid the ring onto her finger. It was gold with a turquoise stone in the center and diamonds stacked on either end to form a marquee shape. Unconventional for an engagement ring.

"Beautiful." She held her hand out to admire it.

"The turquoise is from Elysia. I found it and had it polished. The diamonds are from Eden. Not quite as amazing as the jewelry Iam gave you, but I'll settle for second fiddle."

She glanced down at her bracelet. "Hmm, that's right."

"What?"

"Well. I guess I don't need *you* anymore." She shot him a devious grin and hovered her finger over the amber stone.

"Oh no you don't." He pulled her hand away. "Tonight you'll be coming with *me*."

Before she could protest, his arms encircled her, and they were falling out of the mangroves and into a drastically less romantic setting.

She glanced around at her sad little living room where they'd landed. "Why did you bring us back here?"

"Go get in some dry clothes, something comfortable. I'll meet you back here in ten."

"Then what?"

"Then...we celebrate."

When they returned to Elysia, the sky was a deep indigo color stippled with luminous stars and a crescent moon hung low on the horizon. The light from the moon was just enough to give an impression of the red dirt and rocks on the expansive plain where they stood. Squat, hairy shrubs sprouted at random from the earth, demanding careful steps as the pair wove their way across the plain. Off in the distance stood the dark shadows of desert mesas, their flat tops towering above like step stools for giants.

Harlan led Terra in the direction of an outcropping of rocks that glowed red and appeared to dance in the dark landscape. As they approached, she could see the flickering glow was not coming from the rocks themselves, but a small fire in between. Someone had built a fire pit out here. In the middle of nowhere. Dark figures near the fire stood up as she and Harlan reached the edge of the outcropping.

"Other people?" Her inner introvert shrank into a prickly ball like a defensive hedgehog.

"It's a celebration, remember?" He put his arm around her and guided her into the circle, where she could see their faces in the firelight.

To her, it looked more like a tribal council, and she was about to get voted out. Before she had a chance to start panicking, she caught sight of Ezra among the strangers. He stepped forward and hugged them both.

"Congratulations," he said into her ear. "Welcome to the family."

"Everyone," Harlan announced to the gathering, "this is Terra: our newest reviver, and also my fiancée."

The small crowd erupted in cheers and whoops. She gawked at them, maybe twenty in total, all looking at her as if she belonged here. Then she allowed herself to smile a little, because maybe she did. Harlan took her around the circle, collecting congratulatory handshakes and introductions along the way. She learned these people were the other revivers who lived in the Indy area (and regularly participated in ad hoc desert meetings).

Some were there with their mentors, and some their grand-mentors, like little family units. The youngest of the bunch was a thirteen-year-old girl, who sat close to her mentor and adoptive mother, watching the others with a sort of skittish fascination. The oldest was a man in his seventies, dressed in cowboy boots and a classic Stetson, looking like any minute now he might whip out a six-shooter and lasso. The characters around the fire ran the gamut, from a young woman going hard at the steampunk trend to a Mr. Rogers doppelgänger, but all were indistinguishable from your typical Eden-dwelling human. The only difference was their matching bracelets.

As everyone settled into their chairs, the man in the Stetson, who had introduced himself as Grady, spoke up.

"Always a pleasure to see you all here in our little home away from home. We need this community as much as we need the air we breathe." He addressed the crowd from his camping chair, one leg crossed over the other, the pointed toe of his boot bobbing in the air. "Thanks to Harlan for calling this gathering, even if he did only give us two and half hours' notice." He cast a wry smile in Harlan's direction.

"Hey now, that's all the notice I got from Iam," Harlan said.

"S'okay," Grady said. "We all know how Iam likes to keep us in suspense until the last minute."

Chuckles arose around the fire.

"In any event, I'm glad most all of us could make it out, even Darius over there, who's smack dab in the middle of his annual trip to China. Sorry about the long jump back, buddy."

A tired-looking man nodded in acknowledgement. Harlan leaned over and whispered into Terra's ear. "Takes a full twelve seconds from China, not counting crossover time."

"Yikes," she whispered back. Might as well use a giant catapult to get here from there.

"And Fran, God bless 'er, somehow found time to bake a cake to help us celebrate," Grady said, sounding genuinely bewildered.

Fran called out across the fire. "It's just a sheet cake, and I didn't have time to frost it." She held up a clear container with something white and goopy inside. "But I brought the frosting here, if anyone wants some."

The thirteen-year-old girl's eyes lit up. "Oh, I love cake!" she said in a twitter of a voice, then looked to her mentor with a *can you believe it?* grin. It made Terra wonder whether they had cake back in perfect Elysia. (And could any place be perfect without cake?)

"Yes, I understand a few others here have brought things to share with the two of you. Gifts and such." Grady said, addressing Terra and Harlan. "But before we get into any of that, I thought it fitting to share some reviver insights with our newest member of the gang here."

Terra felt all eyes drawn to her like fuzz to a wet lollipop.

"Now Terra, we're all pretty jazzed about the fact that Iam chose an Edenite. That doesn't happen 'cept once a blue moon. In fact, I only once remember meeting another reviver who was Eden-born, and he was an old man like me now. At the time, I barely knew how to shave. So I can't say I remember too much 'bout him. Anyhow, your unique situation puts us in the position of not quite knowing how to commemorate this day.

"See, usually we get our new revivers straight from the other side of Elysia, and they're just kids. We'd take this opportunity to welcome them to Eden and tell them all about the strange sights and sounds they'd experience in this new place, give 'em advice, and so on. With you, well, I assume you already know a thing or two about the world you grew up in."

She smiled and shrugged. "I guess as much as the next person."

"That's why I figured we'd do things a bit different tonight. So how about we all give you a good laugh by goin' around the circle and sharing our stories from our early days as revivers?"

"Yes. Please." Anything to take all the attention off her.

"I s'pose I'll get the ball rolling. Speaking of expressions, my first year in Eden, I remember someone asking me if I felt under the weather. I got so confused, I looked up at the sky and asked, what for, I'm under the weather just as much as you." He broke into a contagious, rasping laugh and slapped his thigh. All around the circle, a chorus of cackles arose.

*Lean into each other. For every uncertainty, for every doubt, for every unpleasant experience you've acquired in this new life, there are dozens—if not hundreds—of other revivers who have felt the same, thought the same, experienced the same as you. You are not alone.*

*- Elysian Records for the Revivers, Book IV: Acclimation*

# CHAPTER FIFTY

O ne by one, the revivers shared their stories, and Terra was struck by their innocence in those adjustment years. They must have been adorably dorky kids.

One man talked about how in his first year, he tried to give all the kids in his class a hug, and a boy, who was particularly offended by the act, decked him in the mouth. Later, a woman in the group shared how, out of genuine concern, she asked a friend in seventh grade whether her shirt was uncomfortable, because it looked too tight in the stomach. That friend never spoke to her again. That was before she'd understood the Edenites' obsession with body image, of course.

When it came time for Harlan to share, he looked into Terra's eyes and spoke loud enough for the group to hear. "I once saw a woman crying in public and thought I should show I cared by following her around and asking what's wrong. Turns out they don't like that so much. She accused me of stalking her." Everyone chuckled, though only Ezra seemed to catch the reference.

After a few more stories and some *joshing around*, as Grady called it, the group broke into Fran's cake. It was a vanilla cake with orange zest, and to hell with frosting, it was just fine as it was. If there was such a thing as cake in Elysia, Fran had probably smuggled it across the border to bring it here tonight.

Terra swallowed another bite of sugary perfection and asked Harlan, "How'd you guys get all the camping chairs out here?"

The man next to him, who had introduced himself as Wilder, piped up. "If you can carry it, you can jump with it." He had a broad smile worthy of a game show host and hair to match his name. He turned to Harlan. "That reminds me, man. I brought the thing, whenever you're ready for it."

Harlan patted his shoulder. "Later. Thank you."

Terra was about to question him when a man's voice rose behind her.

"A little something for the both of you."

Terra turned to see a couple standing there, the man holding out a bottle of champagne to Harlan.

"Thank you, good sir," Harlan said as he took the bottle and shook the man's hand.

Terra tried not to stare at the real-life reviver couple, but she had so many questions. Was their relationship preordained in Elysia? Did they do all their *reviving* together? Did they still get it on like teenagers? She settled for a safer question. "How long have you two been together?"

"Oh, thirty-seven years now?" The man turned to his wife for confirmation.

"Something like that," the wife said, latching an arm around him. "We met in Eden. Never knew each other in Elysia. Isn't that the darnedest thing?"

"So how'd you find each other?"

"I'm sure Iam had something to do with it," the man said. "She kept showing up wherever I was. I almost thought she was desperate at first." He let out a snicker and leaned into her.

"Hey," Harlan said. "Who brought the cornhole set?" He nodded toward the far end of the outcropping, where a crew of revivers was setting up wooden boards.

Terra and Harlan thanked the couple again and headed off to try a round of the glorified bean bag tossing game. It was pretty much what she'd expected. Just like playing cornhole in Eden, except out in the middle of a desert. After a second round, Terra decided to take a seat and watch the increasingly competitive game from a safe distance. Harlan and three of the other men had taken to flinging the bean bags at each other whenever one of them made a wisecrack.

"Enjoying the show?"

She turned. Ezra had taken a seat next to her.

"My future husband and friends, horsing around like a bunch of juveniles. What's not to love?"

"And how are you feeling about being a reviver?" His blue eyes held hers.

"Well, I—good mostly."

He patted her back. "It's okay if you have doubts."

"It is?"

"We all did in the beginning."

Terra stared at the ground and shrugged. "I don't know what I'm doing. I haven't even *remembered,* or whatever it's called."

"Hey, all that stuff comes with time. You don't have to be an expert. You just have to be available." He handed her a stocky, nondescript book with a black cover.

She read the titled printed in plain text across the spine. "*Elysian Records for the Revivers*?"

"This is what the revivers get when they first cross over. It explains a lot you already know, but you might find some of it helpful."

She flipped through. It looked slightly more readable than her college macroeconomics textbook. "Thanks."

"But you can always come to me if you have questions. We're all here for you, Terra. We're rooting for you."

She studied the sincerity in his eyes. Maybe she had gained a family through this after all. She might never meet Harlan's biological family, but she had the revivers. Overcome by a sudden urge, she leaned forward and hugged him. Then someone yelled *fire in the hole!* as a bean bag came sailing through the air and landed at her feet.

The evening stretched on for another hour or so before the group disbanded and, one by one, used their bracelets to return to their lives in Eden. Amid all the disappearing acts, Wilder made his way over to Harlan and Terra.

"You need me to show you the way?" he asked Harlan.

"Where'd you leave it?"

"On the tallest mesa there." Wilder nodded at the distant formations. "At the top of the canyon."

"I know where to go then," Harlan said.

Terra frowned at him. "What are—"

"Don't worry about it," Harlan said, slipping an arm around her. "You leave the worrying to me."

"You two have fun," said Wilder. "And bring her back in one piece, man, you hear?"

Harlan leaned in for a fist bump. "Of course. Hey, thanks again."

Terra shot Harlan a side eye. "Bring me back in one piece?"

"Oh, he wasn't referring to you." He turned to face her and wrapped both arms around her back.

Before she could ask what the hell *that* meant, they were falling through a tunnel of darkness.

Upon landing, Terra was struck by how strong the wind was. It didn't take long to deduce they were standing at the top of one of the towering, flat mountains she'd seen in the distance. Far below them and miles away, the abandoned embers of the fire pit glowed softly, a speck of red-orange on black canvas.

Harlan tugged at her hand. "Come on. I think it's over here."

"What are we doing?" she asked, certain he still had no intention of telling her.

He twisted his mouth and lowered his dark eyebrows. "Call it a *trust building* exercise."

She matched his expression. "In what way?"

"Well, mostly it will be trust building for *you*. For me, it will be great fun." He tweaked her nose, then ran off ahead before she could bat him away.

"I don't like the sound of that," she called.

"There!" He pointed to a nondescript shape in the dark field ahead of them.

She followed him, stepping over the rocks and brush as she went. He finally slowed enough to let her catch up and wrapped an arm around her shoulders as they walked.

"You see what's out there?"

She eyed the direction he was pointing. The dark shape looked like a small structure jutting out from the ground. "It's too dark."

"No, I mean out there." He pointed past the dark shape and into the horizon.

She searched the inky blackness. "Air?"

"Exactly."

She frowned at him.

"There's a drop-off beyond that slope, and a canyon a few thousand feet below."

"And?"

"We're going to go there...using this." He gestured to the structure, now a few yards away from them.

Terra squinted. It was long and low to the ground, covered with a sort of lustrous fabric in thick strips of black and blue. Its flat top angled to a point and spanned outward from the middle in two oblong triangles stretching some thirty feet across. She walked around to its side for a better angle. Underneath its center was a much smaller geometric skeleton of rods braced together and two small wheels at the bottom. Black straps dangled from the center. Harnesses. For two people.

No. No. Absolutely not.

She stepped back. "Harlan, you're insane."

"I promise you, It's perfectly safe. Now get—"

"Nope." She was dashing in the opposite direction before he could finish.

The sound of his laughter followed her. A second later, she screamed and giggled when his arms wrapped around her waist and pulled her to the ground. She thrashed in his arms as they both rolled to a stop.

"Hey...you're going...to...love it," he shouted between bouts of laughter as he wrestled her into submission. "Hold still."

"You are *not* taking me up in that thing."

He managed to pin her on the ground with two hands on her arms and one shin across her thighs. He looked down at her, beaming triumphantly, and took a minute to catch his breath. "Technically we won't be going *up* so much as *down*."

Terra whimpered underneath him. "Please no."

Harlan leaned in and placed a hand against the side of her face. He held her gaze there until their breathing had slowed. "Trust me."

She envisioned that moment on the bank of the healing pool. His hand stretched out to hers. *Trust me.* She sighed. This wasn't the first time he'd lured her out of her metaphorical hidey-hole where everything was safe and boring. Time to buck up. She wrapped a hand behind his neck, kissed him fiercely, then said, "I really don't like you right now."

"Does that mean you're ready?"

"Yes," she grumbled. She glanced uneasily across the mesa as they stood, wondering where exactly the few thousand feet of canyon began. "How do you know how to fly a hang glider, anyway?"

"I used to fly with my family back in Elysia." Harlan kept a firm grip on her hand as they walked, no doubt wary of a second escape. "We had gliders there too. They looked a little different, of course, but the same concept. Now Wilder lets me borrow his once in a while."

They approached the craft again, and Terra stroked its smooth sail. "Wilder crossed over with this thing?"

"If you can carry it, you can jump with it, remember?"

"And it's sturdy?" She wrapped her fingers around the frame's unnervingly skinny metal rods.

"Of course."

"I really don't want to end up in the healing pool for a third time."

He smirked. "Third time's a charm, right?"

As the tension ratcheted up in the pit of her stomach, she ducked under the sail and allowed him to slip the harness over her torso. After tightening the straps, he showed her where to grip the triangular control bar.

"Go ahead and lift it."

She picked the frame up off the ground. The entire craft felt very light. Light enough to snap in two like a wishbone once airborne. She swallowed hard and watched as Harlan strapped on his own harness. He wrapped one arm behind her jittery shoulders to reach the control bar with both hands. Now they stood side by side, facing the slope.

"Here's the fun part," he said.

"Hmmph?" Terra was too busy quelling the whirlpools of trepidation in her stomach to say anything intelligible.

He leaned into her ear. "We run."

# CHAPTER FIFTY-ONE

Was it possible to die on this side of Elysia?

If you were hurtling through the air, screaming like a lunatic, would a flash mob of cherubs catch you with their dimpled little hands and haul your ass to safety? Or would you simply pancake on the canyon floor while the animals looked on?

These were the questions scrolling through Terra's mind as the desert brush *whapped* against her legs on her race toward the gaping chasm of the night.

Harlan's arm pressed against her shoulders as they ran, reminding her there was no stopping this freight train, whether she dragged her feet or not.

Not that it mattered, because soon enough, the wind swept them into a yawning black hole and her feet lost traction.

At the same time, her stomach nearly lost Fran's cake.

The ground below faded to a blur as the glider peeled off the slope. She tensed at the sudden jolt of updrafts against the glider and squeezed her eyes shut. Harlan's arm moved behind her, adjusting his grip on the control bar and tilting his weight to find their balance in the wild clutches of the wind. Mercifully, the ride smoothed out.

"Look," he said.

"No thanks," she replied, keeping her eyelids firmly in place.

He whispered into her ear. "You're going to miss out if you don't open those beautiful eyes of yours."

"How about you shut that beautiful mouth of yours first?"

When he didn't reply, she took that as her cue to pony up. She forced her eyes open.

They were floating above darkness. But now she could see the walls inside the canyon, just visible in the moonlight. The stone was striated into a rainbow of earth tones. Prickly shrubs clung to every horizontal sliver of dirt along the walls, proving they could grow wherever they damn well pleased. That was some next-level tenacity.

Just when Terra's heart had stopped pounding in her ears, Harlan, with casual ease, tugged the control bar inward until it was under their bodies. To her horror, this action tilted the nose of the glider down and sent them plummeting toward the dark floor of the canyon.

Terra shrieked, then promptly blacked out.

She was floating. In a healing pool? It had to be. She'd just survived a deadly glider crash. She was okay now. Third time's a charm, as Harlan had said. But why was the water blowing through her hair so fast?

Water doesn't blow.

She opened her eyes and almost blacked out a second time. She was dangling from the glider harness like a deflated balloon in a ceiling fan. The canyon floor was rushing by only ten yards beneath. She jerked back into consciousness and seized the glider's bar, aghast that she'd ever let go.

Harlan's voice was in her ear again. "Hey, don't worry. I've got you."

Sure. Just like gravity had her. And she was pretty sure gravity was going to win this one.

She gritted her teeth and watched their surroundings fly by. On this side of the mesa, the dryness of the desert gave way to spring-fed life. Tufts of spindly shrubs were replaced with swathes of grass. A winding stream made its way through the center of the canyon, a sparkly black streak between a patchwork quilt of green.

Harlan pointed toward a mass of dots along the bank ahead. "Water buffalo."

Terra could barely make it out in the faint light, but there they were. An entire herd was resting at the water's edge, looking like black boulders, except with eyes that glistened in the moonlight. They all looked up, twitching their ears and flicking their tails at the odd human torture device passing over their heads.

Harlan tilted the glider and drew close to one of the walls. A strong updraft hit the sail and pushed them upward. When they neared the top of the wall, Harlan began to pull the bar inward again.

Terra clapped her hand over his in a death grip. "Don't you dare."

He eased the bar back out before they could nosedive. "You don't like the drops, huh?"

"What do *you* think?"

"I think that we're going to have to drop back down at some point. Unless you want to end up in the stratosphere."

She loosened her grip on his hand. "Okay. Just...*slowly* this time."

"No problem."

They glided down at a less vertigo-inducing angle and followed the widening river below, soaring past cake-layer walls, waterfalls, and tall pillars of rock, until the chasm opened up into a valley of rolling hills. The glassy surface of the calm waters here reflected the moon and the stars, as if the glider were suspended between two skies. Terra's grip around the bar finally relaxed. It was slick with her sweat.

Harlan wrapped his right arm around her waist and kissed her behind the ear. "Kind of makes it worth all the ups and downs, doesn't it?"

As if on cue, a flock of white geese flew beneath them, casting faint shadows along the river, and Terra realized he was right. This was worth it. For all the scared shitless moments and the passing out, she still wouldn't have wanted to miss this. It made her feel oddly philosophical.

Wasn't that what life itself was? Ups and downs?

Brutal, yes. But something about those downs made it richer. Without fear, without risk, without loss, how else could you appreciate the good? Or feel the thrill of adventure? (And really, how could you know how amazing a rose smells until you've stepped in a giant dog turd?)

As the geese pulled ahead, they filled the night sky with their honking, proving how it was possible for something so lovely to produce such ugly sounds.

Funny how life was a study in contrast, a painting ranging from the darkest of blacks to the brightest of whites. Abuelita had said something about darkness once. About how, one day, the darkness would be a fading memory that would serve to make the light seem that much brighter. Terra hadn't thought much of it at the time, but now it was starting to make sense.

"Your turn." Harlan guided her hands into position on the control bar.

He showed her how to change direction, and how to catch thermal currents like the birds, to keep adrift when they were running out of steam. After the better half of an hour, they glided onto a flat stretch of land next to the river.

Terra's legs were like jelly as they hit the ground, but that was okay with her so long as they were still attached. They spent the rest of the night and into the early morning hours lying in the grass, side by side, staring up at the stars. She couldn't shake that idea of the fading darkness. That it wasn't just that way for the world, but for people too.

Knowing that the light was there inside each heart, waiting to emerge in the final moments, somehow made it easier to accept the darkness, the messiness, the imperfections in people for now. Because it wasn't who they really were. It wasn't forever. As she lay on the ground, hand in Harlan's and heart full, she made her decision.

She would forgive her mother.

*We offer compassion and wisdom to others. But this is a temporary fix, and many Edenites are already accomplishing this task on their own. What we can offer beyond that is this truth: a permanent fix is coming. Traces of it are riding in on the wind. Glimmers of it are flashing in the sea. The silent announcement of its existence stretches across the sky with the rise and fall of the sun. It reminds us to tell them. Tell them all.*

*- Elysian Records for the Revivers, Book V: Our Charge*

# CHAPTER FIFTY-TWO

Terra had to keep reminding herself to slow down.

The Canal Walk stretched out before her like a jet runway, and all she wanted to do was fly. Her legs were primed and pumping like pistons. But she couldn't leave her companion in the dust.

Heavy footsteps plodded behind her. When they began to fade from earshot, she slowed her pace and stepped to the side as a handful of runners passed them from the opposite direction.

The crowds didn't bother her much these days. She'd gotten over the feeling of every stranger's glance in her direction being an affront, every passerby an invasion of personal space. She hadn't taken the time to ascertain why. These things just didn't take up much room in her mind anymore.

Up ahead, the mirrored edifice of the state museum loomed, its multi-pinnacled roof jutting out at odd angles against an overcast sky. Sea-green pedal boats slipped along the canal, their passengers working up a mild sweat under fall jackets. Pristine lawns and shrubs lined the walkway on Terra's right. The dark waters of the canal began abruptly on the left. Little more than common sense guarded against a pedestrian's misguided steps straight into the canal, which left her wondering how many times it had happened before.

The sound of footfalls behind her faded again.

"Hey! Wait up, speed demon," Alexis called out between pants.

Terra transitioned from a lope to a slow jog. "Sorry."

"I remember a time when *I* was the fast one," Alexis muttered. "Now you've got more energy than a seven-year-old on crack."

"Maybe you should take the lead." Terra fell back behind her.

Alexis had given up on asking for the secret formula to her health a while ago, after Terra deflected with a list of random, unpleasant solutions such as coffee enemas and raw sauerkraut. But she still felt guilty. How could she explain? Any talk of Elysia was off the table. That included the healing pools. So what then? Say *God healed me* and leave it at that?

"No, I'd rather take a break. Oh, my savior!" Alexis spied a bench, sat down, and melted onto it like a slice of grilled cheese. "Oh, this feels *so good*. Bench, you are my *favorite* bench." She ran a loving hand along the slatted back support.

Terra watched her with suppressed laughter, then took a seat beside her. "Next time, just tell me when you need a break."

Alexis pulled at her compression garment and rubbed it with furious fingers. "This thing is so damn itchy when I sweat."

"You can't work out without it?"

"I'm not supposed to take it off except to shower. They say the scars won't heal right otherwise."

"Hm." Terra gazed with concern at her friend as she continued to rub the tight fabric. Alexis's other arm was still a splotchy pink from the road rash of three weeks prior. The rash was peeling, little tufts of dead skin decorating the borders.

"Hey." Alexis sprawled across the bench with her legs hanging off the other end and her head on the seat, staring up at the sky. "What do you think about dyeing my compression sleeve to match the color of your bridesmaid dresses? Make it part of the outfit?"

"We can work it in somehow..." Terra twirled a hair around her finger. "What if we got you a fancy—I don't know—sash or something? Wrap it around your arm all the way up?"

"Ooh, I like that. So badass." Alexis held up a thumb and forefinger to the sky and squinted at it, as if pinching a cloud between her fingers. "Like a ninja."

Terra scrunched her face. "Do ninjas wear sashes on their arms?"

"They do if they're sexy Halloween costume ninjas. Ooh. You could make *all* the bridesmaids wear them. You know, solidarity."

"Sure. A whole clan of sexy ninjas."

"We're going to look so good. Let me see that ring again." She snatched Terra's left hand and held it above her face. "*Gorgeous!*" she sang. "My girl's getting married!"

Terra laughed. "Crazy how fast things change."

"Six months ago, you hated him."

"Mind-blowing, right?"

"Yeah." Alexis stretched her mouth into a slow yawn.

"How's the weaning process going?"

"Getting rebound insomnia again. Happens every time we taper the dose. But I guess that's expected."

Terra joined her friend in studying the gray sky. "That sucks. I'm sorry."

"But in other news, those anti-nausea meds are doing their job. Who knew sleeping pill withdrawal could make you feel so sick?"

"You've been handling it like a boss."

"It helps having a friend." Alexis smiled up at her unabashedly. "Thank you for going with me to my appointments. You always know the right questions to ask, and you don't take any bullshit answers either."

"Chalk it up to personal experience, I guess."

The women watched as another pedal boat floated by, its two occupants arguing loudly over who was bearing the brunt of the leg work. A flock of geese flew far above, making their usual honking sounds at a frequency that rivaled a New York block full of cabs. Terra thought about the white geese she'd seen from the hang glider and the often undeniable resemblance between her world and theirs. Lately she was finding it almost easy to forget which world she was in. Almost.

Alexis grew quiet for a while, then craned her neck to look up at Terra. "Hey."

"Yeah?"

"I'm really sorry about all those times in the past...when you were feeling awful, and I kind of blew it off."

Terra looked down at her with a furrowed brow. "That's okay."

"No. I made you go along with things, even when you didn't feel like it. I wasn't very good with the empathy thing back then."

"You didn't make me do anything, Lex. If I hung out with you, it's because I chose to, because you made me forget about the pain."

"Still. Thanks for putting up with me." Alexis extended a fist in Terra's direction. "Put 'er there, partner."

Terra bumped her fist against Alexis's.

Alexis sat up and shook off the cobwebs. "Did I tell you I joined an online burn survivors support group?"

"No. That's *great*."

"They're giving me ideas for things to try for the pain. For better healing. Things my doctor never mentioned." She brought a hand to the side of her mouth and whispered, "And they're all mostly legal."

"Great. I think. Are you still going to sign up for that therapy program at the pain clinic?"

"Worth a shot, I guess."

Terra watched two lone geese flap furiously toward the disappearing flock. Stragglers who'd overslept, she guessed. "Worth a shot."

"Yesterday I finally told Jess I need to back off on some of the workload, just until I can get my head right again."

"How'd she take it?"

Alexis chortled. "I think she was relieved. I've been dropping balls all over the place lately. She knows it's the drugs though." She scrunched her legs onto the bench and rested her chin on her knees. "You know, I keep thinking I can do this on my own. Eventually, I mean. Once I'm feeling better."

Terra, having been lost in the study of her engagement ring, looked up. "Do what?"

"Editing. Freelance."

"Oh, Lex. You could totally do it."

"Hmm..." Alexis nodded thoughtfully, as if Terra herself had made the suggestion. "I could, couldn't I? And you'd be promoted pretty much by default."

"Maybe."

"Are you kidding me? If I were to leave, there'd be nothing stopping you. You'd be Jess's righthand woman. I thought that's what you were hoping for."

She *had* been, not too long ago. Things had changed though. That burning ache she used to feel inside every time she thought about the progress of her career—or lack thereof—had subsided, like water poured over hot coals. "It'll happen when it happens."

Alexis looked at her sideways. "I've never known you to not have a plan."

"Oh, there's a plan in place. I just don't know what it is yet. And I'm okay with that for now."

Alexis stayed quiet, her brows drawing together.

"What is it?" Terra asked.

"This is going to sound weird."

"I promise not to laugh. At least not to your face."

"So...do you think that maybe there's already a plan for each of our lives? One that's set in motion from the day we're born? And all the crap we have to wade through..." She waved a hand around as if gesturing to steaming piles of said crap. "It's all going to somehow make sense in the end?"

Terra looked up at the sky. "Yes."

"It's so bizarre. I had this dream a while back, when the pill addiction was getting really bad. You were with me. And something scary happened. Like we fell out of an airplane or something. But then we were fine. All I know is we had to keep going, wherever the hell we were going. Then I heard someone telling me that what I was going through was the most important thing in my life. Soon it would be over, and when it was, I'd be better than new."

Terra's eyes widened. Alexis remembered more from their little Elysian trip than she'd thought.

"I think this is it, Terra. Maybe this whole surviving-the-fire thing is the best thing that's ever happened to me. Does that make any sense, or am I just crazy?"

Terra squinted in deliberation, then cocked a half smile in her direction.

"Both of those, but you've always been crazy."

"You know me well."

"But I don't think it's going to be like this forever."

"Like what?"

"This." She gestured to Alexis's arm and then to the imaginary steaming piles surrounding them. "All this. You know. The crap of life. I think there's...a perfect *good* that got lost somewhere along the way, and God is planning to bring it back.

Alexis cocked an eyebrow in amusement. "God?"

"Yes."

She shifted in her seat and studied Terra. "Since when are you all buddy buddy with God?"

"A lot has happened in the past few months."

"Oh?" Alexis's inquisitive eyes pierced her own.

Where to start? There were still some things that could be said, right? She didn't have to mention Elysia at all. Flashes of her dream in the desert played in her mind.

*Start there,* an insistent thought told her.

So she did.

*Like humans, they are bound by their geography, only capable of presence in one place at a time. For this reason, the majority of them choose to work a small territory, often inflicting generations of people within the same town or even family before boredom or competition urges them on to a different location.*

*- Elysian Records for the Revivers, Book III: The Subversives*

# CHAPTER FIFTY-THREE

Terra lifted her steaming mug of coffee to eye level and scowled at the writing on the side, which told her to *Talk to the Hand* in faded purple letters.

"Mom, how *old* is this mug?"

"What's that, hon?" Leta asked over the clatter of dishes and silverware she was rinsing in the sink.

Terra halted mid-sip and called out, "Never mind," making a mental note to herself to shop new mugs for her mom's upcoming birthday. "Can I help?"

"Nah. Almost done."

The smell of Leta's cinnamon *crema de maiz*, bacon, and potatoes lingered in the air. By the time she'd heard the news about her daughter's engagement, she was already reaching for her griddle. What better way to celebrate than with some girl talk over a plate of hash (browns, that is)?

It had been the better part of a year since Terra had set foot in her mom's house. She'd forgiven Leta in her heart. Not out loud just yet, because blaming someone for years of childhood distress is not the sort of thing you bring up on the fly, but she'd started by calling to apologize about her outburst in the restaurant. Leta had apologized too. Then Terra had told her about the proposal. Now here she was, drinking coffee in her mom's breakfast nook, like they were a couple of gal pals from way-back-when.

Leta threw the last of the mess in the dishwasher and bumped the door closed with her hip. She stepped around the kitchen counter carrying her own vintage mug, a picture of Joey Tribbiani from *Friends* smiling and winking. A caption at the bottom read *How YOU doin'?* Leta leaned against the edge of the counter and sipped her coffee, then hissed as it burned her tongue. "Always hotter than I expect." She smiled warmly, then gestured to Terra's coffee. "How you like it?"

*About the same as any other coffee,* Terra thought. But she grinned. "It's good," she said, then took another sip as evidence. This was Leta's way of seeking approval. The brunch and coffee, the tidy house. Like she was saying, *See? I've got my life together now.*

Terra had to hand it to her, she really *did* have it together. The house itself was modest in size, but newer and nicer looking than the rental they'd lived in back in Terra's teens. This place was Leta's first stab at a mortgage. A very adult thing to do. And who knew? Maybe by next month, she'd be writing her congressman, or yelling at kids to keep off her grass.

"I was thinking," Leta said, "maybe we can have Harlan and Jeremy join us for brunch next time."

"Of course."

She stared at her daughter until her smile faded a little. "Hey, how about we go sit in the living room? I need to talk to you about something."

"Sure," Terra responded, though a wisp of anxiety flitted through her stomach.

"It's about your Aunt Yanira."

The women sat catty-corner from each other in the small living room. The air felt very still in here, like an unvisited corner of a decrepit library. Terra crossed her legs, then uncrossed them, unable to find a comfortable position. Usually, she would make up some excuse about getting home right after the meal. She glanced over at Leta, who was playing obsessively with a ring on her finger.

Finally, Leta cleared her throat and spoke. "You know I've told you before...about when I found out I was pregnant."

Terra put down her coffee. "Yeah?"

"I was so scared."

"I know. But you decided to keep me."

"But I never told you, Terra, maybe out of embarrassment or because it was too painful to admit." She lowered her eyes back to the ring. "It was Yanira who talked me into it."

Terra blinked.

"One day, I confided in her that..." Leta brought her hand to her mouth and winced. When the seizure of emotion passed, she continued. "I was going to visit the women's clinic for...you know. Yanira sat me down and asked me to think about it. Not about how I felt at that moment, but how I would feel looking back at myself in twenty years. What would I have wanted for myself...and for you?"

Terra swallowed the rising lump in her throat. Their conversations usually waded in the shallows, where deep emotions had no place, but her mom had decided to go scuba diving.

"She was right," Leta said. "Of course, that was back when she had her mind still. When she could think clearly. She promised me she would help raise you, and Abuelita would too, and it would all be okay. She changed my mind." Leta looked away as she swiped at her cheek with the side of her hand. "I'm sorry I never told you all that."

Terra dug her fingernail into a chip in her coffee mug and drew a ragged breath. When she finally summoned the composure to look up, she saw Leta was still facing away and sniffling quietly. "Mom, it's okay."

"Such a shameful thing."

"Hey." Terra reached out a tentative hand to her arm, unsure of how to touch her but knowing it was what she needed. Then she pulled her into a hug that was both awkward and sincere. "I forgive you. I forgive you for everything."

Finally, she'd had the chance to say it. And mean it. No need to rehash what all was encompassed in that word *everything*. For now, this was enough.

It took a moment for Leta to respond. When she did, it was with a shaky voice, barely above a whisper. "Thank you."

Without another word, Leta patted her daughter on the back, then stood from her chair. She crossed the room and opened the mahogany cabinet—an old musty thing she'd nabbed from Huelo and Abuelita's house before the estate sale—and shoved aside the piles of timeworn magazines, yearbooks, and photo albums within. Far in the back, behind a tray of dusty, half-burned candles, was a small cardboard box. She slid the artifact out with great reverence and placed it on the coffee table before Terra like a peace offering. "I thought you might like to see these."

Terra peered into the box. A disheveled stack of old three-by-five prints lay inside. A glance at the top photo made her heart tense painfully in her chest. It was Aunt Yanira, younger than Terra remembered, maybe early twenties. She wore a yellow tank top and ripped denim shorts, one hand propped on her hip, and a smile with enough sass to confirm her inheritance of the Burgos family genes. She stood in front of Abuelita's flower bed, a Pabst Blue Ribbon in her other hand, a burgundy ring of lipstick on the rim of the can to match the burgundy color of her lips.

Terra picked up the photo and peeked at the one beneath it. This was more recent. Terra's three-year-old self stood in the foreground, a rainbow necklace draped across her like a sash and a stuffed animal of unidentifiable species tucked under her arm (she'd always ran her stuffies ragged.) Yanira sat behind her, chin resting on her head, arms wrapped around her chest. They were both laughing. The quality was dim and fuzzy, but the emotion it transmitted was powerful.

"They're all of her," Leta said. "I kept thinking I would make a scrapbook someday, but then..." She lifted one of the photos out of the box and studied it before setting it back down. "Life got in the way."

Terra took in the sight of her aunt in a royal blue satin prom dress. "I've never seen these. I hardly remember seeing any photos of her."

"Well," Leta said with a sigh, "here they all are. It was my fault for hiding them away like that. It's just that every time I'd go to take them out of the cabinet, I'd feel like I was grieving all over again. It got to be too much."

Terra ran her finger over a photo of Yanira standing in the kitchen with Abuelita, tostones frying on the stove behind them. "So what changed?"

"You got me thinking about her again. I had to admit to myself that, while I had worked so hard to improve every other part of my life, this one thing had stayed the same. It was eating me up inside and I had to find a way to make my peace with it. Abuelita always told me I'd have to walk through the fire before I could escape it."

"What does that mean?"

"It means I need to talk about it. And dammit, Terra, I don't want to." Leta paused and heaved another sigh. "But last night while I was lying awake in bed, something told me I need to talk to you about her. Like a voice in my head. I don't know. Maybe I'm making all this up. I just feel like it's what we both need."

Terra nodded as she pored over the photos, taking each one in with the same fixation as a teenage boy inhaling a bag of Cheetos.

"Before Yanira passed away, there were...red flags."

Terra dropped the photos back into the box and looked up at her mother.

"For the last couple months, she began to lose her mind."

"How?"

"At first it was subtle. She got paranoid about the strangest things. Avoided going to certain places she used to love going to. She didn't like being left alone. That's why she ended up staying with us. Do you remember that?"

"I think so. I remember her sleeping in your bed."

"Yes. She couldn't even fall asleep until I was in the room with her. Then her behavior got stranger. She was jumpy all time. Panicky. She couldn't focus on anything. Ended up getting asked to leave her job at the hospital because she was making mistakes with the patients' records. It's like her mind was crumbling. Abuelita and I took her to see doctors, psychiatrists, but nothing helped."

"So, how did she—"

Leta placed her hand on Terra's. Her other hand covered her own eyes as she struggled for the words. "It was suicide, honey. Completely senseless, but the investigators couldn't come up with any other explanation. I found her in my bathtub with a belly full of vodka and codeine."

Terra choked back the tears. Her mother's face echoed the pain in her own. "That doesn't sound like her at all."

"No. It doesn't. But she was very sick." Leta batted at the hair that stuck to her damp face and reached for the tissue box on the end table.

"I'm sorry I hid it from you all these years, but I didn't want you to grow up wondering how someone in our family could be capable of something like that...and wondering if you might be capable of the same. Besides, how was I supposed to explain all this to my little girl? How could I help you through it when I couldn't even handle it myself?"

"Maybe we were meant to help each other through it."

"Oh honey, I couldn't do that to you. You were so young."

"I know," Terra said, and returned her gaze to the photos in the box. She pulled another one from the stack. Yanira was posing with her hand held out to block the camera's shot and giving the photographer the stink-eye, but there was laughter on her lips. "It's just so strange. I remember her being fearless. She didn't answer to anyone."

Leta nodded. "My sister, the rebel."

"So what could make her so scared like that?"

"All I know is she would wake up screaming at night."

A sudden queasiness came over Terra. "Nightmares?"

"Yes. I couldn't get her to talk about them, except to say that something was always coming after her in her dreams. Like a predator." Leta shuddered. "Gives me the heebie jeebies."

Terra gripped the arms of her chair and felt her coffee rise to the back of her throat. She closed her eyes until the convulsion passed.

"I sometimes wonder if part of her brain just..." Leta shook her head and frowned. "Went bad. An infection or something."

No. It wasn't an infection. Terra's skin crawled with pinpricks.

"Are you okay?"

Terra realized she was hyperventilating. She forced her breathing to slow. "I don't feel well."

Leta leaned forward, worry written all over her face. "Can I get you something?"

"No." Terra stood. "No, I think I need to go home."

"Well, wait a minute. Are you sure you're well enough to drive? Why don't you lay down first? Is it a stomach bug?"

With each question, Terra's blood pressure ratcheted upward. "No. I just want to go home."

Hurt rippled across her mom's features. But she couldn't tell her mom about this. Not about Hulum. Now she knew why Yanira had kept quiet about it too. No amount of psychiatric therapy could exorcise a demon. And no one wanted to end up in the looney bin.

"What's gotten into you?" Leta laid a hand on Terra's shoulder as she edged her way out of the living room. "Was it something I said about Yanira? Oh God, I shouldn't have told you."

Terra shrugged off her hand and bolted for the door. "No, Mom. I just can't talk about this right now. I'm sorry," she called over her shoulder as she charged out onto the front stoop, hands clenched.

The sick son of a bitch. It wasn't enough to mess with one person in her family. He'd been around long before Terra was even aware of his existence. Silently waiting. Stalking her aunt first, then her. And how many more before Yanira? How many had he ruined—or killed? Her coffee threatened to make its way out again, forcing her to take deep breaths to curb the sensation in her throat.

As she started the car, her vision began to blur. She wiped the tears away and risked one last glance at the house. Leta stood motionless in the doorway, eyes hollow with regret.

Terra would call her later to reassure her. Tomorrow. When she was calm. When this overwhelming panic had subsided.

Five minutes out of Leta's neighborhood, Terra's hands were shaking too much to control the wheel any longer. She pulled onto the shoulder, buried her mouth in the thick folds of her sweater, and screamed.

# Chapter Fifty-Four

Terra gazed out her bedroom window. The sky was a dark gray, dark as her mood. Harlan had done everything he could to lift her spirits. But there was a grieving process, and it would take time. No way around that.

Yesterday Aunt Yanira had been resurrected, only to die a second time. Terra's childhood memory of Yanira's demise had been a censored, blurry, black and white photograph. But this—knowing what she knew now—*this* was a full-color, feature-length horror film come to life. It was inescapable.

A solitary bird flitted past her window, unfazed by the threatening sky. She wondered what it saw in Indiana this time of year. *Fly south, you stupid bird. There's nothing here for you.* The bird whirled around and lighted on a branch near her window, defying her with its chirpy little twitters.

Terra's phone rang. She cringed at the caller ID. She'd put off calling too long. It was time to talk.

"Mom," she answered the phone with a heavy sigh. "I'm so sorry."

"Uh, Terra?" The voice on the other end was not Leta's but a man's.

"Who is this?"

"Jeremy."

"Oh. Hi—"

"You need to come over to your mom's house immediately." His voice was flat and urgent.

"Why? Where is she?"

"She's right here. She's threatening to kill herself if you aren't here within half an hour."

"What?" Icicles stabbed the back of her neck. "Let me talk to her."

"She has a knife, Terra." His voice caught in his throat. "She's already cut herself once...when I tried to call the emergency line. All she wants is to see you, she says."

"Oh God." Terra thought of the look on Leta's face as she'd left yesterday. A pang of guilt ripped through her chest. "She's not drinking, is she?"

"No. Please tell me you're on your way."

"Grabbing my keys now. Tell her to go lay down and take deep breaths until I get there." It was her best attempt at calm authority. Truth be told, she had no idea what she was doing.

She wished she could use her bracelet to get there this instant, or have Harlan take her there since she didn't know how to jump with any accuracy yet. But her mom knew the drive there took nearly twenty minutes. No sense in freaking her out worse with a sudden magical appearance. She groaned. Having a superpower you couldn't use for a moment when you most needed it was about as disappointing as a wine glass full of grape juice.

She threw herself into her car and revved the engine, then hesitated. No way in hell could she do this alone. This was too big. She pulled out her cell and called Harlan.

"Can you meet me somewhere in twenty minutes?"

Terra pulled up to the little two-bedroom bungalow in sixteen minutes flat. She was pretty sure she'd run a red light or five on the way, but she could brush up on her driving record later. Jeremy's car was in the driveway, but otherwise, everything looked as it should. Cheery chrysanthemums in red and orange framed the front walkway. A Welcome sign hung on the periwinkle blue door in a grandiose, handwritten font. Robins chirped from the nearby trees, in blissful disregard to the dark event unfolding inside.

She stepped onto the porch and reached for the doorbell. Jeremy opened the door before her finger made contact.

"Thanks for coming." He stepped aside to let her through. Everything about him looked wrong, his face worn and gray. No trace of the idealist left.

"What happened? Where is she?" Terra brushed past him, peeking into the living room.

"She's in the bedroom. We were supposed to go out for lunch today, so I came by to pick her up," he said as he followed Terra down the hall. "She wanted nothing to do with me. She started crying—was hysterical—started asking for you. That's when she grabbed the knife."

"Holy crow."

"I know. I've never seen her like this before. Have you?"

"Never suicidal," she whispered, careful that her voice didn't carry as she approached the bedroom. She stopped at the doorway.

Leta sat serenely at the edge of the bed, arms resting by her sides. Her fingers were wrapped around the handle of a seven-inch chef's knife. A dark crimson line of dried blood was visible on the underside of her opposite forearm, three drips streaking toward her wrist. Terra felt a shock of pain in her own arm at the sight of it.

When Leta saw her, she smiled a triumphant smile, as if this had all been a silly game and she was winning. "There's my darling daughter."

"Mom, what is this all about? Talk to me." Terra kept her eyes downcast. Trying to look directly at her mother in her current state made her sick to her stomach.

"Terra?" Harlan's voice carried down the hall from the entryway.

Leta's smile dropped. "Why is *he* here?"

"He's here to help. He cares about you too."

"I didn't ask for him. I asked for *you*." She drew up her legs and pulled herself farther back on the bed. Reflected light from the knife bounced around on the ceiling as the bed shook under her shifting weight.

Terra scowled. Leta had always been a private person. Summoning Harlan must have felt like an assault on her dignity. But really, she'd lost her right to have a say in the matter the second she'd started playing with knives.

Leta's eyes snapped to Jeremy, who stood behind Terra. "I'd like to speak with my daughter. *Alone.*"

Without a word, Jeremy retreated down the hallway, halting Harlan at the halfway point with a somber shake of the head. After a wary glance toward the bedroom, the men headed into the living room.

"Ah." Leta's features relaxed. "That's better."

"Mom, you hurt yourself."

She regarded the cut with indifference, as if to say *this old thing?* and looked back to Terra. "It's nothing."

"No, this is serious. We need to get you help."

"No. This is between you and me and no one else."

"Look, I'm really sorry about storming out of here yesterday."

"Come talk to me." Leta patted the bed next to her.

Terra eyed the knife warily. "Not until you put that thing down."

"I'll put it down when I'm damn well ready." Her smile was congenial, but her tone burned like acid.

Terra shifted uncomfortably at the door. Issuing an ultimatum wasn't the wisest thing when her mom was already contemplating death, but she didn't like the idea of being manipulated either. She decided to speak her apologies from the doorway instead.

"Mom, I know you're regretting telling me about Yanira, and after the way I reacted, I don't blame you. But I'm glad you told me the truth. I needed to know, as much as it hurt."

"Yanira..." Leta said in a dream-like voice. Then she let out a *hmm* that was somewhere between a laugh and a sigh. "I miss her. But anyway, it's not important now."

"Still, I shouldn't have shut you out like that. We should be able to talk openly with each other. No more avoidance, you know?"

"I agree completely." She offered another reassuring smile. "Now..." Her face turned stern. "If there's something you're not telling me..."

Terra flinched. "Nothing that can't wait."

"Terra, I'm not playing games with you. Spit it out."

"This is not a good time, with you the way you are right—"

"Now is the *perfect* time. Why do you think I've taken a knife to my flesh? It's because my daughter is hiding things from me, and I can sense it."

Guilt. All-consuming guilt raged inside her. She'd have to come clean. "I, um..." Terra fidgeted with the hem of her sleeve. "I think I might know why Aunt Yanira lost her mind."

"Go on."

"A few months ago," she started uneasily, "I began having nightmares just like her, where I was being chased."

"Really?"

This was all wrong. This is not how she wanted the truth to come out. But here it came anyway. "And...I don't know how to explain it to you, but I'm sure it was a demon. A demon was causing the nightmares. I think it might have been the same one that was getting in Yanira's head too."

As Terra spoke, Leta's face gradually shifted from ease to alarm. By the end, she'd covered her mouth with her free hand and was rising slowly from the bed.

"I know that sounds crazy—"

"Oh, Terra. That must have been awful for you."

"Wait. You believe me?"

"Of course." Leta stepped toward her. It made Terra unsettled. Something about the way she continued to clutch the knife at her side like a security blanket. The other hand she kept clapped firmly over her mouth. Behind her hand, her cheeks drew upward, and her eyes crinkled. Her shoulders began to shake. She must have been horrified to the point of tears, and Terra couldn't blame her.

"Mom, are you okay?"

Leta continued in her spasms until she was making muffled hiccoughing sounds beneath her hand. Finally, she removed it, revealing a gaping smile and an eruption of laughter. Not her usual laughter, but something deeper, breathier.

"Mom. Why are you laughing?"

Between gasps for air, Leta replied, "I can't do this any longer."

"What?"

She settled down enough to speak after several breaths. "Now it's my turn to make a confession." She leaned in close, her breath cold against Terra's ear.

"I am Hulum."

*Do not live in fear. Everything here is fleeting, and the end is worth it all.*

*- Elysian Records for the Revivers, Book IV: Acclimation*

# Chapter Fifty-Five

The words hit her like shards of ice, and, for a moment, they froze her in place. Probably not the best reaction when danger was literally breathing down her neck. Terra turned her face to her mother's. A malevolent grin stretched across Leta's lips.

Hulum. In host form. Again.

Terra shrieked and pushed herself off the doorframe, stumbling backward in a frantic bid for escape. She wheeled around and tore down the hallway toward Harlan. Safety. They could jump to Elysia. Take Jeremy with them if they had to. He'd be super confused afterward, but at least he wouldn't be dead.

The two men watched from the edge of the kitchen, eyes wide, as she hurled through the living room and flung herself into Harlan's arms.

He looked down at her with alarm. "What?"

"Hulum."

As if on cue, Hulum-Leta swaggered into the living room and leered at them.

"What's going on?" Jeremy asked.

Hulum ignored him. "Think, Terra, before you do something rash."

Terra turned to face the subversive. Harlan stepped in front of her.

"You can save yourselves…" Hulum drew the chef's knife up to Leta's neck and pressed firmly at the jugular. "But then what would happen to Mom?"

"Leta, no!" Jeremy pushed past the other two and charged toward her.

Hulum stopped him by extending the point of the knife in his direction. "Look, jackass."

Jeremy halted in surprise.

"I don't know you," Hulum continued, "and this has nothing to do with you, but you're really starting to get in the way." He flicked the knife blade toward the kitchen. "Get back where you were before I have a reason to kill you too."

"She's right," Harlan called to him. "You can't help."

Jeremy looked at him in confusion.

"She's possessed," Terra said, then added, "by a demon," just in case it wasn't clear this was a bad thing.

Jeremy turned back to Leta, who grinned at him viciously, teeth bared. He backed away slowly.

"Now this is how it's gonna go down," Hulum announced. "Terra's coming with me. You two clowns are staying here."

"Where are you going?" Harlan asked.

"None of your damn business, Elysian. But I can guarantee you she won't be coming back." Hulum fixed Leta's eyes on Terra's. "We have a little debt to settle."

Harlan gripped Terra's hand behind him. "You know we won't let that happen."

"What choice do you have? Look at me!" He brought the knife back to Leta's neck. "If you follow us, the mom dies. If the police show up, the mom dies. If Terra tries to escape, the mom dies. You see a pattern here?"

"And how would killing Leta benefit you?"

Hulum shrugged. "If you force my hand, I'll just move on to the next host. I'm getting pretty good at it, you know."

Terra glared at the unsettling form of her mother. "Why *her*?"

Leta's lips grinned. "The weak-minded ones are the easiest."

Terra's vision went red. She had some choice words for this dipstick but couldn't seem to get them out with her mother right there in front of her. It was the ultimate paradox.

"Face it." He raised Leta's voice. "Your mother is a pathetic bore. There's a reason I moved on to other families after Yanira all those years ago."

"You killed my aunt," she spat.

"She killed herself," he said with a smirk.

Terra pushed past Harlan with the full intent of strangling the bastard.

"Go ahead." Hulum started into his deep-throated laughter again. "Kill me."

She stopped halfway between the men and Hulum, mind racing. She needed a better game plan. He would never give her up. He was a dog with its chew toy, not content to drop it until it had been ripped to shreds. And—oh God—she was that chew toy, caught in an endless loop of capture-rescue-repeat. This had to end today.

"Terra, what are you doing?" Harlan's panicked voice was behind her.

"I'm thinking."

She could try to wrestle the knife out of Leta's hand. Risky. And then what? Hulum could disappear, only to reappear and pull the same trick at a later date.

She could reason with him. Tell him she didn't break any rule after all. Talk him into letting her live. Hilarious.

She could find a way to end it herself. Maybe that was the only way. With her dead, Hulum would have no reason to kill or manipulate the people in her life any further. But would her mom and Harlan be okay with that choice? Hell, was *she* okay with that choice?

No. No. No.

Hulum feigned a yawn. "I can do this all day, Terra, but I'll admit it's getting a tad monotonous."

Terra's eyes flicked around the room, searching for solutions. As if she would find another rock to throw at him or something, not that *that* had ever panned out.

It was Iam's plan that had saved her the first time. Well, an angel anyway. As much as she enjoyed getting blasted off her feet, she was still working through a bit of post-angelic PTSD. But what then? Did Iam have a plan now?

That's when it hit her. Of *course* he had a plan. She chose to believe it. She chose to trust that somehow this would not end the way it appeared it would, with evil ripping through her world and leaving a meaningless void in its wake.

With that thought, time began to slow, like a music box lazily plunking out its last notes as its gears wind to a stop. Slow...slower...until all became motionless. A hazy light penetrated everything in the room, making it glow softly. And Terra's mind began to float.

The image of her mother before her remained static in this viscous suspension of time, a flash of light from the knife's blade reflected across her face. Terra loved this woman so much; she felt it like a beam of warmth radiating from her chest. Slowly, like moving underwater, Terra looked over her shoulder. Harlan and Jeremy stood frozen in the doorway, shock held captive in their faces. Although she would never know every expression and quirk and mannerism of Jeremy's as well as she knew Harlan's, there was a warmth rising inside her for both of them too.

She felt an avalanche of compassion for all three of them. Forget Hulum and his sinister schemes. It was this fraught little group of human beings that mattered. She wanted desperately to reach out to them and tell them it was okay, that they didn't have to feel anxious or guilty for the circumstances unfolding before them. But she couldn't, because soon, they faded from her vision.

Her mother's living room was gone.

In its place was a forest of ferns and moss, with trees that stretched high above, a dappled canopy in a world of green. She stood on a worn dirt path that ran along a stream. Birdsong, foreign and familiar at the same time, echoed above. The rich scent of black soil filled her nose. Somehow, she knew this place. She stood there for a moment trying to sort it out, feeling a bit senile.

She had been here. She'd walked these paths. Next to someone. Someone who'd loved her with the same urgency that had just seized her back in Leta's home. Someone whose presence had been so comforting, she'd once doubted the very existence of evil. Their love had been so perfect, it had freed her to love herself completely. But she'd lost it.

How do you lose something that precious?

Terra lowered her eyes to her bare feet, the soft mud molding around the edges of her toes like playdough. Then something touched her hand and wrapped around her fingers. Its grip was strong and warm. His hand.

She raised her eyes. He was standing at her side now. The same person she'd met in the desert. His face was no longer covered by a desert scarf, and she could see it clearly, broad and smiling.

He squeezed her hand and laughed. "You remember."

It was a hazy memory. Not even that. It was a vision as familiar as a recurring dream. She knew where she was now, and who he was. Better yet, she knew who *she* was. Garden. Creator. Creation.

You can't miss something you've never had. But she'd been missing this as long as she'd been alive. This reality that was meant to be, but never became. As she studied his eyes—they were fierce but kind—her hopes for what could one day be surged. Sure as the ocean is wet, that light would win out over the darkness in time.

Overcome, she fell forward and hugged him, no holds barred, like her arms had an expiration and she'd better use them all up now. "Iam," she whispered into his shoulder. The folds of fabric in his shirt pressed creases into her cheek as he returned the hug.

She was sure of it now. This was not just an elusive past. It was a certain future. It was not just hers, but everyone's. In his arms, Terra tapped into a connection with every other being in creation—the fortunate and the unfortunate, the strong and the weak, the lovable and the not-so-much—all hanging onto him desperately, waiting for eternity to intersect with the present. She loved them all as if they were an extension of her own heart.

She rested in this moment for what might have been a century, or maybe only a second. Then he bent his head down to her ear.

"Embrace her," he said.

Before the words could sink in, the images around her began to fade. The green of the forest was replaced with the dull grays and whites of her mother's living room, and the sounds of the stream and animals were stifled by the dead silence of suspense. Her awareness returned to the demon-possessed woman standing before her. With a twinge of melancholy, Terra realized her moment with Iam had passed.

But she had *remembered*.

*From his perspective, everything that will ever happen already has. It is laid out before us now like a long and winding path home. All we have to do is follow it, having confidence in where it leads.*

*- Elysian Records for the Revivers, Book V: Our Charge*

# CHAPTER FIFTY-SIX

"**S**top stalling." Leta's voice bludgeoned the silence like a dull knife. "Time to make a decision, Terra. Shall we get this over with today, or does someone get to die for your sake?" Hulum eyed the men at the doorway. "Any takers?"

Terra's momentary euphoria gave way to the heavy weight of crisis as time began plodding forward again. She felt the ache of it in her chest, but she breathed it out and let it fall to the floor. Even if she had to go as a lamb to slaughter to save the people she loved, she knew this couldn't be a defeat, as senseless as that logic seemed, because death was not forever.

*Embrace her.*

His words had confused her in the garden, but now the meaning seized her mind the way roots stake their claim in the soil. There was no avoiding it.

Tears welled at the base of Terra's eyes. She coaxed them out, letting them multiply and flow until her face was tingling with wetness. Hulum would think they were tears of defeat. She'd let the bastard think he'd won. But these were tears of relief.

"Just let me hug her one last time." Her arms shook as she held them out. Iam had given her a solution, but he hadn't promised it was easy.

Hulum sneered through Leta's lips. "That's it, Terra. Accept your fate. Wallow in it. Human willpower is so..." He leaned in and breathed her scent. "Malleable."

Terra resisted the urge to flinch.

Hulum called to the men in the doorway. "Take a look, boys. This is how the soul dies," he hissed, "grasping for something that no longer exists, reaching for pretend comforts, sniveling and feckless."

Terra had to stop herself from glaring. *Karma is a big, hairy bitch, shadow man.*

"Just one hug," she pleaded. She drew close enough to feel the icy chill emanating from Leta's body.

Hulum jerked Leta's head back in disgust and tightened her grip on the knife. "You can't be serious. Do you even hear yourself, Terra?"

Now Harlan and Jeremy were watching Terra with the same incredulous expression, as if to shrug back at the demon like *we don't get it either.* The ruse would be up soon.

Energy pulsed through her legs like a fully charged defibrillator. Now or never. She lunged forward and threw her arms around her mother's torso.

Leta's body tensed. "What the— Get off!"

Terra's fingers floundered behind her mother's back and pushed back the cuff of her sleeve, locating the delicate twists of cords underneath. Leta's free hand was already clawing at her shoulder when Terra's index finger found the amber stone.

She held her breath and pushed.

Falling through the soundless black had long since lost its sting to Terra. It was simply a mode of transportation, no more daunting than a 747 to a flight attendant. But this jump was another story, thanks to the uncertainty of what awaited her on the other end. Not to mention, most flight attendants don't have to carry a wildly thrashing passenger in their arms.

The second she'd pressed the amber stone, Hulum knew. His cry of alarm, a throaty, wholly inhuman cry, had echoed behind them as the dark vortex swallowed them whole. She wasn't sure exactly where the barrier lay, or whether they had crossed it yet. Nor was she sure whether there was still time for Hulum to slip out of Leta's body and scramble back to the safety of Eden. She could only trust that Iam's plan would work.

But Hulum still held the knife.

Just as the thought crossed her mind, a searing pain ripped through her trapezius. Terra belted out a muted scream. The backstabbing, mother-stealing psychopath was trying to break free. Lucky for Terra, Hulum had chosen his host poorly. Leta was a petite woman who loathed exercise, and Terra had no intent of letting go.

Hulum pulled the knife free from her back and took a second stab to the scapula. The white-hot feeling of metal bouncing off of bone made Terra woozy. Her head lolled toward Leta's shoulder. Still, she held on. If her finger slipped from the stone before fully crossing over, they would immediately return to Eden. Then there would be no second chances. And definitely no more hugging.

Undeterred by the second stab, Hulum came in for a third, much deeper puncture between her ribs, and Terra nearly lost her grip. Her body convulsed from the pain. Damn it all, she would die here in this inky black between two worlds if that's what it took. She closed her eyes and pressed her head against her mother's writhing neck. She felt the unwelcomeness in this action, Hulum still pulling away with all of Leta's strength. She felt the hostility, the resentment, then...nothing. Leta's frame collapsed in Terra's arms.

Terra opened her eyes to the sensation of ground under her feet. The Elysian sun shone through a throng of racing clouds, flickering on her face and lighting up the surrounding fields as if the grass were a bubbling river. She laughed breathlessly, to the protest of the bleeding wounds in her back.

Terra pulled back to see Leta's face. Her eyes were closed, her body limp. Hulum was gone. Ezra's comment about subversives crossing the barrier had been true: destroyed on impact. Like a spider in a vacuum cleaner. She lowered Leta carefully to the ground, yelping in pain with each movement of her torso, then lay on her side next to her unconscious mother.

"We did it, Mom," she whispered. "It's over."

Terra began to laugh again, though it became apparent to her ears that it sounded more like sobs than anything joyful. Warm fluid ran down her back, and she began to wonder which way she would need to crawl to reach the nearest healing pool. And why did Elysia have to be so freaking huge?

But her mother's peaceful face was there in front of her, a testament to the feat Terra had accomplished. She had slayed a card-carrying, in-the-flesh subversive. She wanted to lay here a while longer and revel in this moment. And she was kind of tired.

That was probably from the blood loss. And who knew movement could feel so impossible? She kept her eyes focused on Leta's face. It anchored her in the moment and pushed the pain to a far corner of her mind where it could be contained.

Here they were: mother and daughter. Forgiveness heals all. Like a Hallmark moment, but bloodier.

Reflecting on this, she began to sink into oblivion. Meanwhile, the blurry image of Harlan emerged from the background and raced toward her.

She caught a fleeting thought as her vision went dark.

*Third time's a charm, right?*

# WINTER

## (ALMOST)

Terra had zero interest in exploring the upper trail of the falls today. The view from below was nice enough. Yes, she had flown suspended in a hang-glider from heights thousands of feet higher than this cliff, but she wasn't in the mood for all that being brave business today.

Harlan had stayed back in Indy so he could supervise at the clinic but encouraged her to go ahead. It was her day off; they could manage at the clinic without her. She'd brought her car down because she hadn't yet mastered the art of long-distance jumping. (Harlan still teased her about the time she'd tried to bring them both on a day trip to the Dunes and ended up somewhere in the grasslands of Minnesota instead.) She didn't mind the drive. Good to stay rooted in this world anyway.

Hemlock Cliffs had a silence about it this morning, like it was lying in wait for the coming winter. The leaves beneath her feet were all dried and brittle now, already trampled to fragments by the hikers of weeks past. Rays of cool sun shone through interlocking bare branches above. She had passed a pair of hikers on her way in toward the falls, but whether by the deep chill or by some mystique of the nature that surrounded them (or maybe just a lovers' spat), they had been lulled into silence as well.

Terra shoved her hands deep into her coat pockets and sucked in a frosted breath that stung her windpipe. Something about this place made her feel alive. Funny, considering it was where she'd almost died. But since then, she hadn't felt alone.

As the cliff came into view, one of her bootlaces came undone. She stopped and bent down to tie it, feeling a twinge of resistance from the scars on her back. Iam had healed her on her third and—she hoped—final visit to the healing pool, but not completely this time. He'd wanted her to carry the evidence of her struggle with the demon. He'd told her the pink slashes across her skin and the pain they carried were a memento of her act of faith, a reminder to trust. Plus, they looked pretty badass.

A thin stream of water dribbled and splashed its way down the face of the cliff ahead of her, much lighter now since the rains had dried up in the past weeks. Soon, it would be frozen against the rocks, forming stacked icicles like walrus tusks, multiplying and stretching until the spring thaw. She'd talked with Harlan about having the ceremony here, the waterfall as their backdrop, but he didn't seem too keen on the idea. Something about the memory of her mangled body at the base of the falls not being romantic enough.

Instead, they'd agreed it would be somewhere in town, maybe overlooking the canal. Small, sophisticated, simple, and all the other *S* words. She knew that would be a big ask for Leta, who was more likely to go for a Mardi Gras at Liberace's type of theme. But really, it wasn't up to her.

Terra wasn't too worried about having a run-in with her mom. They'd been much more agreeable with each other since the incident with Hulum. (Nothing like some quality mother-daughter bonding over a possession.) There had been a lot of explaining to do, of course. Seeing no way around it, she and Harlan had laid it all out for Leta and Jeremy over a very long and uncomfortable lunch. Other than Jeremy choking on an onion ring and requiring the Heimlich, Terra thought it had gone pretty well.

After one last look at the towering rock wall in front of her, Terra resumed her walk around the loop and headed back toward the main trail. She planned to meet up with Alexis for coffee once back in town. Decaf for the insomniac, of course—Terra wasn't about to derail her friend's progress. The sleep did seem to be getting better lately. Alexis actually stayed *in* bed while she slept now. The pain was still a problem, but Alexis was finding better ways to manage it. She'd also found new friends through her support group that could commiserate with her. That was half the battle, wasn't it? Not having to feel alone in your struggles?

At that thought, the sound of voices materialized on the other side of the ravine.

At first it was casual conversation. A male and female voice. Then the voices were raised, their negative energy stomping all over her carefree hike like a kid in a mud puddle. She stopped where she was on the path and peered through the trees.

A young couple was making their way toward the falls. A rail-thin young woman with fair skin and dark hair walked with her arms crossed as if in a straight-jacket. Her companion was a behemoth of a man, wide across the chest and scruffy with brown curls peeking out beneath his ball cap. He walked with a swagger, plucking twigs off the trees as he passed them and breaking them into pieces with his troll-hands.

"I told you not to bring that up again," he boomed with a dash of country twang.

The girl aimed her inaudible reply toward the ground.

"Ya know, sometimes," he said, "I like you better when your mouth is shut."

Oh, lovely.

As they approached the falls, Terra walked herself back into the cover of the trees and leaned against a poplar, watching the scene unfold. There was a faint shadow of familiarity in the man. Ancient memories of Brock, now what felt like a lifetime removed, bubbled to the surface.

The girl's voice was louder now. "Screw you, Ethan." She darted ahead.

Yeah, screw 'em.

He stopped where he was and stared after her. Terra could swear she saw his nostrils flare from where she stood. He yelled at her. "Oh, it's like *that* now?" Then, he charged.

Oh no. Terra leaned forward, debating. She was no superhero in spandex, but there had to be *something* she could do.

The girl turned in shock and giggled nervously as he descended on her and seized her arm in a death grip. "What are you doing?" she yelled. "It's fine. It's fine! I didn't mean it."

"We're leaving."

"But I don't want to."

"Don't matter." Grip still tight on her arm, he proceeded to drag her away from the falls.

"Hey, cut it out!"

He didn't respond but continued to yank at her as if she were a wayward puppy on a leash.

Finally, she wrenched herself free and belted out, "Stop!"

Ethan took a half step backward, and Terra thought he might be winding up to clock her in the face. But instead, he stood in place, glowering.

Terra snagged a heavy stick from the ground and prepared to chuck it at the scumbag.

After a tense moment, he turned and walked off. The girl stood there looking miserable as he called over his shoulder, "Fine. You can Uber your ass home."

Panicked, she started after him. "Don't be a jerk, Ethan."

He whirled around and spat in the dirt, then mumbled something indistinct but menacing enough to stop her in her tracks.

Then he was gone.

Terra dropped her stick.

The girl, now alone near the center of the falls, crouched and slumped onto a rock. She rested her head in her hands for a long, sullen moment, breaking form only to wipe an arm against her cheek.

Terra took stock of her, as she always did with people and their flaws, but this time, the list was different: anxious, hurting, in need.

Terra sucked in a deep breath. Flipping hell, this bravery stuff was hard to avoid. She could go home now, but then she'd be ignoring the subtle voice nudging her forward. Stepping out from the safety of the trees, she swallowed her cowardice and began walking.

It wasn't until Terra had made it halfway around the curve of the ravine wall that the girl looked up. She immediately turned her face away and cursed, her voice obscured by the echoes of dripping water.

Terra's steps slowed. She tried to summon some reassuring words.

"Hey."

It was a start, anyway.

The girl snorted and rubbed her face with her sleeve. "You saw that?" She looked barely out of her teens. A tiny string of stars was tattooed on the side of her neck.

"Yeah. Sorry. Are you okay?"

The girl hunched over, picked up a rock, and lobbed it into the shallow pool of water below. It made a satisfying *thunk*, splashing water in every direction. "Yeah. He does that sometimes." She wiped her face with her sleeve, then suddenly guffawed. "I sure know how to pick 'em, don't I?"

Terra stepped closer to the woman and lowered herself onto a rock. "I was with someone like that for a while."

The girl's eyes met hers. "Did he ever ditch you at a national park?" The side of her lips rose into a forced grin of camaraderie.

"Not exactly. But he did a lot of other dipshit things."

"Like what?"

"He cheated on me, for starters."

She nodded in understanding.

"He made me feel like all our relationship problems were my fault. Like I was the only one who needed fixing."

This she had no response to. She frowned down at the ravine, then chucked a second rock into the water below.

"I'm Terra, by the way. What's your name?"

"Savannah."

"Where do you live, Savannah?"

"Bedford." She wrapped her arms around herself.

"That's on my way home. Need a ride?"

Savannah hesitated, her stick-straight hair hanging across her face as she fixed her eyes on her shoes. Eventually, she lifted her head and nodded. "Yeah. Thanks."

Terra smiled and helped pull her to her feet. "It's nothing." But it wasn't nothing. She was going to be late for coffee with Alexis. But it was all good. She would buy Alexis her favorite latte to make up for it. And one of those ginormous muffins she liked, even if it meant she'd have to sit there and listen to Alexis lament about her stomach pooch the whole time. "Let's go. We can talk more in the car."

"Wait."

Terra turned back to face her. "What?"

"I'm not ready yet." Savannah turned her eyes to the top of the falls. "Is there a way to get up there?"

"Yeah..." Terra eyed her, gauging her level of intent. And whether she might be half mountain goat. "But it's pretty steep."

"I don't mind." She glanced around. "Where is it?"

Terra lifted her eyes to the path that wound around the back of the falls. She sighed heavily. No one should be hiking up there by themselves.

A defeated smile spread across her face. "Come on. I'll show you the way."

## Please leave a review...

Indie authors like me depend on them. If you have one minute to spare, kindly post an honest review using the QR code below. I read and appreciate every review!

## ... and follow me.

I love connecting with my readers! You can get all the latest updates and extras by signing up for my newsletter scanning this QR code:

# ACKNOWLEDGEMENTS

I never set out to write a book, but well, here we are. I certainly didn't get here on my own.

I suppose it only makes sense to start with the people who brought me into this world and let me live in their house for two decades. Thank you to my parents, Barry and Alice. I appreciate all the love and encouragement over the years, and—when I went to college and announced I'd be majoring in accounting—thank you for gently expressing your disappointment that I didn't choose something more creative. Sorry to disappoint, but I kind of wanted a stable income. I'm sure you're happy to know I'm making up for lost time now.

Thank you to my fantastic editor, Lauren Humphries-Brooks, for her sharp eye and dedication to eliminating all the ridiculous and ineffective verbiage from my manuscript. If it weren't for you, my characters would be face-planting in exhaustion from all the shrugging and sighing I had them doing.

Thank you to my long-suffering alpha readers: Katie Potter, Karyn Savory, Heather Surdick, and Sharon Tjaden-Burkes. You read the absolute worst, cringe-worthy first version of this book and still somehow managed to give me positive feedback. Hats off to you. Special thanks to Sharon, a talented writer and author herself, for not accepting any BS and setting me straight on some of the book's worst faults. I wish you only the very best with your future projects and publications.

Thank you to the host of beta readers who read the various revisions of Terra's Fall, some of whom I don't even know your first name, just your user ID. All the same, I felt connected with you through the lines of text we shared. Reading each comment and reaction gave me the fuel I needed to keep at this story until it was the flawless version we have today. Just kidding. It was always flawless... just less so.

Thank you to the talented artists at Miblart, or as I like to refer to them, my favorite Ukrainians. You did a most excellent job of bringing my vision of this book's cover to life, despite all my vague descriptions and waffling. Blessings to you and prayers for peace to come to your country soon.

Thank you to the good people of Atlanta Writers Club and the ASPC for providing the resources and education needed for this new author to bloom.

A massive thank you to my hubs, Anthony. I know it's been a looooong journey for this random hobby I picked up, and I appreciate the countless nights you took over getting the boys to bed while I concentrated on my "writing" (i.e. sitting with my laptop, staring into space). Thanks for talking up my book to everyone and for reading the whole thing, even though I know you have zero time for pleasure reading, which isn't even your thing. Somehow you made time, and you gave me the encouragement I needed to make Terra's Fall a reality. You're the best, and you're also my favorite person.

And most of all, thank you to God, who essentially inspired me to write this book, prodded me forward when I thought nothing would come of it, and miraculously provided a way through each time I hit writer's block so crippling that it brought me to my knees in prayer.

This book was a personal journey for me and a testament to how I've experienced the character of God. Whether you live in the real world or Elysia, he is not far from any one of us. And you'll find he's got some pretty cool tricks up his sleeve if you're willing to put your trust in him.

# ABOUT THE AUTHOR

Amanda D'Errico is a thriving survivor (a *sur-thriver*?) of chronic illness and disability and can tell you a thing or two about uncovering joy in dark places. After becoming disabled from a mysterious connective tissue disorder and finding herself stuck on the couch for most of her days, she turned to her first love, writing. She is also a frequent artistic dabbler, an epic slideshow creator, and a big fan of sleep, despite regular dreams of being stuck inside a sci-fi action film. She lives with her husband and two sons in Atlanta, Georgia.